AN UNCERTAIN

Fred Vargas was born in Paris in 1957. A historian and archaeologist by profession, she is now a bestselling novelist.

Siân Reynolds is a historian, translator and a former professor at the University of Stirling.

FRED VARGAS

An Uncertain Place

TRANSLATED FROM THE FRENCH BY
Siân Reynolds

VINTAGE BOOKS
London

Published by Vintage 2012

2 4 6 8 10 9 7 5 3 1

First published with the title *Un lieu incertain* in 2008 by Éditions Viviane Hamy, Paris

First published in Great Britain in 2011 by Harvill Secker

Vintage
Random House, 20 Vauxhall Bridge Road,
London SW1V 2SA

www.vintage-books.co.uk

Addresses for companies within The Random House Group Limited can be found at: www.
randomhouse.co.uk/offices.htm

The Random House Group Limited Reg. No. 954009

A CIP catalogue record for this book
is available from the British Library

ISBN 9780099552239

This book is supported by the French Ministry of Foreign Affairs as part of the Burgess
programme run by the Cultural Department of the French Embassy in London.
www.frenchbooknews.com

Liberté • Égalité • Fraternité
RÉPUBLIQUE FRANÇAISE

Ouvrage publié avec le soutien du Centre national du livre – ministère français
chargé de la culture

This book is published with support from the French Ministry of
Culture – Centre National du Livre

MIX
Paper from
responsible sources
FSC® C016897

Typeset in Sabon by Palimpsest Book Production Limited,
Falkirk, Stirlingshire

Printed and bound by CPI Group (UK) Ltd, Croydon, CR0 4YY

AN UNCERTAIN PLACE

I

COMMISSAIRE ADAMSBERG KNEW HOW TO IRON SHIRTS. HIS mother had shown him how you should flatten the shoulder piece and press down the fabric round the buttons. He unplugged the iron and folded his clothes into his suitcase. Freshly shaved and combed, he was off to London, and there was no way of getting out of it.

He pushed a chair into the patch of sunlight falling on the kitchen floor. Since the room had windows on three sides, he spent his time moving his seat around the circular table, following the light, like a lizard on a rock. He put his bowl of coffee on the east side and sat down with his back to the warmth.

Going to London was fine by him: he would find out whether the Thames smelt of damp washing the way the Seine did, and what kind of sound the seagulls made. Perhaps they had a different call in English. But he would hardly be allowed time for that. Three days of conference, with ten papers per session, six debates, and a reception at the Home Office. There would be a hundred or so top brass, representing police forces from all over Europe, crammed into a big hall; cops from twenty-three countries, seeking to foster closer police links in an expanded Europe and, more precisely, to 'harmonise the management of migratory flows'. That was the subject of the conference.

As chief of the Serious Crimes Squad in Paris, Adamsberg was obliged to turn up, but he wasn't greatly concerned. He would be participating in a virtual, hands-off way: first because of his ingrained hostility to any 'management of flows', and secondly because he had never been able to remember a word of English. He finished his coffee contentedly, reading a text message from *Commandant* Danglard: '*Rdv 80 mins GdNord eurostar gate. Fckin tnnl. Have smart jkt + tie 4 U*'.

Adamsberg pressed 'delete', wiping away his deputy's anxiety like dust from furniture. Danglard was not cut out for walking or running, still less for travelling. Crossing the Channel by tunnel was as distressing for him as flying over it in a plane. But he would not for all the world have given up his place on the mission to anyone else. For thirty years, the *commandant* had been wedded to the elegance of English clothes, on which he banked to make up for his lack of good looks. And from this vital choice he had extended his gratitude to the rest of the United Kingdom, becoming the typical Anglophile Frenchman, addicted to good manners, tact and discreet humour. Except, of course, when he let himself go – revealing the difference between an Anglophile Frenchman and a true Englishman. So the prospect of a trip to London had over-joyed Danglard, migratory flows or not. He just had to get past the obstacle of the *fckin tnnl*: it would be his first experi-ence of it.

Adamsberg rinsed out his coffee bowl, snatched up his suit-case, and wondered what sort of *jkt + tie* Danglard had chosen for him. His elderly neighbour, Lucio, was knocking loudly on the glass door, his weighty fist making it rattle. Lucio had lost his left arm in the Spanish Civil War when he was nine years old, and it seemed that his right arm had grown so large to compensate that it had the strength of two. Pressing his face to the pane, he was summoning Adamsberg by his imperious expression.

'Come along,' he said gruffly and peremptorily. 'She can't get them out, I need your help.'

Adamsberg stepped outside and put his suitcase down in the unkempt little garden he shared with the old Spaniard.

'I'm just off to London,' he said. 'I'll give you a hand when I get back, in three days.'

'Not in thrrrreee days! Now!' said the old man.

And when Lucio spoke in this tone of voice, rolling his r's, he produced a great rumbling sound that seemed to Adamsberg as if it was issuing from the very earth. He picked up the suitcase, his mind already on its way to the Eurostar departure lounge at the Gare du Nord.

'What can't you get out?' he said distantly, locking his front door.

'The cat in the tool shed. You surely knew she was having kittens?'

'I didn't even know there was a cat there, and I certainly don't care.'

'Well, you know now, *hombre*. And no way will you not care. She's only managed three so far. One's dead and two others are still stuck, I can feel their heads. I'll massage her belly, and you can pull them out. And be careful, gently does it. A kitten, you can break it in half like a biscuit if you're too clumsy.'

*　*　*

Anxious and impatient, Lucio was scratching his missing arm by moving his fingers in the air. He had often explained that when he had lost his arm, aged nine, there had been a spider bite on it which he hadn't finished scratching. And on account of that, the bite was still itching sixty-nine years later, because he hadn't been able to give it a really good scratch and have done with it. This was the neurological explanation provided by his mother, and it had become Lucio's philosophy of life: he adapted it to every situation and every feeling. You either finish something, or you don't start. You have to go through to the bitter end, and that applies in matters of the heart too. When something was intensely important to him, Lucio scratched the interrupted bite.

'Lucio,' said Adamsberg clearly, walking across the little garden, 'my train goes in an hour and a quarter, my deputy is having kittens himself at the Gare du Nord, and I'm not going to be midwife to your wretched cat when a hundred top cops are waiting for me in London. Do it yourself, you can tell me about it on Sunday.'

'How am I supposed to manage like this?' cried the old man, waving his stump in the air.

Lucio held Adamsberg back with his powerful right arm, thrusting forward his prognathous jaw, worthy of a Velázquez painting, according to Danglard. The old man couldn't see well enough these days to shave properly, and his razor always missed a few bristles. White and tough, they glittered in the sunshine in little clumps, like a silvery decoration made of thorns. Every now and then, Lucio caught a bristle between thumb and fingernail and pulled it out, as he might a tick. He never gave up till he got it out, observing the spider-bite philosophy.

'You're coming with me.'

'Let me go, Lucio.'

'You've got no choice, *hombre*,' said Lucio darkly. 'It's crossed your path now. You have to come. Otherwise it'll scratch you all your life. It'll only take ten minutes.'

'My train's crossing my path too.'

'Time for that afterwards.'

Adamsberg dropped the suitcase and groaned impotently as he followed Lucio into the shed. A tiny head, sticky with blood, was emerging between the cat's hind paws. Under the old Spaniard's instructions, he caught hold of it gently while Lucio pressed the mother cat's stomach with a professional gesture. She was miaowing piteously.

'You can do better than that! Pull harder, *hombre*, get hold of it under its shoulders and pull! Go on, don't be afraid, but be gentle, don't squash its skull, and with your other hand, stroke the mother's head, she's panicking.'

'Lucio, when I stroke someone's head, they go to sleep.'

'*Joder!* Go on, pull!'

Six minutes later, Adamsberg was putting two red and squeaking little rats alongside the others on an old blanket. Lucio cut the cords and placed them one by one at their mother's teats. He looked anxiously at the mother cat, which was whimpering.

'What did you mean about your hand? You put people to sleep?'

Adamsberg shook his head.

'I don't know how. If I put my hand on their heads they go to sleep. That's all.'

'And you do that with your own kid?'

'Yes. And people go to sleep when I'm talking too. I even have suspects drop off when I'm questioning them.'

'Well, do it for this mother cat. *Apúrate!* Make her sleep.'

'Good grief, Lucio, can't you get it into your head that I've got a train to catch?!'

'We've got to calm the mother down.'

Adamsberg couldn't have cared less about the cat, but he did care about the black look his old neighbour was giving him. He stroked the – very soft – head of the cat since, it was true, he really had no choice. The animal's panting gradually subsided as his fingers rolled like marbles from its muzzle to its ears. Lucio nodded his approval.

'Yes, she's sleeping, *hombre.*'

Adamsberg gently removed his hand, wiped it on some wet grass and backed away quietly.

As he went up the escalator at the Gare du Nord, he could still feel something sticky drying on his fingers and under his nails. He was twenty minutes later than agreed for the *rdv.* Danglard hurried towards him. Danglard's legs always looked as if they had been wrongly assembled, and that they would be dislocated from the knee if he tried to run.

Adamsberg raised a hand to pre-empt his reproaches, and stop him running.

'I know, I know,' he said. 'Something crossed my path and I had to deal with it, or I'd have had to scratch it for the rest of my days.'

Danglard was so used to Adamsberg's incomprehensible sentences that he rarely bothered to ask questions. Like others

in the squad, he let it pass, knowing how to separate the interesting from the useful. Puffing, he pointed to the departure
gate, and set off back in that direction. As he followed without
haste, Adamsberg tried to recall what colour the cat had been.
White with grey patches? Ginger patches?

II

'You get some weird goings-on in France too, don't you?' remarked Detective Chief Inspector Radstock, in English, to his Parisian colleagues.

'What did he say?' asked Adamsberg.

'He said we get weird things happening back home as well,' Danglard translated.

'Very true,' said Adamsberg, without taking much interest in the conversation.

What concerned him just now was the possibility of taking a stroll. He was in London, it was a fine evening in June, and he wanted to walk about a bit. The two days of conference he had sat through were beginning to get on his nerves. Staying seated for hours on end was one of the rare experiences that disrupted his habitual calm, and made him undergo the strange state other people called 'impatience' or 'feverishness', usually foreign to his nature. The previous day he had managed to escape three times, and had explored the surrounding district, after a fashion, committing to memory the brick housefronts, the white columns, the black-and-gold lamp posts. He had taken a few steps into a little street called

St John's Mews, though heaven only knew how you were meant to pronounce 'Mews'. A flock of seagulls had flown up in the air, calling (mewing indeed) in English. But his absences had been noticed. So today he had had to stay the course, sitting in his place, unresponsive to the speeches of his colleagues and unable to keep up with the rapid translation by a simultaneous interpreter. The hall was crammed full of police officers, all of whom were displaying much ingenuity in devising a grid intended to 'harmonise the flow of migrants', and to cover Europe with a net through whose meshes it would be impossible to slip. Since he had always preferred fluids to solids, the flexible to the rigid, Adamsberg naturally identified with the movements of the 'flow' and was inventing ways of outflanking the fortifications which were being perfected under his very eyes.

This colleague from New Scotland Yard, DCI Radstock, seemed to know all about nets, but did not seem to be fanatical about their efficiency. He would be retiring in under a year, and cherished the very British notion of spending his time fishing in some northern loch, according to Danglard, who understood everything and translated everything, including things that Adamsberg had no wish to know. He would have liked to tell his deputy not to bother with these superfluous translations, but Danglard had so few treats and he seemed so happy revelling in the English language, rather like a wild boar wallowing in a favoured spot of mud, that Adamsberg hadn't the heart to deprive him of the least scrap of enjoyment. At this point, the *commandant* seemed to have attained a state of bliss, almost to have taken wing, his usually shambling body gaining stature, his drooping shoulders squared, displaying a posture which almost made him impressive.

Perhaps he was nursing a plan to retire one day with this new-found friend, and go fishing for something or other in the northern loch.

Radstock was taking advantage of Danglard's bonhomie to describe to him what it was like working in Scotland Yard, but he was also regaling him with a string of the kind of 'spicy' stories he thought suitable for his French guests. Danglard had listened to him throughout their lunch without any sign of boredom, while making sure to check the quality of the wine. Radstock called him 'Donglarde', and the two policemen were matching each other anecdote for anecdote, drink for drink, leaving Adamsberg far behind. Of all the hundred officers at the conference, Adamsberg was the only one who didn't have even the slightest grasp of the English language. So he was following along in a marginal way, exactly as he had hoped, and few people had gathered quite who he was. At his side was the young junior officer, *brigadier* Estalère, with his wide-open green eyes, which made him look perpetually surprised. Adamsberg had insisted on taking him along on the mission. He maintained that Estalère would wise up one of these days, and from time to time he expended some energy trying to bring this about.

Hands in pockets and for once smartly turned out, Adamsberg was taking full advantage of this long stroll, as Radstock paraded them round the streets to show them the oddities of London by night. Such as a woman sleeping under a canopy of umbrellas sewn together, and clutching in her arms a three-foot-high object described as a 'teddy bear'. 'It's a toy bear,' Danglard had translated. 'Yes, I did gather that,' said Adamsberg.

'And here,' said Radstock, pointing down a long, straight avenue, 'we have Lord Clyde-Fox. He's an example of what you might call an eccentric English aristocrat. Not many left. They don't make 'em like this any more. Quite a young specimen.'

Radstock stopped to allow them time to observe this individual, with the satisfaction of someone showing off a rather unusual phenomenon to his guests. Adamsberg and Danglard obediently observed him. Tall and thin, Lord Clyde-Fox was hopping clumsily about on the spot, first on one foot then on the other, barely avoiding falling over. Another man was smoking a cigar about ten feet away, swaying slightly and contemplating his companion's trouble.

'Er, interesting,' said Danglard politely.

'He's quite often around here, but not every evening,' said Radstock, as if his colleagues were benefiting from a rare sighting. 'We get on all right. He's very amiable, always a friendly word. He's a sort of fixture, a familiar figure of the night. Seeing the time it is, he's probably had an evening out and is trying to get home.'

'He's drunk?' queried Danglard.

'Not quite. He makes it a point of honour to see how far he can go, finds his limit, and then hangs on there. He says that if he walks along a ridge, balancing between one slope and another, he may suffer but he will never be bored. Everything all right, sir?'

'Everything all right with you, Radstock?' rejoined the man, waving a hand.

'A joker,' the chief inspector confided. 'Well, if he wants to be. When his mother died, two years ago, he tried to eat a whole box of photos of her. His sister barged in to stop him, and it turned nasty. She finished up in hospital and him down at the station. The noble lord was absolutely furious because he had been prevented from eating the photos.'

'Really, really eating them?' asked Estalère.

'Yes, really. But what are a few photos? I think, in Paris one time, some chap tried to eat a wardrobe, didn't he?'

'What did he say?' asked Adamsberg, seeing Radstock's frown.

'He says there was some Frenchman once who tried to eat a wardrobe. Actually there was. He managed it over a few months, with the help of some friends.'

'Weird, eh, Donglarde?'

'You're quite right, it was in the early twentieth century.'

'Ah, that's normal,' said Estalère, who often chose exactly the wrong expression. 'There was this man I heard about, he ate an aeroplane, and it took him a year. Just a year. A small plane.'

Radstock nodded gravely. Adamsberg had noticed that he liked to make solemn pronouncements. He sometimes came out with long sentences which – from their tone – were passing judgement on the whole of humanity and its probable nature, good or bad, angelic or devilish.

'There are some things,' Radstock began – Danglard providing a simultaneous translation – 'that people can't imagine themselves doing until some crazy individual has tried it. But once something's been done for the first time, good or bad, it goes into the inheritance of the human race. It can be used, it can be copied, and people will even try to go one better. The chap who ate the wardrobe made it easier for that other chap to eat the aeroplane. And that's how the vast dark continent of madness opens up, like a map, as people explore unknown regions. We're going forward in the gloom, with nothing but experience to guide us, that's what I tell my men. So Lord Clyde-Fox over there is taking his shoes off, and putting them back on, over and over again. Goodness knows why. When we do know, someone else will be able to do the same thing.'

'Greetings, sir,' said the chief inspector now, going closer. 'Is there a problem?'

'Greetings, Radstock,' said Clyde-Fox mildly.

The two men made signs of recognition to each other, two nightbirds, familiars who had no secrets. Clyde-Fox put one stockinged foot on the pavement, holding his shoe in his hand and looking intently inside it.

'A problem?' Radstock repeated.

'I should say so. Perhaps you should go and take a look – if you've the stomach for it.'

'Where?'

'At the entrance to Highgate Cemetery.'

'It's not a good idea to go poking around in a place like that,' said Radstock in disapproving tones. 'What were you doing there?'

'Beating the bounds with a few chosen friends,' the noble lord explained, gesturing with his thumb towards his cigar-smoking companion. 'The boundary between fear and common sense. Well, I know the place like the back of my hand, but he wanted to take a look. Be careful, chief inspector,' said Clyde-Fox lowering his voice. 'My pal over there's as tight as a tick, and he's as fast as lightning. He's already taken out a couple of fellers in the pub. Teaches Cuban dance. Highly strung. Not from here.'

Lord Clyde-Fox shook his shoe in the air again, put it back on and took off the other.

'Right, sir. But your shoes – is there something inside them?'

'No, Radstock, I'm just checking them.'

The Cuban said something in Spanish which seemed to indicate that he had had enough and that he was off. The lord gave him a casual wave of the hand.

'In your view, officer,' Clyde-Fox said, 'what should there be inside a shoe?'

'A foot,' Estalère intervened to say.

'Exactly so,' said Clyde-Fox, nodding approvingly at the young Frenchman. 'And it's just as well to check that the feet in your shoes are your own, eh? Radstock, if you had such a thing as a torch, you might help me clear this up.'

'What do you want me to do?'

'See if there's anything inside these.'

As Clyde-Fox held up both shoes, Radstock methodically looked inside them. Adamsberg, completely forgotten, was pacing around slowly. He was thinking about the man who had chewed up his wardrobe, month after month, splinter after splinter. He wondered which he would prefer to eat, a wardrobe or an aeroplane – or photos of his mother. Or anything else – was there some other exploit that might reveal a new section of the dark continent of madness that DCI Radstock had referred to?

'Nothing there,' concluded Radstock.

'You're quite sure?'

'Absolutely.'

'That's good,' said Clyde-Fox, putting the shoes back on. 'Nasty business. Go on Radstock, old chap, it's your department. Go and look. Just at the gates. A load of old shoes on the pavement. But steel yourself. About twenty of 'em, you can't miss 'em.'

'That sort of thing's *not* my department, Your Lordship.'

'Oh yes it is. They're lined up carefully, all the toes pointing to the cemetery as if they wanted to walk in. I'm talking about the old main gate now.'

'But the old cemetery has nightwatchmen. It's closed to the public after dark, and it's closed to their shoes too.'

'Well, the shoes want to go in all the same, and their whole attitude is most unpleasant. Go on, go and look, do your job.'

'I'm afraid, sir, that I have better things to do than inspect a load of old shoes.'

'Wrong, Radstock! Wrong! Because there are feet inside them.'

There was a sudden silence, a ghastly shock wave. A small whimper came from Estalère's throat. Danglard tensed his arms. Adamsberg stopped pacing and looked up.

'Bloody hell,' whispered Danglard.

'What did he say?' Adamsberg asked.

'He says there are some old shoes, looking as though they want to walk into the cemetery, and he says Radstock is wrong not to go and take a look, because they've got feet inside them.'

'Take no notice, Donglarde,' Radstock interrupted. 'He's had too much to drink. You've had a drop too much, sir, you ought to go home.'

'There. Are. Feet. Inside. Them,' enunciated Lord Clyde-Fox, clearly and calmly, to indicate that he was walking with perfect assurance along the ridge. 'Cut off at the ankles. And the feet are trying to get into the cemetery.'

'As you say, sir, and they're, er, trying to get in, are they?'

Lord Clyde-Fox was carefully combing his hair, a sign that his departure was imminent. Now that he had the problem off his chest, he seemed to have returned to normal.

'Pretty ancient shoes,' he added, 'about fifteen or twenty years old, I'd say. Men's and women's, both.'

'But the feet?' asked Danglard discreetly. 'Are the feet just bones now?'

'Leave it, Donglarde, he's been seeing things.'

'No,' said Clyde-Fox, tucking away his comb and ignoring Radstock. 'The feet are almost intact.'

'And they're trying to get into the cemetery?'

'Precisely, old man.'

III

DCI RADSTOCK WAS UTTERING A CONSTANT STREAM OF growls and grumbles, and gripping the wheel tightly, as he drove fast up to the old cemetery in north London. Of all things, they had had to bump into Clyde-Fox. First this nutter wanted them to check whether someone else's foot had got into his shoes. And now they were on their way to Highgate because His Lordship had fallen off his ridge and had a vision. There wouldn't be any shoes in front of the cemetery, any more than there were strange feet in Clyde-Fox's own footwear.

But Radstock certainly didn't want to go up there alone. Not when he was a few months from retirement. He had had some difficulty persuading the amiable 'Donglarde' to go with him: it was as if the Frenchman was reluctant to embark on this particular expedition. But how would a Frenchman know anything about Highgate, anyway? On the other hand, he had had no trouble with Adamsberg, who was perfectly willing to agree to a detour. This French *commissaire* seemed to go around in a peaceful and conciliatory state of being only half awake. One wondered whether even his profession engaged his attention. Their young colleague, however, was the exact opposite: his wide eyes were glued to the window, as he goggled at the sights of London. In Radstock's view, this Estalère fellow was a halfwit: it was a wonder they had let him come to the conference at all.

'Couldn't you have sent a couple of your men?' asked Danglard, who was still looking vexed.

'I can't send a team off just because Clyde-Fox has started seeing things, Donglarde. After all, he's a man who tried to eat pictures of his mother. But we do have to go and check, don't we?'

No, Danglard didn't think they were obliged to do any such thing. He was happy to be in London, happy to be dressed like an Englishman, and especially happy that a woman had been paying him attention, from the first day of the conference. He had given up expecting such a miracle years ago, and having fatalistically accepted that he would never have any more dealings with women, had not made the first approach himself. She had come up to him, had smiled at him, and found excuses to meet up with him at the conference. If he was not much mistaken, that is. Danglard was wondering how such a thing could be possible, torturing himself with questions. He found himself endlessly going over the tiniest signs that could confirm or invalidate his hopes. He classified them, estimated them, manipulated them to see how reliable they were, as one tries the ice gingerly before venturing on to it. He was examining them for consistency, for possible meaning and trying to decide whether they were encouraging, yes or no. So much so that the signs were becoming more insubstantial the more he worried away at them. He needed some further clues. And at this very moment, the woman in question was no doubt in the hotel bar with the other people from the conference. Now that he had been whisked off on Radstock's expedition, he would miss her.

'Why do we need to check? Your Lord Clyde-Fox was indeed as drunk as a lord,' said Danglard, proud of his command of English idiom.

'Because it's Highgate,' said the chief inspector through gritted teeth.

Danglard gave a start, feeling cross with himself. His intense speculation about the woman at the conference had prevented him reacting to the name 'Highgate'. He looked up as if to reply, but Radstock cut him off with a wave of the hand.

'No, Donglarde, you wouldn't understand,' he said in the sad, bitter and resigned tones of an old soldier, who can't expect other people to share his war memories. 'You weren't at Highgate. I was.'

'But I do understand. Both why you didn't want to go there, and why you're going there all the same.'

'With respect, Donglarde, that would very much surprise me.'

'I know what happened at Highgate Cemetery.'

Radstock shot him a look of astonishment.

'Danglard knows everything,' Estalère explained contentedly from the back of the car.

Sitting next to his young colleague on the back seat, Adamsberg was listening to the conversation, picking up the odd word. It was clear that Danglard knew quantities of things about this 'Highgate', of which he, Adamsberg, was quite ignorant. That was normal, as long as you regarded the prodigious extent of Danglard's knowledge as normal.

Commandant Danglard was very different from what might be called a 'normal educated man'. He was a man of phenomenal erudition, controlling a complex network of infinite and encyclopedic knowledge which, in Adamsberg's opinion, had ended up by taking over his entire being, replacing each of his organs one by one, so that you wondered how Danglard managed to move around like an ordinary mortal. Perhaps that was why he did find it hard to walk, and never strolled. On the other hand, he was sure to be able to tell you the name of the man who had eaten his wardrobe. Adamsberg looked at Danglard's imprecise profile, at that moment subject to a kind of trembling which indicated the ongoing process of knowledge retrieval. No doubt about it, the *commandant* was quickly passing in review his compendious collection of facts about Highgate. At the same time he was desperately preoccupied by something else: the woman at the conference of course, on account of whom his mind was dealing with a whirlwind of questions. Adamsberg turned towards the British colleague whose name he could never remember. Something Stock. *He* was not thinking about a woman, nor scanning his mind for information. Stock was quite simply scared.

'Danglard,' said Adamsberg, tapping him on the shoulder, 'Stock doesn't want to go and see these shoes.'

'I've already told you that he can pick up bits of French. Speak in code please.'

Adamsberg obeyed. In order not to be understood by Radstock, Danglard had advised him to speak very fast and in an even tone, slurring his syllables, but this kind of exercise was impossible for Adamsberg, who pronounced his words as slowly as he placed his feet when pacing about.

'No, he doesn't want to go at all,' said Danglard in this same fastspeak. 'He has certain memories of the place and he wants nothing to do with it.'

'What do you mean, "the place"?'

'One of the most romantic and baroque cemeteries in the Western world, absolutely over the top, an artistic and macabre fantasy. It's full of Gothic tombs, burial vaults, Egyptian sculptures, excommunicated people and murderers. All tangled together in one of those rambling English gardens. It's unique, a bit too unique, a place where madness lurks.'

'OK, I get it, Danglard. But what happened in this tangled garden?'

'Ghastly events, and yet nothing much. But it's the kind of "nothing much" that can traumatise anyone who witnesses it. That's why they put watchmen on it at night. That's why our colleague doesn't want to go there on his own, that's why we're in this car, instead of having a nice quiet drink in our hotel.'

'A nice quiet drink. Who with, Danglard?'

Danglard pulled a face. The complex threads of other people's lives did not escape the notice of Adamsberg, even if those threads were whispers, minute sensations, puffs of air. The *commissaire* had spotted the woman at the conference. And while Danglard had been going over every little incident obsessively, so much so as to blank them out, Adamsberg must already have formed a firm impression.

'With her,' said Adamsberg into the silence. 'The woman who chews the arms of her red spectacles, the woman who keeps looking at you. It says "Abstract" on her badge. Is that her first name?'

Danglard smiled. If the only woman who had ever made

eyes at him in ten years was called 'Abstract', that would have been painfully appropriate.

'No, it's her job. She's supposed to collect and distribute summaries of the papers. They call them "abstracts".'

'Ah, I see. So what *is* her name?'

'I haven't asked.'

'But you need to know her name before anything else.'

'No, before anything else I want to know what's going on inside her head.'

'Because you don't know?' asked Adamsberg, genuinely surprised.

'How would I know? I'd have to ask her. And I'd have to know *whether* I could ask her. And I wonder how I would know that.'

Adamsberg sighed, giving up the struggle when faced with Danglard's intellectual ramblings.

'Well, she certainly has something serious going on inside her head,' he began again. 'And one drink more or less at the hotel bar won't change that.'

'What woman are you talking about?' asked Radstock in French, exasperated by the other two excluding him from their conversation, and in particular realising that the little *commissaire* with dark untidy hair had guessed at his fear.

By now the car was going past the cemetery, and Radstock suddenly wished that the scenario painted by Clyde-Fox would not turn out to be imaginary after all. Then that laid-back little Frenchman, Adamsberg, would be drawn into the nightmare of Highgate Cemetery. Let him get involved, by God, and we'd soon see if the little cop was as calm as he made out. Radstock pulled up at the kerb, but didn't get out. He lowered the window a few inches and poked his torch out.

'OK,' he said, looking in the mirror at Adamsberg. 'Let's all share this.'

'What's he saying?'

'He says he wants you to share Highgate.'

'I didn't ask to do anything.'

'You've no choice,' said Radstock grimly, opening the driver's door.

'I get it,' said Adamsberg, silencing Danglard with a gesture.

The smell was ghastly, the scene was appalling, and even Adamsberg stiffened, standing back a little behind his English colleague. From the ancient shoes, with their cracked leather and trailing laces, projected decomposed ankles, showing dark flesh and white shinbones which had been cleanly chopped off. The only thing that didn't match Clyde-Fox's account was that the feet were not trying to get into the cemetery. They were just there, on the pavement, terrible and provocative, sitting inside their shoes at the historic gateway to Highgate Cemetery. They formed a carefully arranged and unspeakable pile. Radstock held a torch in his outstretched hand, face twisted in denial, lighting up the damaged ankles emerging from the shoes, and vainly trying to sweep away the smell of death in the air.

'You see,' said Radstock, in a resigned yet aggressive voice, turning to Adamsberg. 'You see. That's Highgate for you. A place of the damned, and has been for a hundred years.'

'A hundred and seventy years in fact,' said Danglard quietly.

'Right,' said Radstock, seeking to pull himself together. 'You can go back to your hotel, I'm putting a call through to the Yard.'

He took out his mobile and smiled uneasily at his colleagues.

'The shoes look pretty cheap,' he said, as he punched in the call. 'With any luck they'll be French.'

'And if the shoes are, so are the feet,' Danglard completed the thought.

'Yes, Donglarde. What Englishman would bother to buy French shoes?'

'So if it was up to you, you'd bounce this horrific case across the Channel?'

'You bet! Dennison? Radstock here. Send a homicide team to the old gate of Highgate Cemetery. No, no actual body, but a pile of rotten shoes, about twenty of them. With feet inside. Yes, a whole crime scene team, Dennison. OK,' the chief inspector finished in a weary tone, 'put him on.'

Superintendent Clems was at the Yard; it was a busy night. It sounded as if some discussion was going on, as Radstock waited, holding his phone. Danglard took advantage of it to explain to Adamsberg that only French feet would fit French shoes, and that DCI Radstock fervently wished to send them this case across the Channel, straight to Paris. Adamsberg nodded, his hands clasped behind his back, and walked slowly round the macabre deposit, looking up from time to time to the high cemetery wall, as much to give his mind some air as to imagine where these dead feet wanted to go. They knew things that he didn't.

'About twenty, sir,' Radstock was repeating. 'I'm standing right here looking at them.'

'Radstock!' came the sceptical voice of Superintendent Clems. 'What the hell is all this rubbish about shoes with *feet inside them*?'

'Give me patience,' muttered Radstock to himself. 'I'm in Highgate, sir, not Queen's Lane. Are you going to send me some men, or are you going to leave me alone with this monstrosity?'

'Highgate? Oh, you should have said so before, Radstock.'

'That's what I've been saying for the past twenty minutes.'

'OK, OK,' said Clems, suddenly conciliatory, as if the word Highgate had set off alarm bells. 'The team's on its way. Are we talking about men or women?'

'Both. Adult feet. In the shoes.'

'Who put you on to it?'

'Lord Clyde-Fox. He stumbled across this horror, and went off to down several pints to get over it.'

'Right,' said Clems quickly. 'And the shoes. Quality? Age?'

'I'd say about twenty years old. And they're shoddy-looking too,' he went on sarcastically. 'With a bit of luck we might be able to palm this off on the Frenchies –'

'None of that nonsense, Radstock!' Clems interrupted him. 'We're in the middle of an international conference and waiting for results.'

'I know, sir, I've got the policemen from Paris with me now.'

Radstock laughed briefly again, and looked at Adamsberg before adopting the same linguistic device as his colleagues, speaking spectacularly fast. It was obvious to Danglard that the chief inspector, feeling humiliated now that he had asked them to accompany him, was aiming a volley of cheap shots at Adamsberg by way of revenge.

'Did you say Adamsberg himself was with you?' Clems cut him off.

'Yep, that's him, little fellow, looks half asleep most of the time.'

'In that case, hold your tongue and keep your distance, Radstock,' Clems ordered him. 'The little fellow, as you call him, is a walking timebomb.'

Danglard might look passive but he was not a calm man, and few nuances in the English language escaped him, despite Radstock's precautions. His defence of Adamsberg was unwavering, except for any criticisms he might formulate himself. He snatched the mobile from Radstock's hand and introduced himself to the superintendent, walking away from the smell of decaying feet. It appeared to Adamsberg that gradually the man at the other end of the line was turning into a better potential fishing companion than Radstock.

'As you say,' said Danglard sharply.

'Nothing personal, *Commandant* Danglard,' said Clems. 'I'm not trying to excuse Radstock, but he was there thirty years ago. It's bad luck coming across this when he's six months off retirement.'

'That was all a long time ago, sir.'

'Nothing worse than things from a long time ago, as you well know. Ancient stumps poke up through the grass and they can last centuries. A little sympathy for Radstock, please, because you don't understand.'

'Yes, I do. I know about the Highgate affair.'

'I'm not talking about the murder of the hiker.'

'Neither am I, sir. We're talking about historical Highgate, 160,800 bodies, 51,800 tombs. We're talking about the nocturnal hunts in the 1970s, and even about Lizzie Siddal.'

'All right,' said the superintendent after a pause. 'Well, if you know about that, you should also know that Radstock was there for the last escapade, and at the time he was young and new to the job. So cut him a little slack.'

The crime scene investigation team had arrived. Radstock took charge. Without a word, Danglard switched off the phone and slipped it in his British colleague's pocket. Then he rejoined Adamsberg, who was leaning on a black car and seemed to be supporting Estalère. The young officer was in a state of shock.

'What are they going to do with them?' asked Estalère in a shaky voice. 'Find twenty people without feet and stick them back on? How would they do that?'

'Ten people,' Danglard pointed out. 'Twenty feet, ten people.'

'All right,' admitted Estalère.

'In fact, it appears there are just eighteen, so nine people.'

'Yes. OK. But if the English had already found nine people whose feet had been cut off, they'd know about it, wouldn't they?'

'If they were living people, yes,' said Adamsberg. 'But if the feet came from corpses, they might not necessarily.'

Estalère shook his head.

'If the feet had been cut from dead bodies,' Adamsberg went on, 'that would mean nine corpses. The Brits may well have nine corpses somewhere without feet, but there's no way they would know that. I wonder,' he went on, 'if there's a special word for cutting off feet. We say decapitate for heads, eviscerate for innards, emasculate for testicles, but there isn't a special word for feet, or is there?'

'No, there isn't,' said Danglard. 'The word doesn't exist because the act doesn't exist. Well, not until now. But one individual has just created it, on the dark continent.'

'Like the wardrobe-eater – there isn't a proper word for that either.'

'A thekophagist?' suggested Danglard.

IV

WHEN THE TRAIN ENTERED THE CHANNEL TUNNEL, DANGLARD took a deep breath and clenched his teeth. The journey out had not relieved his apprehensions and this passage under water still seemed to him to be unacceptable, and his fellow travellers strangely insouciant. He distinctly pictured himself speeding through this conduit covered by tons of seawater overhead.

'You can feel the weight of it,' he said, his eyes fixed to the roof of the carriage.

'There isn't any weight,' said Adamsberg. 'We're not under water, we're under rock.'

Estalère asked how it was possible for the weight of the sea not to press down on the rock so hard that the tunnel collapsed. Adamsberg patiently and determinedly drew a diagram for him on a paper napkin: the water, the rock, the shorelines, the tunnel, the train. Then he did the same diagram without either the tunnel or the train, to show that their existence did not modify anything.

'All the same,' said Estalère, 'the weight of the seawater must be pressing down on something.'

'Yes, on the rock.'

'But then the rock must be weighing on the tunnel.'

'No,' said Adamsberg, starting another diagram.

Danglard made a gesture of irritation.

'It's just that you *imagine* the weight. A monstrous mass of water over our heads. The idea of being swallowed up. Sending a train under the sea is a demented idea.'

'No more than eating a wardrobe,' said Adamsberg, perfecting his diagram.

'What the heck has the wardrobe-eater done to get under your skin? You've done nothing but talk about him since yesterday.'

'I'm just trying to imagine his thought processes, Danglard. I'm trying to see how they think, the wardrobe-eater, the foot-amputator, or that man whose uncle was eaten by a bear. The thoughts of mankind are like drills opening up tunnels under the sea that you never expected to come into existence.'

'Who was eaten by a bear?' asked Estalère, suddenly waking up.

'This guy's uncle was on an ice floe,' Adamsberg told him. 'About a hundred years ago. All that was left of him were his glasses and his shoelaces. And this nephew was fond of his uncle. So he flipped. He killed the bear.'

'Well, you would, wouldn't you?' commented Estalère.

'Yes, but then he brought the bearskin back to Geneva, and gave it to his aunt, the widow. Who put it in her sitting room. Danglard, your colleague Stock gave you an envelope at the station. His preliminary report, was it?'

'Radstock, yes,' said Danglard gloomily, still looking up at the ceiling of the carriage and watching out for the weight of the sea.

'Interesting?'

'What does it matter? They're his feet, he can keep them.'

Estalère was twisting a paper napkin in his fingers and concentrating hard, looking down at his knees.

'So I suppose this nephew wanted to bring some relic of his uncle back to the widow?' he asked.

Adamsberg nodded and turned back to Danglard.

'Tell me all the same, what does the report say?'

'When will we get out of the tunnel?'

'Another sixteen minutes. What did Stock find, Danglard?'

'But logically,' Estalère said hesitantly, 'if the uncle was inside the bear . . . and the nephew . . .'

He stopped and looked down again, puzzled and scratching his blond head. Danglard sighed, whether for the sixteen minutes, or the ghastly feet, which he would rather leave far behind, forgetting all about the cemetery gate in Highgate. Or because Estalère, who was as slow-witted as he was curious, was the only member of the squad unable to distinguish between the valuable and the pointless among Adamsberg's remarks. For the young officer, every word his *commissaire* let drop had meaning and he was now pursuing it. And to Danglard, whose elastic mind leapt over ideas extremely fast, Estalère represented a constant and irritating waste of time.

'If we hadn't gone for a walk with Radstock two days ago,' Danglard said, 'and if we hadn't bumped into that crazy Clyde-Fox character, we wouldn't know a thing about those revolting feet and we'd have left them to rot in peace. They belong to the Brits, full stop.'

'There's no rule against being interested,' said Adamsberg, 'when something crosses your path.'

He felt pretty sure that Danglard had not parted with the

woman in London on as reassuring a note as he might have wished. So his anxiety was taking over again, slipping into the recesses of his being. Adamsberg imagined Danglard's mind as a block of fine limestone, where rain, in other words questions, had hollowed out countless basins in which his worries gathered, unresolved. Every day, three or four of these basins were active simultaneously. Just now, the journey through the tunnel, the woman in London, the feet in Highgate. As Adamsberg had explained to him, the energy Danglard expended on these questions, seeking to empty out the basins, was a waste of time. Because no sooner had he cleared out one space than it made way for something else, for another set of agonising questions. By digging away at them, he was stopping peaceful sedimentation from taking place, and the natural filling up of the excavations, which would happen if he forgot about them.

'Don't worry, she'll be in touch,' Adamsberg told him.

'Who?'

'Abstract.'

'Logically,' Estalère interjected, still following his train of thought, 'the nephew ought to have left the bear alive, and brought some of its droppings to the aunt. After all, the uncle was inside the bear, but not in its skin.'

'Yes, indeed,' said Adamsberg, looking satisfied. 'It all depends on the attitude the nephew had both to the uncle and to the bear.'

'And to his aunt,' added Danglard, who was feeling calmer on hearing Adamsberg's certainty about Abstract getting back in touch. 'We don't know the aunt's reactions either, whether she would rather have had the bearskin or the droppings.'

'It all depends on what was going on in the nephew's mind.

Was it that his uncle's soul had gone into the bear, right to the tips of its fur? And what idea did the thekophagist have of the wardrobe? And what was the foot-chopper thinking about? Whose soul is inside the wooden panels, or on the ends of people's feet? What did Stock say, Danglard?'

'Forget the feet, *commissaire*.'

'They remind me of something,' Adamsberg said in a hesitant voice. 'A picture somewhere, a story?'

Danglard stopped the attendant passing with the drinks trolley and took some champagne for himself and for Adamsberg, and put them both on his side of the table. Adamsberg drank very rarely and Estalère not at all, since alcohol went to his head. It had been explained to him that that was exactly the point, and he had been astonished. When Danglard had a drink, Estalère looked at him with intense puzzlement.

'Perhaps,' Adamsberg went on, 'it's some vague story I seem to recall about a man looking for his shoes in the night. Or who came back from the dead to find his shoes. I wonder if Stock knows it.'

Danglard quickly knocked back his first glass of champagne, and wrenched his gaze away from the carriage roof to look at Adamsberg, half enviously, half in despair. There were times when Adamsberg converted himself into a compact and dangerous attacker. Not often, but when he did it was easy to counter him. On the other hand, it was less easy to seize hold of him when his mental equipment was dislocated into several moving parts, which was his usual state. But it became completely impossible when this state intensified to the point of dispersal, as at present, assisted by the movement of the train which shook up any coherence. Adamsberg at such times seemed to move like a diver, his body and mind swooping gracefully without any precise objective. His eyes followed the movement, taking on the look of dark brown algae and conveying to his interlocutor a sensation of indeterminacy, flow, non-existence. To accompany Adamsberg in these extremes of his activity was like swimming into deep water, alongside slow-moving creatures, slimy mud, floating jelly-fish, a world of vague outlines and swirling colours. Spend too much time with him and you might go to sleep in the warm water and drown. At these particularly aqueous moments, there was no point in arguing with him any more than with foam, mist or sea spray.

Danglard was furious with his boss for pulling him towards this liquidity just as he was suffering from the double anguish of the Channel Tunnel and uncertainty about Abstract. He was also furious for allowing himself to be drawn so often into Adamsberg's misty moods.

He swallowed down the second glass of champagne, the one for Adamsberg, and recalled Radstock's report quickly in order to extract from it some precise, clear and reassuring factual details. Adamsberg could see that, and was himself not anxious to explain to Danglard the state of terror into which the sight of those feet had thrown him. The wardrobe-eater and the story about the polar bear had been trivial distractions to help him blot out the image of what he had seen on the pavement in Highgate, to take him out of himself and away from the impressionable Estalère.

'There were actually seventeen feet,' Danglard said. 'Eight matched pairs and one isolated foot. Nine people then.'

'People or corpses?'

'Corpses. It seems that the feet were amputated after death, with a saw. Five men, four women, all adults.'

Danglard paused, but the deep-sea gaze of Adamsberg was intensely waiting for more details.

'The feet were definitely taken from the cadavers before they were buried. Radstock has made a note "In the morgue? Or in the cold stores of the undertakers?" and also, according to the styles of the shoes, though that has to be checked, it looks as if all this happened between ten and twenty years ago, spread over a long period. In short, this was someone who cut off a pair of feet here, then another there, from time to time.'

'Until he got tired of his collection.'

'What's there to say he got tired?'

'The event we've witnessed. Just cast your mind back, Danglard. This man amasses his trophies for ten or twenty years, a diabolically difficult thing to do. He fanatically stores them in a freezer. Did Stock say anything about that?'

'Yes, he says they had been frozen and defrosted several times.'

'So the foot-chopper took them out now and then to look at them for God knows what purpose. Or perhaps to move them.'

Adamsberg leaned back against his seat and Danglard glanced up at the roof again. Another few minutes and they would be out from under the sea.

'And one night,' Adamsberg went on, 'despite all the trouble he had taken to build up his collection, the foot-chopper abandons his precious loot. Just like that, on a public street. He leaves it all behind as if it doesn't interest him any more. Or – and that would be even more disturbing – as if it wasn't *enough* for him any more. Like those collectors who junk one lot of stuff to go off in search of something new, moving up a stage. The foot-chopper switches to a more worthwhile quarry. Something better.'

'Or worse.'

'Yes. He's going deeper into his tunnel. No wonder Stock is upset. If he follows this trail, he'll get to some worrying levels.'

'Where will he get to?' asked Estalère, meanwhile closely observing the effect the champagne was having on Danglard.

'He'll go on until he reaches some unspeakable, cruel, devastating event, the one that has triggered the whole story, a story that ends in cut-off feet, or eating wardrobes. Then the dark tunnel opens up with its stairways and its caves, and Stock will have to go down into it.'

Adamsberg closed his eyes, passing without any visible transition to an apparent state of sleep or escape.

'We can't say that the foot-chopper has moved on to a new phase,' Danglard interjected, before Adamsberg escaped from him altogether. 'Or that he is getting rid of his collection. What we do know is that he deposited it outside Highgate Cemetery. And, good grief, that's not a matter of indifference. It's almost as if he were making an offering.'

The Eurostar sped out into the daylight, and Danglard's brow cleared. His smile encouraged Estalère.

'But, *commandant*,' Estalère whispered, 'what *did* happen in Highgate?'

As so often and without meaning to, Estalère was putting his finger on the crucial spot.

V

'I DON'T KNOW THAT IT'S A GOOD IDEA TO TELL THE HIGHGATE story,' said Danglard, who had by now ordered a third glass of champagne, for Estalère, and was drinking it on his behalf. 'Perhaps it's better not to keep telling it. It's one of those dark tunnels people dig, isn't it, *commissaire*, and this one is very old and long-forgotten. Perhaps we should just let it collapse into itself. Because the problem, when some madman opens up a tunnel, is that other people can get into it, which is really what Radstock was telling us in his own way. And that's what happened in Highgate.'

Estalère was waiting for him to go on, with the happy expression of a man who is about to hear a good story. Danglard looked at his bland, naive face and was unsure what he should do. If he took Estalère into the Highgate tunnel, he might damage that innocence. In the squad they tended to refer to Estalère's 'innocence' rather than to his stupidity. Four times out of five, Estalère just didn't get it. But his naivety sometimes generated the unexpected benefits of unsullied innocence. His blunders sometimes opened up avenues so obvious that nobody else had thought of them. Most of the time, though, Estalère's questions merely held things up. People tried to treat them with patience, partly because they liked Estalère, and partly because Adamsberg had decreed that one of these days he'd come out of it. The others made an effort to believe this, and the collective effort had become a habit. In fact, Danglard liked talking to Estalère when he had plenty of time, because he could expound vast quantities of knowledge without the young man becoming impatient. He glanced over at Adamsberg, whose eyes were closed. But he knew the *commissaire* wasn't sleeping and could hear every word he said.

'Why do you want to know?' he asked. 'The feet are for Radstock to deal with. They're behind us on the other side of the Channel now.'

'You said it might be an offering. Who to? Is the cemetery owned by someone?'

'In a manner of speaking. There's a master.'

'What's he called?'

'The Entity,' replied Danglard with a smile.

'Since when?'

'The west end of the cemetery, the oldest part, where we were the day before yesterday, was opened in 1839. But of course the master might have lived there before that.'

'Right.'

'Some people say that it was because the Entity lived there already in the ancient chapel on Highgate Hill that the place was chosen as a site for a cemetery.'

'A woman?'

'No, a man. More or less. And it was his power that drew the dead and the cemetery towards him, you see?'

'Yes.'

'They don't bury anyone now in the west section, it's become a well-known historical site, it's famous. There are extraordinary monuments there, strange things of all kinds, and the graves of famous people like Marx.'

A flicker of anxiety crossed the face of the young *brigadier*. Estalère never tried to conceal either his ignorance or the great embarrassment it caused him.

'Karl Marx,' Danglard explained. 'He wrote an important work on the class struggle, the economy, that kind of thing. He's the father of communism.'

'Right,' said Estalère. 'But is that something to do with the owner of Highgate?'

'Call him the Master, most people do. No, Marx is nothing to do with him. It was just to show you that West Highgate Cemetery is famous worldwide. And feared.'

'Yes, Radstock was afraid. But why?'

Danglard hesitated. Where to begin this story? If he told it at all.

'Well,' he said, 'nearly forty years ago, in 1970, two girls were coming home from school and they took a short cut across the cemetery. They arrived home in distress, saying they had been chased by a black shape, and that they had seen the dead rise from their graves. One of the girls fell ill and started sleepwalking. When she did this, she used to go into the cemetery and always walked towards the same catacomb, the Master's catacomb, as they called it. The Master must have been calling her. They kept a watch and followed her, and found several dead animals drained of all their blood. The neighbourhood began to panic, the rumour spread, the papers got hold of it and it snowballed. So some sort of self-styled priest decided to go along with other people who were equally worked up to exorcise the Master of Highgate. They went into the vault and found a coffin without a name, somewhat apart from the others. They opened it up. You can guess the rest.'

'No.'

'There was a body in the coffin, but it looked neither living nor dead. It was lying there perfectly preserved. A man, but an unknown and nameless person. The exorcist hesitated to put a stake through his heart, because the Church forbids it.'

'Why would he want to do that anyway?'

'Estalère, don't you know what one's supposed to do to vampires?'

'Ah,' the young man said, 'so this was a *vampire.*'

Danglard sighed, and wiped some condensation from the train window.

'Well, that's what the people thought, and they'd come along with crucifixes, garlic and stakes. And their leader pronounced an exorcism in front of the open coffin: "Get thee gone, wicked being, bearer of all evil and falsehoods! Depart this place, creature of vice."'

Adamsberg opened his eyes wide.

'You know this story?' said Danglard, slightly combatively.

'Not this one, I know others. At this moment in the story, there's usually an unearthly cry.'

'Precisely. There was a great sound of roaring in the vault. The exorcist threw some garlic in and got out, and they stopped up the entry to the catacomb with bricks.'

Adamsberg shrugged.

'You don't stop vampires with bricks.'

'No, and it didn't work. Four years later, there was gossip that a nearby house was haunted, an old Victorian house in

Gothic style. The same exorcist searched the house and found a coffin in the basement, which he recognised as the very same one he had bricked up four years earlier.'

'And was there a body inside?' asked Estalère.

'That I don't know.'

'There's an even older story, isn't there?' asked Adamsberg. 'Or Stock wouldn't have been so frightened.'

'I don't want to get into that,' muttered Danglard.

'But Stock knows it, *commandant*. So we ought to know about it too.

'It's his problem.'

'No, we saw it too. So when does the old story go back to?'

'Eighteen sixty-two,' said Danglard with extreme reluctance. 'Twenty-three years after the cemetery was created.'

'Go on.'

'That year, a certain Elizabeth Siddal, known as Lizzie, was buried there. She'd overdosed on laudanum. A kind of dope they had in Victorian times,' he added, for Estalère's benefit.

'I see.'

'Her husband was a famous man, Dante Gabriel Rossetti, a Pre-Raphaelite painter and a poet. Some manuscripts of her husband's poems were buried with her in the coffin.'

'It's not long till we get there,' said Estalère, looking suddenly alarmed. 'Will we have time for this?'

'Don't worry, it won't take long. Seven years later, the husband had the grave opened. Then there are two versions of this. The first says that Rossetti regretted his romantic gesture and wanted to get his poems back in order to publish them. According to the second version, he couldn't bear living without his wife, and he had this rather scary friend, called Bram Stoker. Have you heard of him, Estalère?'

'No, never.'

'Well, he's the creator of Count Dracula, a very powerful vampire.'

Estalère looked alarmed once again.

'It's only a novel,' Danglard explained, 'but we do know that the whole subject had an unhealthy fascination for Bram Stoker. He knew all these rituals that relate the living to the undead. So anyway, he was a friend of Dante Gabriel Rossetti's.'

In his effort to concentrate, Estalère was twisting another paper napkin, anxious not to miss a word.

'Some champagne?' Danglard asked. 'We've got plenty of time. It's not a nice story but it's quite short.'

Estalère shot a glance at Adamsberg, who seemed indifferent, and accepted. If he was making Danglard tell the story, it would be only polite to drink his champagne.

'Bram Stoker was passionately interested in Highgate Cemetery,' Danglard continued, stopping the drinks trolley again. 'He made one of his heroines, Lucy, go wandering there, and he made the place famous. Or perhaps, some people say, he was driven to it by the Entity itself. According to the second version, it was Stoker who persuaded Rossetti to look once more at his dead wife. Well, anyway, Rossetti did break open the coffin seven years after her death. And it was then, or perhaps earlier, that the Highgate catacomb was first opened.'

Danglard stopped speaking, as if he too were caught up in Dante Gabriel's dark wanderings, faced with the keen gaze of Adamsberg and the bemused expression of Estalère.

'Right,' said Estalère, 'he broke open the coffin – and he saw something?'

'Yes. Well. He discovered with dread that his wife was

perfectly preserved. She had kept her long auburn hair, her skin was as fresh and pink and her nails as long as if she had just died, even better than she had looked in life. That's the truth, Estalère. As if the seven years had done her nothing but good. Not a trace of decomposition.'

'Is that really possible?' asked Estalère, gripping the plastic cup.

'It's what happened in any case. She had the "rosy glow" of the living – in fact, she was rosier than ever. It was described by witnesses, I'm not making this up.'

'But the coffin was normal? Just a wooden one?'

'Yes. And the miraculous conservation of Lizzie Siddal caused a big scandal in England and beyond. People immediately started connecting it with the Master – the Highgate Vampire – and saying he had taken possession of the cemetery. There were ceremonies, people saw apparitions, they chanted incantations to the Master. From that time, the catacomb was open.'

'So people went in.'

'They certainly did, thousands of them. Until the two girls who were followed, more recently.'

The train braked, as they approached the Gare du Nord. Adamsberg sat up, shook out his jacket which he had rolled into a ball, and patted down his hair.

'And what's Stock's connection to all that?' he asked.

'Radstock was part of a team of policemen sent up there when they heard about the exorcism sessions in the 1970s. He saw the preserved body of the man, and he heard the exorcist addressing the vampire. I guess he was young and impressionable at the time. And then finding these dead people's feet in the same place the other day must have upset him a lot. Because they say the Entity – or the Vampire if you like – still reigns in the dark reaches of Highgate.'

'Is that why you talked about an offering?' asked Estalère. 'The foot-chopper was making an offering to the Entity?'

'That's what Radstock thinks. He's afraid some madman wants to start the whole nightmare up again, and "revive" the powers of the sleeping Master. But I guess it isn't really likely. The foot-chopper wants to offload his collection, right? He can't just chuck it all in the bin, any more than we can bear to throw away our childhood toys. He wants to find a suitable place for them.'

'And he chooses a place worthy of his fantasies,' said Adamsberg. 'He chooses Higg-Gate, where the feet could go on living.'

'Highgate,' Danglard corrected. 'It doesn't necessarily mean the foot-chopper believes in the Vampire. It's the character of the place that counts. Well, anyway, all that's well behind us now, and on the other side of the Channel.'

The train pulled in to the platform and Danglard seized his bag brusquely, as if to mark with a decisive action an end to the numbing effect of his story.

'But when you've seen something like that,' said Adamsberg softly, 'a bit of it sticks and stays inside you. Any experience that's too beautiful or too horrific always leaves some fragment of itself in the eyes of people who have witnessed it. We know that. In fact, that's how you recognise it.'

'Recognise what?'

'Something either overwhelmingly beautiful or overwhelmingly terrible, Estalère. You recognise it by the shock, the little splinter that remains.'

As they walked back up the platform, Estalère tapped the

commissaire on the shoulder, Danglard having parted from them in haste, as if regretting having said too much.

'The little fragments of things we've seen, what happens to them?'

'You put them away, you scatter them like stars in the big box we call memory.'

'You can't get rid of them?'

'No, that's not possible, the memory doesn't have a compartment marked trash.'

'So what happens if we don't like them?'

'Either you have to lie in wait for them and destroy them, like Danglard, or you leave them well alone.'

In the metro, Adamsberg wondered in which compartment of his memory the ghastly feet in London were going to lodge, on which galaxy of stars, and how long it would take for him to think he had forgotten them. And come to that, where would the wardrobe man go, or the bear and the uncle, or the girls who had seen the vampire and were trying to get back to him? What had happened to the one who had gone to the catacomb? And the exorcist?

Adamsberg rubbed his eyes, looking forward to getting a good night's sleep. Ten hours, why not? But in the event, he got only six hours.

VI

SEVEN THIRTY NEXT MORNING. THE *COMMISSAIRE*, THUNDER-struck, was sitting on a chair, and gazing at the crime scene, under the anxious eyes of his colleagues – so abnormal was it for Adamsberg to be thunderstruck, or indeed to be sitting on a chair. But he remained where he was, his face expressionless, and his eyes darting around, as if he had no wish to see, and was projecting his gaze far away so that nothing should lodge in his memory. He was forcing himself to think back, to 6 a.m., when he had not yet seen this room drenched in blood. When he had been dressing quickly, after the phone call from *Lieutenant* Justin, putting on the white shirt from the day before and the elegant black jacket lent to him by Danglard, both of them completely inappropriate to the situation. Justin's choked voice had foretold nothing good; it was the voice of someone who was sick to the stomach.

'We're using all the platforms,' he had said. That meant the plastic stands which were put on the ground to prevent any contamination of a crime scene by people's feet. 'All the platforms'. That meant the whole surface of the crime scene could not be trodden on. Adamsberg had left home hurriedly, avoiding Lucio, the tool shed, and the cat. Up to that point, he had been quite all right, he had not yet entered that room, he had not yet sat down on this chair, in front of carpets soaked in blood and strewn with entrails and splinters of bone, between four walls spattered with organic matter. It was as if the old man's body had literally exploded. The most revolting thing was perhaps the scraps of flesh on the black shining lid of the half-size grand piano, as if on a butcher's slab. Blood had also dripped on to the keys. This was another phenomenon for which there was no word: someone had reduced the body of another man to mincemeat. The word 'killer' was inadequate and derisory.

Leaving the house, he had called up his most trusty *lieutenant*, Retancourt, who in his view was the person best able to stand up to anything under creation. To thwart or redirect things as she wished.

'Retancourt, get over there to Justin, they've got all the platforms out. I don't know what's happened. The address is a villa on a private road in Garches, leafy suburb, old man, and apparently an indescribable scene in the house. From Justin's voice it sounded really bad. Fast as you can.'

With Retancourt, Adamsberg alternated between '*tu*' and '*vous*' without thinking about it. Her first name was Violette, an unlikely one for a woman who stood over 1m 80 and weighed 110 kilos. Adamsberg called her by her first name, or her surname, or her rank, depending on which was uppermost in his mind: his respect for her enigmatic abilities or his warm appreciation for the safe refuge she offered him – when she was so moved, and *if* she was so moved. This morning he was waiting for her, in a passive state, making time stand still, while his men spoke in low voices in the room and the blood dried on the walls. Perhaps she had been held up by something crossing her path. He heard Retancourt's heavy tread before he saw her.

'Bloody tailback all the way down the boulevard,' Retancourt was grumbling. She did not appreciate being held up.

Despite her remarkable size, she trod nimbly over the platforms and sat down heavily at his side. Adamsberg gave her a grateful smile. Did she know that to him she represented his tree of salvation, a tree with tough and miraculous fruit, the kind of tree you put your arms round without being able to encircle it, the kind of tree you climb up into when the mouth of hell opens? You build yourself a tree house in its highest branches. She had the strength, the ruggedness and the self-contained quality of a tree concealing a monumental mystery. Her shrewd gaze now took in the room, the floor, the walls, the men.

'It's like a slaughterhouse! Where's the body?'

'Everywhere, *lieutenant*,' said Adamsberg, stretching out his arms to encompass the whole room. 'It's been chopped up, pulverised, scattered. Wherever you look, you see parts of it, and when you see it all, you can't see any of it. There's nothing but the body, but the body isn't there.'

Retancourt inspected the scene in a more systematic manner. From one end of the room to the other, organic fragments were scattered on the carpets, the walls, in ghastly chunks alongside the legs of the furniture. Bones, flesh, blood, something burnt in the fireplace. A disaggregated body, which did not even arouse disgust, in the sense that it was impossible to associate these elements with anything resembling a human being. The officers were moving around cautiously. Every step carried the risk of touching some unseen piece of the invisible corpse. Justin was talking in a low voice to the photographer – the one with freckles whose name Adamsberg could never remember – and his short blond hair was soaked and clinging to his scalp.

'Justin's in shock,' said Retancourt.

'Yes,' said Adamsberg. 'He was the first to get here, and he'd no idea what he'd find. The gardener had raised the alarm. The duty officer at Garches called his boss, who called us when he realised what they were up against. Then Justin walked right in on it. You should relieve him. Can you co-ordinate the takeover with Mordent, Lamarre and Voisenet? We'll have to do a spot check, inch by inch, make a grid and collect the remains.'

'How on earth did he do it? Think how long it must have taken.'

'At first sight, it looks like he had a chainsaw and a blunt instrument of some kind. Between eleven last night and four this morning. He was able to get on with it because these villas are quite a long way apart, with big gardens and hedges. No very close neighbours and most of them are away for the weekend anyway.'

'An old man, you say. What do we know about him?'

'That he lived here, alone, and that he had plenty of money.'

'Plenty of money, yes,' agreed Retancourt, looking at the tapestries on the walls, and the baby grand which took up a third of the room. 'But alone? Surely you don't get massacred like this if you're really alone in the world.'

'That's if it's him at all, Violette. But we're nearly certain about that. The hair looks the same as we found in the bath-room and bedroom. So if it was him, his name was Pierre Vaudel, seventy-eight, former journalist, specialised in legal affairs.'

'Ah.'

'Yes, but according to the son, he didn't have any serious enemies. Just a few disputed cases and some vague grudges.'

'Where's the son?'

'On his way by train – he lives in Avignon.'

'He didn't say anything else?'

'Mordent says he didn't burst into tears.'

Dr Roman, the police pathologist, who had returned to work after a long time off sick, came and stood in front of Adamsberg.

'No point trying to get the family to identify him. We'll do it by DNA.'

'Obviously.'

'This is the first time I've ever seen you sit down on a case. Some reason you're not standing?'

'Because I'm sitting, Roman, that's all I want to do. What would you deduce from this carnage?'

'Some body parts haven't been entirely crushed with a heavy implement. There are recognisable sections of thighs, arms, just bashed about a bit. But the murderer took special care to demolish the head, hands and feet. They're completely shattered. The teeth too. It's a very thorough job.'

'Have you ever seen anything like this?'

'Sometimes you get faces and hands being obliterated to avoid identification. But that's got much rarer since we have

DNA checking. I've seen plenty of bodies that've been damaged or burnt, and so have you. But such a ferocious way of dismembering the body? No, it's quite beyond comprehension.'

'Where does it take us, Roman? Insanity?'

'Sort of. It's as if he went on repeating gestures over and over until he could do no more, as if he were afraid of leaving something undone. You know, it's a bit like when you go back ten times to make sure you've locked the door. He didn't only crush everything, bit by bit, and started again more than once, he chucked the pieces all over the place. No one fragment ended up next to another, even the toes aren't together. It's almost as if he was scattering corn in a field. Did he think there was a chance the old man could come to life again, or what? Don't ask me to try and reassemble the body, it's impossible.'

'I agree,' said Adamsberg. 'He was out of control, panicking, in some kind of endless rage.'

'There's no such thing as an endless rage,' his colleague, *Commandant* Mordent, interrupted aggressively.

Adamsberg stood up, shaking his head, and stepped on to a platform, then on to the next, carefully. He was the only one moving. The other officers had stopped to listen, standing still on their own platforms like so many pawns, as a key piece moved on the chessboard.

'Normally, no, Mordent, but here, yes. This man's rage, or panic or madness, goes beyond what we can see, taking us into unknown territory.'

'No,' the *commandant* insisted. 'Rage and anger burn up quickly, then they're over. This looks like hours of work. Four hours at least, and that's not the way rage works.'

'Well, what is it then?'

'Hard labour, obstinacy, calculation. Maybe even setting up a scene for us.'

'Impossible, Mordent, nobody could fake this.' Adamsberg crouched down to look at the floor. 'He was wearing boots? Big rubber boots?'

'Yes, that's what we thought,' Lamarre confirmed. 'Looks like a sensible precaution, given what he was going to do. The soles have left some good prints on the carpet. And there are some fragments of stuff from the ridges in the boots, mud or something.'

Mordent murmured 'hard labour' again, and stepped diagonally like a bishop, while Adamsberg moved two paces forward and one to the side, accomplishing a knight's move.

'What did he use to do the crushing?' he asked. 'Even with a heavy club or something, he couldn't do that on the carpet.'

'We've got a patch on the carpet hardly stained,' Justin pointed out, 'a rectangular shape. He might have put something on a block of wood or some metal plate, to act as an anvil.'

'That's a lot of heavy equipment to carry around: a chainsaw, a club, a block of wood. Plus spare clothes and shoes.'

'You could get it all into a big sack. I think he must have changed outside in the back garden. There are some specks of blood on the grass, where he must have put down bloodstained clothes.'

'And now and again,' Adamsberg remarked, 'he sat down for a rest. He chose this armchair.'

Adamsberg looked at the chair, its carved arms and its pink velvet seat now stained with blood.

'That's a very fancy chair,' he said.

'That,' said Mordent, 'is not just a very fancy chair, it's Louis XIII, no less. Early seventeenth century.'

'All right, *commandant*, it's Louis XIII,' said Adamsberg evenly. 'And if you're going to nitpick all day, please go home. Nobody wants to work on a Sunday, and nobody likes having to wade through this slaughterhouse. And you've had more sleep than some of us.'

Mordent made another bishop's move, away from Adamsberg. The *commissaire* clasped his hands behind his back and looked again at the chair. 'This was the murderer's refuge, so to speak. He takes a break. Looks around at the destruction he's causing, but he wants a few moments of relief and satisfaction. Or perhaps he's just out of breath.'

'Why are we saying "he"?' asked Justin conscientiously. 'A woman could have brought in the material if she parked near enough.'

'This is a man's work, a man's mind. I don't see an ounce of woman in this. And look at the size of the boots.'

'The victim's clothes,' said Retancourt, pointing to a pile on a chair. 'He didn't tear them off, or rip them up. They've just been taken off, as if he were putting the man to bed. That's unusual too.'

'Because he wasn't in a rage,' said Mordent from the corner to which he had retreated.

'Did he take them all off?'

'Except the underpants,' said Lamarre.

'That's because he didn't want to see,' said Retancourt. 'He took the victim's clothes off so as not to foul up the saw, but he couldn't bring himself to strip the man naked. The idea upset him.'

'In that case,' said Roman, 'at least we can say he wasn't a doctor or nurse or a paramedic. I've stripped hundreds of bodies in my time, doesn't bother me.'

Adamsberg had put on gloves and was rolling between his fingers one of the little balls of earth from the boots.

'There's a horse somewhere,' he said. 'This is horse manure, stuck to the boots.'

'How can you tell?' asked Justin.

'By the smell.'

'So should we start looking for people who work with horses, racehorse trainers, stud farms, riding stables?'

'Come off it,' said Mordent. 'Thousands of people go near horses, the killer could have got that on his boots just walking down any road in the country.'

'Well, that's already something, *commandant*,' said Adamsberg. 'We know the killer may have been in the country, or near horses anyway. When does the son get here?'

'He should be at HQ in less than an hour. He's called Pierre, like his father.'

Adamsberg looked at his two watches.

'I'll send you a relief team at midday. Retancourt, Mordent, Lamarre and Voisenet, you deal with collecting evidence. Justin and Estalère, you start investigating the personal background. Accounts, diary, notebooks, wallet, telephone, family photos, medicines, all that stuff. Who he knew, who he called, what he bought, clothes, food, what he liked doing. Get everything you can, we'll have to reconstruct it as fully as possible. This old man wasn't just killed, he was reduced to nothingness. He didn't simply have his life taken, he was literally demolished, wiped out.'

The image of the polar bear flashed suddenly into his mind. The bear must have left the uncle's body in a state something like this, but cleaner. Nothing left to bring back or bury. And the son Pierre would certainly be unable to bring the murderer's skin back to the widow as a trophy.

'I don't think what he ate is going to be very relevant,' said Mordent. 'It would be more to the point to see what legal cases he wrote about. And his family and financial situation. We don't even know if he was married. We still don't even know it's *him*.'

Adamsberg looked around at the tired faces of the men standing on platforms.

'Break for everyone,' he said. 'There's a cafe down the road. Retancourt and Roman will stay on duty.'

Retancourt walked Adamsberg to his car.

'When the place has been cleaned up a bit, call Danglard. Get him working on the victim's background, but don't let him near the crime scene.'

'Of course not.'

Danglard's squeamishness at the sight of blood or death was well known and uncritically accepted in the squad. They usually didn't call him in until the worst had been cleaned up.

'What's eating Mordent?' asked Adamsberg.

'No idea.'

'He doesn't seem himself at all. Putting on a front and making snide remarks.'

'Yes, I noticed.'

'The way the killer threw everything around, does it ring any bells?'

'Reminds me of my grandmother, not that she's got anything to do with it.'

'Tell me all the same.'

'When she was losing her marbles, she started laying things out in patterns. She couldn't bear one thing touching another. She separated newspapers, clothes, shoes.'

'Shoes?'

'Anything made of cloth, paper or leather. Shoes had to be ten centimetres apart; she lined them up on the ground.'

'Did she say why? Was there some reason?'

'An excellent reason. She thought that if these objects touched each other they might catch fire because of the friction. As I said, nothing to do with this Vaudel business.'

Adamsberg raised his hand to indicate he was taking a message, listened carefully, then pocketed his phone.

'A few days ago,' he explained, 'I helped deliver two kittens. It was a difficult birth. The message says the cat is doing OK.'

'Oh, right,' said Retancourt after a pause. 'I suppose that has to be good news.'

'The killer might have been like your grandmother. He might have wanted there to be no contact, to keep all the elements separate. But that's the opposite of making a collection,' he added, thinking of the London feet again. 'He crushed everything to bits, destroying any coherence. And I wonder why Mordent is being such a pain in the backside today.'

Retancourt didn't like it when Adamsberg's remarks became inconsequential. These non sequiturs and distractions might make him deviate from his purpose. With a wave, she went back to the house.

VII

ADAMSBERG ALWAYS READ THE NEWSPAPER STANDING UP, while he took a turn around the desk in his office. It wasn't even his own newspaper. He borrowed it every day from Danglard, and gave it back in a crumpled state.

An article on page 12 described the progress made by a police investigation in Nantes. Adamsberg knew the *commissaire* in charge quite well: a solitary and tight-lipped man when on the job, but the life and soul of the party after work. Adamsberg tried to recall his name as a mental exercise. Since London, and perhaps since Danglard had presented such an encyclopedic account of Highgate Cemetery, the *commissaire* had been feeling he ought perhaps to try harder to remember names, phrases, sentences. His memory for them had always been poor, though he could recall a sound, a facial expression or a trick of the light years later. What was that cop's name? Bollet? Rollet? He could keep a tableful of twenty people amused, something Adamsberg admired. And just now he felt envious of this Nolet (having just read his name in the article) because he was dealing with a nice obvious murder, whereas Adamsberg couldn't rid his mind of the Louis XIII armchair with its stained velvet seat. Compared with the chaos in Garches, Nolet's inquiry was bracing. A clean killing, two bullets to the head, the victim had opened the door to the killer. No complications, no rape, no madness, a woman of fifty killed, a professional job: you've-pissed-me-off-I'm-going-to-kill-you. Nolet just had to find a husband or lover and tie the case up, without having to wander over several square metres of carpet covered with flesh. Without venturing into the territory of madness, Stock's dark continent. Stock wasn't his real name either, Adamsberg knew that, the British cop who wanted to retire and go fishing. With Danglard perhaps, who knew? Unless that woman, Abstract, succeeded in hauling Danglard off somewhere else.

Adamsberg raised his head as the office clock made a click. Pierre Vaudel, son of Pierre Vaudel, would be here in a few minutes. The *commissaire* went up the wooden stairs, avoiding the irregular step which made people trip, and went into the annexe with the coffee machine to get himself a strong espresso. The little room was more or less the den of *Lieutenant* Mercadet, a man with a gift for statistics and various logical exercises, but suffering from mild narcolepsy. Some cushions in a corner allowed him to take a nap every now and again to refresh himself. Just now he was folding his blanket and rubbing his eyes.

'Sounds like we're wading through a bloodbath out there,' he commented.

'Not exactly wading, we're using platforms six centimetres above the floor.'

'Yeah, but we've got to deal with it, haven't we? Sounds a God-awful case.'

'Yes. If you've got the stomach for it, go and see it before they're out of there. It's slaughter without any rhyme or reason. But there is some obsessive idea behind it. As *Lieutenant* Veyrenc might say: a steel thread vibrating in the depths of the pit. I don't know, some kind of invisible motive, perhaps only poetry could reveal it.'

'Veyrenc would have come up with something better than that. We miss him, don't we?'

Adamsberg swallowed down his coffee, surprised. He hadn't thought about Veyrenc since he had left the squad. He was not inclined to dwell on the stormy events that had set them against each other in a previous case.

'Perhaps you're not bothered though,' said Mercadet.

'Perhaps. Mainly it's that we don't have time for that sort of thing, *lieutenant*.'

'I'll get over there,' said Mercadet with a nod. 'Danglard left a message for you. Nothing to do with the Garches affair.'

Adamsberg finished page 12 as he went down the stairs. Aha, the witty Nolet was not getting on as well as all that. The ex-husband had an alibi, the inquiry was at a standstill. Adamsberg folded up the paper contentedly. In reception, the son of Pierre Vaudel was waiting for him, sitting upright, alongside his wife. He looked no more than thirty-five. Adamsberg paused. How do you tell a man his father has been chopped into pieces?

The *commissaire* avoided getting to the point for some time, as he went through the formalities of identity and family. Pierre was an only child, and a late one. His mother had become pregnant after sixteen years of marriage, when his father had been forty-four. And Pierre Vaudel senior had been unrelentingly furious about this pregnancy, without giving his wife any reason. He was implacably opposed to having children, this child was not to be born and he wasn't going to discuss it further. His wife had given in and gone away to have an abortion. In fact, she stayed away six months and allowed the pregnancy to go to term, and Pierre, son of Pierre, was born. His father's anger had finally subsided after five years, but he always refused to let the child and his mother come and live with him.

Pierre junior had only seen his father now and then as a child, and had been petrified by this man who had refused his existence with such determination. And this fear was entirely because of his having been born against his father's wishes, since Pierre senior was apparently a perfectly reasonable man in other respects, generous according to his friends and affectionate according to his wife. Or at least he had been at one time, since a gradual withdrawal from contacts made it hard to discover his feelings. From the age of fifty-five, he would only see very few visitors, and over time detached himself from all those in his previously quite wide circle of friends. Later on, as a teenager, Pierre junior had managed to gain occasional entry, coming to play the piano on Saturday mornings, choosing pieces he thought would please his father. Then as a young man, Pierre junior had managed to get some serious attention. For the last ten years, especially since his mother's death, the two Pierres had met fairly regularly. The son had become a lawyer and his professional knowledge had been helpful to his father when he was researching legal cases. Working together had allowed them to avoid having too much personal conversation.

'What was his interest in these cases?'

'Well, it was his living. He made all his money from it. He did law reports for several papers and specialist periodicals. Then he would go in search of miscarriages of justice. He was a scientist by training and he used to complain all the time about how sloppy the judicial system was. He said that the law was ambiguous and could be twisted one way and another, so the truth got lost in these endless and sickening arguments. He said you could tell at once if a verdict was right or wrong, if it clicked into place satisfactorily or not. He operated like a locksmith, working by ear. If it squeaked he looked for the truth.'

'And did he find it?'

'Several times, yes. He was responsible for the posthumous exoneration of the Sologne murderer, remember that? And other famous cases too where people got released: K. Jimmy Jones in the US, a banker called Trevenant, Madame Pasnier. He got Professor Glérant acquitted. His articles really counted. As time went on, many lawyers started to worry about his going into print. He was offered bribes, which he refused.'

Pierre junior rested his chin on his hand, looking annoyed. He was not particularly handsome, with his domed forehead and pointed chin. But his eyes were rather remarkable, with a blank, dull glare, impenetrable shutters, possibly not open to pity. Leaning forward, with drooping shoulders and consulting his wife with a glance, he looked an apparently easy-going, docile man. But Adamsberg judged that there was intransigence somewhere behind the fixed glass of his eyes.

'Were there some less happy endings?' he asked.

'He said the truth was a two-way street. He was also responsible for getting three men found guilty. One of them hanged himself in jail after protesting his innocence.'

'When was this?'

'Just before my father retired, about thirteen years ago.'

'Who was it?'

'Jean-Christophe Réal.'

Adamsberg nodded, indicating that he recognised the name.

'Réal hanged himself on his twenty-ninth birthday.'

'Were there any letters after that, threatening vengeance?'

'What's all this about?' asked Pierre's wife, who, unlike her husband, had regular and unremarkable features. 'Father's death wasn't from natural causes. Is that it? You've got doubts about it? If so, say so. Since early this morning, the police haven't given us a single clear fact. Father's dead, but we don't even know if it's him. Your colleague says we can't see the body. Why?'

'Because it's difficult.'

'Are you telling us that Father – if it is Father – died in embarrassing circumstances? In bed with a prostitute? I hardly think so. Or some upper-class woman? Is this a cover-up, to protect people in high places? Because yes, my father-in-law did know a lot of those people who think they're untouchable, the ex-minister of justice for a start. Totally corrupt.'

'Hélène, please,' said Pierre, but he was allowing her to go on.

'Let me remind you, this is Pierre's father we're talking about, and he has a perfect right to see anything and to know anything there is to know, before you, and certainly before people in high places. We see the body, or we don't answer any more questions.'

'That seems reasonable, doesn't it?' said Pierre, in the manner of a lawyer finding a satisfactory compromise.

61

'There *is* no body,' said Adamsberg, looking straight at the wife.

'No body,' repeated Pierre mechanically.

'No.'

'Well, then how do you know it's him?'

'Because he's in the villa.'

'Who's in the villa?'

'The body.'

Adamsberg opened the window and looked out at the lime trees. They had been in flower for a few days and their scent floated in on a breath of air.

'The body's in pieces,' he said. 'He was' – what word to choose? chopped up? pulverised? – 'cut into pieces and scattered round the room. The big room with the piano. There's nothing left to identify. I don't recommend that you see it.'

'There's some kind of cover-up going on,' the wife insisted. 'You're hiding something. What are you doing with him?'

'We've collected what's left of him, by going over every square metre of the room and placing what we find in numbered containers. Forty-eight square metres, forty-eight containers.'

Adamsberg turned back from the lime-tree blossom and towards Hélène Vaudel. Pierre was still looking down, leaving matters to his wife.

'People do say that it's hard to grieve properly unless you have seen with your own eyes,' Adamsberg went on. 'But I've known cases where people have regretted it, and all things considered would prefer not to have seen. Still, the photos taken when the police arrived are available here,' he said, passing his mobile to Hélène. 'And we can send you to Garches in a car, if you insist. But perhaps you should have some inkling what's there before you decide. These aren't good quality, but they'll give you an idea.'

Hélène seized the mobile and started viewing the images, She stopped at the seventh which showed the piano.

'Very well,' she said, putting it down with an altered expression.

'No car?' said Pierre.

'No car.'

This was issued like a command and Pierre nodded. Not a sliver of rebellion, although it was his father they were discussing. No curiosity about the photos. Apparently simple and direct neutrality. A provisional and deliberate submission before he took back the reins again.

'You don't happen to ride a horse by any chance?' Adamsberg asked.

'No, I follow racing a bit in the papers. My father used to be a heavy better at one time. But for years now, he'd only had a flutter about once a month. He'd changed, he'd shrunk into himself. He hardly ever went out.'

'Did he ever go to a trainer's stables or a racecourse? Did he go out into the country? Could he have brought any horse manure home on his shoes?'

'Papa? Horse manure in the house?'

Pierre sat up as if this idea had jolted him despite himself.

'Are you telling me there's horse manure in his house?'

'Yes, on the carpet. Just a few bits from the sole of someone's boot.'

'He never put boots on in his life. He didn't like animals, or nature, the earth, flowers, even daisies fading away in a vase, anything like that. Did the murderer come in with boots covered in dung?'

Adamsberg excused himself to answer his mobile.

'If you've still got the son there,' Retancourt said, without preliminaries, 'ask him if the old man had a pet, a cat or dog. We found some hairs on the Louis XIII armchair. But there's no sign of an animal, no cat litter or dog food. So if he didn't, the hairs could have come off the murderer's trousers.'

Adamsberg turned away from the couple, shielding them from Retancourt's abrupt tones.

'Did your father by any chance have a pet animal? Dog, cat?'

'I just told you, he didn't like animals. He didn't put himself out for people, still less for an animal, too much bother.'

'No, not at all,' said Adamsberg into the phone. 'But check it out, *lieutenant*, it could be from a rug or a coat. Check the other chairs as well.'

'Or tissues? Did he use them? We found one crumpled up in the grass outside, but there aren't any in the bathroom.'

'Tissues?' Adamsberg asked.

'No, never,' said Pierre, raising his hands as if to push away this further aberrant suggestion. 'Only cotton handkerchiefs, folded in three one way and in four the other. He was fussy about them.'

'No, just cotton handkerchiefs,' Adamsberg relayed.

'Danglard is insisting on talking to you. He's walking around on the grass in circles with something on his mind.'

That was spot on, thought Adamsberg, as a description of Danglard's temperament. Prowling around the basins in the limestone where his worries were becoming calcified. He ran his fingers through his hair, trying to remember what stage the interview had reached. Oh yes, boots, horse manure.

'No, not boots *covered* in manure,' he explained. 'Just a few little fragments that must have fallen off the soles, from the damp.'

'Have you seen the handyman, the man who did the garden? He must have boots.'

'Not yet. We've been told he's a rough customer.'

'A ruffian, an ex-convict and a halfwit,' Hélène completed. 'Father was besotted with him.'

'Oh, I wouldn't say he was half-witted,' Pierre intervened. 'Why,' he asked cautiously, 'was the body treated that way? Killing him, all right, one can perhaps understand. The family of the man who committed suicide, there could be a possible cause there. But why destroy the body? Is this a common modus operandi?'

'Not until this particular killer came along. He wasn't copying anyone, he seems to have created something entirely unprecedented.'

'Anyone would think you were talking about a work of art,' said Hélène with a disapproving frown.

'Well, why not?' said Pierre suddenly. 'It would be a sort of rough justice. He was an artist.'

'Who, your father?'

'No, Réal, the suicide.'

Adamsberg made another apologetic sign as Danglard came on the line.

'I knew we were going to be up shit creek,' the *commandant* was saying in a studied voice, which told Adamsberg that he had already had several drinks and was making an effort to pronounce clearly.

They must have let him into the room with the piano.

'Have you visited the crime scene, *commandant*?'

'No, the photos are quite enough. But it's just been confirmed, the shoes are French.'

'The boots you mean?'

'No, the shoes. And there's something worse. And when I saw that, it was as if someone had lit a match in the catacomb, as if someone had cut off my uncle's feet. But we don't have any choice, I'm on my way now.'

More than three drinks, Adamsberg guessed, and knocked back in short order. He looked at his watches: only four o'clock. Danglard would be no good to anyone for the rest of the day. 'Don't worry, Danglard, just leave the villa, I'll catch up with you later.'

'That's what I'm saying.'

Adamsberg put the phone away, wondering absurdly what was becoming of the cat and kittens. He had told Retancourt that the mother was recovering, but one of the kittens, one of the two he had delivered, a female, was not doing well. Had he squeezed her too hard? Had he damaged something?

'Jean-Christophe Réal,' Pierre reminded him insistently, as if he feared the *commissaire* wouldn't find his way back alone.

'The artist,' Adamsberg agreed.

'He worked with horses, he used to hire them. The first time it was to cover a horse with bronze paint to make a sort of living statue. The owner sued him, but that's how he made his name. He did more after that. He painted everything, it took colossal amounts of paint: grass, trees, stones, leaves one by one, as if he was petrifying the whole landscape.'

'That won't interest the *commissaire*, Pierre,' said Hélène.

'Did you know Réal at all?'

'I visited him in prison. Actually, I was determined to get him released.'

'What did your father accuse him of?'

'Of painting this woman – she was his patron – who had left him money in her will.'

'I don't get it.'

'He painted her, literally, with bronze paint, and sat her on one of these horses to be a living equestrian statue. But the paint blocked her pores, and before they could clean it off, she died of asphyxiation on horseback. Réal did inherit.'

'How weird,' said Adamsberg. 'And the horse – that died too, I suppose?'

'No, it didn't, that's the whole problem. Réal knew perfectly well what he was doing, of course, he used porous paint. He wasn't mad.'

'No,' said Adamsberg sceptically.

'Some forensic scientist said the paint must have reacted with her make-up and that led to the poisoning. But my father claimed to have proof that Réal had switched the paint after doing the horse, and that he had set out to kill her.'

'And you didn't agree.'

'No,' said Pierre, thrusting out his chin.

'And was your father's claim founded?'

'Maybe, who knows? My father was abnormally fixated on this guy. He hated him for no obvious reason. He just set out to destroy him.'

'No, you're wrong,' said Hélène, suddenly disagreeing. 'You knew Réal was a megalomaniac, and he was deep in debt. He must have killed that woman.'

'Oh, for God's sake,' said Pierre. 'My father went after him to get at *me*. When I was eighteen, I wanted to be a painter. Réal was a few years older than me, I admired his work, I'd been to see him twice. When my father found out, he went berserk. He thought Réal was a greedy ignoramus, that's what he called him, whose grotesque artworks were destabilising civilisation as we know it. My father was a man from the dark ages, he believed in the ancient foundations of the world, and Réal infuriated him. So with his notoriety in legal matters, the old bastard pestered the authorities, had him charged, and caused his death.'

'*The old bastard*?' repeated Adamsberg.

'Yes,' said Pierre unblinkingly. 'If you really want to know, my father was a chateau-bottled shit.'

VIII

THE NAMES HAD BEEN NOTED OF ALL THE RESIDENTS IN THE nearby villas, and inquiries in the neighbourhood had begun, a necessary and wearisome task. Nothing they found so far contradicted what Pierre had said. No one else quite dared describe Pierre Vaudel as a chateau-bottled shit, but the witness statements all portrayed him latterly as a withdrawn, eccentric, intolerant man, entirely self-sufficient. He was clever, but to no one else's advantage. He avoided people and by the same token didn't bother anyone. The police went from door to door, explaining that an unpleasant murder had taken place, but without telling them that the old man had been butchered. Would he have opened the door to his attacker? Yes, if the reason had been something technical, like repairs, but not just to have a chat. Even after dark? Yes, he wouldn't have been afraid, he was, well, sort of invulnerable. Or that was the impression he gave.

Only one man, the gardener, Émile, described him in any other terms. No, he said, Vaudel wasn't a curmudgeon. His only suspicions were of himself and that was why he didn't want to see people. How did the gardener know that? Because

Vaudel said so himself, with a funny little smile sometimes. How had they met? In court, when Émile was up for the ninth time for GBH, about fifteen years ago. Vaudel had taken an interest in his violent career, and gradually they had become acquainted. Until in the end he had hired him to look after the garden, fetch logs for the fire, and later on to do shopping and odd jobs. Émile suited him because he didn't try to chat. When the neighbours had found out about the gardener's past, they had not been best pleased.

'Can't blame 'em. Put yourself in their place. "Basher", that's what they call me. So course, the people round here, they keep out of me way.'

'They don't want to meet you at all?' asked Adamsberg.

The gardener was sitting on the top step of the stairs up to the house, where the June sun had warmed the stone. He was a small, wiry man, his overalls hanging loosely off him, and did not look particularly threatening. His lived-in face was worn and rather ugly, expressing neither strong will nor confidence. He kept up a series of defensive gestures, wiping his nose, which was crooked from previous violent encounters, and shading his eyes. One ear was bigger than the other, and he rubbed that too, rather like a nervous dog, and this movement alone indicated either that he was upset, or perhaps that he was bewildered. Adamsberg sat down beside him.

'You from the cops?' asked the man, looking intrigued at Adamsberg's clothes.

'Yes, and my colleague says you don't agree with the neighbours about Monsieur Vaudel. I don't know your name.'

'I told them about twenty times: Émile Feuillant.'

'Émile,' Adamsberg repeated, trying to fix it in his mind.

'Aren't you going to write it down? The others, that's what

they done. Stands to reason, I suppose, or you keep telling 'em the same thing over. Course, *they* keep saying the same thing. Always gets me going, that. Why do cops always have to say everything twice. You tell 'em, Friday night I was down the Parrot, and the cop goes: "So where were you Friday?" Just gets you all worked up.'

'Yes, that's the point, it gets you worked up, so in the end the man stops talking about the Parrot, and tells the cops what they want to hear.'

'Yeah, stands to reason. I get it.'

Stands to reason, doesn't stand to reason, Émile seemed to divide the world up on either side of this demarcation line. By the way he was looking at him, Adamsberg had the feeling that Émile was not putting him on the side of things that stood to reason.

'Are they all afraid of you round here?'

'Yeah, suppose so, except for Madame Bourlant next door. See, I've been in a hundred and thirty-eight street fights, not counting when I was a kid. So there you are.'

'Is that why you're saying the opposite of the neighbours? Because they don't like you.'

This question seemed to surprise Émile.

'See if I care if they *like* me or not. Just I know more than they do about old Vaudel. Can't blame 'em, stands to reason they're afraid of me. I'm a man with "a violent past of the most reprehensible kind". That's what he used to say,' he added, with a laugh that revealed a couple of missing teeth. 'Mind, he was a bit out of order, cos I never *killed* nobody. But "violent past", yeah, he wasn't far wrong.'

Émile brought out a packet of tobacco and efficiently rolled himself a cigarette.

'This violent past, how much time have you done for it?'

'Eleven years and six months, seven different sentences. That wears you out. Well, now I'm over fifty, it's not so bad. Just the odd fight now and then. No more. And I've paid the price, haven't I? No wife, no kids. Like kids all right, but I wouldn't want any myself. When you're like me, quick with my fists, wouldn't be such a good idea. Stands to reason. That was something else we had in common, Monsieur Vaudel and me. He didn't want no kids either. Well, not that he said it like that. What he said in his plummy voice was: "No descendants, Émile." Still, he did have a kid an' all, without meaning to.'

'Do you know why?'

Émile dragged on his cigarette and looked at Adamsberg in surprise.

'Didn't mind out, did he?'

'But why didn't he want "descendants"?'

'Just didn't. But what I'm thinking now is what'm I going to do? I've not got a job, or a roof over my head no more, I used to live in the shed.'

'And Vaudel wasn't afraid of you?'

'Not him. He wasn't afraid of anything, even dying. He used to say, only thing about dying, it takes too long.'

'And you never felt like being violent towards him?'

'Yeah, sometimes, at first. But I preferred to get him at noughts and crosses. I taught him how to play. I never thought to find someone didn't know how to play noughts and crosses. I'd come in the evening, light the fire, pour out a couple of Guignolets. That's something he showed *me*, drinking Guignolet. And we'd sit down and play noughts and crosses.'

'And who won?'

'Two times out of three it was him in the end. Because he was really crafty, and he invented this special version, very big, with long pieces of paper. Really hard, you see?'

'Yes.'

'So he wanted to go even bigger, but I didn't.'

'Did you do a lot of drinking together?'

'No, just a couple of Guignolets, that was it. But what I'll miss is the winkles we used to eat with it. He used to order them every Friday, we had a little pin each, mine had a blue top, his had an orange top, never mix them up. He said I'd be . . .'

Émile rubbed his nose trying to remember a word. Adamsberg recognised this kind of search.

'Yeah, that I'd be nost-al-gic when he weren't there no more. But he was right an' all, crafty old thing. I *am* nostalgic.'

Adamsberg had the sense that Émile was proudly assuming the complex state of nostalgia and the unfamiliar word to honour it.

'When you were violent in the past, was it when you were drunk?'

'Nah, that's just it. Sometimes I'd have a drink *after*, to get over it, like. And yeah, before you ask, I seen lots of shrinks, they made me see 'em, like it or not, ten or more. They didn't know what I was doing it for. They poked about, asking about my parents, father, mother, nothing. I was happy enough as a kid. That's why Monsieur Vaudel, he used to say, nothing to be done about it, Émile, it's in your genes. Do you know what that is, genes?'

'Sort of.'

'No, properly?'

'No.'

'Well, *I* know, it's bad seed as comes down to you. So, you see. It wasn't any point him and me trying to live like other people. It was down to genes.'

'You think Vaudel had genes too?'

'Of course,' said Émile with an air of annoyance, as if Adamsberg was making no effort to understand. 'But like I said, I don't know what I'm going to do now.'

He concentrated on cleaning his nails with the end of a matchstick.

'No,' he said, shaking his head. 'He wouldn't have anyone talk about it.'

'Émile, what *were* you doing on Saturday night?'

'Told you, I was at the Parrot.'

Émile gave a wide provocative grin as he threw away his match. He was no halfwit.

'Come on.'

'I took me mother out for supper in this cafe. Always the same place, it's near Chartres. I told 'em, the cops, the name an' all. They'll tell you. I go there every Saturday. And let me tell you, me mum, I've never lifted a finger against her. Well, would be the end, wouldn't it? And me mum, she thinks the world of me. Stands to reason, don't it?'

'But your mother doesn't stay out till four in the morning, does she? And you got home at five.'

'Yeah, and that's when I saw there wasn't no lights on at the house. He always left his lights on all night.'

'When did you leave your mother?'

'Ten o'clock on the dot,' said Émile. 'Like every Saturday. I went to see me dog after.'

Émile pulled out a wallet and showed a well-thumbed photograph.

'That's him,' he said. 'Sit in my pocket, he could, like a kangaroo, when he was little. When I was in prison the third time, my sister she said she didn't want to look after him no more, so she gave him away. But I knew where he was. With these cousins, Gérault their name is, it's a farm out Châteaudun way. So after supper with me mum, I take me van and go and see him, with dog food and presents and stuff. He knows I'm coming. He waits for me in the dark, he jumps the gate, and he comes and sits all night in the van with me. Rain or shine. He knows I'll be there. And he's no bigger than that an' all.'

Émile held his hands in a shape the size of a child's football.

'Are there any horses on this farm?'

'Gérault, he does mostly cattle, three-quarters dairy, quarter beef. But he's got a few horses an' all.'

'Who knows about this?'

'That I go see the dog?'

'Yes, Émile, we're not talking about the farm animals. Did Vaudel know?'

'Yeah, he'd never let me have a dog here, but he understood. He let me have Saturday nights off: me mum and me dog.'

'But Vaudel's not around any more to back up your story.'

'No.'

'Nor the dog either.'

'Yeah, *he*'s around. You come with me any Saturday night and you'll see I'm not making it up. You'll see, he'll jump the gate, and come to the van. That proves it.'

'No. That isn't proof you went there *this* Saturday night.'

'No, OK, you're right, but you can't expect a dog to know which Saturday it was. Even a dog like Cupid.'

Cupid, eh, said Adamsberg to himself.

He closed his eyes, resting against the stone lintel of the doorway, turning his face to the sun, like Émile. Behind the thick wall, the collection of evidence was coming to an end, the platforms were being folded up. The square metres of carpet had been numbered and their contents put in containers. Now they would have to start looking for some meaning in all this. It was possible that Pierre junior might have wanted to kill the old bastard. Or the daughter-in-law, who seemed a strong-willed type, risking everything on her husband's behalf. Or Émile. Or the family of that painter who covered horses in liquid bronze, and had unfortunately done the same to a woman. Painting your patron in bronze was one more thing that had never been heard of, on Stock's dark continent. On the other hand, killing an old man with plenty of money had been known about for a long time. But why reduce him to mincemeat and scatter his remains? Why? There was no answer to that. Until you have the reason, you won't find the man.

Mordent came towards them with his awkward gait, his long neck thrust forward, his grey hair cropped close to his skull, his eye movements rapid, just like a crafty heron on the lookout for fish. He came over to Émile and looked at Adamsberg without indulgence.

'He's asleep,' whispered Émile. 'Stands to reason, anyone can see that.'

'Was he just talking to you?'

'So what, it's his job, isn't it?'

'Yes, of course. But we're still going to wake him up.'

'Strewth,' said Émile bitterly, 'can't a man kip for a few minutes without getting a bollocking?'

'I'm hardly likely to give him a bollocking, since he's my boss. That's the *commissaire*.'

Adamsberg opened his eyes as Mordent tapped his shoulder. Émile stood up, and put some distance between them. He was rather shocked to learn that this man was the *commissaire*, as if the proper order of things had been disturbed and beggars could become kings without warning. It was one thing to chat about your bad genes and your dog Cupid with an ordinary cop, quite another if he was a *commissaire*. In other words someone who knew all the sneaky techniques of interrogation. And this one was supposed to be an ace, or so he had heard. And he had just been rabbiting on, and probably saying far too much.

'Stay where you are,' Mordent said, holding Émile back by the sleeve. 'This is going to interest you. *Commissaire*, we've been on to the solicitor. Vaudel made a will three months ago.'

'Leave a lot of money?'

'I'll say. He owned three houses out here in Garches, another in Vaucresson and a big building let out for rent in Paris. Plus about the equivalent in stocks and insurance.'

'Nothing too surprising about that,' said Adamsberg, getting up and brushing his trousers.

'Apart from the legal requirement for the son's share, he left it all to someone outside the family. Émile Feuillant.'

IX

ÉMILE SAT DOWN AGAIN ON THE STEP, LOOKING STUNNED. Adamsberg remained standing, leaning against the doorpost, head bowed and arms crossed on his stomach, the only visible sign that he was thinking, according to his colleagues. Mordent paced up and down, swinging his arms, his eyes darting here and there. Adamsberg was not in fact lost in thought, but was telling himself that Mordent looked more than ever like a heron that's just pounced on a fish and is still happily holding it in its beak. A fish called Émile in this case. Who broke the silence, as he started, clumsily this time, to roll himself another cigarette.

'Don't stand to reason that, to cut out his own kid.'

He had too much paper at the end of the roll-up, and it flared up, singeing his grey hair.

'Whether he liked it or not, that was his kid,' Émile went on, rubbing the lock of hair which smelt like burnt pork. 'And he didn't like *me* that much. Even if he knew I'd be nost-algic, and I *am* nost-algic. It should've gone to Pierre.'

'You're a one-man charity, are you?' asked Mordent.

'No, I'm just saying it should've gone to him, stands to

reason. But I'll take my share, gotta respect the old man's wishes.'

'Respect – that's handy for you.'

'Not just respect, the law.'

'Ah. The law's handy too.'

'Yeah, sometimes. Will I get this house?'

'This one or the others,' Adamsberg intervened. 'On the part of the estate that comes to you, you'll have to pay big death duties. But you'll probably end up with a couple of houses and quite a lot of money.'

'I'll get me mum to come and live with me, and I'll buy back me dog.'

'You're getting organised very fast,' said Mordent. 'Anyone'd think you were expecting it.'

'So? Stands to reason to get your mother a proper house, doesn't it?'

'I'm saying you don't seem all that surprised. I'm saying that you're already making plans. You could at least observe a decent interval to take it in. That's the normal thing.'

'Normal thing be buggered. I've taken it in already. Don't see why I'd be hours taking it in.'

'What I'm saying is you knew quite well that Vaudel was going to leave you his money. I'm saying you knew about the will.'

'No, I never. But he did promise me I'd be rich one day.'

'Same thing,' said Mordent, curling his lip, as if moving in for an assault from the side. 'He good as told you you'd inherit.'

'No, he never. He read my hand. He knew how to do that, and he showed me an' all. See,' said Émile putting out his right hand palm up, and pointing to the base of his ring finger. 'That's the bit told him I was going to be rich. Didn't mean to say it was *his* money, did it? I play the lottery, thought that'd be it.'

Émile suddenly fell silent, looking at his palm. Adamsberg, watching the cruel game of heron and fish, saw a trace of an ancient fear cross his face, one that had nothing to do with Mordent's aggressive questions. The stabs from the *commandant*'s beak had neither troubled nor irritated him. No, it was this business of reading his palm.

'Did he see anything else in your hand?' asked Adamsberg.

'No, not much, just that I'd come into some money. He said my hands looked ordinary, and that was a bit of luck, I wasn't bothered. But when I wanted to see his hand, no, that wasn't allowed, he closed 'em both up, and said there was nothing to see, no lines. As if he could have no lines! He looked so cross, wasn't worth going on, and we didn't play our game that night. But no lines, that ain't normal. If I could see the body, I'd see if it was true.'

'No one gets to see the body. Anyway, the hands are unrecognisable.'

Émile shrugged regretfully, and watched *Lieutenant* Retancourt come over to them, with her long ungainly strides.

'She seems nice,' he commented.

'Don't you believe it,' said Adamsberg. 'She's the most dangerous wolf in the pack, and she's been here since early yesterday morning, without a break.'

'How does she do that?'

'She can sleep standing up.'

'That don't stand to reason.'

'No,' Adamsberg agreed.

Retancourt stopped in front of them and nodded to the two men. 'Yes, it's OK,' she said.

'Right,' said Mordent. 'Shall we get on with it, *commissaire*? Or do we do a bit more chiromancy?'

'I don't know what that means, chiromancy,' said Adamsberg shortly.

What on earth was up with Mordent? Good old bird, with ruffled feathers, normally so benign and competent? Irreproachable at work, an expert on stories and legends, talkative and conciliatory. Adamsberg knew that of his two *commandant*s, he had chosen Danglard to go to London, and that Mordent had been miffed. But he was due to be on the next foreign trip, to Amsterdam, which was fair, and Mordent was surely not the sort of man to harbour resentment or to begrudge Danglard a trip to his beloved England.

'It's the science of reading hands. In other words, a waste of time. And we're wasting time now. Émile Feuillant, you were wondering where you were going to sleep tonight, well, we've got the answer now.'

'In the house,' said Adamsberg.

'No, in the shed,' said Retancourt. 'The house is still sealed.'

'In the police cells,' said Mordent.

Adamsberg detached himself from the wall and took a few steps down the path, hands in pockets. The gravel crunched under his feet, a sound he rather liked.

'That's not up to you, *commandant*,' he said, detaching every word. 'I haven't called the *divisionnaire* yet, and he hasn't spoken to the examining magistrate. Too soon, Mordent.'

'No, too late, *commissaire*. The *divisionnaire* telephoned me, to say the magistrate has ordered Émile Feuillant's arrest.'

'Really,' said Adamsberg, turning round, with folded arms. 'The *divisionnaire* called, and you didn't pass the call to me.'

'He said he didn't want to speak to you. I had to do what he said.'

'Not normal procedure.'

'Well, you don't exactly play by the book yourself.'

'Right now I am. And procedure says this arrest is premature and without sufficient cause. One might as well pull the son in for questioning, or someone from the painter's family. Retancourt, what's that family like?'

'They're devastated, they all think the same way, still hell-bent on revenge. The mother killed herself a few months after the son. The father's an engine driver, two other sons are away somewhere, one's a truck driver, the other's in the Legion.'

'What do you say to that, Mordent? Worth checking out surely? And Pierre, the disinherited son? Do you think he didn't know about the will? What could be easier than to accuse Émile and get the whole of the estate? Did you tell the *divisionnaire* that?'

'I didn't have that information. But it was the magistrate who insisted. Because Émile Feuillant's got a record as long as your arm.'

'And since when do we pull someone in on a hunch? Without waiting for forensics? Without any serious evidence?'

'We do have two serious pieces of evidence.'

'Right, I agree to be informed about them. Retancourt, are you up to speed on this?'

Retancourt scraped the gravel with her toe, like a restless animal. She had many remarkable qualities, but was not gifted for social relations. An ambiguous or tense situation, requiring subtle reactions or pretence left her looking awkward and disarmed.

'What is all this bullshit anyway, Mordent?' she asked hoarsely. 'Since when is the judicial system in such a hurry? And who's behind it?'

'I don't know, I'm just following orders.'

'You're following them a bit too closely,' said Adamsberg. 'So what are your two pieces of evidence?'

Mordent looked up. Émile was making himself inconspicuous, fiddling about setting fire to a twig.

'We contacted the retirement home where Feuillant's mother lives.'

'S'not a retirement home, it's a death camp.'

He was still blowing at the twig trying to kindle it. Too green, thought Adamsberg, it won't catch.

'The matron confirmed it. At least four months ago, Émile told his mother that they would soon be going somewhere else and they'd be able to live off the fat of the land. Everybody knew about it.'

'Course they did,' said Émile. 'I told you, Vaudel told me I'd be rich, and I told my mother. Stands to reason, don't it? Do I have to tell you twenty times? Man could go barmy here.'

'All right,' said Adamsberg calmly. 'And the other element, Mordent?'

This time Mordent smiled. This time, he's sure of himself, thought Adamsberg, he's got the fish belly-up now. Looking closely, he thought Mordent's face was showing signs of strain. There were dark rings under his eyes, and his cheeks were drawn.

'There was horse manure on the floor of his van.' He pointed to Émile.

'So what?' said Émile, stopping blowing on the twig.

'We found at least four little balls of manure at the crime scene. The killer must have had it on his rubber boots.'

'I don't have no rubber boots, that's got nothing to do with me.'

'The judge thinks it does.'

Émile stood up, abandoning the twig, and pocketed his tobacco and matches. He bit his lip, looking suddenly panicked. Discouraged, piteous, as still as an old crocodile. Too still. Was it at that moment that Adamsberg realised? He never quite knew. What he did know for sure was that he took a step back from Émile, creating a gap that left his way clear. And Émile reacted with the unreal speed of a crocodile, attacking with a lightning strike. Before you can say knife, it's seized the antelope by the leg. And before you could say knife, or see how Émile had struck them, both Mordent and Retancourt were on the ground. Adamsberg saw him sprint down the path, jump the wall and cross a garden, all so fast that only Retancourt might be able to catch him. The *lieutenant* was off to a late start, but got up, clutching her stomach, then ran after the man, throwing her weight into the pursuit, heaving her 110 kilos over the wall with ease.

'Immediate reinforcements,' Adamsberg said into the car radio. 'Suspect escaping west-south-west. Secure the perimeter.'

Later – but he never got a clear answer – he wondered if he had put enough conviction into his voice.

At his feet, Mordent was clutching his genitals and moaning with pain, tears running down his cheeks. Mechanically,

Adamsberg leaned over him and clasped his shoulder as a sign of understanding.

'Bad move, Mordent. I don't know what you were trying to do exactly, but next time you'll have to find a better way to do it.'

X

Supported by the *commissaire*, Mordent was limping back to join the rest of the team. *Lieutenant* Froissy had now replaced Lamarre and had immediately taken charge of rations, providing everyone with lunch on a table in the garden. You could always count on Froissy, who treated the question of provisions as if there was a war on. Thin and always hungry, her obsession with nourishment had led her to install various food stores in the headquarters of the squad. They were believed to be even more numerous than Danglard's caches of white wine. Some people even claimed that they would still be finding these food stores in the remains of the building in two hundred years' time, whereas Danglard's bottles would long since have been emptied.

Lieutenant Noël had his own theories about Froissy. Noël was the toughest member of the team, with a crude attitude to women and an aggressive one towards men. Suspects he always treated with contempt. He caused more harm than good on balance, but Danglard considered his presence necessary, maintaining that Noël catalysed the darkness that lay inside every police officer and in that way he allowed others to behave better. Noël shrugged and accepted his role. But oddly enough, he was better informed than anyone about his colleagues' intimate secrets, whether because his brusque and direct approach overcame their inhibitions, or because they felt no shame in letting him view the murky depths of their lives, since Noël's own past made him unshockable. At any rate his interpretation of Froissy's dietary insecurity was, he said, linked to the fact that when she was a baby her mother had fainted and lost consciousness and she had been left for four days without nursing. So Froissy, he concluded with a knowing laugh, was still looking for the breast and giving it to others at the same time, which explained why she never put on any weight.

It was three in the afternoon and they had to wait till they had eaten before they could relax and tell each other what exactly had been happening outside the villa. They knew that Retancourt had gone in pursuit of someone – which was generally bad news for the pursued – and that she had been backed up by a squad from Garches, three patrol cars and four motorcyclists. But there had been no word from her, and Adamsberg had reported that she had set off with three minutes' handicap, after receiving a punch to the midriff. And the someone in question, otherwise known as Émile or 'Basher', eleven years inside and 138 known brawls, was the kind of guy who would escape even Retancourt. He summarised, but without going into details, the disagreement between himself and Mordent which had caused the suspect to run for it. Nobody asked why Émile hadn't punched the *commissaire* or why Adamsberg hadn't gone after him himself. Everyone knew that Retancourt was the fastest on her feet of all the squad, so they considered it normal that she had set off alone. Mordent wiped his plate, still looking grim, but that was put down to concern for his testicles. In Émile's file, rapidly checked, nobody had failed to see one item, namely that 'Basher' had destroyed the manhood of a racing driver with a single blow of his elbow. That fight alone had fetched him a year in jail, plus compensation and damages yet to be finalised.

Adamsberg observed his colleagues' expressions of doubt, questioning and hesitating between the instinctive sympathy they all felt for their fellow officer who had received such an intimate injury, and a cautious prudence. Everyone, even Estalère, had understood that Mordent had stepped out of line in an incomprehensible way: he had jumped the gun by ordering a suspect to be taken into custody without first referring to Adamsberg, and had then panicked the suspect by tackling it in an amateur way.

'Who put the last samples in the truck this morning?' Adamsberg asked.

He unthinkingly poured the liquid from the bottom of a bottle into his glass: it was ochre-coloured and cloudy.

'It's home-brewed cider,' Froissy explained. 'You can really only drink it for an hour after it's opened, but it's very good. I thought it would cheer us up.'

'Thank you,' said Adamsberg, drinking off the thick residue.

Another of Froissy's functions was to try and keep people's spirits up, which was not easy in a team of criminal investigators who were chronically short of sleep.

'Froissy and me,' said Voisenet, in answer to his question.

'We need to retrieve the horse shit. I want to see it.'

'That went off yesterday to the lab.'

'No, I don't mean that sample, I mean the stuff they found in Émile's van.'

'Oh,' said Estalère, 'you mean Émile's horse shit.'

'Easy enough,' said Voisenet, 'it's stacked in the priority box.'

'Should we put someone on to the mother's nursing home?' Kernorkian asked.

'Yes, we ought to, for form's sake. But even a Neanderthal would realise it would be watched.'

'And he is a Neanderthal,' said Mordent, as he went on wiping his plate.

'No,' said Adamsberg, 'he's a nostalgic. And nostalgia can give you ideas.'

Adamsberg hesitated. There was one almost fail-safe way of catching Émile: by going to the farm where Cupid was kept. All he had to do was post a couple of men there and they'd pick him up, this week or next. He was the only person who knew about Cupid's existence, or the farm's, or its approximate location, and the name of the owners, which his memory had miraculously retained. The Gérault cousins, three-quarters dairy, one-quarter beef. He opened his mouth, then closed it again, haunted by uncertainty, wondering whether he believed Émile to be innocent, whether he was brooding over some kind of revenge against Mordent, whether for the last two hours, or perhaps since the London trip, he had gone over to the other shore, siding with the migrants who were trying to get across frontiers illegally, giving a hand to wrongdoers, and resisting the forces of order. These questions flowed through his mind like a flock of starlings, but he didn't attempt to answer them. As the others got up, having eaten and been brought up to date, Adamsberg stood apart and motioned to Noël. If anyone knew, he would.

'Mordent. What's the matter with him?'

'He's got problems.'

'I'm sure he has. What kind of problems?'

'It's not for me to say.'

'Vital to the inquiry, Noël. You saw for yourself. Go on.'

'If you insist. His daughter. Only daughter. Sun shines out of her. Mind you, ask me, she's not much to look at. Anyway, she was picked up two months ago, living with half a dozen dropouts, doped up to the eyeballs, in a squat in La Vrille. Know it? One of those stinking holes on the estates where rich kids go when they start doing drugs.'

'And?'

'One of these six wankers is her boyfriend, a skinny so-and-so, rotten to the core. They even call him "Bones". Twelve years older than her, plenty of form for mugging pensioners, that kind of thing, total scumbag, but good-looking, and a big player in the Colombian network. The girl had run away from home, leaving a note, and our poor old Mordent's gnawing his balls off about it.'

'Well, how are his balls anyway?'

'He's called the doctor, they say leave it for a day or two. Hope he gets them back, not a foregone conclusion with that Basher's record. Not that he has much call for them, his wife's having it off with the piano teacher, and she rubs his nose in it.'

'Why didn't he tell me when the girl left home?'

'He's like that, the old storyteller. He spins us any number of yarns, but he keeps shtum about real life. If you remember, we were doing all that stuff with the graves we opened. And take it any way you want, but people don't like to tell you this kind of thing.'

'Why not?'

'Because they're never sure you'd be listening. And even if you listen, they expect you'll forget. So no point, is there? Mordent doesn't want to get into the clouds. But you're sitting up in them.'

'I know what they say. But I think my feet are on the ground.'

'Well, different ground from the rest of us, is all I can say.'

'Perhaps, Noël. Anyway, what's happened about the girl?'

'Elaine, she's called. Mordent went over to the squat when the Bicêtre cops called him in, and it was a real hell-hole, you can imagine. Teenagers there eating dog food out of tins. It was one of them panicked and called the emergency services, because somebody OD'd. Mind you, dog food isn't as bad as all that, it's just meat stew. Any rate, Mordent's kid was totally out of it, high as a kite, and the cops found enough coke there to slap on a charge of dealing. But the worst thing was they found weapons – a couple of handguns and flick knives. And one of the guns was traced to a case from some months back in the north of Paris, shooting of a dealer, name of Stubby Down. And the witnesses had said there were two attackers involved, one of them a girl with long brown hair.'

'Oh dammit.'

'In the end, they kept three of the kids in on remand, and Elaine Mordent's one of them.'

'Where is she now?'

'Fresnes jail, and she's on methadone. She could get two to four years minimum, more if they prove she was really involved in this Stubby Down murder. Mordent says when she comes out she'll be finished for good. Danglard's trying to keep him going by watering him with white wine like a plant, but it just makes him worse. As soon as he can get away from work, he's down there, in Fresnes or outside, looking at the walls. So, you can imagine.'

Noël turned round, thumbs in his belt, and jerked his chin towards the villa.

'And with this God-awful scene in there, it's no wonder he's going off message. Perhaps we'd better get Danglard to come along, now we've cleaned it up. Voisenet's looking for you, he's found Émile's horse shit, as that halfwit Estalère called it.'

Voisenet had put the sample on the garden table. He passed Adamsberg a pair of gloves. The *commissaire* opened the plastic sachet and sniffed the contents.

'They labelled it "horse manure" but it could be something else.'

'No, that's what it is,' said Adamsberg, holding a chunk in his hand, 'though it doesn't look the same as the stuff in the house. That was in pellets.'

'Yeah, but that's because the pellets formed in the soles of the boots. And with all the blood and stuff on the carpet, they came out.'

'No, Voisenet, it wasn't the same horse. At least what I'm saying is, it's not the same horse shit, so it wasn't the same horse.'

'Maybe there were two horses,' Justin hazarded.

'What I mean is, not a horse from the same farm. Therefore not the same shoes. At least I think not.'

Adamsberg pushed back a lock of hair. It was annoying that they kept getting back to shoes. His mobile rang. Retancourt. He dropped the sample on to the table.

'*Commissaire*, nothing doing. Émile got away from me in the car park of Garches hospital, two ambulances got between us. I'm sorry. There are some motorbike cops trying to pick up the scent.'

'Don't blame yourself, *lieutenant*, he had a good start.'

'That wasn't all he had,' said Retancourt. 'He knows the area like the back of his hand, he went streaking through gardens, alleyways, as if he'd built them himself. He's probably hiding behind some hedge. It'll be hard to dislodge him unless he gets hungry, which he might soon. I'm stopping here, because I think he cracked one of my ribs when he took off.'

'Where are you, Violette? Still at the hospital?'

'Yes, the cops have gone round it searching for places he might be hiding.'

'Get inside and see a doctor about the rib.'

'Will do,' said Retancourt and rang off.

Adamsberg snapped his mobile shut. Retancourt had no intention of getting herself examined.

'Émile may have broken her rib,' he said. 'Painful.'

'Could have been worse, he could have kicked her in the balls.'

'That'll do, Noël.'

'Not the same horse farm?' Justin chipped in.

Adamsberg took up the piece of horse manure again, biting back a more angry retort to Noël, who never stopped needling Retancourt, saying she wasn't a woman at all, but an ox or something. Whereas for Adamsberg, if Retancourt wasn't exactly a woman in the ordinary sense, it was because she was a goddess. The polyvalent goddess of the squad with as many talents as the God-knows-how-many-armed goddess Shiva.

'How many arms does that Indian goddess have?' he asked his juniors, still holding the scrap of dung.

The four *lieutenants* shook their heads.

'Always the same,' said Adamsberg. 'When Danglard's not here nobody knows the answer to anything.'

He closed up the sachet again, shut the zip and gave it to Voisenet.

'We'll have to call him to get an answer. Now, what it is, I think *this* horse, the one that produced this shit, familiarly known as Émile's horse shit, was out in a field and has eaten nothing but grass. And I think the other one, the origin of the pellets in the villa, which we'll call "the killer's horse shit", was fed in a stable on granules.'

'How can you tell?'

'I spent my childhood collecting horse manure for fertiliser, and cowpats for burning in the fireplace. I still do that, and I can assure you, Voisenet, that depending on what they've been fed, you get a different kind of horse manure.'

'OK,' agreed Voisenet.

'When will we get the lab results?' asked Adamsberg, as he punched in Danglard's number. 'Give them a kick up the pants: we need this stuff urgently – the shit, the Kleenex, fingerprints, body parts, all that.'

He walked away as Danglard came on the line.

'Nearly five o'clock, Danglard. We need you for this Garches mess. It's all cleared up, we're on our way back, we're going to do the first summary. Oh, one second, how many arms has that Indian goddess got? The one that sits inside a ball? Shiva?'

'Shiva's not a goddess at all, *commissaire*. He's a god.'

'A god! It's a man,' added the *commissaire* for his *lieutenants'* benefit. 'So Shiva's a man, and how many arms does he have?' he asked Danglard.

'Depends on the different images, because Shiva's powers are immense and contradictory, covering practically the whole spectrum, from destruction to blessing. Sometimes two, sometimes four, but it can go up to ten. Depends what he's embodying at the time.'

'And roughly speaking, Danglard, what does he embody?'

'Well, to cut a long story short, "at the vacuum in the centre of Nirvana-Shakti is the supreme Shiva whose nature is emptiness".'

Adamsberg had turned up the speaker, and looked at his colleagues who seemed as lost as he was and were making signs to forget it. Finding out that Shiva was a male deity was quite enough for one day.

'Has this got anything to do with Garches?' asked Danglard. 'Not enough arms?'

'Émile Feuillant's inherited Vaudel's estate, except the legal share that goes to Pierre junior. Mordent broke the rules and told him he was about to be arrested. So Émile, aka Basher, floored him and made a break for it.'

'And Retancourt couldn't catch him?'

'She didn't manage it. She can't have had all her arms working, and he'd broken one of her ribs when he took off. We're expecting you, *commandant*. Mordent's out of it more or less.'

'I dare say. But my train doesn't leave until nine twelve in the evening. I don't think I can change my ticket.'

'What train, Danglard?'

'The train that goes through the goddam tunnel, *commissaire*. Don't imagine I'm doing this for my own amusement. But I saw what I came to see. And if he didn't cut off my uncle's feet, it came pretty close.'

'Danglard, where are you?' asked Adamsberg slowly, sitting back down at the table and turning off the speaker.

'Where the heck do you think I am? I'm in London, and they're pretty sure now, the shoes are almost all French, some good quality, some bad. Different social classes. Believe me, we're going to get the whole lot on our plate, and Radstock is already rubbing his hands.'

'But what the devil took you back to London?' Adamsberg almost shouted. 'Why the hell did you have to go and get mixed up with the damned shoes again? Leave them in Higg-Gate, leave them to Stock!'

'Radstock you mean. *Commissaire*, I told you I was going and you agreed, it was necessary.'

'Don't mess me about, Danglard, it was that woman Abstract, and you swam the Channel to see her.'

'No, I did not.'

'Don't tell me you haven't seen her again!'

'I didn't say that, but that's got nothing to do with the shoes.'

'I certainly hope not, Danglard.'

'If you thought that someone had cut off your uncle's feet, you'd want to go and take a look too.'

Adamsberg looked up at the sky which was clouding over, watched as a duck flew across the horizon, and turned back to the phone more calmly.

'What uncle? I didn't know there was an uncle involved.'

'I'm not talking about a living uncle, I'm not talking about someone walking around with no feet. My uncle died about twenty years ago. My aunt's second husband, and I was very fond of him.'

'Without wanting to upset you, *commandant*, nobody would be capable of recognising their uncle's dead feet.'

'Not his feet, no, the shoes. As our friend Lord Clyde-Fox rightly said.'

'Clyde-Fox?'

'That eccentric English lord we met.'

'Ah. Yes,' said Adamsberg with a sigh.

'I saw him again yesterday, incidentally. He was down in the dumps because he's mislaid his new Cuban pal. We had a few drinks, he's a specialist on Indian history. And as he quite rightly said, what can you put into shoes? Feet of course. Usually your own. And if the shoes belonged to my uncle, there was every chance the feet did too.'

'A bit like the horse shit and the horse,' Adamsberg commented. Fatigue was starting to give him a backache.

'Like the container and the contents. But I'm not sure whether it's actually my uncle or not. It could be a cousin, or someone from the same village. They're all cousins of some kind over there.'

'OK,' said Adamsberg, sliding along to the end of the table. 'Even if some nutter *has* made a collection of French feet and his path unfortunately crossed that of your uncle, or his cousin, what the hell has that got to do with us?'

'You said yourself that there was no rule against taking an interest,' said Danglard, sounding disgruntled. 'You were the one who wouldn't let the Highgate feet drop.'

'While we were there, yes, maybe. But now we're in Garches and I'm not interested. And that was a big mistake to go back, Danglard. Because if these feet are French, Scotland Yard will want us to collaborate. It could have been sent to a different squad, but now, thanks to you, our squad is the one with its head above the parapet. And I need you here, for this blood-bath in Garches, which is a damn sight more scary than some necrophiliac who went round cutting off feet right and left twenty years ago.'

'Not "right and left". I think they were selected.'

'Did Stock tell you that?'

'No, that's my idea. Because when my uncle died, he was in Serbia, and so were his feet.'

'And you're wondering why the amputator went all the way to Serbia to collect feet, when there are sixty million of them in France.'

'A hundred and twenty million. Sixty million people, a hundred and twenty million feet. You're making the same mistake as Estalère in reverse.'

'But what was your uncle doing in Serbia anyway?'

'He was a Serb himself, *commissaire*. His name was Slavko Moldovan.'

Justin arrived, out of breath.

'There's this guy outside demanding an explanation. We rolled out the crime scene tapes, but he wouldn't listen. He wants to come in.'

XI

Lieutenants Noël and Voisenet were standing facing each other and, with their outstretched arms blocking the door, forming a barrier in front of the man, who did not look particularly intimidating.

'How do I know you're policemen?' he kept repeating. 'How do I know you're not burglars – especially you,' he said, pointing at Noël, whose head was close-shaved. 'I've got an appointment, five thirty, and I'm always on time.'

'Yeah, well, your appointment can't see you!' said Noël with an aggressive sneer.

'Show me your police badges. You haven't shown me any proof.'

'We've already explained,' Voisenet said. 'Our badges are in our jackets and our jackets are inside, but we have to keep this door shut, so that you can't go in there. The whole site is forbidden to the public.'

'But of course I'm going inside!'

'Can't be done.'

As Adamsberg approached from inside the house, he judged that the man was either singularly obtuse or else rather brave, given his average height and corpulent figure. If he really did think they were burglars, he'd have done better to stop arguing and get away fast. But he looked like someone from the professional classes, self-confident and self-possessed, with the pompous air of a man doing his duty or at any rate his job, whatever the circumstances, at least if it didn't harm his fee. Was he an insurance agent, an art dealer, a lawyer, a banker? His manner of approaching these two policemen with their shirt-sleeved arms indicated a clear class reflex. He wasn't somebody who could be sent packing, and certainly not by the likes of Noël and Voisenet. Negotiating with them would be beneath him, and perhaps it was that social conviction, that basic caste scorn, which made him brave beyond foolishness. He had nothing to fear from his social inferiors. Apart from his present attitude, his shrewd and old-fashioned face might be quite attractive in repose. Adamsberg laid a hand on the plebeian arms and nodded to the newcomer.

'If this really is something to do with the police, I'm not leaving till I see your superior officer,' the man was saying.

'I am their superior officer, *Commissaire* Adamsberg.'

Astonishment, disappointment. Adamsberg had seen these all too often on people's faces. But almost immediately afterwards there would be submission to the superior rank, in however odd a form it had appeared.

'Enchanté, *commissaire*,' said the man, holding out his hand. 'Paul de Josselin. I'm Monsieur Vaudel's doctor.'

Too late, thought Adamsberg, as they shook hands.

'I'm sorry, doctor, but you can't see Monsieur Vaudel.'

'So I gather. But as his doctor, I surely have the right and indeed the duty to be informed about it. Is he ill, in hospital? Dead?'

'He's dead.'

'And he died at home? Is that why there's all this police presence?'

'Correct, doctor.'

'But when? How? I examined him a couple of weeks ago, and he was in good health.'

'The police are obliged to keep details confidential. Normal procedure in a murder case.'

The doctor frowned, muttering 'murder!' to himself. Adamsberg realised that they were talking to each other across the outstretched arms, like neighbours talking across a fence. The two *lieutenants* had maintained their stiff attitude without anyone thinking to change it. Adamsberg tapped on Voisenet's shoulder and lifted the barrier.

'Let's go round into the garden,' he said. 'We mustn't contaminate the floor.'

'I understand, I quite understand. So you can't tell me anything about it?'

'I can tell you as much as the neighbours have been told. It was during the night from Saturday to Sunday, and we discovered the body yesterday morning. The alarm was raised by the gardener when he got home at about five o'clock.'

'Why did he raise the alarm? Did he hear cries?'

'According to the gardener, Vaudel normally left his lights on all night. But when he arrived back, there were no lights showing – he said his employer had a pathological fear of the dark.'

'I know, it goes back to his childhood.'

'Were you his doctor or his psychiatrist?'

'I was his GP, but also his somatopathic osteopath.'

'I see,' said Adamsberg, who didn't. 'Did he tell you much about himself?'

'No, absolutely not, he hated the idea of psychiatry. But what I could feel in his bones told me a lot. I was actually very attached to him, medically speaking. Vaudel was an exceptional case.'

The doctor stopped speaking abruptly.

'Yes, I see,' said Adamsberg. 'You won't tell me any more if I don't tell you any more. Our professional secrecy makes it stalemate.'

'Precisely.'

'You do realise I will have to ask you what you were doing between eleven on Saturday night and five on Sunday morning.'

'No offence taken, I'm quite willing to tell you. Given that most people are asleep at that time, and since I don't have a wife or children, what can I say? At night I'm in bed, unless I get called out to an emergency. You must know that.'

The doctor thought for a moment, pulled out his diary from his inside pocket and carefully rearranged his jacket.

'Ah, Francisco,' he said, 'our concierge. He's paraplegic, I don't charge him for treatment – he called me at one in the morning. He'd managed to fall between his wheelchair and the bed and got his tibia at an angle. I sorted his leg out and put him to bed. Two hours later he called me again, the knee was swollen. I was rather sharp with him, and said you'll just have to put up with it, and I called to see him again in the morning.'

'Thank you, doctor. You know Vaudel's handyman, Émile?'

'Émile? The noughts and crosses specialist? Fascinating case. I took him on as a patient too. He was very resistant, but Vaudel took an interest in him and told him to come and see me. In three years I'd gradually brought his violence level down.'

'Yes, he did mention that, but he put it down to getting older.'

'Not at all,' said the doctor with amusement, and Adamsberg recognised the shrewd and forthcoming face he had detected under the pompous exterior. 'Age usually increases neuroses. But as I was treating Émile, I was gradually reaching zones that were stiff, and making them more supple, although he kept shutting doors behind me. But I'll get there in the end. His mother beat him as a child, you know, but he'll never admit it. He idolises her.'

'So how do *you* know that?'

'This way,' said the doctor, putting his index finger just up and to the right of the back of Adamsberg's neck, touching the base of his skull.

He felt something like a sting, as if the doctor's finger had a spike on it.

'Ah, another interesting case,' Josselin noted under his breath, 'if you'll allow the observation.'

'Émile?'

'No, you.'

'I wasn't beaten in my childhood, doctor.'

'I didn't say you were.'

Adamsberg stepped to the side, removing his head from the doctor's curiosity.

'Our Monsieur Vaudel – I'm not asking you to infringe professional secrecy – but did he have any enemies?'

'Yes, plenty. And that was the root of the problem. He had enemies who were threatening and even deadly.'

Adamsberg stopped on the gravel path.

'I can't give you any names,' the doctor said quickly, 'and it would be useless anyway. It would fall outside your investigation.'

Adamsberg's mobile vibrated, and he excused himself to take the call.

'Lucio,' he said crossly, 'you know I'm at work.'

'I never call you, *hombre*, this is the first time. But one of the kittens won't feed, she's wasting away. I thought perhaps you could come and stroke her head.'

'Too bad, Lucio, I can't do anything about it. If she won't feed, that's life, it's a law of nature.'

'But you could calm her down, get her to sleep.'

'That still wouldn't make her suckle, Lucio.'

'You're a real bastard and a son of a bitch.'

'And above all, Lucio,' said Adamsberg, raising his voice, 'I'm not a magician. And I've had a bloody awful day.'

'Well, so have I. Can't even light my cigarettes. Because of my eyesight, can't see the tip properly. And my daughter won't help me, so what am I to do?'

Adamsberg bit his lip, and the doctor came closer.

'Is it a baby who won't feed?' he asked politely.

'No, a five-day-old kitten,' said Adamsberg curtly.

'If whoever you're talking to would like, I could try something. It's probably the MRP of the lower jaw that's blocked. Not necessarily a law of nature but possibly a post-natal and post-traumatic dislocation. Was it a difficult birth?'

'Lucio,' said Adamsberg sharply into the phone, 'is it one of the two we had to deliver?'

'Yes, the white one with a grey tip to the tail. The only girl.'

'Yes, doctor,' Adamsberg confirmed. 'Lucio had to press and I had to pull her out by the jaw. Perhaps I pulled too hard. It's a female kitten.'

'Where does your friend live? If he's willing of course,' said the other, raising his hands as if a life in the balance suddenly made him humble.

'Paris, 13th arrondissement.'

'I'm not far, I'm in the 7th. If you agree, we could go there together and I could treat the kitten. If there's anything to be done, that is. Meanwhile, what your friend should do is sprinkle water all over her body, but without making her soaking wet.'

'We're on our way,' said Adamsberg, feeling as if he was sending a signal for an urgent police operation. 'Sprinkle her with water, but not too much.'

Feeling a little dazed, as if he had now left the bridge, and was being besieged by bashers, migratory flows, doctors and one-armed Spaniards, Adamsberg told his colleagues to clear things up and drove back with the doctor.

As they entered the ring road, he said, 'This is ridiculous. We're going to give medical assistance to a kitten, while all hell has broken loose on Vaudel.'

'A nasty crime, was it? He was very rich, you know.'

'Yes, I guess it will all go to the son,' said Adamsberg, feeling his voice ring false. 'Do you know him?'

'Only through his father's mind. Desire, refusal, desire, refusal, both of them, same thing.'

'Vaudel didn't want a son.'

'He especially didn't want to leave behind him vulnerable descendants who would be exposed to his enemies.'

'What enemies?'

'If I told you it wouldn't help. They were the mad imaginings of the man, created over the years and lodged in the caverns of his mind. It's medical, not police work. At the point he'd reached, you'd have to be a speleologist.'

'Imaginary enemies, you mean?'

'You don't want to go there, *commissaire*.'

Lucio was waiting for them in the tool shed, his huge hand stroking the kitten, which was rolled up in a damp towel on his knees.

'She's going to die,' he said hoarsely, his voice full of tears which Adamsberg could not understand, since it was a mystery to him how anyone could be so affected over a cat. 'She can't feed. Who's this?' Lucio asked ungraciously. 'We don't need an audience, *hombre*.'

'This gentleman is a specialist on cats with dislocated jaws who can't feed. Mind out, Lucio, and give him the cat.'

Lucio scratched his absent arm, and obeyed, still looking suspicious. The doctor sat down on the bench and took the cat's head in his thick fingers – he had enormous hands for his size, not unlike Lucio's large single hand. He felt her slowly all over, back and forth. Charlatan, Adamsberg was thinking, now feeling more upset than he should have been, as he looked at the kitten's limp little body. Then the doctor moved to the pelvis, and put his fingers on two points, as if playing a trill on a piano, and they heard a weak mew.

'Her name's Charm,' Lucio said grudgingly.

'We can fix the jaw,' said the doctor. 'Don't worry, Charm, we'll have you right in a minute.'

The large fingers – to Adamsberg they were getting more and more enormous, like the ten arms of Shiva – came back to the jaw and held the kitten's head in a pincer grip.

'Now, now, Charm,' he murmured, as he moved his thumb

and finger. 'Did you get your jaw blocked when you were born? Did the *commissaire* twist your head? Or were you frightened? Just a few minutes more and we'll be on the way. There now. I'm going to press your TMJ.'

'What's that?' asked Lucio warily.

'The temporo-mandibular joint.'

The kitten relaxed, as if it was made of plasticine, and allowed itself to be put to the mother's teat.

'There, there,' crooned the doctor gently. 'The jaw joint was dislocated caudally left and cephalically right, so of course it couldn't move, the injury was stopping the sucking movement. Seems to be fine now. Let's just wait a little, to see if it stays that way. I also adjusted the sacro-iliac joint. All consequences of a slightly eventful birth, don't worry. She'll be a tough little thing, take good care of her. No harm in her, she's got a sweet nature.'

'Yes, doctor,' agreed Lucio, who had become respectful, as he watched the kitten sucking away like a steam engine.

'And she will always want her food because of the five days.'

'Ah, like Froissy,' said Adamsberg.

'Another cat?'

'No, one of my colleagues. She eats all the time, and hides stashes of food, but she's as thin as a rake.'

'An anxiety disorder,' said the doctor wearily. 'She should get it seen to. So should everyone, me included. You wouldn't have a glass of wine or something, would you?' he broke off suddenly. 'If it's not too much trouble. It's that time of day. It may not look it, but this stuff uses up a lot of energy.'

Now he looked nothing like that professional pompous bourgeois Adamsberg had first seen across the arms of the *lieutenant*s. The doctor had loosened his tie and was rumpling his grey hair with his fingers, looking like a simple man who had just finished a good job of work, and hadn't been sure whether he'd manage it an hour earlier. He'd like a drink, and the request made Lucio react at once.

'Where's he going?' asked the doctor as Lucio shot off towards the hedge.

'His daughter has banned alcohol and tobacco. So he has to hide them in the bushes. He puts the cigarettes in a double plastic container against the rain.'

'His daughter knows he does that, I bet.'

'Yes, she does.'

'And he knows that she knows?'

'Of course.'

'The way of the world, all these hidden agendas. What happened to his arm?'

'He lost it during the Spanish Civil War when he was nine years old.'

'But there was something else there, a wound that hadn't healed? A bite? I don't know, some unfinished business.'

'Just a minor thing,' said Adamsberg, with a slight gasp of surprise. 'A spider bite that itched.'

'He'll be itching for ever,' said the doctor fatalistically. 'Because it's in there,' he said, tapping his forehead, 'etched into the neurones. They still don't understand that the arm's gone. It lasts for years, and knowing why makes no difference.'

'So what's the point of knowing why?'

'It reassures people, which is something.'

Lucio was on his way back with three glasses arranged between his fingers and a bottle clutched under his stump. He put it all down on the shed floor, and took a long look at the kitten, now firmly clamped on to its mother's teat.

'She's not going to burst now, is she, from feeding too much?'

'No,' said the doctor.

Lucio nodded, filled the glasses and invited them to toast the kitten's health.

'The doctor knew about your arm and the itch,' said Adamsberg.

'Naturally,' said Lucio. 'Spider bite, that'll go on itching till kingdom come.'

XII

'THAT GUY,' SAID LUCIO, 'MAY BE AN ACE, BUT I WOULDN'T want him touching my head. He'd have me back sucking like a baby.'

Exactly what he was doing at that moment, Adamsberg reflected, as Lucio sucked the edge of his glass with a sound like a newborn child. Lucio much preferred to drink straight from the bottle. He had only brought out glasses for the occasion because they had company. The doctor had gone an hour since, and they were sitting in the shed, finishing off the bottle and watching the litter of kittens, now fast asleep. Lucio took the view that you finished a bottle once you had opened it, because the wine would go off. Either you finish or you don't start.

'No, I wouldn't like to have him come near me again either,' agreed Adamsberg. 'He just put his finger here' (he showed the place on the back of his neck) 'and it seemed something funny happened. "Interesting case" he called it.'

'In doctor language, that means something's wrong.'

'Yes.'

'If you agree with the funny stuff, you don't need to worry.'

'Lucio, can you imagine for a minute you're Émile?'

'OK,' said Lucio who had never heard of Émile till this moment.

'You're someone who likes a fight. You're compulsive, fifty-three years old, not unreasonable, but you fly off the handle now and then, you've been rescued from a life of crime by an old eccentric who hires you as a handyman, which includes playing giant games of noughts and crosses, over a glass of Guignolet.'

'Stop there,' said Lucio. 'Can't stand Guignolet.'

'But you have to imagine you're Émile, and that's what the old man gives you.'

'If you say so,' said Lucio reluctantly.

'OK. Forget the Guignolet, imagine something else. It doesn't really matter.'

'Right.'

'Now imagine your old mother's in a home, and your dog's been boarded out at a farm, because you've been in and out of jail, total of eleven years, all in all. And imagine that every Saturday you get in your van, and first you take your mother out for a meal, then you go and see your dog, taking it some meat for a treat.'

'Wait a minute, I can't see the van.'

Lucio poured out the last of the wine.

'Blue, curved corners, battered paintwork, back window dirty and a rusty ladder on the roof rack.'

'Got it.'

'Now, suppose you always wait for the dog outside this farm, he jumps the gate and comes to eat with you, and you spend some of the night with him in the back of the van, then you have to leave at four in the morning.'

'Wait a minute. Can't see the dog.'

'What about the mother, you can see her?'

'Perfectly.'

'The dog's long-haired, off-white with a few patches, floppy ears, and it's quite small, about the size of a football, a mongrel with big eyes.'

'Got it.'

'Now imagine the old boy's been murdered, and he's left lots of money to *you*, cutting out his son. So you're suddenly rich. Imagine the cops suspect *you* could have killed him, and they want to pull you in.'

'No need to imagine that, it's what they'd do, for sure.'

'OK. Now suppose you kick one of these cops in the balls, you hit another one, breaking a rib, and you make off like a shot.'

'All right.'

'What do you do about your mother?'

Lucio sucked his glass.

'I'm not going to see her, the cops are sure to be watching her home. So I'll send her a letter in the post to tell her not to worry.'

'And what do you do about the dog?'

'Do the cops know where the dog's shacked up?'

'No.'

'Well, then I can go and see him, tell him that I've got to lie low, he might not see me for a bit but, not to worry, I'll be back.'

'When?'

'When will I be back?'

'No, when will you go and see the dog?'

'Right away, of course. They might catch me, so I've got

to tell the dog first. But my mother – I suppose my mother's still got her marbles?'

'Yes.'

'Good. Well, if I was in prison, the cops would tell her anyway. But they won't tell the dog. No way. None of them would think to do that . . . So yeah, telling the dog, I've got to do that, and the sooner the better.'

Adamsberg stroked Charm's silky belly, emptied his glass into Lucio's, and got up, brushing the seat of his trousers.

'Now then, *hombre*,' said Lucio, 'if you're going to try and see this guy before he sees the dog and before the dog sees the cops, you'd better put your skates on.'

'I didn't say that's what I'd do.'

'No, you didn't.'

Adamsberg drove slowly, aware that fatigue and the wine had made inroads on his energy. He had switched off his mobile and the car's GPS in case there was a police officer somewhere with the same thought processes as Lucio – which was not likely, even in Mordent's stories and legends. He had no clear plan what to do about the violent Émile. Except what Lucio had suggested: to get to Châteaudun before the cops thought of the dog. Why? Because of the different kinds of horse manure? No. He hadn't known about them when he had let Émile go – if that was what he really had done. So? Was it because Mordent had come galumphing in like a buffalo across his path? No. Mordent was going off his rocker, that was all. Because Émile was a decent guy? No. Émile wasn't a decent guy. Because Émile might starve to death in the sticks somewhere, because a depressed cop had acted stupidly? Maybe. But fetching him back to prison, was that any improvement on dying in the sticks?

Adamsberg was not good at the complications of 'maybe', whereas Danglard loved them, and would go out on a limb in his delight, drawn by the dark abyss of anticipation. Adamsberg was simply heading for the farm, that was all, praying none of the others had overheard his conversation that morning with Émile the Basher, Émile the Lucky Heir Apparent, now owner of houses in Garches and Vaucresson. While Danglard was at that very moment arguing with himself in the Channel Tunnel, getting drunk on champagne, and all because he had this idea that, *maybe*, some lunatic had cut off his uncle's feet, or perhaps the feet of his uncle's cousin, in some faraway mountain village. Meanwhile, Mordent was staring up at the walls of Fresnes prison, and what in the name of all that was holy could they do for Mordent?

Adamsberg parked on the verge, in the shelter of a wood, and went the last five hundred metres on foot, gingerly, trying to get his bearings. The dog was supposed to jump some gate, but which one? He walked for about half an hour around the outskirts of the farm – three-quarters dairy, one-quarter beef – and his legs were getting tired by the time he located the most likely gate. In the distance, other dogs were barking loudly at his approach, and he flattened himself against a tree, standing as still as he could, while checking his bag and his gun. There was a smell of dung in the air, which he found reassuring, as everyone does. Now he must not drop off to sleep, but wait, and hope that Lucio was right.

On the warm breeze, a faint animal sound like a whimper from beyond the gate reached him from time to time, perhaps fifty metres further on. Some woodland creature? A rat or a stoat? Something no bigger than that. He leaned against the tree, and flexed his legs, trying not to fall asleep. He imagined how Émile would get here, walking, hitching lifts with truck drivers who weren't fussy if he offered to buy them a drink. What was Émile wearing? That morning he had worn a greasy jacket with ragged sleeves on top of his blue overalls. He pictured Émile's hands before some words came back to him. Two hands making the shape of the dog. 'No bigger than that.' Adamsberg dropped to one knee and listened more carefully to the distant whining. No bigger than that. The dog?

Cautiously, he made his way towards the sound. From about three metres away he saw a small white shape, the dog, running in panicky movements round a body on the ground.

'Émile! Shit!'

Adamsberg raised him by the shoulder and felt the side of his neck with his fingers. There was a pulse. Through the torn clothes, the dog was anxiously licking the man's stomach, then moving to his thigh, and making its tiny whimpering sound. It stopped to look up at Adamsberg, and made a different kind of yelp that seemed to say: glad to have some help, friend. Then it returned to its task, tearing away the cloth of the trousers, licking the thigh, trying to make it as wet as possible. Adamsberg switched on his torch and shone it on Émile's face, now smeared with mud and glistening with sweat. Émile the Basher, felled, beaten, money doesn't buy you happiness.

'Don't try to talk,' Adamsberg told him. Holding Émile's

head in his left hand, he gently explored the back of the skull with his fingers. No wound there.

'Blink for yes. Can you feel your foot? – I'm pressing it.'

Yes.

'And the other one?'

Yes.

'See my hand? Know who I am?'

'*C-commissaire.*'

'Yep. You're hurt, stomach and leg. What happened? Did you get into a fight?'

'Not a fight, gun. Four shots. Two got me. See the water tower?'

Émile raised his left hand slightly. Turning off the torch, Adamsberg peered into the darkness. The water tower was about a hundred metres away, near the wood through which Émile must have dragged himself to get to the gate, which he had almost reached. Whoever did the shooting might still be there.

'No time to call an ambulance, we're getting out of here.'

He felt all over Émile's back.

'You're in luck. The bullet exited your side, didn't touch the spine. I'm going to get my car. Two minutes. Tell your dog to shut up.'

'Shush, Cupid.'

Adamsberg stopped the car, without headlights, as near Émile as he could manage and lowered the front passenger seat. An official beige raincoat had been left in the back of the car, probably Froissy's since she always took care to dress the part. With his knife, he cut off the sleeves to make two long strips, and found himself bumping against the pockets, which were bulging with objects. He shook the coat and out fell a couple of tins of pâté, some dried fruit, biscuits, half a bottle of water, a few sweets, a 25ml carton of wine and three miniature bottles of brandy, like you get on trains. He had a moment's sympathy for Froissy, then offered up thanks. Her eating disorder was helpful.

The dog was now quiet and stood aside letting Adamsberg take over. He shone the torch on the stomach wound which was now clean, the dog's tongue having licked it all over, pulled away the shirt and removed the mud.

'Your dog's been busy.'

'Dog's saliva. Antiseptic.'

'I didn't know that,' said Adamsberg, binding the wounds with the fabric strips as best he could.

'Don't know a lot, do you?'

'What about you, eh? Bet you don't know how many arms Shiva has. And I knew how to find you here. I'm going to carry you now, try not to yell.'

'Thirsty.'

'Later.'

Adamsberg installed Émile in the car, carefully arranging his legs.

'Guess what,' he said. 'We'll let the dog come too.'

'Ah,' said Émile.

Adamsberg drove the first few kilometres along the lanes without lights, then stopped, keeping the engine running. He opened the bottle of water, but halted his hand in mid-air.

'No, I daren't let you drink,' he said, 'in case your stomach's been touched.'

He set off again and reached a minor road.

'Another twenty kilometres to Châteaudun and the hospital. Think you can make it?'

'Keep me talking, gonna pass out.'

'Keep looking ahead. Guy who shot you, did you see anything?'

'No, behind the water tower. Must have been waiting for me. Four shots. Like I said. Just the two got me. Not a pro. I go down and I hear him coming. So I pretend to be dead. He goes for me pulse, see if that's it. He's panicking, right. Could have put in a couple more though. Make sure.'

'Take it easy, Émile.'

'This car come up the crossroads. He runs off, fast as he can. I wait a bit. Then I try to crawl up to the farm. If I've had it, monsieur, don't want Cupid to wait for ever. Waiting. No way to live. Don't know your name.'

'Adamsberg.'

'Right, Adamsberg. No way to live, eh? Ever do that? Wait a long time?'

'Wait? Yeah, I think so.'

'A woman?'

'You could say so.'

'No way to live, eh?'

'Right,' said Adamsberg.

Émile gave a spasm of pain and gripped the door.

'Only eleven kilometres to go.'

'You talk. I'm all in.'

'Stay with me, Émile, I'll ask you questions, you just say yes or no. Like in the game.'

'No, not like the game,' Émile whispered. 'In the game, you don't say yes or no.'

'No, OK, you're right. So. This guy was waiting for you, right? You tell anyone you were going to the farm?'

'No.'

'Only old Vaudel and me, we were the only people knew where you kept the dog?'

'Yeah.'

'But Vaudel might have told someone? Like his son?'

'Yeah.'

'It wouldn't do him any good to kill you, because your share wouldn't go to him anyway if you died. It's in the will.'

'Angry.'

'With you? Yes, probably. Have *you* made a will?'

'No.'

'You've got no one who would inherit from you? No kids – you're sure about that?'

'*Yeah.*'

'The old man didn't give you anything? Papers, letters, files, confessions, anything he was guilty about?'

'No. Hey, someone could've followed *you*,' Émile gasped.

'Only one person knows,' said Adamsberg, shaking his head. 'An old Spanish man, with one arm and no car. Anyway, they shot you before I got here.'

'Yeah.'

'Only three kilometres. *You* could have been followed too, from the hospital in Garches. Three police cars – that told people you were there. You stayed inside the hospital?'

'Two hours.'

'Where.'

'A & E. Waiting room. Lotta people.'

'Nice one. Nobody following you when you came out?'

'No. Maybe. Motorbike.'

Adamsberg parked by the emergency room, pushed open the plastic curtain, alerted an exhausted intern, and flashed his badge to hurry things up. A quarter of an hour later, Émile was on a trolley, with a tube in his arm.

'Can't keep the dog, sir,' said a nurse, giving him a plastic bag holding Émile's clothes.

'No, I know,' said Adamsberg, disentangling Cupid from Émile's legs. 'Émile, listen to me. No visitors, no one at all. I'll tell them in reception. Where's the surgeon?'

'In the operating block,' said the nurse.

'Tell him to keep the bullet from his leg.'

'Wait,' said Émile, as the trolley started to move. 'If . . . if I snuff it. Vaudel did ask me something, an' all. If he died.'

'Ah, you see.'

'Some woman. Old now, he said. But still. Wrote it in code. Didn't trust me. Post it if he died. Made me swear.'

'Where is it, Émile, and the address?'

'Overalls.'

XIII

THE TINS OF PÂTÉ, THE BISCUITS, THE CARTON OF UNDRINK-able wine and the mini-brandies – these were all Adamsberg could think about as he made his way back to the car park. Any other time, in any other place, he would have found the thought deeply off-putting, but just now they constituted a clear and beautiful promise of satisfaction on which all his energy was concentrated. Sitting in the back of the car, he spread Froissy's treasures on the seat. The pâté could be opened with ring-pulls, there was a straw attached to the wine box – she really was a practical genius, *lieutenant* Froissy, the squad's nonpareil sound engineer. He spread some pâté on a biscuit and gobbled it up: a peculiar sweet and sour mixture. Then one for the dog and another for himself, until he had emptied both tins. He had no problem with the dog. It was clear they had been through a campaign together, and their friendship needed no commentary or past. So Adamsberg forgave Cupid for stinking like a farmyard and smelling out the car. He poured a little water for the dog in the ashtray and opened the wine. This plonk, no other word for it, entered his organism etching in acid all the contours of his digestive system. He drank it all, welcoming the burn, since mild suffering makes life taste sweeter. And since he was happy, happy to have found Émile before he bled to death in the grass with his dog whimpering at his side. Happy, almost euphoric, and he took some time to admire the mini-brandies before pocketing them.

Relaxing in the seat, as comfortable as in a hotel lounge, he called Mordent. Danglard would still be preoccupied with his uncle and he didn't want to wake Retancourt who had gone without sleep for two days. Mordent would no doubt welcome some action to distract him from his distress, which probably explained his otherwise absurd precipitation earlier in the day. Adamsberg consulted his two watches, only one of which was luminous. About 1.15 in the morning. It had been an hour and half since he had found Émile, but that made it about two and a half hours since he had been fired on.

'Take your time to wake up, Mordent, I can wait.'

'Go ahead, *commissaire*, I wasn't asleep.'

Adamsberg put his hand on Cupid's head to stop his yelping and listened to the slight background noise coming across on the phone. A sound of the outside world, not the interior of an apartment. Traffic, a truck rumbling past. Mordent wasn't at home. He was on a vigil in a deserted avenue at Fresnes, looking up at the prison walls.

'I've got Émile Feuillant, *commandant*. He's taken two bullets and now he's in hospital. The attack happened shortly before eleven, twenty kilometres outside Châteaudun, out in the country. Can you get a fix on Pierre Vaudel for me, see whether he's back home yet?'

'He should be, *commissaire*. He was due back in Avignon at about seven this evening.'

'But we're not sure about that or I wouldn't be asking you to check. Can you do that now, before he has time to do anything else? Not by phone, he could have had his calls forwarded. Get the Avignon cops to go round there.'

'With some excuse?'

'He's supposed to be kept under review, with a ban on leaving the country.'

'He wouldn't stand to gain by Émile's death. By the terms of the will, Émile's share would go to his mother if he died.'

'Mordent, I'm just asking you to check and send me the information. Give me a call when you have.'

Adamsberg picked up the bag containing Émile's clothes, and extracted the bloodstained overalls. From the right-hand back pocket, he pulled out a sheet of paper, still in one piece, folded into eight and stuffed down to the bottom. The writing was angular and well formed, that of Vaudel senior. An address in Cologne, Kirchstrasse 34, to a Frau Abster. Then: *Bewahre unser Reich, widerstehe, auf dass es unantastbar bleibe.* Then an incomprehensible word in capitals: КИСЛОВА. Vaudel had a German lady love. They had a special word, like teenagers. Adamsberg put the paper into his own pocket, disappointed, then lay back on the seat and went to sleep immediately, hardly registering that Cupid had settled on his stomach with his head on Adamsberg's hand.

XIV

SOMEONE WAS KNOCKING ON THE CAR WINDOW. A MAN IN A white coat was shouting and making signs to him from outside. Sleepily, Adamsberg propped himself up on his elbow and felt a stiffness in his knees.

'You got a problem?' the man was saying. He looked on edge. 'This your car?'

In daylight, as Adamsberg realised at a glance, the car did indeed look as if it had a big problem. Himself for a start, his hands still speckled with dried blood, his clothes mud-spattered and rumpled. And then there was the dog, with its bedraggled fur and muddy muzzle. The front passenger seat was stained, Émile's clothes were in a blood-drenched bundle, and scattered all around were tins, biscuit packets, an empty ashtray, a knife, and on the car floor the crushed wine carton and his service revolver. It looked like a pigsty belonging to a malefactor on the run. A second paramedic joined the first: he was very tall, very dark and very aggressive.

'Sorry,' he said, 'we had to do something. My colleague's calling the police.'

Adamsberg put out his hand towards the car door to lower

the window, glancing at his watches. Good grief, almost 9 a.m., and nothing had wakened him, not even the call from Mordent.

'You stay in the car,' said the larger man, leaning on the door. Adamsberg pulled out his badge and pressed it to the window, waiting for the two paramedics to hesitate. Then he lowered the window and handed it to them.

'I *am* the police,' he said. '*Commissaire* Adamsberg. I brought a man in last night, with bullet wounds – about one fifteen in the morning, it was. Name of Émile Feuillant – you can check it out.'

The shorter man punched in a three-digit number and moved away to make the call.

'OK,' he said, 'I've had confirmation. You can get out.'

Adamsberg flexed his knees and shoulders, standing in the car park, and quickly brushed his jacket.

'Seems like it was quite a night,' said the tall one, suddenly curious. 'You look a bit of a mess. We weren't to know.'

'My apologies, I didn't mean to fall asleep.'

'There are showers inside, and you can get something to eat if you want. But that's it,' he said, eyeing Adamsberg's clothes, and perhaps his general condition, 'we can't help with anything else.'

'Thanks, I'll take the offer.'

'But the dog has to stay outside.'

'I can't take him inside to clean him up?'

'Afraid not.'

'OK. I'll just park the car in the shade and I'll follow you.'

By contrast with the air outside, the car smelt to high heaven. Adamsberg refilled the ashtray with water, got out some biscuits and explained to Cupid that he would be back soon. He took his gun and holster with him. The car was one of Justin's favourites, and he was very fussy, so it would have to be cleaned to within an inch of its life before he put it back in the car pool.

'It's not your fault, but you really stink,' he said to the dog. 'But then everything in here stinks, including me. So don't fret.'

In the shower, it occurred to Adamsberg that it would be best not to clean Cupid. He smelt of dog, but he also smelt of the farmyard and therefore of manure. Perhaps he had some on his paws or his fur. He put his dirty clothes back on, having brushed them as best he could, and made his way to the paramedics' room. There was some coffee in a Thermos, bread and jam.

'We checked how he's doing,' said the tall man, André, according to his name badge. 'He must be pretty tough, because he'd lost a lot of blood. He's got a perforated stomach, and a tear in the iliac psoas muscle, but the bullet just grazed the bone without breaking it. He's doing pretty well now, apparently out of danger. Did someone try to kill him?'

'Yes.'

'Ah,' said the paramedic, with a kind of satisfaction.

'How soon can he be moved? I'll need to transfer him.'

'Our hospital's not good enough, is that it?'

'On the contrary,' said Adamsberg, drinking up his coffee. 'But whoever wanted to kill him may come looking for him.'

'Got you,' said André.

'And he's to have no visitors. No flowers, no presents. Nothing must get into his room.'

'Got you, I'll see to it. Abdominal surgery's my set of wards. It'll probably be a day or two before the doctor will let him be moved. Ask for Professor Lavoisier.'

'Lavoisier like Lavoisier the scientist?'

'You know him?'

'If it's the same one who was at Dourdan three months ago, yes, he got one of my *lieutenants* out of a coma.'

'Ah, well, he's just been appointed head of surgery here. You can't see him today, he did four operations last night, so he's sleeping.'

'Tell him my name – or better still mention Violette Retancourt – can you remember that? And ask him to keep an eye on Émile, and to find somewhere to hide him.'

'Got you,' said André. 'We'll guard this Émile for you. But if you ask me he looks like a real troublemaker.'

'You're right, he is,' said Adamsberg with a farewell hand-shake.

In the car park, he switched on his mobile. Battery dead. He went back inside, found a payphone and called the squad. *Brigadier* Gardon was on the desk. None too bright, but very keen, wearing his heart on his sleeve, Gardon was not ideally suited to police work.

'Is Mordent about? Put him on, Gardon.'

'If I may, *commissaire*, treat him gently. His daughter banged her head against her cell wall last night until she drew blood. It's not too serious, but the *commandant* is like a zombie this morning.'

'What time was that?'

'About 4 a.m., I think. Noël told me. I'll put Mordent on.'

'Mordent, Adamsberg here. You didn't call me back.'

'No, really sorry, sir,' came Mordent's voice, hollow with depression. 'They didn't want to know in Avignon, they grumbled, they had too much on, couple of car crashes, guy up on the ramparts with a rifle. No spare men.'

'Oh, for heaven's sake, Mordent, didn't you insist? Homicide inquiry?'

'Yes, I did, but they only got back to me at about seven this morning when they'd just been round to his house. He was there then.'

'And his wife?'

'Yes.'

'Never mind, *commandant*, too bad.'

Adamsberg went back to the car, brooding, opened the windows and sat down heavily in the driving seat.

'By 7 a.m.,' he said to the dog, 'you can bet your boots Vaudel had had plenty of time to get home. So we'll never know. Big slip-up. Mordent didn't insist, you can bet on that too. His mind's somewhere else, it's wandering off into the clouds, too distressed to bother. He told the Avignon people to do the check, then he washed his hands of it. I should have guessed that would happen, what with Mordent being so out of it. Even Estalère would have done better.'

When he reached headquarters two hours later, carrying the dog under his arm, nobody really greeted him. An air of suppressed excitement was propelling his colleagues in all directions through the offices like irregular robots. There was a smell of early-morning sweat. They were brushing against each other with curt words and seemed to be avoiding the *commissaire*.

'Has something happened?' he asked Gardon, who did not seem to be affected.

As a rule, disturbances reached this *brigadier* only a few

hours after everyone else and in a milder form, like the wind from Brittany blowing itself out before it reached Paris.

'It's the newspaper article,' he said, 'and the lab results too, I think.'

'OK, Gardon. The beige car, number 9, can you send it off for cleaning? Ask for special treatment: there's blood, mud, awful mess.'

'*That*'ll be a problem.'

'No, it'll be all right. The seats have plastic covers.'

'I meant the dog. Did you find this dog somewhere?'

'Yes, and it's got farmyard muck all over its feet.'

'There'll be trouble with the cat. I don't think we can manage that.'

Adamsberg felt almost envious.

Gardon had this in common with Estalère, that he had absolutely no sense of proportion. He couldn't put things in the correct order of priority. And yet he, like everyone else, had seen the awful butchery at Garches. But perhaps this was his own form of defence mechanism, and if so he was no doubt right. He was also right to be worried about how the dog would get on with the cat – although the huge apathetic tomcat which lived in the office was not disposed to move about much, and preferred to lie stretched out on the warm cover of one of the photocopiers. Three times a day, certain officers – usually Retancourt, Danglard or Mercadet, who was sympathetic to the cat's sleeping habits – took it in turns to lift this huge animal, weighing eleven kilos, down to its feeding dish, then waited while he ate. That was why there was a chair alongside the dish, so that they could carry on working without getting impatient and forcing the cat to hurry up.

This arrangement was organised near the room with the drinks dispenser and it often happened that men, women and office pet all foregathered round the water cooler. Having been told about this unorthodox behaviour, *Divisionnaire* Brézillon had sent an official note requesting the immediate removal of the cat. Before his quarterly inspection – the function of which was simply to get up everyone's nose, since he could hardly complain about the squad's excellent results – there was a rapid tidying up operation. They had to sweep out of sight the cushions Mercadet slept on, Voisenet's ichthyological journals, Danglard's wine bottles and Greek dictionaries, Noël's pornographic magazines, Froissy's food caches, the cat's litter and dish, Kernorkian's aromatherapy oils, Maurel's Walkman, Retancourt's cigarettes, until the office looked extremely operational and totally unsuited to everyday life.

During such purges, the only problem was the cat, which miaowed terribly if shut in a cupboard. So someone would carry it out to the courtyard at the back and wait in a car until Brézillon departed. Adamsberg had refused to get rid of the two gigantic antlers in his office, saying that they were key evidence in an investigation. With the passage of time – since the squad had now been in these offices for three years – the camouflage operation had become longer and more difficult. Cupid's presence would certainly not help, but it could be assumed that he was only there temporarily.

XV

IT WAS ONLY WHEN ADAMSBERG HAD REACHED THE CENTRE of the large hall that people really noticed his filthy clothes, unshaven jowls and the little dog under his arm. A ragged circle of chairs organised itself spontaneously around him. The *commissaire* summarised the night's events: Émile, the farm, the hospital, the dog.

'So you knew where he was going, and let me chase after him?' said Retancourt crossly.

'No, I only remembered about the dog much later,' Adamsberg lied. 'After Vaudel's doctor had come along.'

Retancourt tossed her head, indicating that she did not believe this for a second.

'What did the doctor have to say,' came Justin's high-pitched voice.

'For now he's not told us any more about Vaudel than we've told him about the murder. Professional confidentiality, both of us are stymied.'

'No secret, game over,' said Kernorkian under his breath.

'But the doctor did say that Vaudel had enemies, only he seemed to think they were imaginary. He knows more than he's saying. He's a skilled doctor, at least: he reset a dislocated jaw that was interfering with nursing.'

'Vaudel's?'

Adamsberg didn't really want to look at Estalère. Sometimes you wondered if he was doing it on purpose. But he glanced at Maurel, who was scribbling something in a notebook. He knew that Maurel was collecting stories about Estalère, something which Adamsberg did not regard as innocent fun. Maurel saw him looking and closed the notebook.

'Did someone check whether Pierre junior was in Avignon when Émile was attacked?' Voisenet asked.

'Mordent took charge of that, but the Avignon cops dragged their feet, they didn't check until it was too late to be sure.'

'Mordent should have insisted.'

'He did insist,' said Adamsberg, defending Mordent and his distracted mind. 'Gardon said there were some results from the lab?'

Danglard stood up automatically. The *commandant*'s memory, knowledge and powers of synthesis made him the reporter of choice for summing up scientific data. This was a Danglard who stood up almost straight, whose complexion was almost fresh and whose expression was almost animated, having been regenerated by a second immersion in the British climate.

'Concerning the body, it is estimated that it was cut into about four hundred and sixty fragments, and about three hundred of those were reduced to pulp. Some parts had been hacked off with an axe, others cut off with a chainsaw, using a wooden block as an anvil. The samples show wooden splinters and sawdust. The same block was used to crush body parts. The elements of mica and quartz found in the remains indicate that the killer rested the item on the block, and used a club to beat down on a granite stone. The most savagely attacked parts were the joints: ankles, wrists, knees, elbows, shoulders and hips, as well as the teeth and the feet, tarsals and metatarsals. The big toe had been pounded to pieces, but not the other toes. The least damaged features were the hands, apart from the carpal segments, and the longer bones, the iliac, the ischium, the ribs and breastbone.'

Adamsberg had not managed to take all this in, and he raised a futile hand to stop the recital. But Danglard pressed on.

'The rachis was differently treated from the others, the sacro- and cervical vertebrae were clearly more fiercely attacked than the lumbar and dorsal ones. Of the cervicals nothing is left of the atlas and the axis. The hyoid has been preserved and the shoulder blades barely touched.'

'Danglard! stop!' said Adamsberg, observing the horror on the surrounding faces, and seeing that some had already melted away. 'Let's do a diagram, that will be more helpful for everyone.'

Adamsberg was an excellent draughtsman, and with a few deft strokes of his pen could bring anything to life on paper. He spent many odd moments scribbling, standing up, resting the paper on a notebook or on his thigh, and drawing in blacklead, charcoal or ink. His sketches were lying about in the office because he abandoned them as he came and went. Some of his colleagues, being admirers, discreetly collected them – notably Froissy, Danglard and Mercadet, but also Noël, who would never have admitted to it. Now Adamsberg quickly sketched on the whiteboard the outline of a body with its skeleton, one from the front, one from the back, and gave Danglard two ink markers.

'Mark in red the parts that were particularly attacked, and in green the least damaged.'

Danglard illustrated what he had just been describing, and added red to the head and genitals and green to the clavicles, the ears and the pelvis. Once the drawing had been coloured in, it showed some kind of logic, though a strange one, demonstrating that the killer had not been arbitrary in what he chose to destroy or to spare. But the meaning of this weird series of choices was inaccessible.

'There was some selection in the internal organs too,' Danglard went on. 'The killer wasn't interested in the stomach, intestines or spleen, lungs or kidneys. But he attacked the liver, heart and brain, burned part of the brain in the fireplace.'

Danglard drew three arrows pointing outside the body for brain, heart and liver.

'It's an attempt to destroy his spirit,' hazarded Mercadet, breaking the rather stunned silence of the officers, who were gazing mesmerised at the drawings.

'The liver?' asked Voisenet. 'Does the liver have anything to do with the spirit?'

'Mercadet's got a point,' said Danglard. 'Before Christianity, but afterwards too, people thought of several souls existing inside the body, the *spiritus*, the *animus* and the *anima*. Spirit, soul and movement, which might lodge in different parts of the body, such as the heart and liver, which are seats of fear and emotion.'

'OK,' said Voisenet, since Danglard's fund of knowledge was considered unchallengeable.

'To destroy the joints,' said Lamarre, speaking stiffly as usual, 'would be so that the body would never function again. Like breaking the gears of a machine.'

'What about the feet? Why the feet but not the hands?'

'Same thing,' said Lamarre. 'So that he never walked again.'

'No,' said Froissy, 'that doesn't explain the attention to the big toe. Why smash that in particular?'

'Oh, what the fuck are we doing?' said Noël, getting to his feet. 'Why are we looking for reasons for this goddam butchery? There's no reason in it at all, it's just what was in the killer's mind, and we're not even close.'

Noël sat down again, and Adamsberg nodded.

'Like the guy who ate the wardrobe.'

'Yes,' agreed Danglard.

'What did he do that for?' asked Gardon.

'Same difference. We don't know.'

Danglard came back towards the board and took out a sheet of paper. 'It gets worse,' he said. 'The killer didn't just chuck the bits about in any old order. Dr Roman was right, he arranged them. I won't go into it, you can see the spatial distribution in the report, but to give you an example, the five metatarsals of the foot were thrown into the four corners of the room, and the same for other parts, here and there, a couple under the piano.'

'Perhaps it was just an automatic reflex,' said Justin, 'he threw it all round him.'

'There's no *pattern* in any of this,' Noël said again, angrily. 'We're wasting our time trying to interpret it. This killer was in a mad rage, he demolished this body, he went to town on some bits, and we have no idea why, end of story. We just don't know.'

'The mad rage went on for hours,' Adamsberg pointed out.

'Yes,' said Justin. 'If he went on being angry, perhaps that's why he did all this. He couldn't stop, he just went on and on blindly till he had reduced everything to pulp, like someone who drinks till he collapses.'

Or who scratches a spider bite all his life, Adamsberg thought.

'We need to move to the other evidence,' announced Danglard.

He was interrupted by his telephone, and moved away – rather fast for Danglard – pressing his mobile eagerly against his ear. That'll be Abstract, Adamsberg diagnosed.

'Should we wait for him?' asked Voisenet.

Froissy shifted on her chair. She was getting anxious about eating – it was 2.45 already – and started to clench her arms around herself. Everyone knew that missing a meal brought on a panic attack and Adamsberg had asked his colleagues to watch out for that, because three times when out on a mission she had fainted with fear.

XVI

THEY RECONVENED IN THE CORNET À DÉS (THE DICE SHAKER), a scruffy little bar at the end of the street. At this time of day the classier Brasserie des Philosophes opposite had stopped serving lunch, since it observed conventional hours. According to one's mood and wallet, merely by crossing the street one could opt to be either a bourgeois or a worker, rich or poor, choose lemon tea or a *vin ordinaire*.

The owner passed round fourteen cheese baguettes – there was no choice, all that was left was Gruyère – and the same number of coffees. He put three carafes of red wine on the table, without being asked. He didn't like customers who refused his wine, which was of unknown origin. Danglard said it was a lousy Côtes-du-Rhône and the others believed him.

'This painter who killed himself in prison – are we any further forward with him?' asked Adamsberg.

'Haven't had time,' said Mordent, who was pushing away his sandwich untouched. 'Mercadet's going to do that this afternoon.'

'The horse manure, the hairs, the Kleenex, fingerprints, anything from those?'

'You were right, the two samples of horse manure were different,' said Justin. 'Émile's wasn't the same as the pellets in the house.'

'We can check the dog for comparison,' said Adamsberg. 'Ten to one it comes from that farm.'

Cupid was crouching at his feet – Adamsberg had not yet dared to confront the cat with him.

'That dog stinks,' called Voisenet from the top of the table. 'We can smell him from here.'

'We take a sample first, we clean him up afterwards.'

'What I mean is,' insisted Voisenet, 'he smells bad anyway.'

'Oh, shut up,' said Noël.

'No surprises in the fingerprints,' Justin continued. 'Vaudel's and Émile's are all over the house. Émile's are mostly on the card table, the mantelpiece, the door handles and the kitchen. Émile was a conscientious cleaner it seems, because the furniture isn't dusty. But we've got a partial print from Pierre junior on the desk, and a good one from a chair back. He must have pulled it up when he was working with his father. And there are four prints on the lid of a little writing desk in the bedroom, unknown male.'

'Could be the doctor,' said Adamsberg. 'He would have done the consultation there.'

'And we have another, different man in the kitchen, and a woman's print in the bathroom, on the washbasin.'

'There you are,' said Noël. 'Vaudel had a woman in the house.'

'No, you're wrong, Noël, no woman's prints in the bedroom. The neighbours say he rarely went out. He got everything delivered and he also had his hairdresser, his bank manager and a men's outfitter from the avenue come to the house.

Same result for phone calls, nothing personal. He spoke to his son a couple of times a month, and it was always the son who made the first move to call him. Their longest conversation was four minutes sixteen seconds.'

'He didn't call Cologne at all?' asked Adamsberg.

'In Germany? No, why?'

'Apparently he had an old flame, a German lady, getting on a bit now, a Frau Abster in Cologne.'

'Doesn't mean he didn't sleep with the hairdresser.'

'I didn't say he didn't.'

'No, he didn't have women callers, the neighbours are pretty sure about that. And in this road they all seem to know each other.'

'How do you know about this Frau Abster?'

'Émile gave me a love letter that he was supposed to post to her if Vaudel died.'

'What does it say?'

'It's in German,' said Adamsberg, taking it from his pocket and putting it on the table. 'Froissy, you can handle that, can't you?'

Froissy looked at it and frowned.

'It says, more or less: *Guard our empire, resist to the end, stay beyond attack.*'

'Unhappy love affair,' Voisenet pronounced. 'She was married to someone else.'

'But then there's this word in capitals at the end,' said Froissy, 'and it's not in German.'

'Some sort of code they used?' said Adamsberg. 'Some reference to a moment only they knew about?'

'Oh, here we go,' said Noël. 'Secret words. Load of rubbish, girls like it, drives men up the wall.'

Froissy asked quickly if anyone wanted another coffee and some hands went up. Adamsberg thought that she too probably invented secret words, and that Noël's remark had offended her, given that she had had plenty of love affairs, all of which turned toxic in record time.

'Vaudel obviously didn't think it was rubbish,' said Adamsberg.

'It could be a code,' said Froissy, bending over the scrap of paper, 'but anyway, it seems to be in Russian: КИСЛОВА. That's Cyrillic script. Sorry, I don't know any Russian. Not that many people do.'

'I do a bit,' said Estalère.

There was a stunned silence, which the young man did not seem to notice, since he was stirring his coffee.

'How come you know Russian?' said Maurel, almost accusingly.

'I tried to learn it once. I only got as far as pronouncing the alphabet.'

'But why Russian? Why not Spanish?'

'I just felt like it.'

Adamsberg passed him the letter and Estalère concentrated. Even when he was concentrating, his eyes didn't narrow. They remained wide open, looking on the world in surprise.

'If you pronounce it properly it sounds something like "kisslover",' he said. 'So if it is a secret love message, that would make sense: *kiss, lover*, that's English for "*embrasser*", "*amant*".'

'Of course,' said Froissy.

'Yeah, right,' said Noël, taking the paper to have a look. 'Put it on a letter, get the girls going.'

'I thought you said just now codes were rubbish,' Justin

piped up. Noël smirked and gave the letter back to Adamsberg. Danglard came into the cafe, puffing, his cheeks rather flushed. The conversation went well, Adamsberg thought. She's going to come to Paris, it's just hit him, he's in shock.

'Anyway, all this stuff, love letters, horse shit, is beside the point,' said Noël. 'We're still not getting anywhere. It's like the dog hairs on the chair, long, white ones, Pyrenean mountain dog, the sort that slobbers all over you. And where does that leave us? Still in the dark.'

'No, because it completes the information from the Kleenex,' said Danglard.

Silence fell once more, arms were crossed, and a few furtive glances went round. Ah, thought Adamsberg, that's what the commotion was about this morning.

'Let's have it then,' he said.

'The tissue was recent,' Justin explained, 'and there were traces on it.'

'A tiny speck of the old man's blood,' said Voisenet.

'And it was a used Kleenex . . .'

'. . . so it was snotty.'

'In other words, all the DNA you want.'

'We meant to tell you last night when it came through, and we tried again this morning, but your mobile was off.'

'The battery's run down.'

Adamsberg looked around at their faces in turn and poured himself half a glass of wine, something he rarely did.

'Look out,' said Danglard discreetly, 'it's not very good.'

'So let me try to understand,' said Adamsberg. 'This DNA on the Kleenex wasn't from Vaudel senior, Vaudel junior, or Émile. Is that it?'

'Affirmative,' said Lamarre, who as a former gendarme had

retained his military vocabulary. And since he was also from Normandy, he found it hard to look Adamsberg in the eye.

Adamsberg sipped the wine and shot a glance to Danglard to confirm that yes, the wine had nothing going for it. Still, it wasn't as awful as the stuff he had drunk through a straw from a carton the night before. He wondered in passing whether it hadn't been that plonk that had made him sleep so long, whereas he usually needed no more than five or six hours. He broke off a piece from a sandwich on the table – Mordent's – and slipped it under his seat. 'For the dog,' he explained.

He leaned down to check that Cupid was happy with it, then looked back at the thirteen pairs of eyes fixed on him.

'So we have the DNA of some person unknown,' he said, 'presumably the killer. And you sent this off to the databank without thinking it would amount to anything, but you hit the jackpot. You've got the killer's name and photo, because he's on file.'

'Yes,' Danglard confirmed in a low voice.

'And you know where he lives.'

'Yes,' said Danglard again.

Adamsberg realised that this rapid conclusion was troubling his colleagues, generating a strong emotion of some kind, as if they had had to make a forced landing. But the air of general embarrassment, even guilt, disconcerted him. Somewhere the plane had gone off the runway.

'So,' he continued, 'we know his address, maybe we know where he works, his family, friends. And you found that out less than twenty-four hours ago. So we check his whereabouts, we move in cautiously and we've got him.'

As he spoke he realised that he was completely mistaken.

Either they were not going to catch the suspect, or they had already lost him.

'You can't have missed him, unless he knows he's been identified.'

Danglard put his baggy briefcase on his knees, the one usually bulging with bottles of wine. He pulled out a sheaf of newspapers and passed one over to Adamsberg.

'Yes, he does know,' he said in a weary voice.

XVII

Lavoisier, head surgeon at the hospital, was looking down severely at his patient, as if he blamed him for his own condition. This sudden attack of fever wasn't supposed to happen. It was caused by incipient peritonitis which would gravely compromise his chances of recovery. He was on powerful antibiotics, and the sheets were changed every two hours. The doctor patted Émile's cheeks several times.

'Wake up, old chap, we're going to have to hook you up.'

Émile obeyed painfully and looked up at the little man in white, to him a slightly fuzzy silhouette.

'I'm Professor Lavoisier, like Lavoisier,' said the doctor. 'Hang on in there,' he said, patting the cheek again. 'You're supposed to be nil by mouth, but you must have swallowed something secretly. A piece of paper, something you didn't want us to find?'

Émile moved his head left to right. Negative.

'Come clean, *mon vieux*. I don't care if you've got something illegal in here. It's your stomach I'm worried about, not your criminal record. Understand? You could have killed all four of your grandparents and it wouldn't change the problem

I've got with your stomach. See what I mean? I'm quite neutral. So come on, did you swallow anything?'

'Wine,' Émile whispered.

'How much?'

Émile indicated about five centimetres with finger and thumb.

'Or two or three times that, no?' Lavoisier guessed. 'Ah, that's helpful, now I can see a bit more clearly. Because I don't care how much you drink as a rule, that's your business. But right now, nothing at all. So where did you get this wine? Under the other patient's bed?'

Negative. Vexed.

'Don't drink much. Good for me circulation though.'

'Oh, you think that, do you? And where did you dig that up?'

'They told me.'

'Who? The guy over there with the ulcer?'

'No, wouldn't believe him, he's too dumb.'

'Yes, true, he is dumb,' said Lavoisier, 'so who?'

'White coat.'

'No, impossible.'

'White coat, mask.'

'No doctor on this floor wears a mask. Nor do the nurses or paramedics.'

'White coat. Made me drink, good for me.'

Lavoisier clenched his fist as he remembered Adamsberg's strict injunctions.

'All right, *mon vieux*,' he said, 'I'm going to call your pal the cop now.'

'That cop,' said Émile, lifting his arm. 'If I've had it, tell him something.'

'You want me to give Adamsberg a message?'

'Yeah.'

'Take your time.'

'Code word. On a postcard too. Same thing.'

'Right,' said Lavoisier, writing a few words on the temperature chart. 'That it?'

'Dog, watch out.'

'Watch out for what?'

'Allergic to peppers.'

'That's all?'

'Yeah.'

'Don't worry, I'll pass it all on.'

Once he was in the corridor, Lavoisier called the tall paramedic, André, and the small one, Guillaume.

'From now on, take it in turns to watch his door, don't leave him alone for a second. Some bastard has got him to swallow something in a glass of wine. Wearing a white coat and a mask, simple as that. Immediate stomach pump, tell the anaesthetist and Dr Vénieux, it's make or break.'

XVIII

DANGLARD ASKED ADAMSBERG TO STAY BEHIND WITH HIM in the cafe, and pulled together the newspapers spread all over the table. The most explicit had published a photograph of the killer on the front page. A dark-haired young man, with angular features, eyebrows meeting in a line across his face, a prominent nose, small chin and large expressionless eyes. 'THE MONSTER CHOPPED UP HIS VICTIM'S BODY!' shouted the headline.

'So why didn't you tell me all this as soon as I got here? The DNA, the leak to the press?'

'We were waiting,' said Danglard. 'We hoped we might be able to catch him instead of having to face you with this mess.'

'Why did you ask the others to go back to the office?'

'Because the leak came from inside the squad, not from the lab or the databank. Read the article, and you'll see that there are details nobody but us could have known. The only thing they don't publish is the killer's address, they've got just about everything else.'

'And where's that?'

'Paris, 18th arrondissement, 182 rue Ordener. We identified it at eleven this morning, the team went out and – there was nobody there of course.'

Adamsberg frowned. 'But you know that's Weill's address? Number 182?'

'Our Weill, our *divisionnaire* that was?'

'Yes.'

'What do you think? That the killer did it on purpose? That he liked the idea of living in the same apartment building as a senior policeman?'

'He could even have taken the risk of getting to know Weill as a neighbour. It's quite easy, he holds open house on Wednesdays, and you get good eats.'

Ex-*Divisionnaire* Weill was, if not exactly a friend, at least one of Adamsberg's few highly placed protectors at the quai des Orfèvres. He had retired early from the force, on the pretext of back pains aggravated by his being overweight, but really in order to devote himself to his study of poster art in the twentieth century, on which he had become a world authority. Adamsberg had a meal with him two or three times a year, sometimes to settle something administrative, sometimes just to listen to him talk, reclining on a shabby couch which had once belonged to Lampe, Immanuel Kant's valet. Weill had told him that when Lampe wanted to get married, Kant had dismissed him along with his couch, and had pinned on the wall a note saying 'Remember to forget Lampe'. Adamsberg had been struck by this, since he would have written 'Remember not to forget Lampe'.

He put his hand on the photograph of the young man, spreading his fingers as if to hold it down. 'Anything found in the apartment?'

'No, of course not. He'd had plenty of time to scarper.'

'Once the news got out this morning.'

'Maybe even before that. Someone could have tipped him off and told him to get out. Then the press reports would simply be a cover for the leak.'

'What are you suggesting? That this man has some relative in the squad – a brother, or cousin, or girlfriend? That's ridiculous. Or an uncle? Another of those uncles.'

'No need to go as far as that. One of us tells someone, and that person tells someone else. Garches was a dreadful business. People might feel the need to get it off their chest.'

'Even if that's true, why give away the guy's name?'

'Because he's called Louvois. Armel Guillaume François Louvois. Which is funny.'

'What's so funny, Danglard?'

'Well, the name of course. François Louvois, like the marquis de Louvois.'

'I don't get the point, Danglard. Was he a murderer or something?'

'Yes, you could say that, because he was the man who built up Louis XIV's armies.'

Danglard had dropped the paper and his hands were waving in the air orchestrating the melodies of his encyclopedic knowledge.

'And a brutal realpolitik kind of diplomat. He was the one that sent death squads out against the Huguenots, no choirboy.'

'Frankly, Danglard,' Adamsberg interrupted, laying a hand on his arm, 'I would be very surprised if anyone in our squad (a) knew the first thing about François Louvois, or (b) would find anything remotely funny about it.'

Danglard stopped his arm movements and his hand dropped dejectedly on to the newspaper.

'Just read the article.'

Following a call from the gardener, detectives from *Commissaire* J.-B. Adamsberg's Serious Crime Squad arrived early on Sunday morning in the quiet suburb of Garches. There in a luxury villa, they discovered the atrociously mutilated body of the owner, Pierre Vaudel (78), a retired journalist. The neighbours are in shock. They say they can think of no reason why anyone would carry out such a vicious attack. We are informed that the body had not only been dismembered but chopped up and scattered around the house, making a nightmare scene. The investigation quickly turned up clues which may identify the homicidal maniac, including a paper tissue. Swift DNA analysis has yielded the name of a man the police wish to help them with their inquiries. The apparent suspect is one Armel Guillaume François Louvois (29), an apprentice jeweller. Louvois was on file for his involvement, along with two accomplices, in a gang rape twelve years ago of two underage girls.

Adamsberg stopped as his mobile rang.

'Yes, Lavoisier. Yes, nice to speak with you again, indeed. No. Lots of problems . . . What! Isn't he getting better?'

He stopped to pass the word on to Danglard.

'Some bastard's tried to poison Émile. He's got a very high temperature. Lavoisier, I'm just putting the speaker on for my colleague.'

'Frightfully sorry, *mon vieux*, someone got in wearing a

mask and a white coat, you can't be everywhere at once. Seventeen different departments at the hospital and we're squeezed for cash. I've put two paramedics on now, taking it in turns by his door. Émile's afraid he's going to die, and I have to say it's not impossible. He said he had two messages for you. Got a pen?'

'Hang on,' said Adamsberg and tore a scrap off the newspaper.

'First, the code word is on a postcard too. No idea what that means, I didn't insist, poor man's on the edge.'

'When did this happen?'

'He was fine first thing this morning. The nurse paged me at two thirty this afternoon, his temperature shot up around midday. Second message: for the dog.'

'What about the dog?'

'Allergic to peppers. I hope you know what he's talking about, it seemed to matter a lot to him. Perhaps it's the rest of that code, because why would you give a dog peppers anyway?'

'What's this code word?' Danglard asked, when Adamsberg had shut the phone.

'It's some word in Russian like a billet-doux. "Kiss lover". Vaudel used to be in love with some woman in Germany.'

'Why write "*kiss lover*" in Russian script? It's English.'

'*I* don't know, Danglard,' said Adamsberg, picking up the paper again.

Louvois was acquitted of rape, but the judge gave him a nine-month suspended sentence for being a party to violence and non-assistance to persons in danger. Since that time, Armel Louvois has not been involved in any further offence, at least on paper. His arrest is regarded as imminent.

'Imminent indeed,' said Adamsberg, looking at both his wristwatches. 'Well, he'll be far away by now, this Louvois. But we'd better keep a watch on the flat, not everyone reads the papers.'

From the cafe, Adamsberg phoned through his instructions. Voisenet and Kernorkian were to follow up the family of the artist who painted his benefactor; Retancourt, Mordent and Noël were to check the suspect's apartment; Weill must be warned – he would be aghast to see any cops in his private space, and would be capable of raising Cain; Froissy and Mercadet were to check Louvois's phone and email accounts; Justin and Lamarre were to check his car if he had one; the Avignon police were to be alerted and told to check the whereabouts of Pierre Vaudel junior and his wife. Stations and airports to be watched, picture of suspect to be circulated.

As he spoke, Adamsberg could see Danglard making signs to him which he couldn't interpret, no doubt because he was incapable of doing two things at once: talking and seeing, seeing and listening, listening and writing. Drawing was the only thing he could do as a background activity to anything else.

'We question Louvois's neighbours?' asked Maurel.

'Yes, but go and consult Weill first, he's right on the spot. Concentrate on the flat itself – you never know, Louvois may not have seen the news, he might come back. See where he works, shop, workshop, whatever.'

Danglard had written five words on the edge of the newspaper and was holding it in front of him. 'Not Mordent. Replace by Mercadet.'

152

Adamsberg shrugged.

'Correction,' he said into the phone. 'Mordent to work with Froissy, and Mercadet to go to the flat. That way if he drops off, there'll be two others around, including Retancourt which makes seven in practice.'

'Why did you want me to change Mordent?' he asked.

'He's spooked, I don't trust him,' said Danglard.

'Just because a man is spooked, there's no reason he can't keep an eye on a flat. Anyway, Louvois isn't there.'

'It's not that. There's been a leak.'

'Come on, out with it, *commandant*, if you've got something at the back of your mind. Mordent's been in the force twenty-seven years, he's seen it all. Never a whisper of corruption, even when he worked in Nice.'

'I know.'

'So I don't see it, Danglard. Frankly, I don't see it. You were saying just now that it was probably someone gossiping. Careless talk costs lives. Carelessness, not deliberate treachery.'

'I always put the best complexion on things in public, but I always believe the worst. He short-circuited you yesterday, and he triggered Émile's escape.'

'Danglard, Mordent's head is a million miles from here, because his daughter has banged *her* head against a wall in Fresnes. Of course he's going to make blunders. He's doing either too much or too little, he's tetchy, he's not in control. We just have to put someone alongside him, that's all.'

'He made a mess of checking the alibi in Avignon.'

'So?'

'So that's two professional errors in a row, and not minor ones: one suspect escapes arrest, and an alibi any fool could have dealt with can't now be checked. Who's legally responsible? You are. With those two mistakes, people will be able to say that in less than forty-eight hours, two days, you've made a complete mess of the first stage of the inquiry. With Brézillon after your guts as usual, you could be stood down for less than that. And now this latest disaster: press leak, killer on the run. If someone wanted to have you taken out of circulation, they wouldn't have put a foot wrong.'

'Oh, come on, Danglard. Mordent sabotaging the inquiry? Mordent wanting to land me in the shit? No way. Why would he?'

'Because otherwise you might find the killer. And that would be embarrassing.'

'Who for? Embarrassing for Mordent?'

'No. For someone upstairs.'

Adamsberg looked at Danglard's index finger pointing at the ceiling which was his way of referring to higher authority, though it could equally well mean 'downstairs' in the caves of Hades.

'Somebody up there,' Danglard said, without moving his finger, 'doesn't want this Garches affair to be solved, or for you to carry on investigating it.'

'And Mordent's on their side? That's unthinkable.'

'On the contrary, it's highly thinkable, because his daughter is in the hands of the judicial system. Upstairs, a murder can be covered up easily. Mordent gives them the ammunition to get rid of you, his daughter gets off the charge. Her case comes up in two weeks, don't forget.'

Adamsberg made a dismissive sound.

'He's not the type.'

'Nobody's not the type if their child is under threat. Easy to see you haven't got any kids.'

'Don't start, Danglard.'

'I mean a kid you really look after,' said Danglard bitingly, going back to the major bone of contention between them. Danglard stood on one side, protecting Camille and her child from the very elusive ways of Adamsberg, and Adamsberg on the other, living as he pleased, leaving behind him, almost without noticing, a trail of calamities in other people's lives.

'I do look after Tom,' said Adamsberg, clenching his fist. 'I babysit him, I take him out, I tell him stories.'

'Oh yeah, so where is he now?'

'None of your business, just stop bugging me, Danglard. He's on holiday with his mother.'

'Yes, but where?'

Silence fell on the two men, the dirty table, the empty glasses, the crumpled newspapers and the killer's photograph. Adamsberg was trying to remember where Camille had gone with little Tom, somewhere healthy, that was for sure. Seaside probably. Normandy, something like that. He called them on the mobile every three days, they were fine.

'In Normandy,' he said.

'In Brittany,' said Danglard. 'In Cancale.'

If Adamsberg had been Émile at that moment, he would have punched Danglard on the jaw right away. He imagined the scene, which pleased him. He contented himself with getting up.

'What you are thinking with respect to Mordent, *commandant*, is unworthy.'

'It's not unworthy to want to save your daughter.'

'I said what you are thinking is unworthy. It's what's in your head that's unworthy.'

'Yes, of course it's unworthy.'

XIX

LAMARRE BURST INTO THE DICE SHAKER.

'Urgent, *commissaire*! Vienna wants to talk to you.'

Adamsberg looked at Lamarre in puzzlement. The young *brigadier* was not good with words, and if he had to make a report, his lack of confidence usually meant he had to speak from notes. Had he got a name wrong?

'Who's Vienna?'

'Vienna, the place. Thalberg, name like yours, with berg on the end, like the composer he said.'

'Alban Berg, or more likely Sigismund Thalberg, 1812–1871, Austrian composer,' murmured Danglard.

'But he's not a composer, he's a *police chief*.'

'A Viennese police chief,' said Adamsberg. 'You might have said so.'

He got up and followed the *brigadier* across the road.

'And what does this man from Vienna want?'

'Didn't ask, it's you he wants, sir. Tell me,' said Lamarre, looking back, 'why is the cafe called the Dice Shaker when there aren't any dice players or even tables for them?'

'Well, why aren't there any philosophers in the Brasserie des Philosophes?'

'That's not an answer, just another question.'

'Often the way, *brigadier*.'

Kommissar Thalberg in the Viennese police headquarters had asked for a videoconference, and Adamsberg went into the technical suite, with Froissy to help him get the equipment working. Justin, Estalère, Lamarre and Danglard all squeezed in behind him. Perhaps it was just the mention of the romantic Austrian composer, but it seemed to Adamsberg as if the man who now appeared on screen belonged to an earlier century: a refined and ethereal face, a little pale, set off by his turned-up shirt collar and the perfect blond curls.

'Do you speak German, *Commissaire* Adamsberg?' asked the gracious Viennese colleague, lighting a long cigarette.

'No, afraid not. But *Commandant* Danglard will translate.'

'That is most kind of him, thank you, but I am capable to speak your language. Happy to know you, *commissaire*, and also happy to share. I saw yesterday your case in Garches. It would have been cleared up quickly if the *Blödmänner* of the press had kept their mouths shut. Your man escaped?'

'What does *Blödmänner* mean, Danglard?' Adamsberg whispered.

'Jackals.'

'Yes, he has got away,' Adamsberg confirmed.

'I am regretful for you, *commissaire*, and I hope you keep the inquiry, yes?'

'So far, yes.'

'So maybe I can help you and you also for me.'

'You've got something on Louvois?'

'No. I have got something on the crime. That is, I am nearly sure I too have this crime, for it is not usual, no? I send you pictures, better to see what I mean.'

The blond head disappeared and a village house came up on-screen with half-timbering and a gabled roof.

'This is the place,' Thalberg's mellifluous voice continued. 'Here is Pressbaum, near Vienna, five months and twenty days ago, and one night. A man also, Conrad Plögener, younger than your man, forty-nine only, married with three children. His wife and children had gone for the weekend to Graz, and Plögener was killed. He was a furniture dealer. Killed like this,' he went on, as a picture appeared of a bloodstained room with no visible body. 'I don't know for you, but in Pressbaum the body was so cut up that nothing remained. Also crushed on a stone and scattered in many directions. Do you have similar modus operandi?'

'Looks the same at first sight, yes.'

'I can show you some close-ups, *commissaire*.'

There followed a slide show of about fifteen pictures repeating the nightmarish spectacle of Garches. Conrad Plögener had a more modest lifestyle than Pierre Vaudel, no grand piano or tapestries.

'I was less fortunate than you, we found no trace of the *Zerquetscher*.'

'Crusher,' Danglard explained, twisting his hands against each other to mime it.

'*Ja*,' Thalberg said. 'The people here started calling him *der Zerquetscher*, you know they always like to give a label. I found some footprints of mountain boots. I'm saying that there is a big possibility we have the same *Zerquetscher* as you, even if it is a great rarity that a killer does not act only in his own country.'

'Quite. Was the victim Austrian? No trace of French in his background?'

'I have been to verify that, just now. Plögener was quite Austrian, he was born in Mautern in Styria. Mind you, I am talking just of him, because nobody is completely something, my grandmother came from Romania and so, everybody also. And Vaudel was French? You don't have any Pfaudel or Waudel or anything else with his name?'

'No,' said Adamsberg, sitting chin in hand, and seeming stunned by this new bloodbath at the home of Conrad Plögener. 'We've looked through most of his papers and there's no connection with Austria. Oh. Wait a minute, Thalberg, there is a German connection. A Frau Abster in Cologne, apparently an old sweetheart of his.'

'I'll write down *Abster*. I check his private papers.'

'Vaudel wrote her a letter in German to be posted to her after his death. Give me a moment, I'll get the piece of paper.'

'I can remember it,' said Froissy. '*Bewahre unser Reich, widerstehe, auf dass es unantastbar bleibe.*'

'Then a Russian word that seems to read "kiss lover".'

'I'm writing it. A bit solemn I find, but the French are often eternalists in love, opposite to what people say. So perhaps we have a Frau Abster who dismembers her former lovers. I am just making a joke of course.'

Adamsberg made a sign indicating drink to Estalère, who shot out of the room. He was the coffee specialist in the squad, knowing everyone's preferences – with or without sugar, or milk, espresso or americano. He knew Adamsberg liked the cup with the orange bird on it. Voisenet, who was a bit of an ornithologist, said the bird didn't look like any existing species, and that was how habits got ingrained. It was not servility that made Estalère memorise everyone's tastes but a passion for small technical details, however insignificant, and perhaps that was what made him bad at taking an overall view. He came back with a perfect tray, as the Viennese *commissaire* was offering a diagrammatic image of a body on which the parts most savagely attacked were marked in black. Adamsberg sent in return their own version with red and green.

'I would be convinced that these two cases must be connected.'

'Yes, I would be convinced also,' murmured Adamsberg.

He drank his coffee, registering the marked zones on the Austrian diagram: head, neck, joints, feet, thumbs, heart, liver – yes, almost a carbon copy of their own drawing. Thalberg's face came back on-screen.

'Give me the address of this Frau Abster, I will see that someone visits her in Köln.'

'In that case, you could take her the letter from her friend Vaudel.'

'Yes, that would be polite.'

'I will send you a copy. You will take care how you tell her about his death, won't you? I mean, there's no need to go into detail.'

'Always I take care, *commissaire*.'

'The *Zerquetcheur*,' Adamsberg repeated several times, thoughtfully, when the videoconference was over. 'Armel

Louvois, the *Zerquetcheur*.' He pronounced it as a French word.

'*Zerquetscher*,' Danglard corrected, in German.

'What do you think of this face?' Adamsberg asked, taking up the newspaper Danglard had left on the table.

'Mugshots fix people's features in a rigid pose,' said Froissy, respecting the ethical obligation not to comment on the physical appearance of suspects.

'That's true, Froissy, he does look fixed and rigid.'

'Because he's looking straight at the camera, without moving.'

'Makes him look a bit of a thug,' commented Danglard.

'But what else? Can you see danger in this face? Or fear? Lamarre, would you like to meet him in the corridor?'

'Negative, *commissaire*.'

Estalère took the paper and concentrated, then he gave up and handed it back.

'Well?' asked the *commissaire*.

'Nothing. I think he just looks normal.'

Adamsberg smiled and put down his cup. 'I'm going to visit the doctor,' he said, 'and Vaudel's imaginary enemies.'

He consulted his watches, which were as usual out of sync, took an average, and gathered that he had little time in hand. He picked up Cupid, who looked somewhat odd, since Kernorkian had cut off some of the dog's coat to collect traces of manure, and went across the main office towards the cat and the photocopier. Adamsberg presented the animals to each other, and explained that the dog was just a temporary visitor unless his master died, which was not impossible, because some bastard had given him blood poisoning. Snowball unfolded part of his enormous round body, and glanced briefly at the frantic little creature which was licking Adamsberg's wristwatches. Then he put his head back down on the warm lid of the machine, indicating that so long as his meals continued to be served on time, and so long as he could occupy the photocopier, the newcomer left him indifferent. On condition of course that Retancourt did not become seduced by this dog. Retancourt belonged to him and he loved her.

XX

AS HE REACHED THE DOOR OF THE BUILDING, ADAMSBERG realised that he had not memorised the name of Vaudel's doctor, despite the fact that this man had saved the kitten's life and that they had all had a drink together in the tool shed. He found the brass plate on the wall, *Dr Paul de Josselin Cressent, osteopath and somatopath*, and realised he now had a clearer idea why the doctor had seemed so disdainful towards the policemen who had been blocking his way with their brawny arms.

The concierge was watching television, from his wheel-chair, muffled in blankets. His hair was long and grey, his moustache grimy. He did not turn his head, not apparently intending to be rude, but because, like Adamsberg himself, he seemed to be incapable of watching a film while listening to a visitor.

'The doctor's gone out to see someone with sciatica,' he finally vouchsafed. 'He'll be back in a quarter of an hour.'

'Are you one of his patients too?'

'Yes. He's got magic fingers.'

'Did he come to see you during the night of last Saturday to Sunday?'

'Is this important?'

'Yes it is, if you don't mind.'

The concierge asked for a few minutes' grace, to see the end of the soap he was watching, then turned away from the screen without switching it off.

'I fell on my way to bed,' he said, pointing to his leg. 'I just managed to reach the phone.'

'And you called him out again a couple of hours later?'

'I did apologise. My knee was puffed up like a football. I *did* apologise.'

'The doctor says your name is Francisco.'

'Francisco, that's right.'

'But I need your full name.'

'Not wanting to refuse, but why is that?'

'One of Dr Josselin's patients has been murdered. We have to make inquiries about everything, it's the rule.'

'Your job, eh?'

'Correct. So I need your full name,' said Adamsberg, taking out his notebook.

'Francisco Delfino Vinicius Villalonga Franco da Silva.'

'OK,' said Adamsberg, who had not managed to get any of this down. 'Sorry, I don't speak Spanish. Where does your first name end and your family name begin?'

'It's not Spanish, it's Portuguese,' said the man, with a snap of his jaw. 'I'm Brazilian, my parents were deported under the dictatorship of those sons of bitches, God damn them to hell. Never seen again.'

'I'm sorry.'

'Not your fault. As long as you're not a son of a bitch

yourself. The family name is Villalonga Franco da Silva. The doctor's on the second floor. There's a waiting room on the landing, all you need up there. That's where I'd live too, if I could.'

It was true, the landing on the second floor was as large as an entrance hall. The doctor had installed a coffee table and armchairs, with magazines and books, an antique lamp and a water cooler. A refined and somewhat ostentatious person. Adamsberg sat down to wait for the man with magic fingers, and called Châteaudun hospital, with apprehension, Retancourt and her team, without hope, and Voisenet's team, while trying to keep at bay the unworthy reflections of *Commandant* Danglard.

Professor Lavoisier was slightly more hopeful – 'Well, he's hanging on.' The fever had gone down slightly; the stomach had survived the pumping; the patient had been asking whether the *commissaire* had found the postcard with the word on it –' He seems obsessed with that, *mon vieux*.' 'Tell him we're looking for the postcard,' said Adamsberg, 'and that we're dealing with the dog, the samples of manure. Everything going to plan.'

Must be a coded message, thought Professor Lavoisier, noting down every word. Well, none of my business, I suppose the police have their methods. But with this new inflammation and a perforated stomach, it was still touch and go.

* * *

Retancourt sounded relaxed, almost jovial, whereas all the signs were that Armel Louvois would not be back. He had gone out at 6 a.m. The concierge had seen him leave with a backpack. Instead of their usual friendly morning exchange, the young man had merely waved his hand at her as he went past. It sounded as though he had been heading for a train. Weill was unable to confirm this, since he did not rise until the gentlemanly hour of midday. He turned out to have a certain affection for his young neighbour, and was extremely vexed by the news of the crime. He had fallen silent, appeared to be sulking, and had provided only a few irrelevant scraps of information. Unusually, Retancourt did not seem too affected by this obstruction. It was possible that Weill, who was a connoisseur of fine wines, had distracted the duty patrol by offering them a decent vintage in fancy glasses. With Weill, who had his suits handmade, since he was extremely rich, extremely snobbish and almost spherical in shape, anything was possible, including the suborning of officers on duty, something which would no doubt give him a paradoxical pleasure. Retancourt did not seem to realise she was on guard outside the apartment of a madman, the *Zerquetscher* who had reduced an old man to mincemeat; indeed, it seemed that Weill's indulgent attitude to his neighbour had overcome her vigilance. 'Tell Weill that he dismembered another person in Austria,' Adamsberg ordered her.

The Voisenet–Kernorkian team, on the other hand, now on its way back, was on its knees. Raymond Réal, the father of the artist, had taken ten minutes to put down his shotgun and let them into his semi-basement in Survilliers. Yes, he'd heard the news, and yes, he called down God's blessings on the guy who had taken revenge and wiped out that old bastard Vaudel, and God willing the cops would never catch him. So, the papers had come out in time to warn him, and he'd got away? Good! Vaudel had at least two deaths on his conscience, Réal's son and his wife, and don't you forget it. Did he know who might have killed Vaudel? Could he tell them where his sons were? They must be joking if they thought he'd tell them, even if he knew. What fucking planet were they on? Kernorkian had muttered, 'Planet Deep Shit,' which had seemed to mollify him somewhat.

In fact, Voisenet was explaining, 'he scarcely let us say a thing. He had this gun on the table, only a shotgun, OK, but loaded, right? He had three bloody great dogs and his lair, the only word for it, was full of motors, batteries, hunting stuff.'

'And you don't know where the sons are?'

'What he said, and these are his actual words, was: "One's in the Legion and the other's a truck driver: Munich–Amsterdam–Rungis, so you can bloody well look for them yourselves." And he told us to get out, "because you stink to high heaven". Actually,' Voisenet added, 'he wasn't wrong about that, because Kernorkian had been handling the dog.'

Listening to all this, Adamsberg reached under the glass-topped table to pick up a toy left by one of Dr Josselin's patients – a little heart made of foam rubber covered in red silk, which you could press inside your hand to calm your nerves. As he made his next call, to Gardon, he twirled it on the table to make it spin. Third time round, he got it to spin for a few seconds. The goal was to get the letters on the front

– LOVE – to face the right way when it stopped. He succeeded on the sixth try, as he asked Gardon to get hold of all the postcards from among Vaudel's papers. The *brigadier* read him a message from the Avignon police. Pierre Vaudel had been at the law courts all afternoon, preparing a brief. Information not verifiable. He had returned home at 7.12 p.m. Local bigwig, being protected, Adamsberg thought. He closed the phone and went on playing with the little heart. Was the *Zerquetscher* on the way somewhere else?

'He got away, did he?'

Adamsberg got up heavily, feeling tired and shook hands with the doctor.

'Didn't hear you come in.'

'No harm done,' said Josselin, opening the door to his flat. 'And how is little Charm? The kitten who wouldn't feed,' he explained, seeing that the name hadn't registered with Adamsberg.

'All right, I suppose. I haven't been home since yesterday.'

'With all this fuss in the press, I'm not surprised. Still, can you let me know how she's doing, please?'

'What, now?'

'It's important to follow up one's patients for the first three days. Would you be offended if I receive you in the kitchen? I wasn't expecting you, and I really need something to eat. Perhaps you haven't eaten either, I'd guess? In which case we could share a simple meal? Don't you think?'

I wouldn't say no, thought Adamsberg, who was searching for an adequate way of talking to Josselin. People who said 'don't you think?' always disconcerted him on first acquaintance. As the doctor took off his jacket and put on an old cardigan, Adamsberg called Lucio, who was astonished that he should be asking after Charm. She was fine, her strength was coming back. Adamsberg passed on the message and the doctor snapped his fingers with satisfaction.

It goes to show that you can't rely on appearances and, as they say, we never really know other people. Adamsberg had rarely been received with such simple and natural cordiality. The doctor had left his pompous manner behind, like his jacket on the coat stand, and proceeded to lay the table casually – forks on the right, knives on the left – before tossing a salad with grated cheese and pine nuts, cutting a few slices of smoked ham, and putting on to the plates two scoops of rice and one of pureed figs, using an ice-cream scoop, which had been lightly oiled with his finger. Adamsberg watched him move around, fascinated, as he glided like a skater from cupboard to table, deploying his large hands with the utmost grace, a sight combining dexterity, delicacy and precision. The *commissaire* could have watched him for ever, as one might a dancer accomplishing movements one could never do oneself. But Josselin took a mere ten minutes to get everything on the table. Then he looked critically at the half-full bottle of wine, which was standing on the counter.

'No,' he said, putting it down, 'I so rarely have visitors that it would be a pity.'

He bent down to look under the sink, surveyed what was there, and re-emerged with agility, showing his guest the label on a fresh bottle.

'Much better, don't you think? But to drink it all on one's own would be like having a birthday party with no guests. Rather sad, don't you think? Good wine tastes a lot better if it's shared. So if you'll do me the honour of joining me?'

Sitting down with a contented sigh, he tucked his napkin

familiarly into his collar, as Émile might have done. Ten minutes later, the conversation had become as relaxed as his practised gestures.

'The concierge thinks you're a guru,' said Adamsberg. 'He says you've got golden fingers, can put anything right.'

'Not at all,' replied Josselin with his mouth full. 'Francisco likes to believe in something beyond him, and that's understandable, given that his parents were "disappeared" under the dictators.'

'The sons-of-bitches-God-damn-them-to-hell.'

'Just so. I'm spending a lot of time trying to settle the trauma, but he keeps blowing a fuse all the time.'

'He's got a fuse?'

'Everyone does, more than one as a rule. In his case it's F3. It's a sort of safety valve, like in a security system. It's just science, *commissaire*. Structure, agency, networks, circuits, connections. Bones, organs, connective tissue, the body works like a machine, you understand?'

'No.'

'Take this boiler,' said Josselin, pointing to the wall. 'Is it just a set of distinct elements, tank, water pipes, pump, joints, burner, safety valve? No, it's a synergetic whole. If the pump gets furred up, the valve flips, and the burner goes out. You see? It's all connected, the movement of each element depends on all the others. Well, so if you sprain your ankle, the other leg tries to compensate, you put your back out, your neck gets stiff and gives you a headache, next thing you know you feel sick and lose your appetite, your actions slow down, anxiety creeps in, the fuses blow. I'm simplifying of course.'

'Why did Francisco's fuse blow?'

'He's got a blocked zone,' said the doctor, pointing to the

back of his own head. 'It's his father. That box is shut, the basal-occipital won't move. More salad?'

He served Adamsberg without waiting for an answer, and refilled his glass.

'And Émile?'

'His mother,' said the doctor, munching noisily, and pointing to the other side of his head. 'Acute sense of injustice. So he goes round bashing other people. But much less these days.'

'And Vaudel?'

'Ah, we're getting to the point.'

'Yes.'

'Since the press has revealed so many details, the police can't keep it a secret any more. Can you tell me about it now? Vaudel was horribly chopped up, is what they seem to say. But how, why, what was the killer after? Did you discover any logic, some sort of ritual?'

'No, just a sort of unending panic, a fury that couldn't be resolved. There must be a system there somewhere, but what it is we don't know.'

Adamsberg got out his notebook and drew from memory the diagram showing the points the murderer had attacked most fiercely.

'You're good at drawing,' said the doctor, 'I can't even draw a duck.'

'Ducks are difficult.'

'Go on, draw me one. I'll be thinking about this diagram and the system while you do it.'

'What sort of duck – flying, roosting, diving?'

'Wait,' said the doctor, smiling. 'I'll fetch some proper paper.'

He came back with some sheets of paper and moved the plates aside.

'A duck in flight.'

'Male or female?'

'Both if you can.'

Then he asked Adamsberg to draw a rocky coastline, a pensive woman and a Giacometti sculpture, if possible. He waved the drawings about to dry the ink, and propped them up under the lamp.

'Now *you* really have got golden fingers, *commissaire*. I would like to examine you. But you don't want that. We've all got closed rooms we don't want strangers to walk into, don't you think? Don't worry, I'm not a clairvoyant, I'm just a pragmatic practitioner with no imagination. You're different.'

Carefully putting the drawings on the windowsill, the doctor carried the bottle and glasses through to his sitting room, along with the Vaudel diagrams.

'What did *you* make of this?' he asked, pointing with his large fingers at the elbows, ankles, knees and skull on the diagram.

'Well, we thought the killer destroyed what made the body work, the joints, the feet. But it doesn't take us very far.'

'But also the brain, liver and heart. He was also intent on demolishing the soul, don't you think?'

'That's what my deputy thought. More than a murderer, he's a destroyer, a *Zerquetscher*, as the Austrian policeman said. Because he destroyed someone else, outside Vienna.'

'Someone related to Vaudel, by any chance?'

'Why?'

The doctor hesitated, then, noticing the wine was finished, took out a green bottle from a cupboard.

'Some *poire* eau de vie – like a drop?'

No, he wouldn't like a drop, after such a long day, but it would spoil the atmosphere, if he let Josselin drink the liqueur alone, so Adamsberg watched him fill two small glasses.

'It wasn't a single blocked zone I found in Vaudel's skull, it was much worse.'

The doctor fell silent, hesitating again, as if wondering whether he should go on, then raised his glass and put it down again.

'So what was there inside his skull?'

'A hermetically sealed cage, a haunted room, a black dungeon. He was obsessed with what was in there.'

'And that was ... ?'

'Himself. With his entire family and their secret. All locked up inside there, silent, away from the rest of the world.'

'He thought someone was locking him in?'

'No, you don't understand. He locked himself in, he was hidden away, removed from anyone's view. He was protecting the other occupants of the cell.'

'From death?'

'From annihilation. There were three other clear factors in his case. He was fanatically attached to his name, his family name. And an unresolved tension over his son: he was torn between pride and rejection. He loved Pierre, but he didn't want him to have been born.'

'He didn't leave his property to him, he left it to the gardener.'

'Logical. If he left him nothing, then he had no son.'

'I don't think Pierre junior saw it that way.'

'No, of course not. And thirdly, Vaudel was full of boundless arrogance, so total that he generated a feeling of invincibility. I've never seen anything like it before. That's what I can tell you as a doctor, and you'll understand perhaps why I was so interested in this patient. But Vaudel was very strong-minded, and he resisted my treatment fiercely. He didn't mind if I treated him for a stiff neck or a sprain, and he was even very pleased when I helped him get rid of vertigo and helped with his approaching deafness. Here,' the doctor said, tapping his ear. 'The little bones in his middle ear were blocked solid. But he hated it if I tried to get near to the black dungeon and the enemies he thought were all around.'

'And who were these enemies?'

'All those who wanted to destroy his power.'

'He was afraid of them?'

'On the one hand, he was afraid enough not to want any children, so as not to expose them to danger. On the other hand, he wasn't personally afraid at all, because of that sense of superiority I told you about. It was a sense he had in his dealings with the law courts, when he seemed to have the power of life and death over people. Be careful, *commissaire*, what I'm saying here isn't objective reality, it's what he saw as reality.'

'Was he mad?'

'Totally, if you consider that it's mad to live by a logic that's different from the logic of the rest of the world. But not at all, in the sense that within his own scheme of things he was completely rigorous and coherent, and he was able to make it fit inside the basic framework of the general social order.'

'Had he identified these enemies?'

'All he would say seemed to point to some kind of gang warfare, a sort of endless vendetta. With some kind of power game thrown in.'

'He knew their names?'

'Yes. These weren't enemies who changed, random demons waiting to pounce on him from round some corner. Their location inside his head never varied. He was paranoid, at least in this sense of his power and his increasing isolation. Yet everything about this war he was living was rational and realistic, and he could certainly put names and faces to his adversaries.'

'A secret war and enemies who are fantasies. And then one night, reality strikes, walks on to his private stage, and kills him.'

'Yes. Did he end up by threatening his "enemies" in real life? Did he speak to them, or become aggressive? You know the standard formula, I expect: paranoid people end up by creating the persecution they always suspected. His invention came to life.'

Josselin offered another drop of alcohol, which Adamsberg refused. The doctor went nimbly over to the cupboard and carefully put the bottle back.

'I don't imagine our paths will automatically cross again, *commissaire*, because I've told you all I know about Vaudel. But would it perhaps be too much to ask of you to come back one day?'

'You want to look inside my head, don't you?'

'Yes, indeed. But we might find a less intimidating problem. No back pains? Stiffness, oppression, digestive troubles, circulation problems, sinusitis, neuralgia? No, none of those.'

Adamsberg shook his head, smiling.

The doctor screwed up his eyes.

'Tinnitus?' he suggested, almost like a street trader offering something for sale.

'Yes,' said Adamsberg. 'How did you know?'

'No magic! The way you keep rubbing your ears!'

'I have been to someone. Nothing to be done about it, apparently, I just have to live with it and try to forget it. Which I'm quite good at.'

'You're indifferent, you don't mind too much,' said the doctor, as he accompanied Adamsberg into the hall. 'But tinnitus doesn't fade away like a memory. I could help you with it. Only if you want me to, of course. Why should we carry our burdens round with us?'

XXI

As he walked back from Dr Josselin's house, Adamsberg turned over in his pocket the squashy little silk heart. He stopped under the porch of Saint-François-Xavier's to call Danglard.

'*Commandant*, it doesn't make sense. That code in the love letter, it's all wrong.'

'What love letter, what code?' Danglard asked cautiously.

'The one from Vaudel. "Kiss lover". The message for the old lady in Germany. He just wouldn't say that. He was old, he was cut off from the world, he was a traditionalist, he used to drink Guignolet, sitting on a Louis XIII armchair, he just wouldn't write "kiss lover" on a letter. No, Danglard, and especially not if it was a last message to be read after his death. It's too cheap for his style. He wasn't going to write silly slogans like you get on toy hearts.'

'Toy hearts?'

'Never mind, Danglard.'

'Nobody's above doing silly things, *commissaire*. Vaudel was eccentric.'

'Silly things in Cyrillic script?'

'If he liked secrets, why not?'

'Danglard, this alphabet, is it only used in Russia?'

'No, it's used in other Orthodox countries in Eastern Europe; it's a Slavonic alphabet, derived from ancient Greek.'

'Don't tell me where it comes from, just tell me if it's used in Serbia.'

'Yes, of course it is.'

'You told me you had an uncle who was a Serb. Were all those cut-off feet Serbian too?'

'I'm not sure they were my uncle's, actually. It was your story about the bear made me think that. They could be someone else's.'

'Such as?'

'Well, a cousin maybe, or a man from the same village.'

'But it is a *Serbian* village, isn't it, Danglard?'

Adamsberg could hear Danglard banging his glass down on the table.

'Serbian word, Serbian feet, are you trying to make something of it?'

'Yes. Two Serbian signals in a few days – that doesn't happen very often.'

'They have absolutely nothing to do with each other. Plus, *you* didn't want us to have anything to do with the feet in Highgate.'

'The wind's changed, *commandant*. What can I do? And right now, it's blowing from the east. Find out what this "kiss lover" stuff could mean in Serbian. Start by investigating your uncle's feet.'

'Look, my uncle didn't know many people in France. And certainly not any rich legal eagles in Garches!'

'Don't shout, Danglard. I've got tinnitus and it hurts my ears.'

'Since when?'

'Since Quebec.'

'You never said.'

'Because before it didn't matter. Now it does. I'll fax you Vaudel's letter. Think, Danglard, something starting with *kiss*. Anything. In Serbian.'

'Tonight?'

'He was your uncle, wasn't he? We're not going to leave him inside the bear.'

XXII

His feet up against the brick fireplace, Adamsberg was
dozing in front of the ashes of his fire, his index finger held
tightly against his ear. Not that it helped, because the noise
was inside his ear, humming like high-tension cables. It must
be affecting his hearing by now, and he was already absent-
minded, so maybe one day he would end up like a bat without
radar, understanding nothing about the world. He was waiting
for Danglard to get to work. By now his deputy would surely
have changed out of his elegant daytime wear into the work
clothes his father used to wear down the pit. Adamsberg could
picture him sitting there in his vest and trousers, cursing his
commissaire.

Danglard looked at the Cyrillic word from Vaudel's letter and
did indeed mutter something about his *commissaire,* who unlike
him had not been the least bit interested in the feet when he
was in London. And now, just when he, Danglard, had decided
to leave them in peace, Adamsberg was suddenly opening up

that can of worms again. Without saying why, in his usual impromptu and mysterious way, which was destabilising Danglard's normal defence mechanisms – indeed, undermining them radically, if Adamsberg should turn out to be right.

Which was not impossible, he admitted to himself, as he spread out on the table the few archives he had inherited from his uncle, Slavko Moldovan. And it wouldn't do at all – that was true at least – to leave him inside some bear, without trying to do something. Danglard shook his head in irritation, as he did whenever Adamsberg's vocabulary infiltrated his own. He had been fond of this Uncle Slavko, his aunt's husband, who had made up stories all day, who had put his finger to his lips to keep a secret, a finger smelling of pipe tobacco. Danglard used to believe that this uncle had been specially invented for him, to be at his service. Slavko Moldovan had never tired, or at least had never shown it, of telling him about fantastic and terrifying aspects of existence, full of mystery and weird lore. He had opened windows, shown new horizons. When he went to stay with them, the young Adrien Danglard used to follow him all round the house, his uncle in his gold-stitched moccasins with red pompoms, which he sometimes used to repair with a shiny thread. You had to take care of them, because they were for feast days back home in the village. Adrien helped him, he threaded the needle with the golden thread. So of course he was very familiar with those shoes, and then had found them ignominiously mixed up in the sacrilegious pile in Highgate. True, these pompoms could have belonged to anyone else from the same village, which was what Danglard was fervently hoping. DCI Radstock had made some progress. He had established that the collector must have gone into mortuary buildings, or funeral parlours when a body was laid out. He would take away his fetish feet, then screw down the coffin again. The feet were clean and their nails trimmed. And if this foot-chopper was French or English, which was most likely, why on earth and how the devil had he managed to find the feet of a Serb in an undertaker's parlour? How could he have gone unnoticed in a little village? Unless, that is, he was from the village in the first place.

Slavko had described village life to him in every season. It was a place full of folklore, fairies and demons: his uncle was favoured by the former and fought the latter. There was one great demon, who hid deep in the earth but who prowled around the edge of the wood, he would say, dropping his voice and putting his finger to his lips. Danglard's mother had disapproved of Slavko's stories and his father had scoffed, 'Why're you telling the kid all this stuff? He won't sleep of nights!' 'Just my nonsense,' Slavko would say, 'the kid and me, we're having fun.'

And then his aunt had left Slavko for some cretin called Roger. Slavko had gone back home.

Back over there.

To Kiseljevo.

Danglard gasped, poured himself a glass and dialled Adamsberg's number. The *commissaire* picked up the phone at once.

'So it doesn't mean "kiss lover", eh?'

'No, it means Kiseljevo, which is the name of my uncle's village.'

Adamsberg frowned and pushed a log with his foot.

'Kiseljevo? That doesn't sound the same as Estalère pronounced it. He said "kiss lover".'

'It is the same. In the west, Kiseljevo is called Kisilova. Like Beograd is called Belgrade.'

Adamsberg took his finger out of his other ear.

'Kisilova,' he repeated. 'That is extraordinary, Danglard. There's a chain running from Highgate to Garches, through the tunnel, the dark tunnel.'

'No,' said Danglard, who was putting up a frantic final defence. 'Over there, lots of names start with K. And there's another obstacle, don't you see?'

'I can't see anything, I've got this tinnitus.'

'I'll speak louder. The obstacle is that it would be a truly massive coincidence if there was any link between my uncle's shoes and the bloodbath in Garches. Something linking both of us, you and me, in two different cases. And you know what I think about coincidences.'

'Exactly. So it means we have been gently led by the hand to that pile of shoes in Higg-gate.'

'Who by?'

'By Lord Fox, perhaps. Or more likely by his Cuban friend who disappeared so fast. He knew Stock would be along, and that we would be with him.'

'And pray why would we have been gently led there?'

'Because Garches, being such a catastrophic case, was certain to be sent to us. The killer knew that, and even if he was passing on to some new stage by getting rid of his collection – perhaps it had got too dangerous – he didn't want to just throw it away without getting any recognition. He wanted there to be a trail between the operations of his youth and those of his maturity. He wanted it to be *known*. That we would still be thinking about Higg-gate when Garches happened. The foot-chopper and the *Zerquetscher* belong in the same story. Remember that the murderer paid special attention to the feet of both Vaudel and Plögener. And where's this Kissilove?'

'Kisilova. On the south bank of the Danube, very close to the Romanian frontier.'

'Is it just a little village or a small town?'

'Just a village, only about eight hundred inhabitants.'

'If the foot-chopper had followed a corpse there, people would have noticed.'

'After twenty years, not many people are going to be able to remember.'

'Did your uncle ever say whether there was any kind of vendetta between families in the village, some kind of clan warfare? The doctor said that Vaudel was living with some kind of obsession like that.'

'No, never,' said Danglard, after pausing for thought. 'The place was full of enemies: ghosts, ogres, ogresses, and of course the "great demon" who lived in the wood. But no family feuds. In any case, *commissaire*, if you're right, the *Zerquetscher* is watching us.'

'Since London, yes.'

'And he won't let us get into the Kiseljevo tunnel, whatever's in there. I advise you to take care. I don't think we can handle this.'

'No, probably not,' said Adamsberg, thinking of the blood on the piano.

'Have you got your gun?'

'It's downstairs.'

'Well, keep it by your bed.'

XXIII

THE STAIRS IN THE OLD HOUSE WERE COLD ON THE FEET, being made of traditional red tiles and wood, but Adamsberg didn't mind. It was 6.15 a.m., and he was coming down in peaceful mood, as he did every morning, having quite forgotten his tinnitus, Kisilova and the rest of the world, as if sleep had restored him to a naive, absurd and illiterate state, with his waking thoughts directed exclusively at eating, drinking and washing. He stopped on the last but one stair, as he saw in his kitchen a man with his back to him, framed in the morning sun, and wreathed in cigarette smoke. The intruder was of slight build with dark, curly, shoulder-length hair. Probably young, he was wearing a black T-shirt that looked new, decorated with a white design showing a ribcage from which drops of red blood were dripping.

The silhouette was unfamiliar, and alarm bells went off in his vacant brain. This man's arms looked strong, and he was waiting with a definite purpose. Plus he was fully clothed, whereas Adamsberg was naked, on the stairs, without a plan and without a weapon. The gun that Danglard had advised him to put by his bed was lying on the table within reach of the stranger. If Adamsberg could manage to turn left to the bathroom without making a sound, he would be able to get to his clothes and the P38 wedged between the lavatory cistern and the wall.

'Put some clothes on, scumbag,' said the man without turning round. 'And forget about the gun, I've got it.'

He had quite a high-pitched voice but was talking tough-guy stuff, a bit *too* tough-guy, signalling danger. The man lifted the back of his T-shirt to show the butt of the P38 jammed into the top of his jeans, against his tanned back.

There was no way out through the bathroom, and no way out via the study. The man was blocking the front door. Adamsberg slipped his clothes on, unscrewed the blade from his razor and put it in his pocket. Was there anything else? A nail clipper. Into the other pocket. Laughable, because the guy now had two guns. And if he was not much mistaken, he was face to face with the *Zerquetscher*. The thick hair, the rather short neck. And on this June morning, it was the end of the road. He had not followed Danglard's anxious advice and now daybreak was here, blocked by the outline of the *Zerquetscher* under his repulsive T-shirt. Just on this very midsummer morning, when the light was falling on every blade of grass, on the bark of every tree, with its exalting and universal precision. Yesterday too, the light had been like that. But he could see it better this morning.

Adamsberg was not a fearful man, through some lack of anticipation or emotion, or perhaps because of his way of opening his arms to the chances life offered. He went into the kitchen and around the table. How was it that at this moment he should be capable of thinking of coffee, of wanting to brew some and drink it?

The *Zerquetscher*. So young, good Lord, that was his first thought. So young, but with a face deeply marked, angular, bony and lined. So young, but his features altered by the choice of a fixed path. He was concealing his anger with a mocking smile, just showing off really, a boastful kid. Mocking death too, a mortal combat which gave him that pale complexion and that cruel and stupid expression. Death was displayed on the T-shirt, with another ribcage design on the chest. Under the breastbone, the legend was a mock-dictionary definition: 'Death: end of life, marked by the extinction of breath and the rotting of the flesh. Dead: finished, nothing.' This individual was already dead and he meant to take others with him.

'I'll make some coffee,' Adamsberg said.

'Don't play the fool, mister,' said the young man, drawing on his cigarette and putting one hand on the gun. 'Don't tell me you don't know who I am.'

'Of course I know. You're the *Zerquetscher*.'

'The what?'

'The Crusher, the most vicious killer of the new century.' The man smiled, satisfied.

'I would like some coffee,' Adamsberg said. 'You can shoot me first or after, it doesn't matter. You've got the guns, you're blocking the way out.'

'Huh,' said the man, 'you make me laugh.' He moved the revolver nearer the edge of the table.

Adamsberg put a filter paper in the funnel with three heaped tablespoons of coffee. He measured two bowlfuls of water and poured them into a saucepan. Better to be doing something than nothing.

'You don't have a proper coffee-maker?'

'Tastes better this way. You haven't had any breakfast? As

you like,' said Adamsberg into the silence, 'but I'm going to eat something.'

'You'll eat if I say so.'

'If I don't eat anything, I won't understand what you're saying. I imagine you came here to say something.'

'You think you're so high and mighty,' said the man. The smell of coffee began to fill the kitchen.

'No, I'm just preparing my last breakfast. Does that bother you?'

'Yeah.'

'OK, go ahead and shoot then.'

Adamsberg put two bowls on the table with sugar, bread, butter, jam and milk. He had not the slightest desire to die from a bullet fired by this sinister character who was blocked somewhere, as Josselin might say. Or to get to know him. But talk and get them talking, that was the first rule you learned, before even learning to handle a gun. 'Words,' the instructor had said, 'are the deadliest weapons if you know exactly where to aim them.' He also said it was quite difficult to find the right place in the head to aim the words, and if you were off target the enemy tended to shoot at once.

Adamsberg poured the coffee into the two bowls, pushed some sugar and bread towards the enemy, whose eyes did not move under the black bar of his eyebrows meeting across the middle.

'Tell me at least what you think of it,' Adamsberg said. 'Apparently you're quite a cook.'

'How would you know that?'

'Through Monsieur Weill, your downstairs neighbour. He's a friend of mine. He also likes you, *Zerquetscher*. I'll say *Zerketch* if you don't mind.'

'I know what you're up to, scumbag. You're trying to make me talk, tell you the story of my life, fucking stuff like that, like the fucking over-the-hill cop you are, and then you'll try to confuse me and kick me in the balls.'

'Story of your life, sorry, I don't give a damn.'

'Huh, really?'

'No,' said Adamsberg sincerely, regretting the fact.

'Well, you're wrong,' said the young man through clenched teeth.

'Maybe so. But that's the way I am. Couldn't give a damn about anything really.'

'Not about me?'

'Not about you.'

'So what does interest you, scumbag?'

'Nothing. I must have missed out on something when I was born. See that light bulb up there?'

'Ha, don't try to make me look up!'

'It hasn't worked for months. I haven't changed it, I just get on with things in the dark.'

'Just what I thought about you. Useless fucking wanker.'

'Well, a wanker does want something, doesn't he?'

'Yeah,' admitted the young man after a moment.

'But I don't. Otherwise, yes, I agree with you.'

'And you're chicken, you remind me of this old geezer I know, a real bullshitter, he thinks he knows it all.'

'Too bad.'

'He was in this bar one night. And these six guys come at him. Know what he does?'

'No.'

'He lies down on the ground. Like a wimp! He says, "Go ahead, guys." So they tell him to get up. But he just lies there, hands folded on his belly, like a fucking woman. And in the end they say, "Stuff this for a lark. OK, grandad, come and have a drink." And you know what he says?'

'Yes.'

'You do?' asked the boy.

'Yes, he says: "What kind of drink? Not if it's only Beaujolais."'

'Yeah, that's right,' said the young man, disconcerted.

'So then,' Adamsberg went on, dunking some bread in his coffee, 'the six thugs think, hmm, cool customer, pick the old man up, and after that they're all friends. But I wouldn't call him chicken. I'd say it took some guts. But that was Weill – eh? I'm right, aren't I, it was Weill?'

'Yeah.'

'He's quick-witted. I'm not.'

'He's better than you? At police stuff?'

'Are you disappointed? You want a higher-class enemy?'

'No. They say you're the best cop in the business.'

'So our meeting was written in the stars.'

'More than you think, scumbag,' said the young man with a nasty smile, but swallowing his first mouthful of coffee.

'Would you mind calling me something else?'

'Yeah, I can call you pig if you want.'

Adamsberg had now finished his bread and his coffee. It was the time when he normally set off for the office, half an hour's walk. He felt tired, sickened by this exchange, fed up with this man and with himself.

'Seven o'clock,' he said. 'Now this is when my neighbour will go out and take a leak against a tree. He has to piss every hour and a half, day and night. It doesn't do the tree much good. But I tell the time by him.'

The man gripped the gun and watched Lucio through the window.

'Why does he have to piss so often?'

'Prostate trouble.'

'See if I care,' said the young man furiously. 'I've got TB, eczema, ringworm, enteritis, and I've only got one kidney.'

Adamsberg cleared away the bowls.

'Ah, well, I see why you want to kill everyone then.'

'Yeah. Another year and I'll be dead.'

Adamsberg pointed towards the *Zerquetscher*'s cigarettes.

'Does that mean you want one?'

'Yes.'

The packet slid across the table.

'Yeah, condemned man gets one last smoke, traditionally. But what else do you want? You want answers, you want to understand? You won't find anything. Ask away.'

Adamsberg took out a cigarette and gestured with his fingers for a light.

'You're not scared?'

'So-so.'

Adamsberg inhaled deeply, which made his head swim.

'Just why did you come here?' he asked. 'To walk into the lion's den? To tell me your little story? To get absolution? To take a look at the enemy?'

'Yeah,' said the young man, though it wasn't clear what that referred to. 'I wanted to see what you looked like before leaving. No, it wasn't that. I came here basically to fuck up your life.'

He was threading the holster on his shoulder, but getting entangled in the straps.

'You've got it on the wrong way round. That strap there goes on the other arm.'

The young man started again. Adamsberg watched him without moving. There came a muted mewing sound and claws scratched the door.

'What's that?'

'A cat.'

'You keep pets? How pathetic, only wimps have pets. Yours?'

'No, she belongs to the garden.'

'You have kids?'

'No,' said Adamsberg prudently.

'Easy to say no, isn't it? Easy not to give a damn about anything? To faff about up in the sky while other people have to slog away down here?'

'In the sky?'

'Yeah. Known as the cloud-shoveller.'

'You're well informed.'

'Course I am, it's all on the Internet. Pictures of you, your famous cases. Like when you chased that guy in Lorient and he threw himself into the harbour.'

'He didn't drown.'

There was another more urgent and panicky sound of mewing.

'What the fuck's the matter with that cat?'

'She's probably in trouble. Just had her first litter and doesn't know what to do. Maybe she's lost one of the kittens somewhere. Take no notice.'

'You say take no notice, because you're a cold bastard, you don't care about anyone.'

'OK, *Zerketch*, go and see.'

'Ha! And let you get away, scumbag?'

'All right, lock me in the study, the window's barred. You take your guns with you, and you go and see. If you're not a cold bastard like me, go on, prove it.'

The young man inspected the study, keeping the gun trained on Adamsberg.

'Don't you dare budge from there.'

'If you do find a kitten, lift it from underneath or by the scruff of the neck, not by the head.'

'Ha,' laughed the young man, 'hark at Adamsberg, fussy as the cat's mother.'

He laughed again and locked the study door. Adamsberg listened to what was happening in the garden and heard the sound of wooden boxes being moved and then Lucio's voice.

'The wind blew these boxes over,' he said, 'and there's a kitten trapped underneath. Come on, *hombre*, you can see I've only got one arm. Who are you anyway? And what are all these guns for?'

Lucio's imperious voice was probing the ground.

'I'm a relation. He's teaching me to shoot.'

Not bad, Adamsberg thought. Lucio respected the family. He heard the sound of the boxes being moved and a tiny mewing sound.

'See it?' Lucio said. 'Is it hurt? I can't stand the sight of blood.'

'Yeah, well, I like it fine.'

'*Hombre*, if you'd seen your old grandad shot in the stomach, and if you'd seen your own arm cut off and spraying blood like a fountain, you wouldn't say that. What did your mother teach you? Pass me that kitten, I don't trust you.'

Gently does it, Lucio, Adamsberg muttered to himself, clenching his teeth. That's the *Zerquetscher* you've got out there, can't you see, he could blow up any moment? He might trample on the kitten and cut you up in the tool shed. Shut up, take the kitten and get out of it.

The door banged and the young man came stamping back into the study.

'Stupid bloody kitten under some boxes, couldn't even find its way out. Like you,' he added, sitting down facing Adamsberg. 'Your neighbour's no fun, I prefer Weill.'

'Look, *Zerketch*, I've got to get out. Sitting still too long makes me edgy. It's the only thing that does. But it makes me really edgy.'

'No kidding,' scoffed the young man. waving the gun. 'So the cop's had enough, the cop wants to get out.'

'That's right, you got it. See this bottle?'

Adamsberg was holding a little glass tube filled with liquid, no bigger than a perfume sample.

'If I were you, I wouldn't touch the gun till you hear what I've got to say. See the cork? I take it off and you'll be dead. In less than a second, in 74.3 hundredths of a second to be precise.'

'You bastard,' said the young man. 'Is that why you're so pleased with yourself? Why you aren't scared?'

'I haven't finished explaining. The time it takes for you to slip the safety catch on your gun is 65 hundredths of a second, and then to press the trigger, 59 hundredths. Time for the bullet to hit, 32 hundredths. Total: one point fifty-six seconds. Result, you're dead before the bullet hits me.'

'What's that bloody stuff?' The young man had stood up and was walking backwards, holding his hand towards Adamsberg.

'Nitrocitraminic acid. Turns into a lethal gas on contact with air.'

'So you'll snuff it with me, fucker.'

'I still haven't finished explaining. All us cops in the squad get immunised by a special course of injections for two months, and believe me that's no picnic. If I push the top off, you'll die – your heart will dilate and burst – but what will happen to me is I'll be sick, and empty my guts out for three weeks, and I'll have a skin rash, and lose my hair. But after that I'll recover.'

'You wouldn't do it.'

'In your case, *Zerquetscher*, like a shot.'

'You son of a bitch.'

'Yes.'

'You can't kill a man like that.'

'Yes I can.'

'What do you want?'

'Put the guns down. Open that drawer in the chest, take out two pairs of handcuffs. You put one pair on your wrists, the other on your feet. Hurry up, I said I was getting edgy.'

'Fucking cop.'

'Yes. But get a move on. Maybe I shovel clouds up there, but down here I can be quick.'

The young man swept the table with his arm, scattering papers round the room, and threw the holster on the ground. Then he put his hand behind his back.

'Careful with the P38. If you stick it in your waistband, you shouldn't push it in so far, especially in tight jeans. One false move and you'll shoot yourself in the backside.'

'You think I'm a baby!'

'Yes, you are a baby, a kid who's lost it. But not an idiot.'

'If I hadn't let you get dressed, you wouldn't have that bottle.'

'Correct.'

'But I didn't want to look at you with your kit off.'

'Oh really? Same thing for Vaudel, you didn't want to look at him with his kit off, as you put it, either?'

The young man carefully pulled the P38 from his trousers and dropped it to the floor. He opened the drawer and took out the handcuffs, then turned round suddenly with a burst of strange laughter, as irritating as the cat's mewing earlier.

'You don't get it, do you, Adamsberg? You still don't get it. You think I'd risk getting arrested? Just for the pleasure of seeing you? You don't understand that if I'm here it's because you *can't* arrest me. Not today, not tomorrow, never. Don't you remember why I'm here?'

'You said you wanted to fuck up my life.'

'Yeah.'

Adamsberg had stood up too, holding the bottle in front of him like a chisel, his fingernail under the lid. The two men turned around each other, like two dogs looking for a chance to pounce.

'Give it up,' said the young man. 'You don't know who my father is. You can't kill me, you can't shut me up, and you can't go on chasing me.'

'Why not? Are you untouchable? Who is your father then? A government minister? The Pope? *God* perhaps?'

'No, scumbag, it's you.'

XXIV

ADAMSBERG STOPPED IN MID-MOVEMENT, DROPPED HIS ARM, and the bottle rolled on to the red tiled floor.

'Shit! The bottle!' shouted the young man.

Adamsberg picked it up automatically. He was looking for a word that meant 'someone who makes up a story and then believes it', but he couldn't think of it. Fatherless kids who go round saying they're the son of royalty, or the son of Elvis, or a descendant of Julius Caesar. One notorious gangster had had eighteen fathers, including famous politicians like Jean Jaurès, and he changed them all the time. Mythomaniac, that was it. And people said you shouldn't shatter the illusions of a mythomaniac, it was dangerous, like waking a sleepwalker.

'Well, while you're about it,' he said, 'you might have found a better father than me. Not very interesting, is it, to be the son of a cop?'

'So, *Commissaire* Adamsberg,' the young man laughed as if he hadn't heard a word, 'father of the *Zerquetscher*! Don't like that, do you? But that's how it is, motherfucker. One day the long-lost son comes back, he crushes his father, he takes over the throne. You know stories like that, don't you? So his father has to go away with nothing, and beg on the streets.'

'Yes,' said Adamsberg.

'Now *I'm* going to make the coffee,' said the young man, mimicking him. 'Bring your fucking bottle, and watch me.'

Looking at him pouring water into the funnel, the cigarette hanging from his lower lip, one hand scratching his dark hair, Adamsberg felt something like a depth charge in the pit of his stomach, an acid spurt more biting than the awful wine in Froissy's car, spreading to the roots of his teeth. 'The fathers have eaten sour grapes, and the children's teeth are set on edge.' In his concentration on the coffee, the young man did look very like his own father used to, as he knitted his dark eyebrows while watching a stew on the stove. In fact, he looked like half the young men of the Béarn, or two-thirds of those from the valley of the Gave de Pau: thick curly hair, receding chin, well-shaped lips, a compact body. Louvois, not a name he recognised at all from his home valley. He could equally well be from the other valley where his colleague Veyrenc had been born. Or he could have been from Lille or Reims or Menton. Not London though.

The young man took the bowls and refilled them. The climate had changed since he had dropped his bombshell. He had carelessly tucked the P38 into his back pocket, and put the holster near him on a chair. The confrontational phase was over, like the wind dropping at sea. Neither of them knew what to do, so they stirred their sugar into the coffee. The *Zerquetscher*, leaning forward, tucked his long hair behind his ear. It fell out and he pushed it back again.

'All right, it's quite possible you're from the Béarn,' said

Adamsberg, 'but pull the other leg, *Zerketch*. I haven't got a son, and I don't want one. Where were you born?'

'In Pau. My mother went to town to have me, so people wouldn't know.'

'And what's your mother's name?'

'Gisèle Louvois.'

'No, doesn't ring a bell at all. And I know everyone in the three valleys.'

'You screwed her one night, by the bridge over the Jaussène.'

'A lot of couples went to the bridge over the Jaussène.'

'Then she wrote to you to ask for your help. And you didn't answer, because you couldn't give a damn, or because you're chicken.'

'Never got any letter like that.'

'You probably can't remember the names of the girls you screwed.'

'Number one, I do remember their names. And number two, I wasn't a Jack the Lad in those days. I was shy, and I didn't have a moped. Other boys like Matt, Pierrot, Loulou, Manu, yes, you might well wonder if one of them's your father. They could get any girl they wanted. But afterwards, the girls didn't own up, because it would have ruined their reputations. How do you know your mother's telling the truth?'

The young man felt in a pocket, frowning, and brought out a little plastic envelope which he waved in front of Adamsberg's eyes, before putting it on the table. Adamsberg took out an old photo, the faded colours turning purple: it showed a youth leaning up against a plane tree.

'And who's that?' asked the young man.

'It's either me or my brother. So what?'

'It's you, look on the back.'

His name: *J.-B. Adamsberg*, written in pencil in small round handwriting.

'It looks more like my brother, Raphaël. I don't remember having a shirt like that. So your mother didn't know us very well, and it proves she's making things up.'

'Just shut up – you don't know what my mother's like, she doesn't make things up. If she says you're my father, then it's the truth. Why would she make it up? It's not as if it's something to be proud of, is it?'

'True. But in our village, it was probably better to say it was me than to own up to Matt or Loulou, because they were known as local bad boys, good-for-nothings, piss-artists. In fact, they used to piss out of the windows on warm summer nights. The grocer's wife, they didn't like her, and she got it in the face once. Not to mention Lucien's gang. In other words, even if it's no big deal, it would still be better to pretend it was me than Matt. Look, I'm not your father, I have never known any girl called Gisèle, in my village or in the next one, and she has never written me any letter. The first time a girl wrote a letter to me, I was twenty-three.'

'Liar.'

The youth clenched his teeth, swaying on the plinth of certainty that had suddenly developed cracks. His imagined father, his long-lost enemy, his target, seemed to want to slip between his fingers.

'Look, whether I'm a liar or she is, *Zerketch*, what are we going to do? Stay drinking coffee here for ever?'

'I always knew it would end like this. Well, you *are* going to let me go, free as a bird. And you can stay here with your lousy cats, because you can't do a thing about it. You'll be reading about me in the papers, believe me. Because there's more to come. And you'll be sitting in your office, and you'll be fucked. You'll have to resign because even a cop doesn't shop his own son for a life sentence. When your kid's involved, there aren't any rules. And you won't want to admit you're the *Zerketch*'s old dad, will you, and that it's all your fault that the *Zerketch* has gone crazy? Because you abandoned him?'

'I did *not* abandon you. And I'm not your father in the first place.'

'But you're not sure, are you? See your face? See mine?'

'Yes, we both look like we come from the Béarn, full stop. But there is a way to find out, *Zerketch*. A way to put an end to your little dream. We've got your DNA on file. And we've got mine. We take a look.'

The *Zerquetscher* stood up, put the P38 on the table and smiled calmly.

'I dare you,' he said.

Adamsberg watched as he walked unhurriedly towards the door, opened it and went out. Free as a bird. *I came here to fuck up your life.*

He reached out for the bottle and looked at it. Nitrocitraminic acid. He folded his hands, and dropped his head on to them, closing his eyes. Of course he wasn't immunised. With his thumbnail, he flicked the top off.

XXV

AS HE WENT INTO THE DOCTOR'S SURGERY, ADAMSBERG realised that he reeked of aftershave, and that Dr Josselin had also noticed it with surprise.

'It was a sample I spilt on myself,' he explained. 'Nitrocitraminic acid.'

'Never heard of it.'

'I made the name up, it sounded good.'

There had been one good moment, when *Zerketch* had fallen for it, when he had believed that the nitrocitraminic acid really existed, believed in the little bottle and the hundredths of a second. Just then, Adamsberg had thought he had got him, but the young man had a secret weapon far more powerful. A different trick, a different illusion, but it had worked. He, Adamsberg, the cop, had let Zerketch go, without lifting a finger to stop him. When his revolver was on the table, he could have grabbed it in a couple of steps. Or he could have had the area surrounded in five minutes. But no, the *commissaire* hadn't budged. 'COMMISSAIRE ADAMS-BERG LET THE MONSTER GO FREE.' He could see the headlines. In Austria too. It would begin something like 'KOMMISSAR

ADAMSBERG'. In big letters dripping with blood, like the ribs on the *Zerquetscher*'s T-shirt. Then there would be a court case, people screaming, a lynch mob, a rope from a tree. The *Zerquetscher* would turn up, his fangs red with blood, thrusting his fist in the air and yelling with the others, 'The son crushes the father!' The characters of the headline began whirling into a cloud of black and green spots.

He could taste pear-flavoured alcohol in his mouth; his head was swimming. He opened his eyes and focused on the face of Josselin who was bending over him.

'You fainted. Does that happen often?'

'First time in my life.'

'Why did you want to see me? Is it about Vaudel?'

'No, it was because I didn't feel well. I was leaving the house and I thought I'd come here.'

'You don't feel well? What's the trouble?'

'Sick, confused, exhausted.'

'Does that happen often?' the doctor repeated, helping him to his feet.

'No, never. Yes, once in Quebec. But it didn't feel the same and anyway that time I had drunk way too much.'

'Lie down,' said Josselin, tapping his examination couch. 'Lie on your back and take your shoes off. Maybe it's just a touch of flu, but I'll examine you all the same.'

Adamsberg hadn't really intended, when he had come to the surgery, to end up on the padded table while the doctor moved his large fingers over his head. His feet had simply taken him away from the office and towards Josselin. He had just intended to talk. The fainting fit was a serious warning. Never would he tell anyone that the *Zerketch* claimed to be his son. Never would he admit to anyone that he had let him go without lifting a finger. Free as a bird. On the way to a fresh massacre, with a smile on his lips and his deathly shirt on his back. *Zerk* was easier to say than *Zerketch* and it was almost onomatopoeic, a sound of rejection and disgust. Zerk, the son of Matt or Loulou, the son of a pisspot. But all the same, no one had felt any remorse over the grocer's wife.

The doctor put his palm across Adamsberg's face and pressed two fingers against his temples. The immense hand easily covered the distance between his ears. The other hand was cupped under the base of his skull. Under this slightly perfumed hand, Adamsberg felt his eyes closing.

'Don't worry I'm just testing the PRM of the SBS.'

'Oh yes?' said Adamsberg with a slight question in his voice.

'The primary respiratory movement of the sphenobasiliar symphysis, a simple basic check.'

The doctor's fingers continued to move, like attentive moths, on to his nose, his jaws, touching his forehead, going into his ears.

'Right,' he said after a few minutes, 'what we have here is a fibrillation incident, which is hiding your basic state. Some recent event has put the fear of death into you, and that has caused an overheating of the system. I don't know what happened, but you didn't like it. A major psycho-emotional shock. What it's done is immobilise the parietal, block the pre-post sphenoid, and blown three fuses. Major stress episode, no wonder you weren't feeling well. That must be why you fainted. Let's get rid of this first, if we want to check the rest.'

The doctor scribbled a few lines and asked Adamsberg to roll on to his stomach He pulled up his shirt and felt the sacro-iliac joint. 'I thought you said it was in my head.'

'The head has to be reached through the sacrum.'

Adamsberg stopped talking and let the doctor move his fingers up his vertebrae, like kindly gnomes trotting up his back. He kept his eyes wide open, so as not to fall asleep.

'Stay awake, *commissaire*, and lie on your back again. I'm going to relax the mediastinal fascia which are also completely blocked. Do you have some pain between your ribs on the right. Here?'

'Yes.'

'That's good,' said Josselin and put two fingers as a fork under the nape of his neck and then with the flat of his hand stroked his ribs as if he was ironing a shirt.

Adamsberg woke up groggily, with the unpleasant feeling time had passed. It was after eleven, he saw by the clock. Josselin had let him go to sleep. He jumped down, slipped on his shoes, and found the doctor sitting at the kitchen table.

'Sit down, I'm having an early lunch because I've got a patient in half an hour.'

He pulled out another plate and cutlery and pushed the dish towards Adamsberg.

'You put me to sleep?'

'No, you just dropped off. The state you were in, there could be no better solution after the treatment. Everything's back in position,' he added, like a plumber reporting on a repair. 'You were deep inside a well, totally inhibited from action, you couldn't go forward. But it should settle down now. You might feel a bit drowsy this afternoon, and tomorrow you may feel a bit low and have a few aches and pains, but that's only to be expected. Within three days, you ought to be back to normal. Better in fact. I had a go at the tinnitus while I was at it, and maybe a single session will be enough. Now it would be a good idea to have something to eat,' he said, pointing to the dish of couscous and vegetables.

Adamsberg obeyed. He felt a bit stunned but also better, lighter, and very hungry. Nothing like the sickness and the feeling that he was carrying lead weights in his feet that had assailed him earlier. He raised his head to see the doctor give him a friendly wink.

'Apart from that,' he said, 'I saw what I wanted to. What your natural structure is.'

'Oh?' said Adamsberg, who felt somewhat diminished alongside Josselin.

'A bit as I had hoped. I've only ever seen one similar case, in an elderly woman.'

'And?'

'It's a total absence of anguish. A rare case. To compensate of course, your emotional temperature is low. The desire for things is only moderate, there's some fatalism, a temptation to walk away, some difficulty relating to people around you, blank spaces. Well, you can't have everything. Even more interesting, there's a sort of interaction between the conscious and the unconscious. You could say that the airlock is badly adjusted, that sometimes you forget to shut the gate. Take care all the same, *commissaire*. It can result in ideas of genius which seem to come from out of the blue – intuition as it's sometimes wrongly called, for short – immense stocks of memories and images, but it also allows toxic elements to rise to the surface, things that absolutely ought to remain buried in the depths. Do you follow me?'

'Sort of. And if these toxic elements come to the surface, what happens?'

Dr Josselin whirled a finger round near his head.

'Then you can't tell the true from the false, the fantasy from the real thing, the possible from the impossible, in short you will end up mixing saltpetre, sulphur and carbon.'

'Explosive,' Adamsberg concluded.

'As you say,' said the doctor, wiping his hands and looking satisfied. 'Nothing to fear if you keep a grip on things. Keep up your responsibilities, carry on talking to other people, don't isolate yourself too much. Do you have any children?'

'One, he's very little.'

'Well, tell him about the world, take him for walks, hang on to him. That will help you throw down some anchors, you mustn't lose sight of the harbour lights. I'm not going to ask you about women, I can see. Lack of confidence.'

'In them?'

'No, in yourself. That's the only little worry, if it can be called that. I have to leave you now, *commissaire*. Make sure to shut the door when you go out.'

'Which door – the apartment or the one in my head?'

XXVI

THE COMMISSAIRE NOW FELT NO APPREHENSION AT THE IDEA of going to the squad's headquarters. On the contrary. The man with the golden fingers had set him right, had chased away the smoke from the accident, the 'psycho-emotional shock' which had blocked everything out for him only that morning. He most certainly had not forgotten that he had let Zerk go. But he would catch him, in good time, in his own way, just as he had tracked down Émile.

Émile was making progress ('He'll pull through, *mon vieux*' was one of the messages on his desk). Lavoisier had transferred him, but as agreed was not revealing where he was now being treated. Adamsberg read the news about Émile to the dog. Someone had given Cupid a bath – someone kind, or who had lost patience – and his fur was now soft and smelt of soap. The dog rolled over in his lap and Adamsberg stroked his back. Danglard came in and crashed down like a bag of old clothes on to a chair.

'You look well,' he said.

'I'm just back from seeing Josselin. He fixed me like an engineer fixes a boiler. The man's a pro.'

'Not like you to go and consult someone.'

'I meant just to talk to him, but I passed out in his surgery. I'd been through two ghastly hours this morning. A burglar got into the house and got hold of both my guns.'

'Good grief, I told you to keep them by you.'

'And I didn't. So this burglar grabbed them.'

'And?'

'When he realised I didn't have any money, he left in the end. But I felt like a wet rag.'

Danglard looked at him with some suspicion.

'Who washed the dog?' asked Adamsberg, changing the subject. 'Estalère?'

'Voisenet. He couldn't stand the smell any longer.'

'I read the note from the lab. So the horse shit on Cupid matched the lot on Émile. They both picked it up from the same farm.'

'That may take the pressure off Émile a bit, but he's not out of the woods yet. Nor is Pierre junior, because he puts money on horses a lot, so he goes to the races and training stables where there's no shortage of manure. He's even supposed to be buying a horse.'

'He didn't tell me that. How long have you known?'

As he talked, Adamsberg was leafing through the little pile of postcards which Gardon had put on the desk for him, taken from among Vaudel's effects. They were mostly conventional holiday messages posted by his son.

'The Avignon police found that out yesterday, and I did this morning. But hundreds of people go to the races. There are thirty-six major racecourses in France, hundreds of stud farms and riding schools and tens of thousands of race-goers. So there are vast quantities of horse manure all over the place. It's one of the most widely distributed materials there is.'

Danglard pointed to the floor under Adamsberg's desk.

'More widespread, for instance, than pencil shavings and powder from pencil leads. If one were to find that at a crime scene, it would be a much better bit of forensic evidence than horse manure. Especially since people who like drawing don't choose their pencils by chance. You don't, for a start. What kind of pencil do you use?'

'Cargo 401-B and Seril-H.'

'So here on the floor, that would be shavings from Cargo 401-B and Seril-H? Bit of charcoal too perhaps?'

'Well, naturally, Danglard.'

'So that would be much more helpful at a crime scene, wouldn't it? Better than some damn horse shit.'

'Danglard,' said Adamsberg, fanning himself with a postcard, 'get to the point.'

'I'm not that keen to. But if something's going to fall on us, better get there first. Like in cricket, you have to dash to catch the ball before it hits the ground.'

'All right, dash for the ball, Danglard, I'm listening.'

'A team went to look for the spent cartridges, on the ground, out at the farm where Émile got shot.'

'Yes, that was a priority.'

'And they found three.'

'Well, for four shots, that's pretty good.'

'And then they found the fourth,' said Danglard, getting up and clenching his fingers in his back pocket.

'Where was that then?' asked Adamsberg, stopping fanning himself with the postcard.

'At Pierre's house, Pierre the son. It had rolled under the fridge. But they couldn't find the revolver.'

'So who found it? Who asked for his house to be searched?'

'Brézillon. Because of the link between Pierre and the horses.'

'And who told the *divisionnaire* about that?'

Danglard spread his hands in a gesture of ignorance.

'So who went to look out at the farm for the cartridges?'

'Maurel and Mordent.'

'I thought Mordent was supposed to be with Froissy.'

'Well he wasn't, he wanted to go with Maurel.'

There was a silence, and Adamsberg ostentatiously sharpened a pencil over his waste-paper basket, letting shavings of Seril-H fall there before blowing on the lead, and fetching a piece of paper to rest on his thigh.

'So what does all this mean?' he asked quietly, as he began to draw. 'Pierre fired four shots, but only took one cartridge away with him?'

'They think it might have got stuck in the barrel.'

'Who's "they"?'

'The Avignon police.'

'And that doesn't bother them? Pierre gets rid of the gun, but first he ejects a jammed cartridge? Then he saves this precious little cartridge? Until he stupidly drops it in his kitchen, where it rolls under his fridge. And why did they go to such lengths in the search? Moving a fridge? Did they know there was something underneath?'

'The wife apparently said something to them.'

'Now that would really amaze me, Danglard. The day that woman betrays her husband, Cupid will have given up on Émile.'

'Well, precisely, that's what bothered them. Their top guy isn't the sharpest knife in the box, but he got to thinking maybe someone had planted it. Especially since Pierre is swearing black and blue he's innocent. So they got out the whole shenanigans: vacuum cleaner, sieve, microscopic samples. And they found something. That,' said Danglard, pointing to the floor.

'That what?'

'Bits of pencil lead and shavings probably off someone's shoes. But Pierre never uses pencils. We've only just received this information.'

Danglard was now tugging at his shirt collar, and went into his own office to get a glass of wine. He was looking deeply unhappy. Adamsberg waited.

'They're going to send the stuff to the lab, expecting results in two or three days – what kind of lead, what make of pencil. It's not simple apparently. Of course, it would be easier if they had a sample to compare and I think they are quite soon going to know where to look.'

'For pity's sake, Danglard, what are you thinking?'

'The worst. Like I said. I'm thinking what *they'll* think. That *you* planted the cartridge under Pierre Vaudel's fridge. Of course they'll have to prove it. So they'll have to analyse the shavings, identify the pencil, compare it to the sample. So probably it'll be four days before they start asking you questions. Four days to catch the ball before it hits the ground.'

'OK, let's just get this clear, Danglard,' said Adamsberg, with a fixed smile on his face. 'Why would I want to implicate Pierre junior?'

'To save Émile?'

'And why would I want to save Émile?'

'Because he's going to inherit a fortune which mustn't be contested by the natural heir.'

'But why would he contest it?'

'Because the will could be a forgery.'

'Oh really? Do they think Émile is capable of forging a will?'

'No, he would have had an accomplice. An accomplice who was handy with a pen. An accomplice who'd get fifty per cent.'

Danglard drank off his glass of white wine in a single gulp.

'For pity's sake,' he said, 'it's not rocket science. Do I have to spell it out? Émile and his accomplice, let's call him Adamsberg, they prepare a false will. Émile lets the son know – *he's going to cut you out of his will* – which alarms Pierre Vaudel. Then Émile kills the old man, puts down some horse manure to incriminate Pierre, and makes it look like a murder by some complete madman, to distract people from the money. A smokescreen which leaves in the shadows a simple plan. Then Adamsberg, according to a prearranged scenario, shoots Émile, a couple of serious shots to make it look convincing, and immediately rushes him to hospital. He leaves three cartridges on the spot, then plants one in Pierre's house and that way Pierre is guilty of attempted murder of Émile. On the lie detector, they find that Pierre knew about the will. Then Émile declares he saw Pierre junior leave the house at night. Pierre killed his own father, so of course he can't inherit now. And his *whole* share also goes to Émile, as per the will. Adamsberg and Émile share it out, not forgetting their old mothers. That's the scenario. The end.'

Adamsberg, stunned, looked at Danglard who seemed on

the verge of tears. He felt in his pocket, found the cigarettes left behind by Zerk and lit one.

'But,' Danglard was going on, 'the investigation opens and some disturbing facts begin to pile up, and the Émile–Adamsberg plot starts to unravel. First of all, why did this old Vaudel, who hates everyone, leave his money to Émile? Anomaly number one. Shortly afterwards, Vaudel dies. Anomaly number two. There is too much horse manure in the picture. Anomaly number three. On the Sunday, after Mordent had warned him, Adamsberg lets Émile escape. Anomaly number four. Then that very night, without telling anyone, Adamsberg knows exactly where to find Émile. Anomaly number five.'

'You're getting on my nerves with these anomalies.'

'Adamsberg arrives just in time to save him, just after someone has taken a shot at him. Anomaly number six. Then a cartridge is found in the residence of Pierre Vaudel. Anomaly number seven. Very big anomaly. The cops start to think somebody is pulling a fast one somewhere, and they go through the flat with a toothcomb. What do they find? Some pencil shavings. Who benefits from this crime? Émile. Could Émile have forged the will? No. Has he got a friend who's good with a pen, who could imitate handwriting? Yes, Adamsberg, who's looking after him like a baby at the hospital, and who's had him transferred to a secret location so the cops can't question him, matter of national security. Anomaly number eight. Does Adamsberg make a habit of sharpening pencils? Yes. They compare the sample and it's a one in a thousand chance, but it matches. When could Adamsberg have got to Avignon to hide the cartridge? Last night for instance. The *commissaire* disappeared last night, he only came into the office at half past twelve. Alibi? Yesterday he was with the doctor. This morning? He was with the doctor. He fainted, something which doesn't ever happen. So the doctor's in on it too. These three have concocted it between them, Adamsberg, Émile and Josselin. They only met three days ago so-called, but they seem to get on very well with each other. Anomaly number nine. Result: Émile gets life or at least thirty years for the murder of Vaudel senior and fraud relating to the will. Adamsberg gets the sack and falls off his pedestal, on account of forgery and complicity in homicide, and tampering with evidence. Twenty years. That's it. Now Adamsberg has four days to try and save his skin.'

Adamsberg lit another cigarette off the first one. Good thing Josselin had put his boiler right that morning when he had been on the brink of a total emotional breakdown. Zerk and now Danglard, both of them living in fantasy land.

'And who would believe that, Danglard?' he said, carefully stubbing out the butt.

'You're smoking again?'

'Only since you started talking.'

'Better not. It's a sign of changed behavioural patterns.'

'Danglard,' said Adamsberg, in a louder voice, 'Who. Would. Believe. That?'

'Nobody yet. But in four days, maybe three, Brézillon might and the Avignon police as well. Then the others. Because cartridge or not, Pierre Vaudel is not under arrest at the moment.'

'And *why* would they believe all that?'

'Because it was a set-up. It's obvious, good grief.'

Danglard suddenly looked at Adamsberg with a disgusted expression.

'You don't think I b-believe this, do you? he said stuttering, which was rare for him.

'How would I know, *commandant*? You're very convincing with your little scenario. I almost believe it myself.'

Danglard went out of the room again and returned with his wine glass full.

'I am being very convincing,' he said, detaching every word, 'in order to convince you of what those who are being made to believe it will believe.'

'Speak plain French, Danglard.'

'I told you yesterday. Someone's out to get you. Someone who will do anything to stop you finding the Garches murderer. Someone whose life will be ruined if you do. Someone with a long arm, someone way up in the hierarchy. Probably some relation of the real killer. You've got to be moved off the case, and someone else has to be the fall guy for the *Zerquetscher*. Simple, isn't it? The first blunders in the investigation didn't get you taken off the job. That's why they moved on, and gave the supposed *Zerquetscher*'s name to the press, so that he could escape. Then they planted the cartridge in Pierre's kitchen with your pencil shavings. Now they've got you. Automatically. But to do all that, the man up in the hierarchy has to have an accomplice, someone who's here on the spot. Who could have got hold of the pencil shavings? Someone in the squad. Who had access to the cartridges? Mordent and Maurel. Who has disappeared from circulation this morning, nervous breakdown, off sick, no visitors? Mordent. I warned you about this in the cafe, and you said I was having unworthy thoughts. I told you his daughter's case was coming up in a couple of weeks. She'll get off, you'll see, and that's all fine and dandy for her and for her father. But you'll be under lock and key by then.'

Adamsberg blew out his smoke with more force than necessary.

'Do you believe me?' Danglard asked. 'You see what's going on?'

'Yes.'

'Cricket,' repeated Danglard, who took no interest in sport. 'Catch the ball. Three or four days at the outside.'

XXVII

'So it means we have to find Zerk by then,' said Adamsberg.

'Zerk?'

'The *Zerquetscher*. Thalberg sent us his file.'

'Yes, it's here,' said Danglard, lifting up his wine glass and pointing to a pink folder with a wet ring on it. 'Sorry about the stain.'

'If stains on files were all we had to worry about, Danglard, life would be a breeze. We could smoke fags and drink wine all day, and go fishing in your friend Stock's loch. We could make as many wine stains as we liked on tables, we could go boating with your kids and my little Tom, and we could spend old Vaudel's money with Émile and his dog.'

Adamsberg gave a broad smile, the kind that always reassured Danglard, however bad things seemed. Then he frowned.

'But what on earth can they say about the Austrian murder? This person with the long arm – what can he say? Is Émile supposed to have committed that too? It won't wash.'

'They'll just say that has nothing to do with it. They'll say

Émile carried out a copycat murder on the Austrian model, because he lacks imagination.'

Adamsberg reached out to take a mouthful from Danglard's wine glass. Without Danglard and his relentless logic, he wouldn't have seen this coming.

'I'm going to London,' Danglard announced. 'The shoes will lead us to him.'

'No, you're not going anywhere, *commandant*. I'm going. And I need someone to take charge of the squad. Make your contacts with Stock by telephone or video link.'

'No. Put Retancourt in charge.'

'She's too junior in rank, and I don't have the right to promote her. We've got enough trouble on our hands as it is.'

'Where will you go?'

'You already said it: the shoes will lead us to him.'

Adamsberg showed him the postcard: a picturesque village against a background of mountains and blue skies. Then he turned it over. In Cyrillic script, in capital letters, the name КИСЕЛЕВО: Kisilova, the demon's village. 'Who was it that prowled at the edge of the wood? That's what this word КИСЕЛЕВО means?'

'Yes, Kiseljevo originally. But we already talked about that. Twenty years on, nobody will be able to remember the foot-chopper.'

'That's not what I'm after. I'm going to try and find the dark tunnel that links Vaudel to this village. We have to find it, Danglard, go right in and dig up the history and tear out its roots.'

'So when are you going?'

'In four hours from now. I couldn't get a direct flight at this notice, so I'm flying to Venice, and getting the night train to Belgrade. I've reserved two places, and the embassy is trying to find me a translator.'

Danglard shook his head, looking hostile. 'You'll be too exposed. I'm coming with you.'

'No, no way. It isn't just the problem of the squad. If they really want to get me, and you come with me, you'll go down with the ship. And if they do try to take me in, you're the only person who could get me out of jail. It could take you ten years, so hang on in there. But meantime, keep away from me, keep right outside this. That way, I'm not going to contaminate you, or anyone else in the squad.'

'I give in. If it's a translator you want, Slavko's grandson might fit the bill. Vladislav Moldovan. He works as an interpreter for research institutes. He's a nice guy, like his grandfather. If I say it's for Slavko, he'll engineer some time off. When does the Venice–Belgrade train leave?'

'Nine thirty-two this evening. I'm going home now to pick up a packet and my watches. It bothers me not to have the time.'

'So what? – your watches are never right.'

'That's because I set them by Lucio – he goes out to piss in the garden every hour and a half. But it's a bit approximate.'

'You just need to do the opposite. Set your watches by a clock and then you'll know the exact time Lucio pisses.'

Adamsberg looked at him in surprise.

'But I don't need to know when Lucio pisses. What use is that to me?'

Danglard signalled 'drop it', and handed him another file, a green one.

'Here's Radstock's latest report. You can read it on the train. It's augmented by the interrogation of Lord Clyde-

Fox and some doubtful information about the Cuban friend, so-called. They've done some more precise analysis. All the shoes are French, except my uncle's.'

'Or maybe some cousin of your uncle, a Kisslover, or a Kisilovian.'

'A Kiseljevian.'

'How are these shoes supposed to have crossed the Channel?'

'Smuggled in, by boat I guess, how else?'

'It seems a lot of trouble to go to.'

'But worth it. Highgate's a very special place. Some of the shoes, four pairs at least, are no more than twelve years old, but Radstock has had problems trying to date the others. Twelve years could correspond to the time the *Zerquetscher* has been in action, assuming he started collecting around the age of seventeen. Which is a bit young to start creeping into undertakers' parlours and cutting off feet. But chronologically, it could fit, because it would correspond to the gothic craze, heavy metal, old lace, horror movies, devil worship, sequins, zombies in evening dress and all that. It could be a sort of sympathetic impregnation.'

'What on earth do you mean, Danglard?'

'Goths,' said Danglard. 'Never heard of them?'

'Gothic, like in the Middle Ages?'

'No, goths as in the 1990s, and still today. You must have seen them. Young people who wear T-shirts with death's heads and skeletons and blood.'

'Oh. Yes. I know exactly what you mean,' said Adamsberg, who had a vivid and ineradicable memory of Zerk's T-shirt. 'So Stock has a problem with the other shoes?'

'Yes,' said Danglard, rubbing his chin, which was clean-shaven on one side but had stubble on the other.

'Why did you only shave on one side of your face?' asked Adamsberg, interrupting himself.

Danglard stiffened, then went to the window to look at his reflection.

'The bathroom light's gone, I can't see much on the left. I ought to get it fixed.'

Abstract, thought Adamsberg.

Danglard was waiting.

'Do we have any here? Bayonet bulbs, sixty watt?'

'In the store cupboard. Look here, time's passing,' said Adamsberg, tapping his wrist.

'You changed the subject yourself. There are some feet that don't fit a twelve-year time frame. Some of them belong to women with varnished toenails, a kind of varnish from before the 1990s. The analysis seems to point to the middle 1970s.'

'Is Stock sure about that?'

'Pretty much, he's asked for more tests. There's one pair of men's shoes in ostrich leather, something very rare, very dear, and they stopped making them when our *Zerquetscher* was only ten. He'd have to be very precocious. And it gets worse. Some of them are maybe twenty-five or thirty years old. I know what you're going to say,' Danglard said, fore-stalling Adamsberg by lifting up his glass. 'In your wretched village in the Pyrenees, even little boys used to make toads explode when they were practically in their cradles. But still.'

'No, I wasn't going to mention the toads.'

The idea of the toads, which small boys like himself used to make explode with a horrible burst of blood and guts, by forcing them to smoke a cigarette, brought Adamsberg back to the packet he had inherited from Zerk.

'You really have started again, haven't you?' said Danglard, as Adamsberg lit his third cigarette.

'That's because you mentioned the toads.'

'It's always because of something. I'm giving up white wine. It's over. This is my last glass.'

Adamsberg was dumbstruck. That Danglard should be in love, fine. That it was reciprocated, yes, one had to hope so. But if it was making him give up white wine, that was unbelievable.

'I'm switching to red,' the *commandant* announced. 'It's more vulgar but it's less acid. The white's destroying my stomach.'

'Good thinking,' said Adamsberg, who was curiously reassured by the thought that, after all, nothing changes, at least with Danglard.

Things were already bad enough without that.

'Did you buy that packet?' Danglard asked. 'English cigarettes. Pretty stylish.'

'It was my burglar from this morning. He left them behind. So anyway, either Zerk was such a precocious child that he could cut people's feet off when he was two years old. Or some older figure took him on these morbid expeditions, and then he went on with it when he grew up. He could have been acting under someone's influence since childhood.'

'Manipulated?'

'Why not? One can easily imagine some father figure behind all this, guiding him, filling some lack.'

'Possibly. He's registered as father unknown.'

'We need to check out his background, see who he was in touch with, who he saw. He cleared his flat, left no clues.'

'Naturally he would. You didn't think he'd come and see us, did you?'

'What about his mother, have they found her?'

'Not yet. We have an address in Pau up to four years ago, then nothing.'

'Her family?'

'For now we can't find anyone in the region called Louvois, but it's only two days ago, *commissaire*, and we haven't got all that many people on the job.'

'What about Froissy and the phone records?'

'Nothing doing. Louvois didn't have a landline. Weill says he had a mobile, but we can't find one registered in his name. Either someone gave it him, or he stole it. Froissy'll have to check out the networks around his address, but that takes time.'

Adamsberg stood up abruptly, feeling impatient.

'Danglard, can you tell me who's in the Avignon team?'

Among Danglard's feats of memory – who knew why he did it? – was that he could tell you more or less who was in all the police teams throughout France, adjusting his mental card index as people moved around to different postings.

'Calmet is running the inquiry on Pierre junior. I don't know whether it's because of his name, but he's a placid fellow, doesn't go looking for trouble. Like I said, he's not quick off the mark. So I'd say more like four days than three. Maurel said there was a *lieutenant* and a *brigadier*, Noiselot and Drumont. Don't know about the rest.'

'Get me the full list, Danglard.'

'Are you looking for anyone in particular?'

'There's a Vietnamese officer I worked with at Mésilly once. Dozy little place, but I loved it when we were posted there.

He could blow smoke rings and levitate several centimetres – at least it looked that way to me. He could play tunes by tapping wine glasses and he could imitate any animal you like.'

Twenty minutes later, Adamsberg was looking through the list of names in *Commissaire* Calmet's team.

'I've reached Slavko's grandson,' Danglard said. 'He's leaving Marseille now, he'll be at Venice Santa Lucia station by twenty-one hours, standing in front of coach 17 of the Belgrade train. He's perfectly happy to have a trip to the village. Vladislav's always perfectly happy.'

'How will I know him?'

'Very easily. He's thin, and very hairy, he's got long hair and it grows into the hair on his back, pitch black.'

'*Lieutenant* Mai Thien Dinh,' said Adamsberg, stabbing a name on the list. 'He wrote to me last December. I knew there was some talk of him going to Avignon. He often sends me a card when he's on holiday, with mystic Eastern proverbs, like "Don't eat your hand when there's no bread left".'

'That's stupid.'

'Yes, well, he makes them up.'

'And you write back?'

'Oh, I can't make up proverbs,' said Adamsberg, as he tapped in *Lieutenant* Mai's number.

'Dinh? Hello, it's Jean-Baptiste. Thanks for the card in December.'

'This is June. But you're always slow replying. The slow man goes less quickly than the quick man. You know we're on the same case, this Vaudel thing?'

'The little cartridge under the fridge?'

'Yes, and the dope who dropped it walked across a carpet with some pencil shavings on his shoes. Don't worry, we've let Vaudel go for now, and we'll catch your pencil man sooner than that.'

'Yes, well, Dinh, that's just it. I'd prefer if you didn't go too fast on this one. Just moderately fast. Or indeed moderately slowly.'

'Why?'

'Can't tell you.'

'Ah. The wise man gives nothing away to fools. Can't be done, Jean-Baptiste. Just a minute, I'm going out of the room. Now what do you want me to do?' said Dinh after a pause.

'Just to slow things down.'

'Not on the level.'

'Not on the level at all, Dinh. Look, some bastard has just dropped me in shit creek.'

'It happens.'

'And I'm getting in really deep. See what I mean?'

'With perfect clarity.'

'Good. Because imagine that you're right there on the river-bank. Strolling along, levitating, whatever. You see me, and you stretch out your hand.'

'So I put my own hand in the shit for you, without knowing why?'

'That's right.'

'Can you be a little more precise?'

'These pencil shavings. When do they go to the lab?'

'In an hour, they're just putting together the other samples.'

'Can you stop them going? Give them two days' handicap.'

'How'm I supposed to do that?'

'How big is the sample?'

'Size of a lipstick.'

'Who goes with the driver to the lab?'

'*Brigadier* Kerouan.'

'Take his place.'

'We don't look a bit alike.'

'Give your Breton a mission, and you escort the driver instead. As you want to take special care of this lipstick, you put it in the pocket of your tunic for greater security.'

'Then?'

'Then you fall ill on the way. A touch of fever, a dizzy spell, it just comes over you. You deliver everything safely except the tube, but you tell the office you're going home. Where you stay in bed for two days, aspirins, nothing to eat, you can't keep anything down. That's for your visitors of course. In reality you can get up.'

'Thanks a lot.'

'This attack of sickness made you forget the tube in your pocket. The third day, you're feeling better, it all comes back to you. The sample, the lab, the pocket. One of two things might have happened. Either some keeno at the station realises the tube hasn't got to the lab, or nobody has noticed anything. Either way, you bring the tube in, you explain and offer your sincere excuses, but you were ill. That way we'll have gained one and a half to two and a half days.'

'Well, you'll have gained them, Jean-Baptiste. But what's in it for me? Wise is he who seeks his reward on earth.'

'You get two days off. Thursday and Friday, then it's the weekend. Plus it's a rain check for a future good turn from me.'

'For instance?'

'For instance when they find some of your straight black hair at a crime scene.'

'I see.'

'Thanks, Dinh.'

During this conversation, Danglard had fetched his bottle directly into Adamsberg's office.

'More straightforward that way,' said Adamsberg, pointing to the bottle.

'I've got to finish it, because I'm going over to red.'

'Lucio would agree with you. You have to finish it, or else don't get started.'

'You're crazy asking Dinh to do that. Anyone finds out, you've comprehensively had it.'

'I've already comprehensively had it. But they won't find out because the man of the East does not chatter like a frivolous blackbird. As he once wrote to me.'

'OK,' said Danglard. 'Say we've got five or six days. Where will you stay in Kiseljevo?'

'Little hotel, does bed and breakfast.'

'I don't like it. Going off on your own.'

'I'll have your nephew-several-times-removed with me.'

'Vladislav's no fighter. I don't like it,' Danglard repeated. 'Kiseljevo and the dark tunnel.'

'The edge of the wood,' said Adamsberg with a smile. 'You're still frightened of that. More than of the *Zerquetscher*.'

Danglard shrugged.

'Who is on the loose somewhere,' Adamsberg added in graver tones. 'Free as a bird.'

'Not your fault. What shall we do about Mordent? Should we turf him out of his cosy nest? Shake him down, make him spit out everything, how he's comprehensively betrayed us?'

Adamsberg stood up, put a big elastic band round his green and pink files, lit a cigarette which he left hanging on his lower lip, screwing up his eyes against the smoke. Like his father. Like Zerk.

'What shall we do about Mordent?' he repeated slowly. 'First of all, we let him get his daughter back.'

XXVIII

His rucksack was buckled, the front pocket bulging with the three files: French, English and Austrian. Finding himself back in the kitchen had brought flooding into his mind, in no particular order, images of Zerk that morning, their long confrontation and the way he had let the man go. Go on, Zerk, off you go. Off you go, cool as you like, to kill again. The *commissaire* didn't lift a finger to stop you. 'Inhibition of action' was what Josselin had called it. Perhaps it had already been at work when he had stood to one side on Sunday and given Émile his chance to run, if that was really what he had done. But the inhibition was over now, the man with the golden fingers had removed it. Now he had to go down into the Kisilova tunnel, and plunge into this village crouching over its secret. He had had a good report on Émile, his temperature had dropped. He strapped on both watches and lifted the rucksack.

'You've got company,' said Lucio, knocking on the window.

Weill walked calmly into the room, blocking the exit with his large girth. It was customary for others to make the effort to visit Weill, never the contrary. He was a neurotic homebody, and for him to cross Paris was a painful undertaking.

'I almost missed you,' he said, sitting down.

'I haven't got much time now,' said Adamsberg, clumsily shaking hands, since Weill had the habit of holding his hand out limply as if for a kiss. 'I'm catching a plane.'

'Time enough for a beer?'

'If it's a quick one.'

'That's what we'll do then. Sit down, *mon ami*,' Weill said, pointing to a chair, in the slightly disdainful tone he liked to take, as if he was at home wherever he happened to be. 'You're leaving the country? Wise decision. Where to?'

'Kisilova. It's a little village in Serbia on the Danube.'

'This still the Garches case?'

'Yes, still the same one.'

'You smoke?' Weill asked, as he lit Adamsberg's cigarette for him.

'Began again today.'

'Worries,' said Weill.

'Probably.'

'Certainly. That's why I needed to talk to you.'

'Why didn't you phone?'

'You'll understand. The storm is brewing over your head, don't go to sleep under a tree and don't walk out holding a spear. Stay in the shadows and run fast.'

'Details please, Weill, I need them.'

'I've got no proof.'

'Well, give me your hunch then.'

'This Garches killer is being protected by someone.'

'High up?'

'Very. Some heavyweight with no scruples. They don't want

you to solve the case. They want you out of the way. A rather flimsy file has been opened on you, for allowing a suspect to escape – Émile Feuillant – and for failing to check an alibi. They've asked for you to be stood down temporarily. The idea was that Préval would take over.'

'Préval's for sale.'

'Famous for it. I've managed to lose your file.'

'Thanks.'

'They've worse things they can do, and my humble power will be no good. Have you got anything in mind? Apart from flying the coop, that is?'

'Keep one step ahead of them, catching the ball before it hits the ground.'

'You mean you're going to catch the killer by the scruff of the neck, and present everyone with the proof? Nonsense, *mon ami*. You still believe they can't tamper with evidence?'

'No.'

'Right. So you need a triple plan. Plan A, yes, agreed, find your killer, everyone can agree about that, but it's not a priority because the truth won't necessarily get you out of jail free, especially if someone doesn't want that. Plan B, find out who it is up there who wants you out of the way, and prepare a counter-offensive. Plan C, prepare your escape route. Via the Adriatic perhaps.'

'You don't sound very cheerful, Weill.'

'We're not dealing with cheerful people here.'

'I have no way of identifying the man up there. The only way I can get to him is by getting closer to the killer.'

'Not necessarily. What happens up aloft is hidden from us lesser mortals. So start at the bottom. Because the top people always use those lower down the scale who want promotion.

Then work your way up. You know already who's on the lowest rung, the bottom level?'

'My *commandant*, Mordent. They're using him, with a promise to get his daughter off a charge. Her case comes up in a couple of weeks, she's accused of dealing.'

'Or murder. The girl was apparently pretty out of it when Stubby Down was killed. Her friend Bones could very well have put the gun in her hand and pulled the trigger.'

'And that's what happened, Weill, is it? Really?'

'Yes. Technically, she fired the shot. So Mordent has to deliver something really big to get a deal. Who's on the next rung up? In your view.'

'Brézillon. He's giving Mordent orders. But I can't think he's involved in any plot.'

'Never mind. Third rung of the ladder has to be the judge who's agreed in advance to get the Mordent girl off. What does he get out of it? That's what you need to know, Adamsberg. Who asked him to go easy on her, who's he working for?'

'Sorry,' said Adamsberg, finishing his beer. 'I haven't had time to worry about all this. Danglard was the one who twigged. I've been dealing with cut-off feet, that bloodbath in Garches, Émile getting shot, the Austrian murder, the Serbian uncle, my own fuses blowing, the cat out there having kittens, so, sorry, I've got no idea and I've had no time to study this ladder you're talking about, with all these people on it.'

'But they've had plenty of time to worry about *you*. You're way behind.'

'I can believe that. Shavings from my pencil are already with the Avignon police, picked up in Pierre junior's kitchen.

All I've been able to do is stall the procedure. I've got about five or six days before they'll be on to me.'

'It's not that I really want to get into this,' said Weill slowly, 'but I don't like these people. They work on my mind like bad cooking on my stomach. Since you need to make yourself scarce, I could probe some of the rungs on the ladder for you.'

'The judge?'

'Beyond the judge, I would hope. I'll call you. But not on your regular number or mine.'

Weill put two brand-new mobiles on the table and slid one across to Adamsberg.

'Yours, mine. Don't switch it on until you're over the frontier, and never when you're using your other phone. Your regular mobile doesn't have GPS, does it?'

'Yes. I need Danglard to be able to get hold of me if my mobile gives out. What if I'm all alone at the edge of the forest?'

'What's the problem?'

'Nothing,' Adamsberg said, smiling. 'Just this demon who prowls around at Kisilova. And then there's Zerk who's on the loose somewhere.'

'Who's Zerk?'

'The *Zerquetscher*. That's what the Viennese call him. The Crusher. Before Vaudel, he massacred someone in Pressbaum.'

'Well, *he* won't be looking for you.'

'Why not?'

'Neutralise the GPS, Adamsberg, you're being imprudent. Don't give them a way to reach and arrest you, or cause some accident, you never know. I repeat: you're looking for a murderer and someone wants at all costs to stop you finding him. Keep your regular phone switched off as much as possible.'

'There's no risk, only Danglard has the GPS signal.'

'Trust no one, when the high-ups get started with their bribes and their deals.'

'Danglard is the exception.'

'Nobody's an exception. Every man has his price, his demons, everyone has a grenade under the bed. It makes a great chain of people around the globe who've got each other by the balls. Let's call Danglard an exception, if you like, but someone somewhere will be watching Danglard's every movement.'

'What about you, Weill? What's your price?'

'Well, I have the good fortune to be very fond of myself. It reduces my greed and what I can ask the world for. All I want is to live in grand style, in a big eighteenth-century town house, with a staff of cooks, a live-in tailor, two cats purring at my feet, my own personal orchestra, a park, a terrace, a fountain, a few mistresses and chorus girls about the place, and the right to insult anyone I like. But no one is about to give me anything like that. So they don't try to buy me, I'm too complicated and far too expensive.'

'I can give you a cat. There's a little girl-cat here, one week old, as soft as cotton wool. She's always hungry, precious and delicate, she'd fit your grand house very well.'

'I haven't got the first brick of the house yet.'

'It's a start, the first rung on the ladder.'

'I might be interested. But get rid of the GPS, Adamsberg.'

'I'd have to trust you.'

'Men who are dreaming of ancient glories don't make good traitors.'

Adamsberg passed him the phone and drank the very last drop of beer. Weill removed the battery and took out the location chip with his thumbnail.

'That was why I had to see you in person,' he said, giving it back.

XXIX

COACH 17 FOR BELGRADE HELD A LUXURY COMPARTMENT:
two bunks were made up with white sheets and red blankets, and there were bedside lamps, polished side tables, a
washbasin and towels. Adamsberg had never travelled in such
luxury before, and checked his tickets. Yes, berths 22 and 24.
There must have been some mistake at the accounts department of Travel and Foreign Missions at police headquarters,
and there would be hell to pay at some point. Adamsberg
sat down on his couchette, feeling as satisfied as a burglar
who happens on a fortune. He settled in as if in a hotel,
spread out his files on the bed, examined the menu for dinner
'alla francese' which would be served at ten: cream of
asparagus soup, solettes à la Plogoff, blue cheese from the
Auvergne, tartufo, coffee and Valpolicella to drink. He felt
just the same jubilation as when he had returned to his foul-
smelling car in Châteaudun and found Froissy's surprise
provisions. So, he mused, it's not the actual quality that gives
pleasure but the unexpected well-being, regardless of the
components.

He went on to the platform to light one of Zerk's cigarettes.

The young man's lighter was black too, with a red design on it depicting the circuits of the brain. He had no difficulty spotting Uncle Slavko's grandson, whose hair was as straight and black as Dinh's, tied back in a ponytail, and whose eyes were amber-coloured and narrow over high Slavic cheekbones.

'Vladislav Moldovan,' the young man who was about thirty introduced himself, with a grin that covered his whole face. 'You can call me Vlad.'

'Jean-Baptiste Adamsberg. Thank you for agreeing to accompany me.'

'On the contrary, it's my pleasure. Dedo only took me twice to Kiseljevo, the last time I was fourteen years old.'

'Dedo?'

'My grandfather. I'll go and visit his grave and tell him stories like he used to me. Is this our compartment?' he asked, hesitating.

'Foreign Missions must have mixed me up with someone important.'

'Wow,' said Vladislav, 'I've never slept like someone important before. You need that if you're going to confront the demons of Kiseljevo. I know some people who would rather stay hidden in a hut.'

Chatty fellow, said Adamsberg to himself, thinking that this was probably a professional deformation in someone who worked as a translator and interpreter. Vladislav translated from nine languages, and for Adamsberg, who could hardly remember Stock's full name, this kind of brain was as strange as Danglard's encyclopedic equipment. He was only afraid the young man with the sunny disposition would engage him in endless conversation.

'Adrien Danglard – Adrianus, my grandfather used to call

him – didn't tell me why you're going to Kiseljevo. As a general rule, people don't go to Kiseljevo.'

'Because it's a small place, or because it has demons?'

'Do you come from a village?'

'Yes, Caldhez, a tiny place in the Pyrenees.'

'Are there demons in Caldhez?'

'Two: a nasty troll in a cave, and a singing tree.'

'Wow. And what are you looking for in Kiseljevo?'

'The roots of a story.'

'It's a very good place for roots.'

'Have you heard about the murder in Garches?'

'The old man who was chopped to bits?'

'That's it. Well, we found a note in his writing with the name of Kiseljevo in Cyrillic script.'

'What has this got to do with my dedo? Adrianus said this was for Dedo.'

Adamsberg looked out of the window, trying to come up with an instant idea, which was not his strong point. He should have thought earlier of a plausible explanation. He didn't intend to tell the young man that some Zerk had cut off his dedo's feet. Things like that might pierce holes in the soul of a grandson, and destroy his sunny disposition.

'Danglard listened to a lot of Slavko's stories. And Danglard collects information the way a squirrel collects nuts, much more than he would need for twenty winters. He thinks he recalls that this man Vaudel – that was the victim's name – went to live at some point in Kisilova, and that it was your Slavko who told him about this. It seemed perhaps that Vaudel was getting away from some kind of enemy by going to Kisilova.'

Not a very brilliant cover story, but it was enough, since just then a bell rang to say dinner was served. They decided to eat it in their compartment like really important people. Vladislav asked what 'solettes à la Plogoff' meant. And the steward explained in Italian that this meant sole cooked in the Breton fashion, with a sauce of oysters specially flown in from Plogoff, a village on the Pointe du Raz, the furthest western point in Brittany. He took their order, seeming to consider that this young man in a T-shirt and ponytail, with black hair covering his arms, was not a really important person, any more than his travelling companion.

'If you're as hairy as I am,' Vlad said, once the steward had disappeared, 'people send you to ride in a cattle truck. I inherited this on my mother's side,' he said sadly, pulling at the hairs on his forearm before breaking into a peal of laughter as abrupt as a vase shattering.

Vladislav's laugh was deeply infectious and he seemed capable of laughing at anything without any assistance.

After the solettes à la Plogoff and the Valpolicella and the dessert, Adamsberg stretched out on the couchette with his files. He had to read everything and start from scratch again. This was the most wearing aspect of his work for him. Notes, files, reports, formal statements, where you couldn't get through to any real sensation.

'How do you get on with Adrianus?' Vladislav interrupted, as Adamsberg was painfully deciphering the German file and conscientiously reading the report on Frau Abster, domiciled in Cologne, seventy-six years old. 'And did you know that he reveres you,' he went on, 'but at the same time you're driving him to distraction?'

'Danglard is easily driven to distraction. He can do it without anyone's help.'

'He says he doesn't understand you.'

'Like earth, air, fire and water. All I can tell you is that without Danglard, our squad would long since have been shipwrecked on some terrible reef somewhere.'

'Like the Pointe du Raz and Plogoff. That would be cool. You'd be shipwrecked with Adrianus and you could eat solettes like on the Venice–Belgrade train to console yourselves.'

Adamsberg was making no progress with the file. He was stuck on line 5 of the information about Frau Abster, born in Cologne, daughter of Franz Abster and Erika Plogerstein. Danglard hadn't warned him about Vladislav's non-stop talking, which was disturbing his concentration.

'I have to read some of this standing up,' said Adamsberg, getting up.

'Wow.'

'I'll take it out into the corridor.'

'Go ahead, have a walk and do your reading. Does it bother you if I smoke? I'll air the compartment afterwards.'

'Go ahead.'

'I may be hairy but I don't snore. Like my mother. What about you?'

'Sometimes.'

'Too bad,' said Vladislav, getting out his roll-ups and all his materials.

Adamsberg slipped outside. With a bit of luck, on his return, he would find Vladislav floating on waves of cannabis, and unable to speak. He took his pink and green files and walked up and down until the lights went out a couple of hours later.

Vladislav was fast asleep with a smile on his face, shirtless, his torso covered with dark hair like a cat of the night.

Adamsberg felt as if he had dropped off to sleep quickly but superficially, his hand on his stomach, the fish perhaps being hard to digest. Or else the prospect of the next five or six days. He would go off to sleep for a few minutes, then wake up again with scraps of dreams about Plogoff oysters which seemed to be going round and round in his head. Frau Abster's description superimposed itself on the menu, getting mixed up with the solette, written with the same typeface, *Frau Abster born in Plogoff to Franz Abster and Erika Plogerstein*. The words were stupidly entwined and Adamsberg turned on his side trying to shake himself free of them. Or maybe they weren't so stupid. He opened his eyes, alert to the familiar alarm signal that he sometimes felt before he realised what it was telling him.

It was the name: *Frau Abster, born to Franz Abster and Erika Plogerstein*, he thought, switching on his bedside lamp. There was something about her mother's maiden name, Plogerstein, which must have got confused with the solettes à la Plogoff. But why was that significant? Sitting up, he felt in his rucksack for his files, and the name of the Austrian victim suddenly emerged to join the Plogerstein/Plogoff mixture. Conrad Plögener. Adamsberg pulled out the description of the man who had been killed in Pressbaum, and held it under the lamp. Yes, *Conrad Plögener, domiciled at Pressbaum, born 9 March 1961 to Mark Plögener and Marika Schüssler.*

Plogerstein and Plögener. Adamsberg put the pink file on

the bed and pulled out the white file, the French one. *Pierre Vaudel, born to Jules Vaudel and Marguerite Nemesson.*

No, nothing there. Adamsberg shook the shoulder of the long-haired cat lying on the other bunk in an elegant pose suitable for a luxury compartment.

'Vlad, tell me something!'

The young man opened his eyes, surprised. He had undone his ponytail and his straight hair was loose over his shoulders.

'Where am I?' he asked, like a child waking in a strange bedroom.

'You're in the Venice–Belgrade train. You're with a French cop and we're on our way to Kisilova, your grandfather's village, Dedo's village.'

'Yes,' said Vladislav firmly, finding the connections again.

'I'm waking you up, because I need some information.'

'Yes,' repeated Vladislav, and Adamsberg wondered if he was still high.

'Your dedo, who were his parents? Did their names start with "Plog"?'

Vladislav burst out laughing in the dark, and rubbed his eyes. 'Plog,' he said, sitting up. 'No Plogs, no.'

'What was your dedo's father called? Your great-grandfather. What was his name?'

'Milorad Moldovan.'

'And his mother? Your great-deda.'

'Not deda, Adamsberg. Baba.'

Vladislav laughed again briefly.

'Baba was called Natalja Arsinijević.'

'And anyone else he knew, his friends, his cousins? No Plogs anywhere?'

'*Zasmejavaš me*, you make me laugh, *commissaire*, I really like you.'

And Vladislav lay down again, turning his back, continuing to chuckle into his hair.

'No, wait!' he said suddenly, sitting bolt upright. 'There was a Plog. His old history teacher – he used to talk about him all the time. Mihail Plogodrescu. Actually he *was* a cousin, born in Romania, who came to teach in Belgrade, then he went to live in Novi Sad, but he retired to Kiseljevo. The two of them were inseparable, like brothers with an age difference of fifteen years. The weird thing was that they died just one day apart.'

'Thanks, Vlad, go back to sleep.'

Adamsberg slipped out into the corridor in his bare feet walking on the dark blue carpet and looked at his notebook. Plogerstein, Plögener, Plogoff, Plogodrescu. A great catch, from which the solettes must of course be eliminated, because they had nothing to do with anything. A pity though, thought Adamsberg, crossing out the Breton name regretfully, because he wouldn't have got as far as this without them. His two watches were showing 2.25 and 3.45 a.m. He woke up Danglard, who was apt to be tetchy at night.

'What is it now?' muttered the *commandant* grumpily.

'Danglard, forgive me. Your nephew keeps laughing and I can't sleep on this train.'

'He was like that as a kid. He has a sunny disposition.'

'Yes, you told me. Listen, Danglard, can you find something for me urgently? The names of the grandparents of Pierre Vaudel senior. Both sides and if necessary go back further, as far as you have to, until you find a Plog.'

'What do you mean, a Plog?'

'A surname starting with Plog. Like Plogerstein, Plögener, Plogoff, Plogodrescu. Frau Abster's mother's maiden name was Plogerstein, the man killed in Pressbaum was called Plögener and your uncle Slavko had a Romanian cousin called Plogodrescu. It must be his feet that are in Highgate, not your uncle's. If that's any consolation.'

'And Plogoff?'

'Just the sole we ate tonight, Vlad and me.'

'OK,' said Danglard. 'I presume this is urgent. What's behind it?'

'I think they're all the same family. Remember – the vendetta that Vaudel was afraid of?'

'A vendetta against the Plog family? But why don't they all have the same name?'

'Diaspora, dissimulation, hiding their surname for some good reason.'

With a weight off his mind, Adamsberg managed to sleep for two hours before Danglard called him back.

'Got your Plog,' he said. 'The paternal grandfather, who came from Hungary. He must have changed it to Vaudel.'

'What was his name, Danglard?'

'I just told you – Plog, Andras Plog.'

XXX

Vladislav pressed his nose to the window, giving a running commentary as the train pulled into Belgrade, as if it were a real adventure, now and again saying 'Plog' and laughing to himself. The translator's good humour gave the expedition the feeling of a merry escapade, whereas in Adamsberg's mind it was taking on a darker complexion the nearer they came to the hermetic village of Kisilova.

'Belgrade means "white city"', Vladislav announced as the train pulled to a halt. 'It's very fine but we don't have time to look around because the bus goes in half an hour. Do you often wake people up in the middle of the night to ask if there are any Plogs in their family?'

'The police spend their lives waking other people up in the middle of the night. And being woken up themselves. It was worth it, because there was a Plog.'

'Plog,' said Vladislav, trying it out again as if blowing a bubble. 'Plog. And why did you want to know?'

'Plogerstein, Plögener, Plogoff, Plogodrescu and Plog,' Adamsberg recited. 'If we rule out Plogoff, the other four family names are all linked to the murder at Garches. Two of them are victims, and a third, the woman in Germany, is a friend of a victim.'

'What's this got to do with my dedo? Was his cousin Plogodrescu a victim?'

'Yes, in a way. Take a peep into the corridor. The woman, wearing a beige suit, between forty and fifty, wart on her cheek, trying to look nonchalant. She was in the next compartment. Have a good look at her when we get out.'

Vladislav was the first to step down on to the platform and held out his furry arm to the woman in the suit, to help her with her suitcase. She thanked him without warmth and walked away.

'Elegant, rich, nice figure, pity about the face,' said Vladislav, watching her go. 'Plog. I wouldn't try anything.'

'You went out to the toilet in the night?'

'So did you.'

'She left her door a little bit open, we could see her reading. Yes?'

'Yes.'

'Unusual for a woman travelling alone to leave her door open on a night train.'

'Plog,' said Vladislav, who seemed to have adopted this new onomatopoeic word to mean 'yes', or 'agreed', or 'obviously', Adamsberg wasn't sure which. The young man seemed to enjoy this made-up word as if it were a new kind of sweet, which one eats too many of at first.

'Perhaps she was waiting for someone,' Vladislav suggested.

'Or she was trying to overhear someone. Us for instance. I think she was on the same flight as me to Venice.'

The two men got into the bus. 'Stopping at Kaluderica, Smederevo, Kostalac, Klicevac and Kiseljevo,' the driver announced, and these strange names gave Adamsberg the sensation of being completely lost, which pleased him. Vladislav glanced at the other passengers.

'She's not here,' he said.

'If she's following me, she won't be here, it's too obvious in a bus. She'll take the next one.'

'But how will she know where we're getting off?'

'Did we mention Kisilova while we were having dinner?'

'Before,' said Vladislav, adjusting his ponytail and holding the rubber band between his teeth. 'When we were drinking champagne.'

'Did we leave our door open?'

'Yes, because of the cigarettes. But a woman travelling alone has a perfect right to go to Belgrade.'

'Who in this bus doesn't look as if they're a Slav?'

Vladislav went looking down the length of the bus, pretending to have lost something, then sat back down by Adamsberg.

'The businessman is probably French or Swiss. The backpacker is from Germany; the couple are either southern French or Italian. They're about fifty and are holding hands which isn't usual for a Serbian couple in an old Serbian bus. And tourists aren't coming much to Serbia at the moment.'

Adamsberg made a vague sign without replying. 'Don't mention the war.' Danglard had dinned this into him several times.

Nobody else got off at the stop for Kiseljevo. Once they were outside, Adamsberg glanced quickly up at the window and it seemed to him as if the man in the unusual couple was watching them.

'Alone,' said Vladislav, stretching his arms up to the clear blue sky. 'Kiseljevo,' he added, pointing proudly to the village with its multicoloured walls and close-packed roofs, and its white church tower, nestling in the hills with the Danube sparkling lower down. Adamsberg got out his travel papers and showed him the name of the place they were staying: *Krčma*.

'That's not anyone's name,' said Vladislav, 'it means "inn". The landlady, if she's still the same, is called Danica. She gave me my first sip of *pivo* – beer.'

'How do you pronounce this word?'

'With a "ch": Krchma.'

'Kruchema.'

'That'll do.'

Adamsberg followed Vladislav to the *kruchema*, which was a tall house with wooden timbers painted and carved decoratively. Conversation stopped as they went inside and suspicious faces turned towards them, reminding Adamsberg of the Norman drinkers in the cafe at Haroncourt or the Béarnais in the bistro at Caldhez. Vladislav introduced himself to the landlady and signed the register, explaining that he was Slavko Moldovan's grandson.

'Vladislav Moldovan!' exclaimed Danica, and from her gestures, Adamsberg gathered that Vlad had grown, that last time she had seen him he was only so high.

The atmosphere immediately changed and people came up to shake Vladislav's hand, the body language became more welcoming and Danica, who seemed as gentle as her name, sat them down immediately to eat. It was twelve thirty. Lunch today was *burecis* with pork, she said, putting a carafe of white wine on the table.

'This is *Smeredevka*, a little known but reputed wine,' said Vladislav, pouring out two glasses. 'And how are you going to find any traces of your Vaudel? Show photos? Bad idea. Very bad. Hereabouts they don't like people who ask questions, cops, journalists, nosy parkers. You'll have to think of something else. But they don't like historians either, or film-makers or sociologists, anthropologists, photographers, novelists, nutters or ethnologists.'

'That's a lot of people they don't like. Why don't they like nosy parkers? Because of the war?'

'No, just that they ask a lot of questions and they've had enough questions. All they want is to live in peace now. Except for him,' he said, pointing to an old man who had just come in. 'He's the only one dares to get things going a bit.'

Looking happy, Vladislav crossed the room and caught the newcomer by the shoulders.

'Arandjel!' he cried, '*To sam ja! Slavko unuk! Zar me ne poznaješ?*'

The old man, who was very short, thin and rather unkempt, pulled back to examine him, then embraced Vladislav warmly, explaining with gestures that he had grown a lot, he was only so high last time he'd seen him.

'He can see I've got a foreign friend here, he doesn't want to interrupt,' Vladislav explained, rejoining Adamsberg with flushed cheeks. 'Arandjel was a big friend of my dedo. Not afraid of anything, either of them.'

'I'm going for a walk,' Adamsberg announced after finishing his dessert – some sugary balls whose ingredients he could not identify.

'Have some coffee first, so as not to offend Danica. Where are you proposing to walk?'

'Towards the woods.'

'No, they won't like that. Walk along the river, that would look more natural. They're going to ask me about you, the minute you go. What shall I say? I can't possibly say you're a cop – that won't do you any favours round here.'

'It doesn't do you any favours anywhere. Tell them I've had a nervous breakdown and have been told to take a rest in a quiet place.'

'Why would you come all the way to Serbia for that?'

'Because my baba knew your dedo.'

Vlad shrugged. Adamsberg gulped down his *kafa* and took out a pen.

'Vlad, how do you say "hello", "thank you" and "French" in this language?'

'*Dobro veče, hvala, francuz.*'

Adamsberg made him repeat the words and, as was his habit, wrote them on the back of his hand.

'Not towards the woods,' Vladislav said again.

'I understand.'

The young man watched him move off, then signalled to Arandjel that he was now free to talk.

'He's had a nervous breakdown, he's going to walk along by the Danube. He's a friend of a friend of Dedo's.'

Arandjel put a little glass of *rakija* in front of Vladislav. Danica, with a slightly anxious expression, watched the stranger going off on his own.

XXXI

First, Adamsberg walked round the village three times, his eyes wide open to absorb the new sights. By following his instinctive sense of orientation, he quickly grasped the layout of the streets and lanes, the main square, the new cemetery, the stone staircases, the village fountain and the market hall. The decoration of the buildings was unfamiliar, with notices in Cyrillic script, and red-and-white bollards. The colours, the shapes of the roofs, the texture of the stones, the weeds by the wayside, everything was different, but he could make his way around and even feel at home in these remote places. He worked out the paths leading to other villages, towards the woods and fields as far as the eye could see, and towards the Danube, where a few ancient boats were pulled up on the bank. On the other side, the blue fortresses of the Carpathians cascaded abruptly down towards the river.

He lit one of Zerk's remaining cigarettes, using the red-and-black lighter, and set off westwards, in the direction of the woods. A village woman was pulling a little go-cart along, and as he passed her, he involuntarily shivered at the memory of the woman on the train. They were nothing alike, this one having a rather wrinkled face and wearing a simple grey skirt. But she did have a wart on her cheek.

He consulted the back of his hand.

'*Dobre veče,*' he said. '*Bonjour. Francuz.*'

The woman neither replied nor did she move on. She ran after him, pulling her cart, and caught him by the arm. Using the universal language of yes and no, she explained that he shouldn't be going that way, and Adamsberg made it clear to her that he did intend to head that way. She insisted at first, but finally let him go, looking distressed.

The *commissaire* carried on. He walked into the outskirts of the wood where the trees were still far apart, then made his way across two clearings containing ruined huts, and after a further two kilometres came to a denser band of trees. The path stopped there, on a final space covered with wild flowers. Adamsberg sat on a tree stump, perspiring a little, listening to the wind rising in the east, and lit his last-but-one cigarette. A rustle made him turn his head. The woman was standing there, having abandoned her cart, and was staring at him with a mixture of despair and anger on her face.

'*Ne idi tuda.*'

'*Francuz,*' said Adamsberg.

'*On te je privukao! Vrati se! On te je privukao!*'

She pointed to a spot at the end of the little clearing, where the trees started, then shrugged her shoulders in discouragement, as if she had done all she could and it was a lost cause. Adamsberg watched her go, almost at a run. Vlad's advice and the woman's persistence drove his determination in the other direction, and he looked over at the end of the clearing. Where the trees began in the spot she had indicated, he could see a little mound covered with stones and sawn-off rounds of wood. Where he came from, that might have been the remains of a shepherd's hut. This must be where the demon lived, the one Uncle Slavko had talked about to the young Danglard.

Letting his cigarette hang from his lip, as his father used to, he walked up to the little mound. On the ground, almost covered in grass, four lines of small logs, about thirty of them standing on end, formed a long rectangle. On top of the chunks of wood, someone had placed heavy rocks, as if the logs might fly away. There was a large grey stone at the head of the rectangle, crenellated, roughly dressed and with something engraved on it. It looked nothing like a ruin and much more like a grave, but a forbidden grave, if the woman's insistence was anything to go by. The person buried here, far from anyone else, outside the graveyard, must be under some kind of taboo: perhaps an unmarried girl dead in childbirth, or a disgraced and excommunicated actor, or an unbaptised child. All round the tomb, the shoots of young trees had been cut, forming a dank background of rotting stumps.

Adamsberg sat down in the warm grass and patiently began scraping away at the moss and lichen on the grey tombstone, using twigs and shards of bark. He engaged contentedly in this task for an hour, scratching at the stone with his nails, or using a fine twig to dig into the letters. As he uncovered the inscription, he realised that the characters were foreign to him, a long sentence written in Cyrillic. Only the last four words were in Roman lettering. He stood up, gave the stone a final wipe with his hand and took a step back to read them.

Plog, as Vladislav would have said, and in this case it might have meant something like 'Bingo!' or 'Success!' He would have got there sooner or later in any case. Today or tomorrow, his steps would have brought him here, he would have sat down in front of this stone, looking at the root of Kisilova. The long epitaph in Serbian was indecipherable but the four words in Roman letters were ultra-clear, and quite enough to be getting on with: *Petar Blagojević – Peter Plogojowitz*. Then the dates of birth and death: *1663–1725*. No cross.

Plog.

Plogojowitz, like Plogerstein, Plögener, Plog and Plogodrescu. Here lay the origin of the victim family. Original surname: Plogojowitz or Blagojević. The name must have been adapted or rearranged, according to the countries where his dispersed descendants had ended up. Here lay the root of the story, and the first of the victims, the ancestor banished, out of bounds to visitors, exiled to the edge of the wood. Perhaps murdered too, but back in 1725. By whom? The deadly hunt had not ended, and Pierre Vaudel, the descendant of Peter Plogojowitz had still been dreading it. Enough to warn another descendant of this man, Frau Abster-Plogerstein, with that КИСЛОВА as an alarm signal. '*Guard our empire, resist to the end, stay beyond attack, Kisilova.*'

Nothing to do with love, needless to say. But an imperative warning, a prayer that the Plogojowitz clan must be protected, and that all of them should be on the alert. Had Vaudel known about the death of Conrad Plögener? He must have. So he realised that the vendetta had started again, if it had ever ceased. The old man was afraid of being killed in his turn. He had made his will *after* the massacre at Pressbaum, keeping his son out of his direct line of inheritance. Josselin had been wrong about that, Vaudel's enemies were by no means imaginary. They did have faces and names. They too must have taken root in this place, in the early decades of the eighteenth century. Nearly three hundred years ago.

Adamsberg sat on a stump, and thrust his hands into his hair. He was staggered. Three hundred years later, some kind of clan warfare was still going on, resulting in the heights of savagery. What for? What was at stake? Hidden treasure perhaps, a child might have said. Power, money, an adult might have said, which came to the same thing really. What on earth did you do, Peter Blagojević-Plogojowitz, to leave this kind of fate to your descendants? And what did they do to you? Adamsberg ran his fingers over the stone, warm in the sun, murmuring his questions to himself, and realising that if the sun was on his face and on the back of the stone, it was not facing east towards Jerusalem, but turned round, facing west. A murderer, then? Did you massacre the inhabitants of the village, Peter Plogojowitz? Or one of its families? Did you go round devastating the countryside, looting and terrorising people? What did you do for Zerk to be still fighting you, with his white skeleton on his black T-shirt?

Peter, what did you do?

Adamsberg carefully copied out the long inscription, reproducing the foreign lettering as best he could.

Пролазниче, продужи својим путем, не освђи се и не понеси ништа одабде. Ту лежи проклетник Петар Благојевић, умревши лета гоцподњег 1725 у својој 62 години. нека би му клета душа нашла покоја.

XXXII

HIS BEDROOM HAD A HIGH CEILING, LAYERS OF ANCIENT multicoloured carpets on the floor and a bed with a blue quilt. Adamsberg let himself relax on to it, and put his hands behind his neck. Fatigue from the journey had made his limbs feel heavy, but he smiled, his eyes closed, happy at having unearthed the roots of the Plog clan, but incapable of understanding their story. He didn't have the strength to ring up Danglard and talk about it. He sent him two short text messages instead. Danglard pedantically insisted on using Latin for the plural of text messages, *texti*, since the usual word in French is *texto*. The first message read: '*Ancestor is Peter Plogojowitz*', and the second: '†*1725*'.

Danica, who on closer inspection was buxom and pretty and probably no more than forty-two, knocked on his door, waking him up a little after eight, according to both his watches.

'*Večera je na stolu*,' she said with a broad smile, indicating with gestures that she meant 'come' and 'eat'.

Sign language easily dealt with most basic functions.

People seemed to smile a lot here in Kisilova and perhaps

that was the explanation of the 'sunny disposition' shared by Uncle Sladko and his grandson Vladislav. Family ties made Adamsberg remember his own son. He sent a few thoughts towards little Tom, on holiday somewhere in Normandy, and lay back on the eiderdown. He had immediately taken to it: pale blue with cord piping and worn at the corners, it was nicer than the bright red one his sister had given him. This one smelt of hay, dandelions and possibly even donkey. As he went down the narrow wooden stairs, his phone vibrated in his back pocket like a nervous cricket tickling him. He looked at Danglard's reply: one word – '*Irrelevant*'.

Vladislav was waiting for him at the table, his knife and fork poised for action. '*Dunajski zrezek*, Wiener schnitzel,' he said, pointing to the dish impatiently. He had put on a white T-shirt and his dark body hair looked even more striking. It stopped at his wrists like a wave that has run out of strength, leaving his hands smooth and pale.

'Been looking at the scenery?' he asked.

'I went down by the Danube and then to the edge of the forest. A woman came along and tried to stop me going there. Towards the woods.'

He tried to see the expression on Vlad's face, but he was busily eating, looking down at the food.

'But I went there all the same,' Adamsberg continued.

'Wow.'

'What's this mean?' asked Adamsberg, putting on the table the paper on which he had copied the inscription from the grave.

Vlad picked up his napkin and slowly wiped his lips. 'A load of old codswallop,' he said.

'If you like, but what does it mean?'

Vlad snorted his disapproval.

'You'd have seen it sooner or later. Impossible not to really, once you're here.'

'And?'

'Like I said. They don't like talking about it, that's all. It's already not so good that that woman saw you out there. If tomorrow they ask you to leave, don't be surprised. And if you want to carry on with the Vaudel inquiry, don't provoke them with this stuff. Or with the war.'

'I didn't mention the war.'

'See the guy behind us? See what he's doing?'

'Yes, I noticed. He's drawing on the back of his hand with a felt pen.'

'All day long. He draws circles and squares, orange, green and brown. He was in the war,' Vlad added, lowering his voice. 'And now he does nothing but colour in shapes on his hand without speaking a word.'

'What about the other men?'

'Kiseljevo was relatively spared. Because here, women and children aren't left alone in the village. Some people hid, others stayed. Don't talk about your trip to the woods, *commissaire*.'

'But, Vlad, it has to do with this murder investigation.'

'Plog,' said Vlad, sticking his middle finger in the air, which gave a new meaning to the onomatopoeia. 'Nothing to do with it.'

Danica, her blonde hair now neatly combed, brought them their desserts and put two small glasses in front of them.

'Look out,' Vlad advised. 'This is *rakija*.'

'What's it mean?'

'It's strong spirits, made from fruit.'

'No, I'm talking about the inscription on the gravestone.'

Vlad pushed away the sheet of paper with a smile. He knew the inscription by heart, as did anyone who knew anything about Kiseljevo.

'Only an ignorant Frenchman wouldn't jump with fear at the terrible name of Peter Plogojowitz. The story's so famous in Europe that people don't tell it any more. Ask Danglard, he's bound to know.'

'I did tell him about it. He seemed to know.'

'That doesn't surprise me. And what did he say?'

'Irrelevant.'

'Adrianus never lets me down.'

'Vlad, just tell me what's written on the stone.'

'"You who stand before this stone,"' Vlad recited, '"go your way without listening and cut no plant hereby. Here lies the damned soul Petar Blagojević, who died in 1725 aged 62. May his accursed spirit now make way for peace."'

'Why does he have two names?'

'They're the same name. Plogojowitz is the Austrian version of Blagojević. When he lived here, the whole region was under the Habsburgs.'

'Why was he damned?'

'Because, in 1725, the peasant Petar Blagojević died here, in his native village.'

'Don't start with his death, tell me what he did when he was alive.'

'But it was only after his death that his life was cursed. Three days after his burial, Plogojowitz came to visit his wife at night and asked her for a pair of shoes so that he could travel the world.'

'Shoes?'

'Yes. He had left them behind. Do you want to know any more or is it irrelevant?'

'Tell me the rest, Vlad. I vaguely remember hearing something about a dead man coming back for his shoes.'

'In the ten weeks after that, there were nine sudden deaths in the village, all close relatives or associates of Plogojowitz. They lost their blood, and died of exhaustion. During their death throes, they claimed to have seen Plogojowitz leaning over them, even lying on top of them. The villagers panicked and thought Plogojowitz had become a vampire who was going to suck the life out of everyone. And then suddenly, all Europe was talking about him. It's because of Plogojowitz and Kisilova, where you are sitting drinking *rakija* this evening, that the word *vampyr* first appeared outside this region.'

'Really? As famous as that?'

'Plog. After two months, the villagers had resolved to open his grave and annihilate him, but the Church formally forbade that. Tempers ran high, the Empire sent out some religious and civic officials to try and calm things down. The authorities had to stand by powerless when the exhumation took place. But they observed it and wrote a report. Peter's body showed no sign of decomposition. It was intact, the skin looked like new.'

'Like that woman in London, Elizabeth something, whose husband opened her grave after seven years to get his poems out. She looked like new as well.'

'And she was a vampire?'

'So I was told.'

'Normal then. Plogojowitz's old skin and fingernails were

in the bottom of the grave. And there was blood coming out of his mouth, nostrils and eyes. The Austrian officials wrote it all down scrupulously. He had eaten his shroud and he had an erection, though later versions usually leave that bit out. The peasants were terrified, and they took a stake and plunged it into his heart.'

'And there was a noise?'

'Yes, a horrible scream that could be heard all over the village, and a stream of blood filled the grave. His hideous body was taken out and burnt until nothing remained. And the nine victims, well, the villagers shut their bodies up in a sealed vault, and after that they abandoned that graveyard for good.'

'The old one to the west of the village?'

'That's right. They were afraid of contagion spreading underground. And the deaths stopped. Or so the story says.'

Adamsberg took a tiny sip of *rakija*.

'On the edge of the wood, under the mound, that's where his ashes are?'

'There are two versions. Either his ashes were scattered into the Danube or they were collected and put in that grave, a long way out of the village. There's a general belief that some bit of Plogojowitz survives, because they can hear him munching under the ground. But it means that he's lost his toxicity, since he's sunk to the lower status of shroud-eater.'

'He's become a sub-vampire?'

'A passive vampire who doesn't leave his tomb, but expresses his greed by eating everything around him, his shroud, his coffin, the earth. There are thousands of reports of the shroud-eaters. You can hear their teeth gnashing together under the earth. But you'd still do best not to go too near and to make sure they're blocked inside their tombs.'

'That's what the logs are there for?'

'To stop him getting out, yes.'

'Who puts them there?'

'Arandjel,' said Vlad, dropping his voice, as Danica approached to refill their glasses.

'And why are the trees all cut down around the grave?'

'Because their roots reach down into the earth round the tomb. The wood's contaminated, so it mustn't be allowed to spread. And you shouldn't pick any flowers, because Plogojowitz is in their stems. Arandjel cuts all the vegetation down once a year.'

'He believes Plogojowitz can get out of there?'

'Arandjel is the only person in the village who *doesn't* believe it. Here about a quarter of the people believe it one hundred per cent. Another quarter shake their heads and won't say yes or no, for fear of attracting the vampire's anger by mocking it. The other half of the villagers pretend not to believe it, and say it's just old wives' tales fit to worry people in days gone by. But they're never quite sure, which is why the men didn't leave the village during the war. And only Arandjel truly doesn't believe it. That's why he's not afraid to be an expert on all vampires, every kind: *vârkolac, opyr, vurdalak, nosferatu, veštica, stafia, morije.*'

'That's a lot of vampires.'

'Here, Adamsberg, in a radius of about five hundred kilometres, there were thousands of different vampires. And we're at the epicentre. Where Plogojowitz reigned, the undisputed master of the throng.'

'If Arandjel doesn't believe in it, why does he look after the tomb?'

'To reassure the people here. He changes the logs every

year because the wood rots from underneath. And some people say that's because Plogojowitz has eaten all the earth and is starting on the logs. So Arandjel replaces them, and cuts off any shoots. Of course he's the only person who dares. Nobody else goes near, but on the whole people are reasonable enough. They think Plogojowitz isn't so powerful now, because he's transferred his powers to his descendants.'

'And where are they? Here?'

'You must be joking! Even before they dug Plogojowitz up, the rest of his family fled the village to avoid being massacred. His descendants are dispersed all over the place now, who knows where. Little vampirelets left and right. But some people still think that if Plogojowitz manages to get out of his grave, they will all get together in a great terrible entity. Other people say that part of Plogojowitz may be here, but he's reconstituted himself whole somewhere else.'

'Where?'

'I don't know. All this is what my dedo used to tell me. If you want to know any more, you'll have to ask Arandjel. He's kind of the Adrianus of Serbia.'

'Vlad, do you know if any particular family was destroyed by Plogojowitz?'

'I just told you, his own. There were nine deaths among his relations. Which means there was some sort of epidemic. Old Plogojowitz must have been ill, and passed the infection on to his own family, then it spread to their contacts. It's that simple! But people got scared and looked for a scapegoat, found out who was the first mortal case, stuck a stake in his heart and that was that.'

'And what if the epidemic carried on?'

'Must have happened often. Well, they'd reopen the grave, thinking that the remains of the cursed person were still active, and they'd start again.'

'What if they'd thrown the ashes into the river?'

'Well, then they'd open up some other grave, a man or woman suspected of having saved a bit of the monster from the fire and eaten it, so that they became a *vampir* in turn. And it went on until the epidemic died out. So finally they'd be able to say: "The deaths came to an end."'

'But, Vladislav, the deaths haven't come to an end. A man called Plögener in Pressbaum, and another called Plog in Garches have been killed. Two Plogojowitz descendants, one in Austria, one in France. Can we get something else besides *rakija* to drink? This stuff's eating me up like your shroud-eaters. A beer? Could we have a beer?'

'Some Jelen?'

'Yes, fine, some Jelen.'

'Perhaps something else happened to inspire the vengeance? Suppose that Plogojowitz wasn't a vampire in 1725? What would you say then?'

Adamsberg smiled at the landlady as she brought him his beer and tried to remember how to say 'thank you'.

He consulted the back of his hand.

'*Hvala*,' he said, with a gesture signifying smoking, and Danica produced from the folds of her skirt a packet he didn't recognise, Morava.

'A present,' said Vlad. 'She asked me why you have two wristwatches, when neither of them tells the right time.'

'Tell her I don't know.'

'*On ne zna*,' Vlad translated. And went on, 'She fancies you.'

Danica returned to the office where she did the accounts

and Adamsberg watched her go, her ample hips swaying under the red-and-grey skirt.

'So,' Vlad insisted, 'what if there never was a vampire?'

'Then I'd look for some family saga that led to reprisals and death sentences. A secret murder, a betrayed husband, an illegitimate child, a fortune diverted into the wrong hands. Vaudel-Plog was very rich, and he didn't leave his money to his son.'

'Well, there you are. That's where you ought to look. Where the money is.'

'But there are the bodies, Vlad. They've been taken apart so that they couldn't possibly be reconstituted. Is that what they did to vampires, or did they just stick to the stake and the fire?'

'Only Arandjel can tell you that.'

'So where is he? When can I see him?'

There was a brief exchange with Danica, then Vlad came back, looking somewhat surprised.

'Apparently Arandjel is expecting you to have lunch with him tomorrow and he's going to prepare some stuffed cabbage. He knows you cleaned the tombstone and looked at it – everybody knows about that by now. He says you shouldn't start meddling with that sort of thing. It could be fatal for you.'

'I thought you said Arandjel didn't believe in all that.'

'Fatal for you,' repeated Vlad, emptying his glass of *rakija*, and bursting out laughing.

XXXIII

An unpaved lane led to Arandjel's house on the banks of the Danube, and the two men walked along it without exchanging a word, as if some foreign element had altered their relationship. Unless perhaps Vladislav's evening smokes made him unsociable in the morning. It was already warm. Adamsberg swung his black jacket at the end of his arm, relaxing, letting the noises of the town and the inquiry fade away in the mist of oblivion rising from the river, and blotting out the fierce image of Zerk, the nervous atmosphere in the squad, the deadly threat hanging over him, and the arrow that had been loosed by someone high up, which would soon be reaching its target. Was Dinh still lying in bed with his so-called fever? Had he managed to hold back the samples? As for Émile, and his dog, and the man who had painted his patron in bronze, they were all ghostly images fading into the fog which Kisilova was gently spreading into his mind.

'You were late up this morning,' Vladislav said eventually, in a disgruntled tone.

'Yes.'

'You didn't come down for breakfast. Adrianus says you are always up at cockcrow, like a peasant, you're always four hours earlier than him getting into work.'

'I didn't hear the cock crow.'

'I think you heard the cock crowing very well. I think you slept with Danica.'

Adamsberg walked a few paces in silence.

'Plog,' he said.

Vladislav kicked a pebble with his shoe, hesitatingly, then laughed softly. With his hair now loose on his shoulders, he looked like a Slav warrior about to launch his horse against the West. He lit a cigarette and started talking in his usual bantering way.

'You'll be wasting your time with Arandjel. You'll find out a whole lot of obscure information, but nothing that will help your inquiry, nothing you could write in a report. Irrelevant, like Adrianus says.'

'Not a problem, I can't write reports anyway.'

'What about your boss? What will he say? That you were dallying with a woman on the banks of the Danube, while a killer was on the loose in France.'

'He always thinks I'm doing more or less that. My boss – or whoever up there has some sort of hold over my boss – is trying to get me sacked. So I might as well find out what I can here.'

Vladislav introduced Adamsberg to Arandjel, who nodded and produced a dish of stuffed cabbage, which he put on the table. Vladislav served it out in silence.

'You cleaned Blagojević's stone,' observed Arandjel, starting to eat, and forking huge helpings into his mouth. 'You scraped the moss off. You made the name visible.'

Vladislav was translating so fast that Adamsberg had the impression of holding a direct conversation with the old man.

'I shouldn't have done that?'

'No. You shouldn't touch his tomb, in case it wakes him up. The people round here are scared of him, and some of them might be angry with you for making his name visible. Some people might even think he summoned you here, to be his servant. And they might want to kill you before you bring death to the village. Peter Blagojević wants a servant – you understand? That's what Biljana was afraid of, the woman who tried to stop you. "He's calling you, he's calling you," that's what she told me she said to you.'

'*On te je privukao, on te je privukao*,' Vladislav repeated.

'Ye-es, that is what she said,' Adamsberg admitted.

'Don't set foot in the world of vampires without knowing what you're doing, young man.' Arandjel paused significantly, so that the idea could penetrate into Adamsberg's mind, then poured out some wine. 'Vlad told me yesterday that you were interested in Blagojević's story. Feel free to ask. But don't go walking in the place of uncertainty.'

'What do you mean?'

'The place of uncertainty. That's what they call the clearing where he's buried. It's not poor old Peter who might attack you, but someone who's alive and kicking. You have to understand that the safety of the village is what matters most around here. Eat up before it gets cold.'

Adamsberg obeyed, clearing most of what was on his plate before speaking again.

'There've been two horrible murders, one in France, one in Austria.'

'Yes, I know, Vlad told me.'

'I believe that the two victims belonged to Blagojević's family, that they were descendants of his.'

'Blagojević didn't have any descendants who carried his name. All the members of his family left the village under their Austrian surname, Plogojowitz, so that the people here wouldn't be able to trace them. But the word got out, because someone from the village went to Romania in 1813, and when he got back he added the Plogojowitz spelling to the gravestone. If any descendants are still around they'd be called Plogojowitz. So what's your theory?'

'The victims weren't just killed, their bodies were totally demolished. I was asking Vladislav yesterday what you have to do to destroy a vampire.'

Arandjel nodded several times, pushed back his plate and rolled a bulky cigarette.

'The point isn't so much to destroy the vampire as to make sure he can't come back. He has to be blocked, stopped. There are plenty of ways to do it. What most people think is that you have to put a stake through his heart. But they're wrong, the crucial thing is the feet.'

Arandjel blew out a cloud of acrid smoke and spoke at some length to Vladislav.

'I'm going to put on the coffee,' Vladislav explained. 'Arandjel apologises for not offering you a dessert, but he lives alone and he doesn't like sweet things. Or fruit. He doesn't like getting juice on his hands. And he wants to know if you liked the stuffed cabbage, because you didn't ask for a second helping.'

'It was delicious,' Adamsberg replied sincerely, embarrassed that he had not complimented his host on the food. 'But I never eat much at midday. Please ask him not to be offended.'

Having listened to this reply, Arandjel indicated that he accepted the apology, asked Adamsberg to call him by his first name, and went on with his explanation.

'The most urgent thing to do is to stop the dead man walking. So if in doubt they always dealt with his feet first, so he couldn't move.'

'What do you mean "if in doubt", Arandjel?'

'There could be signs during the wake. If the corpse still looked rosy-cheeked, or if some of the shroud was in his mouth, if he was smiling, if the eyes were open. So then they tied his two big toes together with string. Or they bit the big toe. Or they put pins in the soles of his feet, or tied the legs together. All the same sort of thing.'

'Did they ever cut the feet off?'

'Oh yes. A more radical method, but they didn't hesitate to do that if they still felt uneasy. Of course the Church punished this as a sacrilege. Quite often they would cut off the head and place it between the feet in the tomb, so that the corpse couldn't get hold of it. Or they tied his hands behind his back, or trussed him up on a stretcher, and stopped up his nose, and blocked all the orifices, mouth, ears, the lot. There was no end to it.'

'And the teeth?'

'Ah, well, the mouth, young man, is of course a crucial part of a vampire's body.'

Arandjel stopped speaking, while Vladislav poured out the coffee.

'*Bon mangé?*' Arandjel asked in French with a sudden smile which lit up his whole face – and Adamsberg began to warm to the broad Kiseljevan grin. 'I met this Frenchman when they liberated Belgrade in '44. *Vin, femmes jolies, boeuf mode.*'

Vladislav and Arandjel both burst out laughing and Adamsberg wondered once more how people could find contentment in so little, and wished he were the same.

'The vampire has an insatiable appetite,' Arandjel went on. 'That's why he wants to gobble up his shroud, or the earth in the grave. So they might stop his mouth with stones, or they might use garlic or earth, or tie a cloth round his neck very tightly so that he couldn't swallow. Or they buried him face down so that he would just eat the earth, and that way he'd sink deeper down.'

'And some people eat wardrobes,' said Adamsberg under his breath. Vlad stopped translating, unsure he had heard right. 'Did you say wardrobes?'

'Yes. Thekophagists, the people are called.'

Vlad conveyed this and Arandjel did not look too surprised. 'Do you have many examples of that?' he asked.

'No, but there was a man who ate a whole aeroplane once. And in London, a lord ate the photographs of his mother.'

'Now I once knew a man who ate his own finger,' said Arandjel, sticking his thumb in the air. 'He cut it off and cooked it. But next day he couldn't remember a thing about it and he went round looking for his finger. It happened in Ruma. For a long time people wondered whether they should tell him the truth or pretend that a bear had attacked him in the woods and bitten off the finger. They chanced to come across a dead bear some time later, and they brought him the bear's head. The man was quite happy after that – he thought his finger was inside the bear and he hung on to its head, even when it rotted away.'

'Ah, like the polar bear,' said Adamsberg. 'The one that ate the uncle on the ice floe, and the nephew brought back its skin to his widow, and she kept it too. In her sitting room.'

'Remarkable,' said Arandjel. 'Quite remarkable.'

Adamsberg felt somehow fortified, even if he had had to come all this way to find a man who appreciated the story of the bear as it should be. But now he had lost the thread of the conversation, as Arandjel could tell from his eyes.

'Yes, vampires want to eat the living, and they try to eat their shrouds, the earth they lie in, everything,' he said. 'That's why people didn't trust anyone with abnormal teeth. People whose teeth were particularly long for instance, or babies who were born with one or two teeth.'

'Born with *teeth*?'

'Yes, it isn't as rare as all that. Julius Caesar now, he was born with teeth, and so was your Napoleon and your Louis XIV in France. And plenty of others, who weren't famous. Some people thought it wasn't a sign of being a vampire but that you were a superior being. Take me,' he said, tapping his glass against his discoloured teeth. 'I was born like Caesar.'

Adamsberg waited for the loud howl of laughter from Vladislav and Arandjel to subside, then asked for a piece of paper. He reproduced the sketch he had done for the squad, marking the parts of the body which had been attacked. 'Oh yes, splendid,' said Arandjel, picking up the drawing. 'That's right, the joints, to stop the body moving. Feet, of course, specially big toes, so he couldn't walk. Mouth and teeth. Liver, heart and soul. In the old days, the heart, which is the seat of a vampire's life, might be taken out of the body for special treatment. This is a magnificent piece of destruction, by someone who knew exactly what he was doing,' Arandjel concluded, as if he were judging a professional piece of work.

'Because it wasn't possible to burn the body perhaps?'

'Precisely. But what he did came to the same thing.'

'Arandjel, could it be that someone out there really believes all this sufficiently to make him want to wipe out Plogojowitz's descendants?'

'What do you mean "believes all this"? Everyone believes it, young man. Everyone is afraid that at night a tombstone will fall over and you'll feel a cold breath on your neck. And nobody likes to think of the dead as making good companions. Believing in vampires is just the same.'

'I don't mean an ancient, traditional kind of fear, Arandjel. I mean someone who believes this literally, who thinks all the Plogojowitzes are authentic *vampiri*, and should be exterminated. Is that possible?'

'Yes, undoubtedly, if he thinks this has caused all his misfortune. People look for an external cause for their suffering, and the more they suffer, the greater the cause must be. In this case, the killer's suffering is immense. So his response is on the same scale.'

Arandjel turned round to talk to Vladislav, slipping Adamsberg's drawing into his pocket. He wanted the chairs to be taken outside, underneath the lime tree, overlooking the bend in the river, and to take advantage of the sunshine, with some glasses on the table.

'No more *rakija* . . . please,' Adamsberg whispered.

'*Pivo*? Beer?'

'Yes, if it won't offend him.'

'No bother, he likes you. Not many people come to talk to him about his beloved *vampiri* and you've brought him a new case. It's a great distraction for him.'

The three men sat around under the tree in the warm sunshine, listening to the chuckling of the river, and Arandjel began to close his eyes. A mist had started to rise, and

Adamsberg looked across to the other bank at the peaks of the Carpathians.

'Hurry up before he goes to sleep,' Vladislav warned him.

'Yes, this is where I take my siesta,' the old man confirmed.

'Arandjel, I have two final questions.'

'I'll keep listening as long as there's still some drink in my glass,' said Arandjel, taking a very small sip and looking amused.

Adamsberg felt as if he had been caught in an intelligent trap, where he would have to think quickly before the alcohol started to disappear, like sand running through an hourglass. When the glass was empty, the words of wisdom would dry up. He estimated that the time in front of him was about five mouthfuls of *rakija*.

'Is there any connection between Plogojowitz and the old graveyard in north London, Higg-gate Cemetery?'

'Highgate you mean?'

'Yes.'

'Much worse than a connection, young man. Long before they made the cemetery, people say that the body of a Turk was taken to the top of the hill, in his coffin, and that his was the only grave there for a long time. Well, people get a lot of things wrong: he wasn't a Turk at all, but a Serb, and he's supposed to be the master vampire, Plogojowitz himself. Fleeing his native land to go and reign from London. They even say that it was his presence on the hill that spontaneously caused the building of the cemetery.'

'Plogojowitz, the master of London?' Adamsberg whispered to himself, quite taken aback. 'So the person who put the shoes there wasn't making an offering to him, but provoking him, picking a quarrel, showing him his powers.'

'*Ti to verjueš*,' said Vlad, looking at Adamsberg and shaking his long hair. 'You really believe it. Don't let Arandjel bewitch you with his tales, that's what my dedo always told me. He's just having fun with you.'

Adamsberg once more allowed the gales of laughter to finish, watching the level of the alcohol in Arandjel's glass. Meeting his eyes, Arandjel swallowed another mouthful. Just a centimetre left now. 'Time is passing, ask your second question.' That was what Arandjel's smile seemed to say, like the sphinx testing passers-by.

'Arandjel, was there anyone who was specially singled out for treatment by Plogojowitz? Is it possible that there's some family that thinks it is a particular victim of the Plogojowitz clan's powers?'

'Irrelevant,' said Vlad, repeating what Danglard had said. 'I already told you. It's his own family that was targeted.'

Arandjel raised his hand to tell Vladislav to be quiet.

'Yes,' he said. 'All right,' he went on, pouring himself another small slug of *rakija*. 'You have won the right to a last little glass before my siesta.'

A concession that seemed to suit the old man very well. Adamsberg took out his notebook.

'No,' said Arandjel firmly. 'If you can't remember it's because it's not interesting enough to you, so you won't have missed anything.'

'OK, I'm listening,' said Adamsberg, pocketing the notebook.

'There was one family at least that was persecuted by Plogojowitz. In a village called Medwegya, not far from here, in Braničevo district. You can read all about it in the *Visum et repertum* that Dr Flückinger wrote in 1732 for the military council in Belgrade after they closed the inquiry.'

I'm talking to the Danglard of Serbia, Adamsberg

remembered. He had no idea what this *Visum et repertum* could be or where to find it, and old Arandjel had challenged him not to take notes. Adamsberg rubbed his hands together in his anxiety not to forget. *Visum et repertum* by Flückinger.

'The case caused even more of a sensation than Plogojowitz's. A major scandal throughout the Western world, with people taking sides. Your Voltaire had a good laugh about it, the Austrian emperor got involved, Louis XV ordered his envoys to follow the inquiry, the doctors were tearing their hair out, the priests praying for their salvation, the theologians didn't know what to think. A great outpouring of literature and debate. And to think it all started here,' Arandjel added, glancing round at the hills.

'I'm listening,' said Adamsberg.

'This soldier came back to Medwegya after years of fighting in the Austro-Turkish wars. He wasn't the same as when he went away. He said he had been the victim of a *vampir* during his tour of duty, that he had fought the vampire but it had followed him to the Turkish part of Persia and in the end he had managed to kill the monster and bury it. He had brought back some earth from the grave and he ate it regularly to protect himself from the *vampir*. It's a sign that the soldier didn't think he was safe from the living-dead creature, even if he thought he had killed it. So he lived on in Medwegya, eating earth, wandering around cemeteries and getting his neighbours worked up. Then, in 1727, he fell off a hay cart and broke his neck. In the month after he died, there were four deaths in Medwegya, "in the manner people die when attacked by vampires", and people started to say the soldier had become a vampire too. They made such a fuss that the authorities agreed to his exhumation, forty days after his death. And the rest is well known.'

'Tell me all the same,' said Adamsberg, afraid that Arandjel might stop at this point.

'The body was pink-skinned, fresh blood was to be seen in the orifices, the skin looked new and smooth, fingernails were lying in the tomb, and there were no signs of decomposition. They plunged a stake into the soldier's chest and there was a horrible cry. Or some say not so much a cry as an inhuman sigh. They cut off his head and burnt the body.'

The old man took another mouthful of *rakija* under Adamsberg's watchful eye. Only a third of the second glass left. If Adamsberg had remembered the dates right, the soldier had died two years after Plogojowitz.

'The four victims too were taken from their graves and got the same treatment. But since they were afraid that the contagion of the Medwegya vampire might extend to his neighbours in the graveyard, they went further. An official inquiry was instituted in 1731, they opened forty tombs near the soldier's and discovered that seventeen corpses were still in perfect condition: Militza, Joachim, Ruscha and her child Rhode, Bariactar's wife and her son Stanche, Milo, Stanoicka, and others, they were all taken and cremated. And there were no more deaths.'

Only a few drops of liquor now remained in Arandjel's glass, so everything depended on his rate of drinking. 'If the soldier had been fighting with Peter Plogojowitz –' Adamsberg started quickly – 'because we *are* talking about Plogojowitz, aren't we?'

'So they say.'

'In that case, the members of the soldier's family were – how shall I put it? – unintentional vampires, but they could consider themselves as victims of Plogojowitz, people who had been captured and enslaved. Men and women who were turned into vampires by force, destroyed by the creature.'

'Yes, that's it. That's what they were.'

Arandjel swirled the last drop of *rakija* round and looked at the facets of his glass glinting in the sunlight.

'And the soldier's name?' asked Adamsberg hastily. 'Is that known?'

Arandjel raised his glass towards the blank sky and without putting it to his lips threw the last drop of *rakija* straight into his mouth.

'Arnold Paole. He was called Arnold Paole.'

'Plog,' whispered Vladislav.

'Try to remember it,' said Arandjel, stretching out in his armchair. 'It's the kind of name that slips your mind.'

As if Plogojowitz's breath had made it inconsistent.

XXXIV

ADAMSBERG WAS LISTENING TO WEILL CHATTING INTO HIS mobile, asking him about the local dishes and wines, and had he tasted the stuffed cabbage yet?

He was strolling calmly along in a landscape that now seemed familiar to him, almost as if he belonged there. He recognised a flower here and there, ruts in the path, the view across the rooftops. Finding himself at the fork in the forest road, he was on the point of taking the path to the woods, then shrank back. Drawn towards him, you're being drawn towards him. He took a right turn instead, and found himself on the path along the river again, allowing his eyes to scan the Carpathian peaks.

'Are you listening, *commissaire*?'

'Of course I am.'

'Because I'm doing all this for you.'

'No, you're doing it to get back at the forces of darkness in the hierarchy.'

'Well, maybe,' Weill conceded, since he disliked being caught out expressing honourable sentiments. 'I'll start with the third rung of our ladder, which is now leaning up against the jaws of hell.'

'Er, yes,' said Adamsberg, distracted by a huge flight of white butterflies, playing in the warm air round his head as if he were a flower.

'Right. The judge in Mordent's daughter's case is called Damvillois. Found that out. Incompetent type, mid-career but stalled. Only he has a half-brother in high places. Damvillois can't refuse him anything, because he counts on him to get promotion. Fourth rung is the half-brother, Gilles Damvillois, who's a powerful examining magistrate in Gavernan, high-flyer. Might get to be state advocate. If, that is, the current holder of the post is disposed to back him. Fifth rung, current state advocate, Régis Trémard, who's on hot bricks because he wants to chair the Appeal Court, no less. That's if the current chair puts *him* top of the list.'

By now Adamsberg had taken a path he didn't know, along the bend of the Danube, leading towards an old mill. The butterflies were still with him; either they were following him or perhaps they were a different lot.

'Sixth rung, chair of the Appeal Court, Alain Perrenin. What he's after is the vice-presidency of the Council of State. If the current vice-president backs him. We're getting warm now. Seventh rung. Vice-president of the Council of State, a woman called Emma Carnot. Very warm indeed. She got where she is by using her sharp elbows, never wasted a moment of her life messing about reading philosophy, enjoying herself, or all the other things lesser mortals spend their time on. She's a hundred per cent workaholic, and she has a phenomenal number of contacts and strings she can pull.'

By now Adamsberg had gone inside the old mill. He looked up at the ancient rafters, which were of a different pattern from the mill in his home village of Caldhez. The butterflies had abandoned him to the semi-darkness. Under his feet he could feel a carpet of bird droppings which was a crunchy but pleasant sensation.

'And she wants to be Minister of Justice, I suppose?' asked Adamsberg.

'Or go even higher. There's no limit to her ambition, she's out for all she can get. At my request, Danglard searched Mordent's office. He found Emma Carnot's personal number, pathetically obvious, just stuck on the underside of the desk. Forgivable in a junior officer, but a black mark against someone on the *commandant* grade. I have one golden rule: if you can't memorise a ten-digit telephone number, don't get mixed up in anything dodgy. Second golden rule: don't let anyone slip a bomb under your bed.'

'Agreed,' said Adamsberg, shuddering at the thought of Zerk, whom he had let go, just like that.

That was a real bomb under his bed. It could blow him sky-high like the toads the village boys tortured. But he was the only one who knew that. No, of course Zerk knew it and was determined to use it: *I've come to fuck up your life.*

'So, are you pleased?' asked Weill.

'To find out that the key woman in the Council of State is after my guts? Not really, Weill.'

'Adamsberg, what we have to do is find out why Emma Carnot doesn't want the Garches murderer found at any cost. Is he some dangerous colleague? Her son? Her ex-lover? The word on the street is that these days she's only interested in women, but some people whisper – and I've got a whisperer on the line from the Limoges Appeal Court – that there *was* a husband at one time. One time very long ago. The trail always leads to family secrets. Third golden rule:

keep your private life private, and burn all your papers if you can.'

'That's no doubt what she's trying to do.'

'I've looked, Adamsberg. I can't find any records of a marriage, or of any link between her and the Garches affair, or the Pressbaum one either. No marriage, well, perhaps I'm not entirely sure about that.'

Weill clicked his tongue and savoured the brief pause.

'The page that corresponds to her maiden name at the town hall which should be the right one, because she was born in Auxerre, has been quite simply cut out of the register. The clerk says that a woman from "the ministry" asked to see the register recently, something to do with "national security". I think our Emma Carnot is panicking. I can smell fear. A woman with jet-black hair, the clerk said. Golden rule number four: never use a wig, it's ridiculous. So what we have is a marriage which has been removed from the public record.'

'The killer is only twenty-nine, though.'

'Could be the son of the marriage. She might be protecting him. Or trying to make sure her son's crazy actions don't get in the way of her career.'

'But, Weill, the mother of our Zerk has a name, she's called Gisèle Louvois.'

'Yes, I know. But what if Carnot discreetly had a baby adopted – for a hefty consideration?'

'All right, Weill, so we've arrived at the seventh rung – what do we do next?'

'We get hold of Carnot's DNA, we compare it to the Kleenex from the crime scene and see where that gets us. It's easy, the waste-paper baskets at the Council of State are taken out every morning to the Place du Palais Royal. On days when there's been a meeting, there will be water bottles, plastic cups and so on provided for the members of the council. Hers will be there and we can identify it. They've got a meeting this week. Disconnect your mobile now, *commissaire*, and only put it back on tomorrow morning at nine, without fail.'

'OK, without fail,' said Adamsberg, feeling suddenly greatly relieved to learn that the vice-president of the Council of State might have given birth to Zerk. Because whereas he had no recollection of ever having made love to a girl called Gisèle, he was one hundred per cent certain never to have slept with the vice-president of the Council of State.

He switched off and took the battery out of Weill's mobile.

Tomorrow, nine o'clock. He would have to explain to the landlady of the *kruchema* why he was going out early. He bit his lip. He had sworn to Zerk, in good faith, that he always remembered the names and faces of any women with whom he had made love. And this was only yesterday. He concentrated, trying out all the words he had picked up: *kruchema, kafa, danica, hvala*. Danica, that was it. He stopped at the door of the mill, suddenly struck by a new anxiety. Now, what was the name of the soldier whose life Peter Plogojowitz had fucked up? He had remembered when he started walking by the river. But Weill's phone call had pushed it to the back of his mind. He gripped his head in his hands, but with no result at all.

The noise came from behind, like a sack being dragged along the ground. Adamsberg turned round. He was not alone in the mill.

'Fancy seeing you, scumbag,' came a voice from the gloom.

XXXV

WHAT BROUGHT ADAMSBERG BACK TO CONSCIOUSNESS WAS a series of rasping sounds from a roll of tape. Zerk was trussing him up in the kind of heavy-duty tape removal men use. His legs were already immobilised when he was hauled out of the mill and into a car parked about twenty metres away.

How long had he been lying there, tied up on the floor of the mill? Until darkness had fallen, for it must be about nine at night now. He could move his feet, but the rest of him was firmly wrapped like a mummy. His wrists were pinned together, and his mouth sealed. The man was just a dark shape. But he could hear the leather jacket creaking, and the heavy breathing resulting from the effort of dragging him, just sounds without any meaning. Then came a short ride on the back seat of the car, less than a kilometre he estimated, before they stopped. Zerk was now pulling him by his wrists, as if his arms were the handle of a huge basket. He dragged him about thirty metres, stopping five times; gravel crunched under Adamsberg's body. The man dropped him suddenly, puffing from the exertion and muttering. A door opened.

Gravel under his back, scratching him through his shirt. Where had he seen any sharp gravel in Kisilova? Black gravel, different from the kind you saw in France. The man had turned a key, a large old key by the heavy metallic sound. He came back, took hold of the arm-handle again and brutally hauled Adamsberg down a few stone steps, letting him fall to the ground at the bottom. A beaten earth floor. Zerk cut the tape round his wrists, and removed his jacket and shirt, by cutting them with a knife. Adamsberg tried to react, but he was already too weak. His legs were bound and cold, and the man's boot was on his chest. Then more tape, round his torso now, pinning his arms to his sides. A few steps sounded and Zerk closed the door without a word. The intense cold was a contrast to the warm night outside and the darkness was absolute. It must be some kind of cellar without any grating.

'Know where you are, scumbag? Why couldn't you leave me alone?'

The voice reached him in a distorted form, as if on an old-fashioned radio.

'I know your tricks now, mister policeman, I'm taking precautions. You're in there and I'm out here. I've put a speaker under the door. That's how you can hear me. But if you yell, nobody will hear you, so don't even bother. No one ever comes this way. The door's ten centimetres thick and the walls are like a fortress. It's a real bunker.'

Zerk gave a short expressionless laugh.

'And you know why? Because you're in a tomb, scumbag. In the best sealed tomb in all Kisilova. Nobody ever gets out. I'll tell you where you are because you can't see it, so you can imagine it before you die. You've got four coffins stacked up on one side and five on the other. Nine dead bodies. Nice, huh? And the one to your right, if you were to open it, I don't think you'd find a skeleton. No, perhaps a nice fresh body bursting with juices. She's called Vesna and she's a man-eater. Maybe she'd take a fancy to you.'

Another laugh.

Adamsberg closed his eyes. Zerk. But where had he been hiding these last two days? In the woods, in one of the old woodcutter's cabins perhaps. But what did that matter now? Zerk must have followed him; now he'd found him and it was all over. Unable to move an inch, Adamsberg could already feel his muscles seizing up and the cold penetrating his body. Zerk was right, nobody would come into the old cemetery, absolutely not. The place had been abandoned after the panic of 1725, as Arandjel had explained. People didn't dare go there, not even to prop up their ancestors' tombstones when they fell over. And that's where he was, eight hundred metres outside the village, in the vault where Plogojowitz's nine victims had been entombed, built far away from the other graves, and which nobody would go near. Except Arandjel. But what would Arandjel know about his situation? Nothing. Vladislav? Nothing. Danica might start to worry when he didn't return to the *kruchema*. He had missed the evening meal, *kobasice* she had promised. But what could Danica do? Go and find Vladislav. Who might go and find Arandjel. But what then? Where would they think of looking? Along the banks of the Danube for instance. But who would ever imagine that a dark-intentioned Zerk had tied him up and locked him in a vault in the old cemetery? Arandjel might just think of it as a last resort. But only in a week or ten days. Perhaps he might even have been able to survive that long without food or drink. But Zerk was no fool. Tied up in the cold vault, his blood would congeal in his limbs: he could already feel himself getting numb. He wouldn't last two days. Maybe not even until tomorrow. *Don't go into the world of the vampiri without knowing what you're doing, young man.* With a strength of feeling prompted by deep fear, how he missed it all now. The lime tree, the Carpathians, the sun glinting off the little glass of *rakija*.

'Tomorrow, you'll be dead, scumbag. Just to cheer you up, I went back to your place and I killed that kitten. Just one kick did it. Her blood went all over the place. Making me rescue her, huh, that got up my nose. Now you don't owe me anything. And I got some of your fucking DNA out of your house. So I'll have proof now. Everyone will know that Adamsberg abandoned his kid, and how the kid turned out. Because of you. You. You. And your name will be cursed for generations to come.'

The fathers have eaten sour grapes and the children's teeth are set on edge. Adamsberg was having difficulty breathing. Zerk had wound the tape very tightly round his chest. *Tomorrow you'll be dead, scumbag.* With his limbs unable to move and his lungs constricted, he soon wouldn't be getting much oxygen in the blood. It wouldn't take long. Why did the image of the little kitten being kicked to bits under Zerk's boot give him so much pain? When he was going to die in a few hours anyway. Why was he thinking about the *kobasice*, when he didn't even know what *kobasice* looked like?

Kobasice reminded him of Danica, who reminded him of Vlad and his hair like a cat, who reminded him of

Danglard, and Danglard made him think of Tom and Camille, unsuspectingly enjoying themselves in Normandy, and that made him think of Weill and Emma Carnot, with whom he had certainly never slept. And Gisèle? No, never a girl called Gisèle either. So why at this moment could he not keep his mind on anything, concentrate on a single tragic thought?

The voice spoke again. 'I'll give you one thing,' it said with a tinge of regret. 'I admit you got a long way. You got the point. So I'd keep your head and leave the rest of your body. Anyway, scumbag, I'm going to abandon you now, like you abandoned me.'

Zerk pulled on the wire and the little speaker must have slipped back under the door. The last sound Adamsberg heard. Except for the agonising tinnitus in his ear, which had almost disappeared before, he realised. Unless what he was hearing was the cold breath of the rosy-skinned woman sleeping on the lower shelf, on his right. He caught himself wishing that Vesna the vampire would come out of her coffin and suck his blood, to give him eternal life. Or just to keep him company. But no, nothing doing. Even in the tomb, he believed in nothing. Without his being able to control it, his body went into a spasm of shivering for a few seconds. Several convulsive shudders, the start of the organic breakdown, in all probability. His frantic thoughts went to the doctor with golden fingers and his fuse F3. Could Dr Josselin's treatment help him to resist a little longer than other people? Now that his fuse and parietal bone had been cured? But another shudder froze his blood under the wrappings. No. Not a chance.

What should you think about when you are about to die?

Some lines of poetry came into his mind, although he had never been able to learn any. It was like that word *kobasice* that he had remembered. If he were able to survive till the next day, perhaps he would wake up speaking English, and remembering things, like normal people.

In the night of the tomb, Thou who . . .

One of those lines Danglard muttered to himself, along with thousands of others. But he couldn't remember the rest.

In the night of the tomb . . .

Already he couldn't feel his feet. He would die there like a *vampir*, his mouth sealed and his feet pinioned. That way they can never get out. But Peter Plogojowitz had. He had sped away like a flame from the ashes of his remains. And he had taken possession of Higg-gate, and the wife of that Dante somebody, and the schoolgirls. He had gone on oppressing the vampirised family of the Serbian soldier. A vengeful family, from which that madman Zerk must surely be descended, but he could no longer send a text to Danglard to find out. That bastard Weill had made him switch off the GPS. Why?

In the night of the tomb, Thou who consolest me.

Yes, that was it, the end of the line. He was taking short breaths now, with more difficulty than before. The asphyxia was happening faster than he had thought. Zerk was obviously an expert. But what did 'before' mean? It must be about an hour since Zerk had left the graveyard. He couldn't hear the church clock striking. Too far from the village. And he couldn't see either of his watches. So they couldn't even tell him Lucio's pissing timetable.

In the night of the tomb, Thou who consolest me.

There was more to this poem, something to do with 'the

sighs of the saint' and 'the cries of the siren'. Yes, like Vesna. One breath, then another breath. His own.

Arnold Paole! Yes, that was the name of the soldier over-come by Peter Plogojowitz. He would never forget it now.

XXXVI

Danica came into Vladislav's bedroom without knocking, switched on his bedside lamp and shook him awake.

'He hasn't come in. It's three in the morning.'

Vlad lifted his head and let it fall back on the pillow.

'He's a cop, Danica,' he muttered, without thinking. 'They don't do things like everyone else.'

'A cop!' said Danica, shocked. 'But you said he was a friend of yours who'd had a breakdown.'

'A psycho-emotional episode. Sorry, Danica, it slipped out. But he is a cop. One who's had a psycho-emotional episode.'

Danica folded her arms, looking both worried and offended, revisiting the previous night, which she now learned she had spent in the embrace of a policeman.

'So what's he up to here? Does he suspect someone in Kiseljevo?'

'He's searching for traces of a Frenchman.'

'Who?'

'Pierre Vaudel.'

'Why?'

'Someone might have known him here a long time ago. Let me go back to sleep, Danica.'

'Pierre Vaudel? Never heard of him,' said Danica, biting her thumbnail. 'But I don't remember all the tourists who come here. Have to look in the register. When was this? Before the war?'

'Oh, long before, I think. Danica, it's three in the morning, so just what are you doing in my room?'

'I said. He isn't in yet.'

'And I gave you an answer.'

'It's not normal.'

'With a cop, nothing's normal, you should know that.'

'He hasn't any business being out at night, even if he is a cop. Anyway, Vlad, you shouldn't say "cop", you should say "police officer". You haven't turned into a polite young man. But then your dedo wasn't either.'

'Leave my dedo out of it, Danica. And don't start lecturing me about good behaviour. You haven't exactly gone by the book yourself.'

'What's that supposed to mean?'

Vlad made an effort and sat up in bed. 'Forget it. Are you really worried?'

'Yes. Was it dangerous, what he came here for?'

'I don't know, Danica, I'm tired. I don't know anything about the case, and I don't care, my job's just to translate. All I know is, there was this murder somewhere near Paris, a nasty one. And another before that in Austria.'

'If there are murders involved,' said Danica, attacking her nail more viciously, 'then that means it is dangerous.'

'I know he thought he was being followed in the train. But

all cops are like that, aren't they? They don't look at people the way we do. Maybe he went back to see Arandjel. I think they had plenty of stories to tell each other.'

'Vladislav, you're such an idiot. How is he supposed to talk to Arandjel? In sign language? Arandjel speaks English but not French. And *he* speaks French but not English, that's for sure.'

'How do you know?'

'There are some things one just knows,' said Danica, in some embarrassment.

'Right,' said Vlad. 'So let me go back to sleep now.'

'Look, the police,' Danica went on, by now chewing angrily at both thumbs, 'if they start finding out the truth, the murderer will kill them, won't he? Eh, Vladislav?'

'If you want my opinion, he's getting further from the truth with every step.'

'Why do you say that?' asked Danica, letting go of her thumbs, by now glistening with saliva.

'If you go on biting your nails you'll end up eating a whole finger. Then you'll wonder where it's gone.'

Danica shook her mass of blonde hair impatiently and carried on chewing.

'Why are you so sure he's getting further from the truth?'

Vlad laughed quietly, sat up and put his hands on the landlady's plump shoulders.

'Because he thinks the Frenchman and the Austrian who were murdered were from the Plogojowitz family.'

'And you think that's funny?' exclaimed Danica, starting up. 'Funny?'

'Well, anyone would think that was funny, Danica, including the cops he works with in Paris.'

'Vladislav Moldovan, you've not got the sense you were born with, just like your Dedo Slavko.'

'So you're just like all the others, are you? *Ti to verujé?* You won't go near the place of uncertainty? You won't go and visit the tomb of poor old Peter?'

Danica put her hand over his mouth.

'Be quiet for the Lord's sake, Vlad. What are you trying to do? Attract him here? It's not just that you've got no manners but you're stupid and presumptuous. And you're a lot of things old Slavko wasn't. Selfish, lazy and a coward. If Slavko was here, he'd go looking for your friend.'

'What, at this time of night?'

'And you'd let a woman go off on her own, in the dark, to look, would you?'

'Danica, it's dark, we can't see a thing. Wake me in three hours' time, then it'll be getting light.'

By six in the morning, Danica had augmented the search party with the inn's cook, Boško, and his son, Vukasin.

'He knows the paths round here,' she explained. 'He had gone for a walk.'

'Could have fallen in the river,' said Boško, gloomily.

'You go to the river,' said Danica, 'and Vladislav and I will take the woods.'

'What about his mobile?' wondered Vukasin. 'Does Vladislav have the number?'

'I tried,' said Vlad, who still seemed to think it was a big joke. 'And Danica kept on trying between three and five. Either he's out of range or his battery's dead.'

'Or it's in the river,' said Boško. 'There's a dangerous bit of the path by the big rock a stranger might not know about. The planking isn't safe. But tourists don't think.'

'What about the place of uncertainty?' asked Vlad. 'No one going there then?'

'Just keep your jokes to yourself, young man,' said Boško. And for once the young man did shut up.

Danica didn't know what to think. It was 10 a.m. now, and she was serving breakfast to the three men. She had to admit they might be right. They had found not a trace of Adamsberg. No sounds or cries had been heard. But the floor of the old mill had been trodden on – that seemed clear because the carpet of bird droppings had been disturbed. Then there were traces leading through the grass to the road, where tyre marks were clearly visible on the muddy ground.

'You'd better relax, Danica,' said Boško gently. He was a towering figure, his bald head balanced by a bushy grey beard. 'He's a policeman. He's seen a thing or two and I expect he knows what he's doing. He must have asked for a car and gone off to Beograd to see our *policajci*. You can bet on it.'

'Just like that, without saying goodbye? He didn't even call on Arandjel.'

'That's how they are, the *policajci*,' Vukasin assured her.

'Not like us,' said Boško.

'Plog,' said Vlad, who was beginning to feel sorry for the good-hearted Danica.

'Perhaps something urgent came up. He must have had to go off in a hurry.'

'I could call Adrianus,' Vlad suggested. 'If Adamsberg has gone to see the Beograd cops, he's sure to know about it.'

But no, Adrien Danglard had had no news of Adamsberg. More worrying still, Weill had been due to speak with him by phone at nine, but his mobile wasn't answering.

'No, his battery can't have run down,' Weill insisted to Danglard. 'He didn't have it on, it was a special phone just used between the two of us, and we'd only spoken once, yesterday.'

'Well, he's unreachable and unfindable,' Danglard concluded.

'Since when?'

'Since he left Kisilova to go for a walk, at about five yesterday afternoon.'

'Alone?'

'Yes. I called the police in Belgrade, Novi Sad and Banja Luka. He hasn't been in touch with any police force in the country. And they checked the local taxis – nobody has picked up a customer in Kisilova.'

When Danglard put the phone down, he was trembling and sweat was trickling down his back. He had spoken reassuringly to Vladislav, telling him that, with Adamsberg, an unexpected disappearance was not abnormal. But that wasn't true. Adamsberg had now been missing for seventeen hours, overnight. He hadn't left Kisilova, or he would have let someone know. Danglard opened the drawer of his desk and took out an unopened bottle of red wine. A good Bordeaux, high pH factor, low acidity. He made a face, put the bottle back crossly, and went down the spiral staircase to the basement. There was one last bottle of white, still tucked away behind the boiler. He opened it like a beginner, breaking the cork. He sat down on the familiar tea chest which he used as a seat and swallowed a few mouthfuls. Why, by all the saints, had the *commissaire* left his GPS behind in Paris? The signal was unmoving, coming from his house. In the cool cellar, smelling of damp and drains, Danglard felt he was losing Adamsberg. He should have gone to Kisilova with him, he knew it, and he'd said so.

'What are you up to?' came Retancourt's throaty voice.

'Don't put the bloody light on,' snapped Danglard. 'Leave me in the dark.'

'What's going on?'

'No news from him now, for seventeen hours. Vanished. And if you want my opinion, dead. The *Zerquetscher* has got him in Kiseljevo.'

'What's Kiseljevo?'

'The mouth of the tunnel.'

Danglard pointed to another tea chest as if he were inviting her to take a seat in his salon.

XXXVII

His entire body was now swathed in a shroud of cold and numbness, but his head was still working after a fashion. Hours must have passed, six perhaps. He could still feel the back of his head when he had the strength to move it against the ground. Try to keep the brain warm, try to keep the eyes working, by opening and shutting them. These were the last muscles he could still exercise. And he could slightly move his lips under the tape which had become a little looser with saliva. But why bother? What use were still-seeing eyes attached to a corpse? His ears could still hear. But there was nothing to hear, except the wretched mosquito buzz of his tinnitus. Dinh, now, he could waggle his ears but Adamsberg had never been able to. He felt that his ears would be the last bit of him left alive. They could flap about in this tomb like an ugly butterfly, nowhere near as pretty as that cloud of butterflies that had fluttered around his head until the doorway of the old mill. They hadn't wanted to go in – he should have stopped to think and followed their lead. One should always follow butterflies. His ears picked up a sound from the direction of the door. It was opening. He was coming back! Anxious to see if the job had been properly done. If not, he'd finish it off in his own way, axe, saw, stone. He was the nervous type, he would worry; Zerk's hands were always in motion, clenching and unclenching.

The door opened. Adamsberg shut his eyes to protect them from the shock of the light. Zerk closed the door very cautiously, taking his time, and then took out a torch to examine him. Adamsberg sensed the light playing across his eyelids. The man knelt down and pulled the tape roughly from his mouth. Then he felt his body, touching the tape wound round it. He was breathing heavily now, and feeling inside a bag. Adamsberg opened his eyes and looked at him.

It wasn't Zerk. His hair wasn't the same. Short and very thick with red tufts that showed up in the torchlight. Adamsberg knew only one man in the world with hair like that, dark brown but with auburn stripes, where he had been attacked with a knife when he was a child. Veyrenc. Louis Veyrenc de Bilhc. And Veyrenc had left the squad, after a long battle with Adamsberg. He had been gone for months, back to his village of Laubazac. He was paddling his feet in the streams of the Béarn, and not a word had been heard from him.

The man had taken out a knife and was now attacking the covering of tape that was compressing Adamsberg's chest. The knife did not cut well and progress was slow, so the man was swearing and muttering. Not like the way Zerk muttered. Yes, it was indeed Veyrenc, now sitting astride him and tearing away at the tape. Veyrenc was trying to rescue him, Veyrenc was in the tomb in Kisilova. Inside Adamsberg's head, a great bubble of gratitude formed towards this boy whom he had known from childhood, his enemy of yesterday, Veyrenc, *In the night of the tomb, Thou who consolest me.* Almost a bubble of passion: Veyrenc, the man who spoke in verse, the colossus with tender lips, the pain in the neck, the one and only. He tried to move his own lips and say his name.

'Shut up,' said Veyrenc.

The man from Béarn had managed to make an opening in the shell of duct tape, and was pulling at it with abandon, tearing out hairs from Adamsberg's chest and arms.

'Don't try to talk, don't make a sound. If it hurts that's good, it means you can still feel something, but don't cry out. Can you feel any bit of your body?'

Nothing, Adamsberg managed to mouth slightly moving his head.

'Oh God, can't you speak?'

No, Adamsberg managed the same way. Veyrenc was now working on the lower end of his mummified body, and gradually freeing his legs and feet. Then he impatiently chucked the mass of tape behind him and began slapping Adamsberg all over his body like a drummer embarking on a frantic improvisation. After about five minutes of this, he paused and stretched his arms to loosen them. Under his well-padded body, with its round contours, Veyrenc was actually very strong and Adamsberg could hear, without really feeling them, the slapping of his hands. Then Veyrenc changed his approach: he took hold of Adamsberg's arms, bending and unbending them, did the same with his legs, then slapped him all over again, massaged his scalp and started back on the feet. Adamsberg moved his gelid lips with the feeling that he might begin to utter a few words.

Veyrenc cursed himself for not bringing any alcohol. Why hadn't he thought of that? He felt without much hope in

Adamsberg's trouser pocket, and brought out two mobile phones and a mass of useless bus tickets. He picked up the shreds that remained of the jacket on the floor and felt in those pockets too: keys, contraceptives, ID card; then his fingers found some small bottles. Adamsberg had three miniature shots of brandy on him.

'Froiss-y,' Adamsberg whispered. Veyrenc didn't seem to understand, as he put his ear to his lips.

'Froi-ssy.'

Veyrenc had not known Froissy for long, but he got the message. Good old Froissy, what a woman, the goddess of plenty. He opened the first bottle, raised Adamsberg's head and poured it in.

'Can you swallow?'

'Yes.'

Veyrenc poured in the rest of the bottle, unscrewed a second and put it to Adamsberg's mouth, like an alchemist pouring a miracle cure into a large container. He emptied all three bottles and looked at Adamsberg.

'Feel anything?'

'In-side.'

'Good.'

Veyrenc felt in his rucksack and pulled out his stiff hairbrush, carried because no comb would ever get through his thick hair. He rolled it in a strip of the torn shirt, and rubbed it over Adamsberg's skin, as if he were curry-combing a horse.

'That hurt?'

'Just star-ting.'

For another half-hour, Veyrenc went on with his massaging, bending of limbs and curry-combing, asking all the time, which bit of him was coming back to life? Calves, hands, neck? The brandy had warmed his throat, and speech was returning.

'I'm going to try and stand you up in a minute. You'll never get your feet back otherwise.'

Bracing himself against a tomb, the solidly built Veyrenc pulled him upright with ease, and set him on his feet.

'Can't – feel – the ground.'

'Stay standing, so the blood goes down to your feet.'

'Not feet – horse's hooves.'

As he helped Adamsberg to stay upright, Veyrenc flashed the torch around the vault for the first time.

'How many corpses are there in here?'

'Nine. One – undead. Vesna. Vampire. But – if you're here – you must – know that.'

'Me, I don't know anything. No idea even who put you in this fucking tomb.'

'Zerk.'

'Never heard of him. Five days ago I was still in Laubazac. Keep the blood circulating.'

'How – did you – get – here? Flew off – the mountain?'

'Something like that. How are the hooves?'

'One's – coming – back. Think I can walk – a bit.'

'You got a gun anywhere in this place?'

'*Kruchema*. Inn. You?'

'No, don't have my service revolver any more. We're going to need some reinforcements to get out of here. That guy came back four times in the night to check and listen at the door. I had to wait for him to go away for good, and I waited some more to be sure he wasn't coming back again.'

'Who will come out with us then? Ves-na?'

'There's light showing under the door, a gap of about half

a centimetre. Should be able to get a signal. Stay here, I'm leaving you.'

'Only – one foot. Bit – tipsy – brandy.'

'You should be blessing that brandy.'

'Oh – I am. Bless – you too.'

'Don't be in a hurry to bless me, you might regret it.'

Veyrenc lay down on the floor, pushed his phone against the door and checked it with the torch.

'Yeah, I think I'm getting a signal. Have you got someone's number in the village?'

'Vlad-is-lav. On my – mobile. Speaks French.'

'Good. What's this place we're in called?'

'Tomb of the – victims. Of Plog-o-jo-witz.'

'Charming,' said Veyrenc, tapping in the number. 'A serial killer or what?'

'Chief vam-pire.'

'Your pal isn't answering.'

'Keep – trying. What – time is it?'

'Nearly ten.'

'May – be – still – a bit high. Try – again.'

'You trust him?'

One hand holding on to a tomb, Adamsberg was standing on one leg like a suspicious bird.

'Yeah,' he said in the end. 'I – dunno. He laughs – a lot.'

XXXVIII

ADAMSBERG DROPPED HIS HEAD AS HE CAME OUT INTO THE sunlight, leaning on Veyrenc's shoulder. As they emerged from the vault, Danica, Boško, Vukasin and Vlad watched, the first three dumbstruck with terror, and having crossed their fingers against any evil exhalations that might have accompanied the two men out. Danica was staring petrified at Adamsberg, seeing the green shadows under his eyes, the blue lips, pallid cheeks and the naked torso striped with red marks from the tape and bleeding in places from the hairbrush.

'Come on,' cried Vlad angrily, 'just because they've been in there, they're not the living dead. Help them, for God's sake!'

'No manners, you have,' muttered Danica mechanically.

As she gradually saw signs of life in Adamsberg, she got her breath back. But who was the stranger, and what was he doing in the cursed tomb?

Veyrenc's striped hair seemed to worry her even more than Adamsberg's deathly aspect. Boško moved forward cautiously and took the *commissaire*'s other arm.

'Jack-et,' said Adamsberg, pointing to the door.

'OK, I'll get it,' said Vladislav.

'Vlad!' shouted Boško, as Vlad made to move. 'No son of the village goes in there. Send the foreigner.'

It was such a peremptory order that Vlad stopped in his tracks and explained the situation to Veyrenc. Veyrenc left Adamsberg to Boško and went back down the steps.

'He'll never get out alive,' predicted Danica in her direst tones.

'Why is his hair like that, all stripy like a wild boar?' asked Vukasin.

Veyrenc was out in two minutes, carrying the torch and what remained of the tattered jacket and shirt. He pushed the door closed with his foot.

'We ought to lock it,' said Vukasin.

'Arandjel's the only person with a key,' said Boško.

In the following silence, Vlad translated the exchange between father and son.

'The key'll be no use,' said Veyrenc. 'I broke the lock when I picked it.'

'I'll come back and block it up with rocks,' muttered Boško. 'I don't know how this man spent a night there without getting eaten alive by Vesna.'

'Boško is wondering if Vesna touched you,' Vlad explained. 'Some people think she comes out of her coffin, but others think she's just munching and sighing in the night to frighten the living.'

'Maybe – she sighed,' said Adamsberg. 'The sighs – of the – saint and the – cries of the siren. She didn't – wish me – harm, Vlad.'

* * *

Danica brought out some bowls and filled them with fritters.

'If his foot doesn't wake up, it will get gangrene and have to be cut off,' said Boško bluntly. 'Light the fire, Danica, and get him to warm it up. And some hot coffee with *rakija*. And for heaven's sake let's get a shirt on his back.'

They moved Adamsberg's foot closer to the fire, and brought him coffee laced with *rakija*. His brush with death had put unprecedented thoughts into Adamsberg's head, which did not in any way lessen his warm feeling for this little village lost in the mists of the Danube. On the contrary, he was ready to leave his own country, leave his beloved mountains even, leave for good, and end up here in the mists, if perhaps Veyrenc would stay too, and a few other people: Danglard, Tom, Camille, Lucio and Retancourt. The fat office cat would have to be transported to Kisilova, along with the photocopiers. And Émile too – why not? But the thought of the *Zerquetscher* propelled him back into the centre of Paris, Zerk in his grisly death's head T-shirt, and all the blood in the villa at Garches. Danica was rubbing his numb foot with alcohol in which she had been steeping herbs, and he wondered quite what she was expecting to happen. He hoped that her affectionate gestures were going unnoticed.

'Where were you, you idiot?' came the grumbling voice of Weill into the private mobile, his normal cynicism perceptibly tinged with relief.

'Locked in a vault with eight corpses and one living-dead vampire called Vesna.'

'Are you injured?'

'No, but I was trussed up in tape almost to the point of asphyxiation.'

'Who by?'

'Zerk.'

'And they found you?'

'Veyrenc found me. Veyrenc got into the vault.'

'Veyrenc? The guy built like a barrel who's always spouting verse?'

'The same.'

'I thought he'd left the squad.'

'You're right, he did, but it was him in the vault. Don't ask me how, Weill. I've no idea.'

'Well, I'm glad you're still in one piece, *commissaire*.'

'Not quite, one foot is still not working.'

'OK,' said Weill, embarrassed and unable to express any comforting emotion directly. 'Now, I've been getting close to the vice-president. There *was* a marriage, twenty-nine years ago.'

'And the husband's name is?'

'That I don't have yet. I've placed an ad in the papers. One of the witnesses to the wedding, a woman, was murdered in Nantes a week ago, two bullets to the head. Her daughter replied to my ad. I'm looking for the other.'

Nantes. Adamsberg remembered he had been thinking about Nantes recently. But when? And why?

'Any children?'

'Don't know. But if there was one, she'd have given it up for adoption.'

'You need to look for the child, Weill.'

Adamsberg closed the phone and pointed to his foot. 'I can feel something like pins and needles in it,' he said.

'Praise be,' said Danica, crossing herself.

'We'll be getting along,' said Boško, who was followed at once by Vukasin. 'Can you manage for lunch today?'

'Yes, go and get some rest, Boško. I'm going to put him to bed too.'

'Put a hot-water bottle on his foot.'

While Adamsberg was dropping off to sleep under his blue eiderdown, they got another room ready for the stranger with the stripy hair, whose smile Danica found entrancing. His lip went up on one side, making his face very seductive. His long eyelashes cast a shadow on his round cheeks. Nothing like the mobile and tense features of Adamsberg. The newcomer was making no particular effort to please. But he had the mark of the devil in his hair and everyone knows that the devil can take on the appearance of an enchanter.

XXXIX

Veyrenc allowed the *commissaire* two hours' sleep, then he walked into his room and drew back the curtains, bringing two chairs from the hearth, where Danica had lit a blazing fire. The temperature in the room was stifling, enough to make a corpse perspire, which was Danica's aim.

'How's the hoof now? Are you going to end up a centaur or will you stay human?'

Adamsberg moved his foot and tried wiggling his toes.

'Human,' he said.

> '*He rose into the heavens, floating up to the sky*
> *Yet he was but a man and the dream flew too high*
> *Now a mortal at last, he must fall to the earth.*
> *Alas we know not what illusions are worth.*'

'I thought you'd kicked that habit.'

> '*Many months did I try, and my hopes were in vain*
> *And my demons of old have me captured again.*'

'Always the way. Danglard says he's giving up white wine.'

'You're kidding.'

'He's switching to red.'

There was a silence. Veyrenc knew that this light tone couldn't last and Adamsberg sensed it. A simple handshake before tackling a difficult climb.

'Ask your questions,' said Veyrenc, 'and if I don't want any more of them, I'll say so.'

'All right. Why did you come down from your mountain? To join up again?'

'One question at a time.'

'To join up?'

'No.'

'So why did you come down from your mountain?'

'Because I read the papers. An article on the massacre in Garches.'

'Were you interested in the investigation?'

'Yes. That's why I followed the headway you were making on it.'

'Why didn't you just come back to the squad?'

'I was more interested in keeping a watch on you than in saying hello.'

'You always did put the knife in subtly, Veyrenc. What were you keeping a watch on?'

'Your investigation, your actions, who you met, the direction you were taking.'

'But why?'

Veyrenc made a gesture indicating: next question.

'And you really followed me?'

'I was here when you got to Belgrade with that young man covered in hair.'

'Vladislav, the translator. It's fur really, he inherited it from his mother.'

'So he said. One of my friends was assigned to eavesdrop on you on the train.'

'The elegant woman, wealthy-looking. Nice body, pity about the face, was what Vlad said.'

'She isn't actually wealthy. She was acting a part.'

'Well, tell her to try a bit harder, because I spotted her before we left Paris. But when we got to Belgrade, how did you know where I was going? She wasn't on the bus.'

'Called a colleague in the Overseas Missions Department, who told me where you were going. An hour after you'd reserved your tickets, I knew your final destination was Kiseljevo.'

'You can't trust cops further than you can throw them.'

'No, as you well know.'

Adamsberg folded his arms, and dropped his head. The white shirt Danica had found for him was embroidered around the collar and on the cuffs and he stared at the shiny lace patterns the yellow and red threads made on his wrists. Perhaps that was what Slavko's slippers had looked like.

'Was it by any chance Mordent who passed on the information? And asked you to follow me?'

'Mordent? Why would it be Mordent?'

'You don't know? He's off work with depression.'

'What's that got to do with it?'

'What it's to do with, is his daughter: she's due in court. What it's to do with, is the hierarchy that doesn't want us to catch the killer. And has somehow corrupted the squad. They've got their hooks into Mordent. Every man has his price.'

'Where would you rate mine?'

'Pretty high, I'd think.'

'Thanks very much.'

'Whereas Mordent's treachery is utterly cack-handed.'

'Doesn't have a vocation for it, I expect.'

'Still, he gets there in the end. A little cartridge case planted under the fridge, some pencil shavings on the carpet.'

'No idea what you're talking about. I don't know any details about the case. Was that why you let the suspect go? You were under pressure to?'

'Do you mean Émile?'

'No, the other one.'

'I didn't let Zerk go,' said Adamsberg firmly.

'Who's Zerk?'

'The Crusher, the *Zerquetscher*. The man who killed Vaudel and Plögener.'

'And who's Plögener?'

'The Austrian who suffered the same fate five months ago. I see you don't know anything about all this. And yet it was you that opened the vault in Kisilova.'

Veyrenc smiled. 'You'll never really trust me, will you?'

'If I can get to understand you, I might.'

'I flew to Belgrade, then I took a taxi and got to Kisilova before you.'

'How come you weren't spotted in the village?'

'I slept in a hut in the clearing. I saw you go past the first day.'

'When I found Peter Plogojowitz.'

'Who *is* he?'

And Veyrenc's ignorance seemed genuine.

'Look, Veyrenc,' said Adamsberg standing up, 'if you don't

know who Peter Plogojowitz was, you really have no business here. Unless – and please tell me why – you somehow thought I was in danger.'

'I didn't come here with any intention of getting you out of the vault. I didn't come with any idea of helping you. On the contrary.'

'That's better,' said Adamsberg. 'Now we're getting warmer, I can understand you better.'

'But I couldn't let you die in that tomb. You do believe me about that?'

'Yes.'

'I thought the danger came from you. I followed you when you went to the mill, I saw the hire car on the road, registered in Belgrade. I thought it was yours. I didn't know where you meant to go, so I got into the boot. But I was wrong. I ended up being driven like you to that blessed graveyard. He had a gun and I didn't. I waited and watched. Like I said, he came back several times to check. I couldn't do anything till quite well into the morning. Almost too late. Another couple of hours and you really would have been a centaur. A stone one.'

Adamsberg sat down again and re-examined the embroidery on his shirt. He didn't want to look at Veyrenc's smile, or allow himself to be enveloped by him as surely as in the rolls of duct tape.

'So you saw Zerk.'

'Yes and no. I didn't get out of the boot until a while after you, and I went some distance away. I could see your outlines, that's all. I could make out his leather jacket and boots.'

'Yes,' said Adamsberg, biting his lips. 'That's Zerk.'

'If by Zerk you mean the Garches murderer, OK, yes, it

was Zerk. If by Zerk you mean the young guy who came to see you at home on Wednesday morning, that wasn't him.'

'Were you there that morning too?'

'Yes.'

'And you didn't do anything? But it was the same man, Veyrenc. Zerk is Zerk.'

'Not necessarily.'

'You're not making any more sense than you were.'

'*Have you changed from the past, is clarity your god?*'

Adamsberg got up, took the packet of Morava from the mantelpiece, and lit a cigarette from the fire.

'You smoke now?'

'Zerk's fault. He left a packet with me. And I'll go on smoking till I get him under lock and key.'

'So why did you let him go?'

'Just don't bug me, Veyrenc, he was armed, I wasn't, I couldn't do anything.'

'No? Couldn't you have called up reinforcements when he'd gone? Surrounded the district? Why didn't you?'

'None of your business.'

'You let him go because you weren't certain he was the Garches murderer.'

'I was absolutely certain he was. You don't know anything about the investigation. So let me tell you, Zerk left his DNA in Garches on a Kleenex. And that was the same DNA that came walking in on two legs to my house on Wednesday, with the clear purpose of killing me, that morning or some other time. And let me tell you that boy is bad through and through. He didn't once deny the murder.'

'He didn't?'

'On the contrary, he was proud of it. And he went back

there just to stamp on a kitten with his boot. And he wears a T-shirt covered with vertebrae and drops of blood.'

'Yes, I know about that, I watched him go.'

Veyrenc took a cigarette from the packet, lit it and paced around the room like an obstinate wild boar. All the sweetness had vanished from his face. Adamsberg observed him. Veyrenc was protecting Zerk. So Veyrenc must be in league with Emma Carnot. Veyrenc must be waiting to push him into a hole, like all those others. But in that case, why rescue him from the vault? To get him eliminated legally?

'Let me tell *you* something, Adamsberg. Thirty years ago, a certain Gisèle Louvois got herself pregnant, down by the little bridge over the Jaussène. You know where I mean. And let me tell you that she went to Pau to hide the pregnancy, and gave birth there to a boy, Armel Louvois.'

'Zerk. Yes, I know all that, Veyrenc.'

'Because he told you.'

'No.'

'Yes, he did. Because he's got it into his head that it was you that made his mother pregnant. He must have talked to you about it when he came. He's thought of nothing else for months.'

'All right, yes, he did. All right, he's got it into his head. Or rather his mother must have put it into his head.'

'And rightly so.'

Veyrenc came back to the fireplace, threw his cigarette into the flames and knelt down to poke the fire. Adamsberg now felt no gratitude at all for his former colleague. He had certainly torn off all that tape, but now he was trying to tie him up all over again.

'Spit it out, Veyrenc.'

'Zerk's right. And his mother's right. The young man down by the bridge was Jean-Baptiste Adamsberg. Without any doubt.'

Veyrenc got up, slight sweat breaking out on his forehead.

'So that makes you the father of Zerk, or Armel if you prefer.'

Adamsberg clenched his teeth.

'Look, Veyrenc, how can you know that, if I don't know it myself?'

'It often happens. Life's like that.'

'Listen, only once have I done something and completely lost any memory of it, and that was in Quebec, when I had had too much to drink. This was thirty years ago you're talking about, and I didn't drink then. What are you suggesting? That not only am I amnesiac, but have the power of being everywhere, and I made love to some girl I have *never* met? In my whole life, I have never slept with or even talked to a girl called Gisèle.'

'I believe you.'

'That's better.'

'She hated her name, she told boys she was called something else. It wasn't Gisèle you went with that night, it was a girl called Marie-Ange. Down by the bridge.'

Adamsberg felt himself pitch down a steep slope. His skin was on fire, and his head was throbbing. Veyrenc went out of the room. Adamsberg dug his fingers into his hair. Yes, of course, he had made love to a girl called Marie-Ange, the girl with the urchin haircut, the girl with slightly buck teeth, by the bridge over the Jaussène, a slight rain falling and the wet grass which had almost put an end to it. And yes, of course, there had been a letter, received some time later, a weird letter

317

of which he couldn't make head nor tail, and that was from her. And yes, of course, Zerk did look like him. So this was what it was like to be in hell. To find you have a son of twenty-nine on your back, and to have that back broken on an anvil. To be the father of the man who had chopped Vaudel into bits, the man who had tied him up in the vault. *Know where you are now, scumbag?* No, he didn't know where he was at all, except that he was inside a skin that was sweating and burning, with his head fallen on his knees, and tears stinging his eyes.

Veyrenc had come back in without saying a word, carrying a tray on which were a bottle and some bread and cheese. He put it down looking at Adamsberg, poured out a couple of glasses and spread the cheese on the bread (*kajmak*, as Adamsberg realised). Head still in hands, he watched. A cheese sandwich, well, why not? The stage he'd reached now.

'I'm really sorry,' said Veyrenc, holding out a glass. He pushed it against Adamsberg's hand, as one tries with a child to get it to unclench its fingers and rescue it from its rage or distress. Adamsberg moved his arm and took the glass.

'Well, he's a good-looking boy,' Veyrenc added pointlessly, as if trying to find a drop of hope in an ocean of calamity.

Adamsberg emptied the glass in a single gulp, an early shot of alcohol, which made him cough. That brought some relief. As long as he could still feel his body, he could at least do something. Which hadn't been the case last night.

'How did *you* know I'd slept with Marie-Ange?'

'She's my sister.'

God almighty. Adamsberg held out the glass, and Veyrenc filled it again.

'Have some bread with it.'

'Can't eat a thing.'

'Try all the same, force yourself. No, I've hardly eaten either, since I saw his picture in the paper. You may be Zerk's father, but I'm his uncle. Not a whole lot better.'

'Why is your sister called Louvois and not Veyrenc?'

'She's my half-sister, from my mother's first marriage. You don't remember Louvois? The coalman who went off with an American woman?'

'No. Why didn't you ever mention this when you were in the squad?'

'Because my sister and the kid didn't want anything to do with you. You weren't popular.'

'But why haven't you been able to eat since seeing the paper? You just said Zerk didn't kill the old man. So you're not really sure?'

'No, not at all.'

Veyrenc put another slice of bread into Adamsberg's hand and both of them sadly and conscientiously swallowed mouthfuls of bread slowly as the fire died down.

XL

ARMED WITH A GUN THIS TIME, ADAMSBERG WENT BACK along the riverbank, then towards the forest, avoiding the place of uncertainty. Danica hadn't wanted to let him go, but the need to walk was more imperative than her anxiety.

'I have to come back to life, Danica. I have to understand.'

So he had accepted an escort, Boško and Vukasin following him at a distance. Now and then, he made a little sign to them, without turning round. This was where he should stay, in Kisilova unravished by the flames of war, with these kind and caring people, and not go back to the cities where he would have to dodge the high-ups, try to escape their clutches, and flee from his hellhound of a son. At every step, his thoughts rose and fell in chaos, as they usually did with him, like fish swimming up to the surface then diving back down, and he didn't try to catch them. This was how he always dealt with the fish swimming round in his brain, he just let them swim anywhere they liked, to the rhythm of his footsteps. Adamsberg had promised Veyrenc he would meet him at the *kruchema* to eat a meal, and after half an hour's walking and looking at the hills, the vineyards and the trees, he felt better prepared. He turned round, smiled at Boško and Vukasin, gesturing 'thank you' and 'let's go back'.

'We'll have to do some thinking now,' said Veyrenc, unfolding his napkin.

'Yes.'

'Or we'll be here till the end of our days.'

'Wait a minute,' said Adamsberg, getting up.

Vlad was sitting down at another table, and Adamsberg explained to him that he needed to have a tête-à-tête with Veyrenc.

'Were you scared?' asked Vlad, who still seemed impressed at having seen Adamsberg emerge from the earth looking grey and red: he called it 'the escape from the vault' as if it was one of his dedo's stories.

'Yes, I was scared, and I was in pain.'

'Did you think you were going to die?'

'Yes.'

'Had you lost all hope?'

'Yes.'

'So what did you think about?'

'*Kobasice.*'

'No, please,' Vlad insisted, 'really, what did you think about?'

'I swear to you that's what I was thinking about: *kobasice.*'

'That's crazy.'

'Yes, I guess so. What are *kobasice* anyway?'

'Sausages. What else did you think about?'

'I was concentrating on breathing one breath at a time. And on a line of poetry – "*In the night of the tomb, Thou who consolest me.*"'

'And did anything console you? The thought of heaven?'

'No heaven.'

'Or some person?'

'No, nothing, Vlad. I was alone.'

'If you were thinking about nothing and nobody,' said Vlad, with an edge of anger, 'you wouldn't have thought of that line. Who or what consoled you?'

'I don't have an answer to that. Why does it bother you?'

The young man with the sunny disposition hung his head, mashing up his food with his fork.

'It bothers me that we looked but we didn't find you.'

'You couldn't have guessed.'

'I didn't believe any of it, I didn't care where you'd gone. It was Danica who forced me to go and look. I should have gone with you when you went out yesterday.'

'I didn't want any company then, Vlad.'

'Arandjel had told me to do it,' he whispered. 'Arandjel had told me not to leave you alone for a minute. Because you had gone into the place of uncertainty.'

'And that made you laugh.'

'Of course. I didn't ask myself any questions. I don't believe in that stuff.'

'Nor do I.'

The young man nodded.

'Plog.'

*   *   *

Danica served the two policemen their meal. Looking anxious, her eyes went from Adamsberg to Veyrenc. Adamsberg guessed that there was a hesitation there, due to the presence of another newcomer. He was not offended, since he had now resolved never to sleep with anyone for the rest of his life.

'Did you think while you were walking?' asked Veyrenc.

Adamsberg looked at him in surprise, as if Veyrenc didn't know him at all, as if he were asking the impossible of him.

'Sorry,' said Veyrenc, gesturing that he took back the question. 'I mean, is there anything you want to say?'

'Yes. Once you had seen Zerk's face in the papers, you started following my every move, to stop me setting hands on him. Just because he's your nephew. So I suppose you're fond of him, you must know him well.'

'Yes.'

'When you heard him talking outside the vault, was that his voice?'

'I was too far away. What about you, when he locked you in, was that his voice?'

'He only spoke to me once the door was shut. And the door was too thick to hear through, even if he had shouted, which he didn't want to do. He slid a little speaker under the door. It altered his voice. But his way of talking was perfectly recognisable: "Know where you are now, scumbag?"'

'Oh, I don't think he would say that,' Veyrenc reacted.

'He damn well did, and you'd better believe it.'

'If someone knew him well, they might have imitated him.'

'Yes, one could imitate him. In fact, you might say he imitates himself, sometimes.'

'There, you see.'

'Veyrenc, have you even a shred of evidence on your side?'

'Well, I smell a rat when a murderer leaves something at a crime scene with his DNA.'

'Yes, me too,' agreed Adamsberg, thinking of the cartridge case under the fridge. 'You mean that convenient little tissue in the garden?'

'Yes.'

'Anything else?'

'Why would Armel only have spoken to you *after* he got you locked inside the vault?'

'So as not to be heard by other people.'

'Or so that you wouldn't hear his voice, because it would be a voice you didn't recognise?'

'Veyrenc, this kid has never denied doing the murder. How are you going to get him out of this mess?'

'By knowing what he's like. I do know him. My sister stayed in Pau after he was born. She couldn't come back to the village with a baby and no father. I was still at school, and I stopped being a boarder and went to lodge with her for seven years. Then I did my teacher training, and started work. And I stayed with them all that time. I know Armel like the back of my hand.'

'And you're going to tell me he's a gentle lad who wouldn't hurt a fly.'

'Why not? From when he was little until now, I've hardly ever seen him fly off the handle. Anger isn't part of his make-up, nor is attacking people or insulting them. He's vague, lazy, undisciplined, and doesn't care much about anything. But it's hard to get him worked up. And I think we can agree that the man who did all that to Vaudel was worked up.'

'It could be lurking under the surface.'

'Adamsberg, the core of this killer's mind is destruction.

Armel doesn't think about destroying things, because he doesn't even think of constructing. Do you know how he lives? He makes home-made jewellery and he sells it to market traders. He has no ambition. He just drifts through life without attaching much importance to anything. So tell me, how does a guy like that work up enough rage and energy to spend hours chopping up Vaudel and Plögener?'

'Well, the young man who came to see me wasn't placid at all – I saw the other side of your nephew. I saw someone who was worked up all right – a brute: rude, insulting, full of hate, and saying he'd come to "fuck up my life". And it was him, wasn't it, that you saw leaving my house? Your Armel?'

'Yes,' said Veyrenc, looking distressed, and not even noticing as Danica changed the plates and brought their dessert.

'*Zavitek*,' she said.

'*Hvala*, Danica. Accept it, Veyrenc. Your Armel is a Zerk in disguise.'

'Or perhaps Zerk is an Armel in disguise?'

'What do you mean?'

'I mean: he could be acting a part.'

'Wait a minute,' said Adamsberg, putting his hand out on Veyrenc's arm to interrupt him. 'A part. Yes, that could be it.'

'Because?'

'First, because he was talking this tough-guy "scumbag" language, and laying it on too thick. And second, because the T-shirt looked brand new. Have you ever seen him kitted out like a goth before?'

'No, never. He dresses any old how, whatever comes to

hand. He doesn't bother to try and look good, or original, or classy. A bit like his idea of himself.'

'How did he react when his father was mentioned?'

'When he was little, he was ashamed, when he was older he just looked down.'

'There could be something there, Veyrenc. Better than this too-convenient handkerchief, and better than your faith in your nephew, and better than the new T-shirt. But it depends if you have the information.'

Veyrenc looked closely at Adamsberg. Whatever his bitterness and suspicion in the past he had always admired his boss, always hoped for something from his elegant leaps of intuition, just when you thought his brain was completely overwhelmed, even if you had to sift through barrels of mud to find a gram of gold.

'In your mother's family, among your ancestors, men and women, is there anyone with a name like Arnold Paole?'

Veyrenc felt disappointment surge through him. Just another barrel of mud.

'P-a-o-l-e,' said Adamsberg, detaching each letter. 'It could have been altered into Paoulet, or made to sound more French like Paul, Paulus, whatever. Or any surname that starts with P or A.'

'Paole. What kind of name is that?'

'Serbian, like Plogojowitz, which has been changed into several forms, into surnames like Plogerstein, Plögener, Plog, Plogodrescu. Not Plogoff – that's a place in Brittany, nothing to do with anything.'

'You mentioned this Plogojowitz before.'

'Don't say that name too loudly in here,' said Adamsberg, looking around the dining room.

'Why not?'

'I already told you. Peter Plogojowitz is a vampire, the greatest of them, and he lives here.'

Adamsberg said this quite naturally, as if he was used to the Kisilova beliefs. Veyrenc's worried face surprised him.

'What is it?' he said. 'Don't you understand we have to talk quietly about him?'

'I don't get what you're doing. You're trying to trace a *vampire*?'

'Not exactly. I'm trying to trace the descendant of a vampire who was the victim of another vampire, down all the line of descent since 1727.'

Veyrenc slowly shook his head.

'I know what I'm doing, Veyrenc. You can ask Arandjel.'

'The man with the key.'

'Yes. The man who stops Plogojowitz escaping from his grave. It's in that clearing at the edge of the wood, not far from the hut you slept in. Maybe you saw it.'

'No,' said Veyrenc firmly, as if he was refusing to believe even in the existence of the grave.

'Forget Plogojowitz,' said Adamsberg, waving away the misunderstanding with his hand. 'But just think about your maternal ancestors, and therefore Zerk's. Do you know who they were?'

'Pretty well. I traced the family tree till I got tired of it.'

'Perfect. Write it on the tablecloth. How far do you go back?'

'To about the 1760s, with about twenty-seven surnames.'

'That should do.'

'It's not that difficult. All the ancestors married people from the next village. If they were really adventurous they moved about six kilometres away. I dare say they all went down to the bridge over the Jaussène to make love.'

'That seems to be the tradition.'

Adamsberg tore the paper tablecloth when Veyrenc had finished his list, which had no trace of any name like Paole.

'Listen carefully, Veyrenc. The killer of Pierre Vaudel-Plog and Conrad Plögener belongs to the line of descent from Arnold Paole, who died in 1727, in a place called Medwegya, not far from here. Zerk isn't descended from any Paole. So there are just two possibilities for your nephew.'

'Stop calling him my nephew. He's your son as well.'

'I don't want to say "my son". I prefer to say "your nephew".'

'Yes, I did gather that.'

'Either your nephew did commit these crimes, because he was being manipulated by this Paole. Or it was Paole himself who was the killer, and planted the convenient little tissue belonging to your nephew. Either way, we need to find this descendant of Arnold Paole.'

Danica put two small glasses on the table.

'Watch out,' said Adamsberg, 'it's *rakija*.'

'So?'

'Try it. I tell you, if I'd had some of this stuff in the vault, I'd never have come close to dying.'

'Ah, Froissy,' said Veyrenc with an air of nostalgia, remembering the three little bottles of cognac. 'But how are we going to find a descendant of Paole?'

'We know one thing about him. It must have been a Paole who has some kind of hold over your nephew, and knows him well enough to imitate him. Think of someone in his circle of people, a substitute father figure, whom he sees often, whom he admires or fears.'

'He's twenty-nine. I don't know everything about his life in Paris.'

'What about his mother?'

'She married this man four years ago. She lives in Poland now.'

'You can't think of anyone who might correspond?'

'No. And it doesn't explain why, if he didn't do the murder, he would have boasted about it to you.'

'Yes, it does,' said Adamsberg. 'By reversing their roles, Armel finds he has been transformed into Zerk, a sort of miraculous change. He's no longer weak but strong, no longer good but bad. If there's a Paole manipulating him, he counted on that. The son will crush the father. That's what Zerk said to me. So Armel gets tipped off by Mordent, he obeys, he runs away, and he discovers what's in the papers. Agreed?'

'Yes.'

'His face is all over the front page, suddenly he's become a personality, a celebrity, an impressive monster. And who is he up against? *Commissaire* Adamsberg. At first he goes into shock. But he soon sees it as a golden opportunity. A new power and it's fallen into his lap. A brilliant way to get his revenge on his father. What does he risk by acting the part of the monster for a day? Nothing. What does he get out of it? A lot. He can lay right into his father, show him his sins, make him feel guilt and responsibility. Does he even think about the handkerchief? No. His DNA at the murder scene? No, to him it's just some mistake, they'll find out soon enough. The proof is that he was tipped off, and told to lie low until things settle down. He hasn't much time. This is a chance to be taken, a stroke of fate, and he'd better make the most of it. So he turns up at his father's place dressed for the part. He talks like a killer, he turns into Zerk, he insults this bastard of an Adamsberg, he's going to demolish him. Look, Adamsberg, your son's a monster, your son's got the upper hand now! And it's all your fault, so now you're going to suffer the way I've suffered. No good shouting and saying you're sorry, it's too late. Then once he's put on his little show, he pushes off, leaving remorse and distress in Adamsberg's head. His father's out of action, he's got his revenge. Your nephew's not as sweet-tempered as all that.'

'Not to you, no.'

'Right. So he's feeling quite pleased with himself. But no correction is published about the DNA found in Garches. He's still a wanted murderer. The little drama goes into reverse. He needs his father now, but he's confessed to the murder, claimed it. So now he's scared stiff, is Armel, and he has to make a getaway. An outcome that any manipulative man with an ounce of sangfroid could have predicted. So who? It must be someone who's known him a while, someone with a hold over him.'

'The choirmaster,' said Veyrenc, banging his glass down on the table. 'Germain. He has a hold over him. I never liked him, nor did my sister, but Armel thinks the sun shines out of him.'

'Tell me about it.'

'Armel's a tenor, he's sung in a choir ever since he was twelve: Notre-Dame de la Croix-Faubin. I often used to take him to choir practice and listen. The choirmaster had his claws into him. That's the kind of man he is.'

'What do you mean?'

'Well, by blowing hot and cold, alternating compliments and criticism, so Armel got to be like putty in his hands. Mind you, he wasn't the only one, Germain had over a dozen of them round him like that. Then he was transferred to Paris and it stopped. No more choir. But when Armel went to Paris as well, it started up again. He sang a solo in a Rossini Mass and got a lot of praise. He loved it. At twenty-six, he was back under Germain's thumb. But a year or two back, Germain was charged with sexual harassment and the choir was dissolved. And like a dope, Armel was broken-hearted.'

'Did he go on seeing him?'

'He swears not, but I suspect he's lying. Maybe the guy asks him round, gets him to sing for him. It's flattering, just like when he was a kid. Armel feels important to the father, whereas it's the father who possesses him.'

'What do you mean "father"?'

'In the religious sense. Father Germain.'

'What's his real name?'

'I don't know, that's what they called him.'

Danglard had left the office, gone home and taken off his elegant suit. Now he was slouching in his vest in front of the television's blank screen, chewing cough drops one after another to keep his jaws occupied. In one hand he held his mobile, in the other his glasses, and checked about every five minutes to see if there was a message. Finally after several hours, 00 381 bleeped. He mopped his face with his handkerchief and deciphered the text message: '*Risen from tomb. Run check Fr Germain choirmaster N-D Croix-Faubin.'*

What tomb for heaven's sake? With sweating hands, Danglard tapped in his reply, his throat tight with rage, but his muscles relaxing with relief. *'Why no message B4?'*

'No sgnl wrong time so slept.'

True, thought Danglard guiltily. He had only come out of the basement when he had been dragged out by Retancourt.

'What tomb?' he texted.

'Vault 9 victims Plogojowitz. V cold. Feet recvrd.'

'Uncle's cousin's feet?'

'Mine. Back tomorrow.'

XLI

ADAMSBERG WAS NOT A MAN WHO WENT IN FOR EMOTION: he skirted around strong feelings with caution, like swifts who only brush past windows with their wings, never going in, because they know it will be difficult to get out. He had often found dead birds in the village houses back home, imprudent visitors who had ventured inside and never again found their way back to the open air. Adamsberg considered that when it came to love, humans were no wiser than birds. And in most other respects birds were a lot more canny. Like those butterflies that had refused to go into the mill.

But his stay in the vault must have dealt him a blow, sending his emotional responses into turmoil, so that leaving Kisilova tugged at his heartstrings. Kisilova, the only place where he had been able to memorise new unpronounceable words, which was something rare for him.

Danica had washed and ironed the beautiful white embroidered shirt for him to take back to Paris. Everyone had lined up in front of the *kruchema* to say goodbye, standing stiffly to attention and smiling. Danica, Arandjel, the woman with the cart and her children, the regulars from the hotel, Vukasin,

Boško and his wife, who hadn't let him leave her side since the day before, plus a few unknown faces. Vlad was going to stay on a few days. He had carefully combed his dark hair and tied up his ponytail. Ordinarily incapable of showing affection, Adamsberg hugged them each in turn, saying that he would be back – *vratiću se* – that they were all his friends – *prijatelji*. Danica's sadness was diluted a little, in that she now didn't know which one she would miss most, the dancer or the enchanter. Vlad said a final 'plog', and Adamsberg and Veyrenc made their way to the bus which would take them to Belgrade. Their flight would see them in Paris by mid-afternoon. Vladislav had written out a sheet of phrases they would need at the airport. As they went down the path carrying a bag of provisions from Danica which would easily last them two days, Veyrenc muttered:

'He must now leave this place and its sweet fragrant air.
He leaves broken-hearted, lamenting his fate.
And his son, whom he found, but already too late.'

'You know, Mercadet says that you don't observe all the rules for alexandrines properly – you don't always have exactly twelve syllables for instance.'

'He's right.'

'Something's wrong, Veyrenc.'

'Yes, I know, that second line doesn't scan.'

'No, I'm talking about the dog hairs. Your nephew had this dog, and it died a few weeks before the Garches murder.'

'Tintin, a stray he'd taken in. His fourth. That's what abandoned kids do, they rescue stray dogs. So what's the problem about its hairs?'

'They compared them with Tintin's hairs from his flat, and they were the same.'

'The same as what?'

The bus started its engine.

'In the room where the Vaudel murder took place, the killer sat on this velvet armchair. A Louis XIII armchair.'

'Why does it matter that it was Louis XIII?'

'Because Mordent was keen on it, never mind what he's been up to since. And the killer sat on it.'

'To get his breath back, I suppose.'

'Yes. He had some horse manure on his boots, and there were a few traces of that too.'

'How many bits?'

'Four.'

'See, Armel isn't keen on horses. Had a fall when he was little. He really isn't a get-up-and-go sort of person at all.'

'But does he ever go to the country?'

'Well, he goes back to the village every couple of months to see his grandparents.'

'There could be horses on some of the paths out there,' said Adamsberg with a frown. 'And he wears boots.'

'Yes.'

'To go out for walks?'

'Yes.'

They both looked out of the window for a minute, saying nothing.

'These hairs you were talking about, then.'

'The killer left some on the chair. Velvet – they stick to that. So he could just have had them on the seat of his trousers, from the flat. If we imagine that someone planted the handkerchief, we'd also have to suppose that the dog hairs were planted too.'

'I see,' said Veyrenc dully.

'It's not that easy even to get someone's handkerchief, but how do you get the hairs of his dog? By picking them up off the floor of his apartment one by one, while Zerk watches you?'

'No, by going in when he's out.'

'We checked. There's a door code, and an entryphone. So it suggests whoever it was must have known him well enough to know at least the code. OK. But then you have to get through the house door, then Zerk's front door. No locks were forced. Worse, our friend Weill and the neighbour opposite both say Zerk didn't have any visitors. He doesn't have a girlfriend?'

'Not since last year. You talking about Weill who used to be at headquarters?'

'Yes.'

'He's involved is he?'

'He lives in the same building as your nephew. They get on quite well. Perhaps Zerk liked to hobnob with cops.'

'No, no. It was me, through Weill, that *got* him the flat when he went to live in Paris. But I didn't know they actually met socially.'

'Well, they do. And Weill seems to be fond of him. At any rate, he's defending him.'

'Was it him that called you yesterday when you were still getting your foot back to life. On your other phone?'

'Yes, he's been involved from the start. He says he's keeping tabs on the hierarchy. He gave me that phone and made me take out my GPS when I left,' Adamsberg said after a moment.

'Pity he did that.'

'Plog,' said Adamsberg.

'What does "plog" mean?'

'It's a word Vlad uses, but it can mean different things in context. It can mean "yes", "precisely", "I understand", or sometimes "rubbish". It's a sort of drop of truth falling.'

The lunch Danica had provided was so copious that it was spread out on a large table in the cafe at Belgrade airport, accompanied by beer and coffee. Adamsberg munched his *kajmak* sandwich and was reluctant to pursue his thoughts.

'One has to say,' Veyrenc began carefully, 'that if we have Weill in the picture, that would solve that entryphone question. He lives in the building, he's got keys to it, he knows Armel. And he's intelligent and sophisticated, unquestionably bossy, the sort of person who could well acquire a hold over someone like Armel.'

'The front door hadn't been forced.'

'No, but Weill's a cop, he'll have pass keys. Easy lock?'

'Yes.'

'Did he ever go to see Armel?'

'No, but we've only got Weill's own word for it. On the other hand, Zerk quite often went round on Wednesday evenings when Weill held open house.'

'So he could quite easily have got hold of a handkerchief and some dog hairs. Not the boots with dung on, though.'

'Yes, he could. The concierge polishes the stairs, and she doesn't like people going up and down with muddy boots. So she gets people to put any dirty shoes in a little cupboard under the stairs on the ground floor. They all have keys to it. Shit, Veyrenc, Weill was at headquarters for twenty years.'

'Weill couldn't care less about the police, he likes being

337

provocative, he likes cooking, he likes art, and not just classic art either. Have you ever been to his flat?'

'Yes, several times.'

'So you know what it's like, it's splendid and over the top, unforgettable once you've seen it. The statue of the man with a top hat and an erection, juggling bottles? The mummified ibis? The self-portraits? Kant's couch?'

'Kant's valet's couch.'

'All right, Lampe the valet. The chair the bishop died in. The yellow plastic cravat from New York. In a bazaar like that, knocking out the Plogojowitz clan by an old eighteenth-century Paole might look like an artistic happening. As Weill says himself, art's a dirty business but someone has to do it.'

Adamsberg shook his head.

'But he's the one who's investigating the rungs of the hierarchy that leads to Emma Carnot.'

'The vice-president of the Council of State?'

'The same.'

'What on earth has she got to do with all this?'

'She's got her hooks into the president of the Appeal Court, who's bought the prosecutor, who's bought a magistrate, who's bought another magistrate, who's bought Mordent. His daughter's case comes up in a few days and the charge couldn't be more serious.'

'Oh hell. But what does Carnot want from Mordent?'

'Obedience. It was him that leaked the information to the press to cover Zerk's escape. Since the morning we discovered the murder, he's been putting obstacle after obstacle in the way of the inquiry, and in the end he planted some stuff on Vaudel's son, which is intended to incriminate me instead of the killer.'

'The pencil shavings you talked about?'

'That's right. Emma Carnot is somehow linked to our murderer. The page in the register for her marriage has been torn out, so we have to assume that if anyone knew about this marriage, her career would be over. One of the witnesses has already been killed. They're looking for the other. Carnot would trample on anyone to protect her interests.' As he spoke, Adamsberg remembered the little kitten under Zerk's boot and shivered. 'She's not the only one. That's why her war machine will run smoothly, because they all get something out of it. Except Paole's future victims, except Émile, and except me, because I'm for the high jump in three days. Like the toads. With the cigarettes.'

'You mean the ones we used to force-feed cigarettes to, back in the days?'

'Yes.'

'Did they analyse the pencil shavings or something?'

'A pal of mine slowed down their trip to the lab. He faked an illness.'

'So you've got what? Another couple of days?'

'If that.'

The plane was about to take off, and they fastened their seat belts. Veyrenc waited until they had been airborne for some time before speaking again.

'Mordent started behaving this way on the Sunday morning, as soon as the Garches murder was discovered. You're sure about that?'

'Yes. He was trying to get the gardener arrested, taking orders direct from the examining magistrate.'

'But that suggests that Carnot already knew who had massacred Vaudel. On the Sunday morning. And she was already in touch with Mordent. If not, how could she have got the machinery working so fast? She'd already got to Mordent. That would mean at least a couple of days' preparation. She must have known on the Friday.'

'The shoes,' said Adamsberg suddenly, drumming his fingers on the porthole. 'It wasn't the Garches murder that alerted Carnot. It must have been whoever cut off the feet we found in London. And some of those were far too old for Zerk to have been involved.'

'I don't know about all this stuff,' said Veyrenc.

'I'm talking about the seventeen feet cut off at the ankles that were found, still in their shoes, in front of Higg-gate Cemetery in London, ten days ago.'

'Who told you about them?'

'No one. I was there. With Danglard. Higg-gate belongs to Peter Plogojowitz. His body was taken there before they ever built the cemetery, to get him away from the fury of the people of Kisilova.'

The stewardess kept returning to them, evidently fascinated by Veyrenc's striped hair. The spotlight over his head lit up all the red strands. She brought two of everything for them – champagne, chocolates, towelettes.

'When we were in London,' Adamsberg said, after telling Veyrenc as succinctly as he could about the whole Highgate saga, 'there was a fat man with a cigar standing in the distance behind this lord who was fussing about his shoes. The "Cuban", so-called, must have been Paole, is what I'm thinking. Who had just deposited his collection of feet as a sort of challenge on Plogojowitz's territory. And he was using Lord Clyde-Fox to lure us there.'

'But why would he do that?'

'To make the link. Paole needs to associate his collection to the destruction of the last Plogojowitzes. He took advantage of French police being there to get us involved, knowing that the Garches murder would come to us anyway. He couldn't have guessed that Danglard would recognise a foot from Kisilova in the pile, whether it was really his uncle's or a neighbour's. Danglard's uncle by marriage was Vladislav's dedo, that is his grandfather.'

Veyrenc put his champagne glass down, and closed his eyes with a flutter of his eyelashes, a reflex he often had.

'Forget all that for a moment,' he said, 'and simply tell me how it's going to bring anything new to bear on Armel.'

'There were pairs of feet there that had been severed when Zerk was a child, a baby even. Whatever I might think of him, I don't believe your nephew went round as a five-year-old robbing the back parlours of undertakers.'

'No, that figures.'

'And I think that what Emma Carnot knew about was a shoe,' said Adamsberg, catching a new fish that was wriggling around in his brain. 'A shoe with a foot in it, that she'd seen somewhere, a long time ago. And she made the connection with Higg-gate, and after that with Garches. A connection that leads to her. Because we took our eye off that one entirely.'

'What one?' said Veyrenc, opening his eyes.

'The missing one. The eighteenth foot.'

XLII

Adamsberg had telephoned ahead from the airport to convene a meeting of the squad – exceptionally, given that it was a Sunday evening. Three hours on, they had all more or less assimilated the latest episodes of the inquiry, rather at random and in some confusion, rendered greater by the *commissaire*'s state of exhaustion. Some people whispered during a break that it was obvious he had spent a night mummified in a freezing tomb and on the point of suffocation. His aquiline nose looked pinched, and his eyes had sunk even deeper into the distant depths. They greeted Veyrenc warmly, slapped him on the back and congratulated him. Estalère was particularly perturbed by the account of Vesna, a corpse almost three hundred years old but looking lifelike, alongside whom Adamsberg had spent the night. He was the only one in the squad who knew the story of Elizabeth Siddal, and he had remembered every detail of Danglard's story. He was still not sure about one point. Had Dante Gabriel Rossetti opened his wife's grave out of love, or to retrieve his poems? His answer varied depending on the day and his state of mind.

There were some gaps in the *commissaire*'s account of the

past few days, on which he did not seem disposed to elaborate. One of them was the inexplicable presence of Veyrenc in Kisilova. Adamsberg had no intention of revealing to the squad that he had a son whom he had abandoned, that this son had suddenly turned up like a figure from hell, aka Zerk, and that everything pointed to his being the author of the atrocities in Garches and Pressbaum. Nor had he mentioned the ambiguous questions raised by the intervention of Weill. And apart from Danglard, no one in the team knew about the danger emanating from Emma Carnot. That would have obliged Adamsberg to reveal the treacherous activity of Mordent, which he was not ready to do. The daughter – Elaine, wasn't it? – was due to stand trial in a few days. Dinh had managed to hold up the lab tests for three whole days without being disciplined. His talent for levitation, real or imagined, no doubt explained the indulgence of his colleagues.

On the other hand, Adamsberg had described in detail the enmity between the Plogojowitz and Paole families. So, not to put too fine a point on it, as Retancourt said, there was some all-out war going on between two clans of vampires, each trying to annihilate the other, after the original clash three hundred years before. And since, ahem, vampires did not exist, what were they supposed to do about it and where was the investigation heading?

At this point, the antagonism which divided the members of the squad resurfaced: the materialist positivists were seriously annoyed by Adamsberg's vague wanderings, sometimes to the point of rebellion, while the more conciliatory group did not object to a spot of cloud-shovelling from time to time. Retancourt, who had at first beamed with pleasure on finding Adamsberg alive, had gone into a sulk at the first mention of *vampiri* and the place of uncertainty. She had had to admit, as Adamsberg pointed out, that there were a lot of Plogs in the surnames of the victims and their entourage. And that Vaudel senior, who was the authentic grandson of an Andras Plog, had written to Frau Abster, a half-Plogerstein, to warn her and to keep Kisilova free from attack – in other words to protect the Plogojowitz family. And that he, Adamsberg, had been well and truly locked in the vault holding Plogojowitz's nine victims. That the severed feet in London – feet cut off to prevent the dead coming back to life – had been deposited in Plogojowitz's English domain, Highgate Cemetery. That one of those pairs of feet belonged to a certain Mihail Plogodrescu. That the massacre of Pierre Vaudel/Plog and Conrad Plögener corresponded strictly to the method of exterminating a vampire; as had already been ascertained, they hadn't just been killed but annihilated, and more especially their thumbs, teeth and feet. That their functional, spiritual and manducatory organs had been systematically destroyed. That everything indicated that this triple destruction was meant to prevent any possible reconstitution of the body from a single fragment and the recomposition of the accursed whole. As the dispersal of the fragments showed, comparable to the practice of placing a vampire's head between its feet. That Arandjel, the Danglard of Serbia, as Adamsberg called him to provide authority for his remarks, had identified the family of the soldier Arnold Paole as being the tragic and unquestionable victims of Peter Plogojowitz.

The positivists were shattered, while the conciliatory group were acquiescent and were taking notes. Estalère was following Adamsberg's pronouncements with passionate intensity. He had never missed a word his boss let drop, whether pragmatic or irrational. But during these moments of confrontation between the *commissaire* and Retancourt, a woman he idolised, his mind was divided into two warring halves.

'We're not looking for a vampire, Retancourt,' said Adamsberg firmly, 'we're not going out into the streets to search for some creature who got a stake through his heart in the early eighteenth century. Surely that's clear enough for you, *lieutenant*.'

'No, not really.'

'What we're doing is looking for some deranged descendant of Arnold Paole, who knows the whole story of his ancestor. Who has identified some other person as the source of his own suffering, and who has decided it must be the old enemy, Plogojowitz. And who has set about destroying all the remaining descendants of that man, in order to escape from his own destiny. If a man went around killing black cats because he was convinced they were bringing him bad luck, you wouldn't think that absurd, would you, *lieutenant*? Unthinkable? Impossible to understand?'

'No-oo,' admitted Retancourt, encouraged by a few grunts from other positivists.

'Well, it's the same thing. But on a much bigger, monumental scale.'

After the second coffee break, Adamsberg set out his instructions. They were to trace the Plogojowitz line, find any possible members of the family, and put them under police protection. They should alert *Kommissar* Thalberg and have him move Frau Abster to a safe place.

'Too late,' came Justin's high-pitched voice, laden with regret.

'What, like the others?' asked Adamsberg, after a silence.

'Same thing. Thalberg called us this morning.'

'It must be the work of Arnold Paole,' said Adamsberg, deliberately looking Retancourt in the eye. 'So let's protect the others. Work with Thalberg to find out if there are any more members of the family.'

'What about Zerk?' asked Lamarre. 'Do we get reinforcements in? Showing the photos around hasn't brought any results yet.'

'This bastard's good at slipping the net,' said Voisenet. 'He must be on his way back from Cologne now, but where's he going? Who's he going to dismember next?'

'It's possible,' said Adamsberg hesitantly, 'that the bastard is only Paole's executioner, a henchman. He doesn't have any Paoles in the maternal line.'

'Yeah, right,' said Noël, 'but what about his father's family?'

'Could be,' said Adamsberg in a whisper.

Zerk's photo had been circulated to all police stations, gendarme headquarters, stations, airports and public spaces, in both France and Austria. In Germany, where the massacre of the old lady in Cologne had caused an outcry, the same was being done. Adamsberg didn't see how the young man would be able to escape the net.

'We need a rapid and thorough investigation of this choirmaster, Father Germain. Maurel and Mercadet, can you get on with it?'

'What about Vaudel junior?'

'Still at liberty,' said Maurel, 'and he's got a very loud-mouthed lawyer.'

'What does Avignon say?'

'Oh, that shower that managed to lose the samples,' said Noël.

'What samples?' asked Adamsberg innocently.

'Some pencil shavings left by whoever planted the cartridge case that rolled under the fridge.'

'They've lost them, have they?'

'No, found 'em in some *lieutenant*'s pocket. It's not a station down there, it's a holiday camp. They got them off to the lab in the end. Three days lost like that, pff!'

'Pff,' echoed Adamsberg, hearing in his ears Vladislav's 'plog'.

'And Émile?'

'Professor Lavoisier sent us a secret note, very conspiratorial. Émile's being rehabilitated. He even asked for winkles to eat – which he didn't get, naturally – and he'll be out in a few days. But not before there's some way to keep him secure, the doctor says. He's waiting for instructions.'

'Not before we find Paole.'

'Why would Émile be in any danger from Paole?' asked Mercadet.

'Because he's the only person that Vaudel-Plogojowitz really talked to.'

A danger both for Paole and for Emma Carnot, Adamsberg thought. The clumsy shooting near Châteaudun was looking like an operation on behalf of the hierarchy.

'We don't call him Zerk any more, do we?' Estalère asked his neighbour, Mercadet. 'We call him Paole?'

'One and the same, Estalère.'

'Oh, all right.'

'Or not.'

'I see.'

XLIII

DANGLARD, VEYRENC AND ADAMSBERG ARRANGED TO MEET discreetly for dinner in a restaurant some distance from the squad, like three conspirators. Veyrenc had told Danglard about the question marks looming over Weill's interest in the case. The *commandant* ran his fingers over his fleshy cheeks and Veyrenc found that he looked different. Must be the Abstract effect, Adamsberg had warned him. There was more energy in Danglard's pale eyes, his shoulders were more firmly squared, taking up the cut of his suit better. Neither of them knew that in his anguish at Adamsberg's possible death, Danglard had postponed a visit from Abstract.

'Shall we just call Weill?' said Veyrenc.

Adamsberg had ordered stuffed cabbage to rekindle Kisilova memories, but it was so inadequate that he was regretting his choice.

'Risky,' he said.

'Nothing ventured, nothing gained,' said Danglard.

The three heads nodded and Adamsberg tapped in Weill's number, signing to the others to stop talking.

'The Avignon sample went off to the lab yesterday,' said

Adamsberg into his phone. 'Just two days left. Where are we now, Weill?'

'Just a moment, while I rescue my lamb roast.'

Adamsberg put his hand over the phone.

'He's seeing to his lamb.'

The other two nodded, understandingly.

Adamsberg switched on the loudspeaker.

'I don't like interrupting the flow when I'm cooking,' said Weill, coming back on. 'You never know how it will turn out.'

'Weill, Emma Carnot knows who the Garches killer is. But only indirectly. The man she has really latched on to is the one who put seventeen severed feet outside Higg-gate Cemetery.'

'Highgate you mean.'

'We forgot about the eighteenth foot. I think that's the one she saw.'

'If you won't let me tell you anything myself, Adamsberg, I'll get back to the lamb.'

'I'm listening.'

'Right. I got on to someone from the police in Auxerre, the place where the marriage register was clipped. A rather intriguing report was made there twelve years ago. A woman had been shocked by finding a severed foot, still in its shoe, lying on a path in the woods, no less. The foot was decomposed and had been attacked by birds and animals. This woman, according to the officer I spoke to, had just evicted her ex-husband from her country house. She was only going down there, after he'd left, to change the locks. And she found this foot about fifteen metres from the front door, on the path leading to the house.'

'And at the time, Carnot didn't suspect the ex-husband?'

'No, or she wouldn't have gone to the police. But there were several reasons why she ought to have been suspicious. It was a private path, no one else would normally be there. The husband made use of the house at weekends, and had been doing so for over fifteen years. He liked hunting there. And this husband, a lonely oddball, according to the people in the village, used to keep his game in a locked freezer. He wouldn't accept any help from the locals when Emma Carnot finally forced him to move out. You can imagine what the freezer held. One foot must have got dislodged when he was in a hurry, loading his van on his own. Emma Carnot must surely have realised that the foot couldn't have fallen out of someone's pocket, or been dropped by a bird. But she didn't want to understand. She probably began to realise only some time later, and then she made the connection right away. The investigation got nowhere – they decided it must have been a bodysnatcher and the affair was buried.'

'Until the discovery made at Higg-gate. Then she understood right away.'

'Obviously. Seventeen severed feet outside a cemetery, and she knew where the eighteenth was. If it got out that she had married a man who had cut the feet off nine corpses, her career was shot. Unfortunately, you happened to be on the spot in London. So her next step was to demolish you, as completely as she could. It took her less than a day to find out where Mordent's pressure point was, and she got her hooks into him. When the Carnot machine gets going, nothing moves faster, and especially not you, *commissaire*. The Garches affair came to light on the Sunday, and she had linked it to Highgate before you did. How, I don't know. Perhaps because of the dismemberment. She sabotaged the investigation, she got someone to shoot Émile, she had already told Mordent to engineer the flight of the suspect, and to plant the cartridge case and the pencil shavings in Vaudel junior's house. She wanted the real culprit to get away, and she wanted you to go down with all hands.'

'So what *is* her ex-husband's name, Weill?' asked Adamsberg slowly.

'No idea. The house in Burgundy is in her mother's name, and has been in the Carnot family for generations. And in the hamlet near it, as they do in the countryside, they give the husband the family name he married into. They used to call him Monsieur Carnot, or Madame Carnot's husband. He only went there for the hunting anyway.'

'But for heaven's sake, there must be a married name somewhere – when she made her statement, for instance.'

'No, because when she went to the police, she'd already been divorced long before. When she embarked on her legal career, aged twenty-seven, she was using her original name Emma Carnot. So she's been using her maiden name for twenty-five years now at least. The marriage was a short-lived youthful aberration.'

'We need her statement, Weill. It's the only element against her that we have.'

Weill just laughed and asked for a minute or two to baste the lamb.

'Honestly, Adamsberg, you don't seem to realise the powers these people have. Of course, there's no longer any record of the statement. I got it verbatim from the officer in Auxerre who dredged it up. No paper trail left. They do these things thoroughly.'

'Weill, what about the other witness to the marriage?'

'Nothing so far. But Emma Carnot's mother is still alive. She must have known who the young husband was, even if she only met him briefly. That's Marie-Josée Carnot, and she lives at 17 rue des Ventilles, Bâle, Switzerland. I think it would be a good idea to put her under protection.'

'What, her mother?!'

'Yes. We're talking about Emma Carnot here. The witness who was killed in Nantes was her first cousin. Tell your colleague Nolet that, if he dares pursue it.'

'What is your message, Weill?'

'Protect the mother.'

'How would Carnot have known where Émile was headed?'

'She caught up with him in her own time, and at her own speed, to deal with him.'

'But the cops in Garches lost track of him.'

'Adamsberg, you really aren't cut out for dealing with the hierarchy. They never lost track of him at all, and they knew perfectly well where he was when he took refuge in the hospital. But they had orders from high up to let him go and just follow him, report where he went to ground, and then vanish. Which they did. That's what they do, they obey orders.'

Adamsberg ended the call and twiddled his phone on the table. He had given the little foam heart to Danica.

'Danglard, you take the mother, get Retancourt on to protection duty straight away.'

'Not her own mother?' said Veyrenc in a horrified whisper.

'Some people eat wardrobes, Veyrenc.'

Danglard went to phone Retancourt. She was ordered to leave for Switzerland immediately. As soon as they knew she was on her way, the three men sighed with relief and Danglard ordered an armagnac.

'I'd prefer a *rakija* after my *kafa*, like in the *kruchema*.'

'How is it, *commissaire*, that you manage to remember half a dozen words in Serbian, when you can't be bothered even to remember an easy name like Radstock?'

'I specially memorised those Kiseljevan words,' said Adamsberg. 'No doubt because it was a place of uncertainty, Danglard. Where strange things happen. *Hvala, dobro veče, kamak.* And in the vault, I was thinking of *kobasice.* But don't expect anything lofty, they're just sausages.'

'Spicy ones,' Veyrenc pointed out.

Adamsberg was not surprised that Veyrenc already knew more than he did.

'Weill seems to be on the level,' observed Danglard.

'Yes,' said Veyrenc, 'but that doesn't mean anything. Weill always plays at the top of his game. On the side of the police or not.'

'But why would he be after Carnot's guts?'

'To shoot her down. She makes mistakes, so she's dangerous.'

'Weill isn't Arnold Paole. He can't be the ex-husband.'

'Why not?' said Veyrenc, though he did not sound too sure. 'The young man of thirty years ago wouldn't look the same. He could have metamorphosed into what he is today, sophisticated, fat and with a white beard.'

'I can't put anyone to spy on Weill officially,' said Adamsberg, 'but, Veyrenc . . .'

'OK, I see.'

'Get a gun from Danglard. And please cover up your hair.'

XLIV

A STRIP OF LIGHT WAS SHINING UNDER THE DOOR OF THE tool shed. Lucio was feeding the mother cat. Adamsberg joined him and sat cross-legged on the floor.

'Ah, you,' said Lucio, without looking up. 'You've been far away.'

'Further than you think, Lucio.'

'Exactly as far as I think, *hombre*. *La muerte*.'

'Yes.'

Adamsberg didn't dare to ask after the little kitten called Charm. He looked left and right but couldn't recognise her among the kittens which were wriggling about in the semi-darkness. '*Killed that kitten. Just one kick did it. Her blood went all over the place.*'

'Any problems?' he asked, uneasily.

'Yes.'

'What?'

'Maria found my beer hidden under the bush. Have to find a better hiding place.'

One of the kittens tottered towards Adamsberg and bumped into his leg. He picked it up and looked at it. Its eyes were only just open.

'Is this one Charm?' he asked.

'Don't you recognise her? You brought her into the world, didn't you?'

'Yes, of course.'

'Sometimes I despair of you,' said Lucio, shaking his head.

'No, it's just I was worried about her. I had a dream.'

'Tell me about it, *hombre*.'

'No.'

'In the dark night of the past, was it?'

'Yes.'

Adamsberg spent the next two days lying low. He came into the office for a few minutes at a time, used the phone, took messages and went off again, not to be contacted. He took time out to call on Josselin about his tinnitus. The doctor had checked his ears with his fingers, and diagnosed a recent shock: 'Shattering, I'd say, a brush with death perhaps? But it's almost healed now,' he remarked with surprise.

The man with golden fingers had removed the tinnitus and Adamsberg reacquainted himself with the street noises now no longer jammed by the high-level buzzing in his ears. Then he resumed the search for Arnold Paole. The attempt to investigate Father Germain was not going well. He refused to tell them anything about his family tree, as was his perfect right. His real name (Henri Charles Lefèvre) was such a common one that Danglard wasn't getting anywhere trying to trace any ancestors. Danglard had confirmed Veyrenc's judgement of him: Father Germain was an unusual and authoritarian person, physically very strong, in a way that might seem impressive to the young: he was unattractive to adults, but might well have some hold over impressionable choirboys. Adamsberg listened to the report, looking distracted, and had once more offended Danglard's susceptibility.

Retancourt was looking after things at the Swiss end, relayed by Kernorkian. Veyrenc had moved into Zerk's former apartment. He was watching Weill like a hawk. He had dyed his hair dark brown to hide the red stripes, but in sunshine they inevitably appeared again, provocatively refusing to be concealed.

Seek not in the darkness to hide what once was done;
The past will reappear by the light of the sun.

Weill spent his time paying (brief) visits to the quai des Orfèvres, then went off doing the rounds of purveyors of the exotic foodstuffs and products he liked best, such as soap scented with the purple rose of Lebanon. Weill had immediately invited the new neighbour round to his Wednesday 'open house', and Veyrenc had declined from a distance, in tones verging on the rude. There had still been party noise coming from Weill's at three in the morning, and Veyrenc would have gladly abandoned his disguise, had it not been for his extreme anxiety about his nephew.

Adamsberg now slept with a gun under his pillow. On the Wednesday evening, he called the station in Nantes again, his earlier messages having remained unanswered. The duty officer, *Brigadier* Pons, refused, as his colleagues already had, to give him *Commissaire* Nolet's private telephone number.

'*Brigadier*,' said Adamsberg, 'I'm talking about a woman who was shot dead eleven days ago in Nantes. Françoise

Chevron. You've arrested an innocent man, and I know that the killer is still at large.'

A *lieutenant* approached the junior officer with a questioning look. 'It's Jean-Baptiste Adamsberg from Paris,' the junior whispered, covering the phone. 'The Chevron case.'

By twirling his finger close to his head, the *lieutenant* indicated his opinion of Jean-Baptiste Adamsberg. Then, as a flicker of doubt seized him, he picked up the phone.

'*Lieutenant* Drémard.'

'Can I have Nolet's private number, Drémard?'

'*Commissaire*, we've tied up the Chevron affair, all the papers are on the examining magistrate's desk. Her husband beat her up regularly, she'd taken a lover. Straightforward case. We can't disturb *Commissaire* Nolet at home, sir, he hates that.'

'He'll hate having an extra victim on his hands even more. Give me his number please, Drémard, move!'

Drémard ran through the many contradictory opinions he had heard about Adamsberg, genius or disaster area, and fearing he'd get a rocket one way or the other, opted for prudence.

'You've got a pen, sir?'

A couple of minutes later, Adamsberg had the witty *Commissaire* Nolet on the line. He was entertaining friends and the sound of background music and chatter muffled his voice somewhat.

'Terribly sorry to disturb you, Nolet.'

'On the contrary, Adamsberg,' said Nolet heartily. 'Are you in our area? Come and join us.'

'It's about your Chevron case.'

'Fine, go ahead.'

Nolet must have asked someone to turn the volume down. Now Adamsberg could hear him better.

'Chevron was witness to a marriage at Auxerre, twenty-nine years ago. And the ex-wife doesn't want anyone to know it ever took place.'

'Any evidence?'

'The page in the register has been torn out.'

'And she'd go to the lengths of killing the witness?'

'Absolutely.'

'OK, I'm interested, Adamsberg.'

'We questioned the wife's mother in Geneva. She denies her daughter was ever married. She's terrified and under police protection.'

'So we should find and protect the second witness?'

'Exactly, but the problem is we haven't managed to identify one yet. A press ad didn't produce anything. But we need you to ask around among Françoise Chevron's friends and family. You're probably looking for a man, because as a rule people choose a witness from each sex.'

'And what's the name of the ex-wife, Adamsberg?'

'Emma Carnot.'

Adamsberg heard Nolet move out of the room, closing the door behind him.

'Right, Adamsberg. I'm alone now. You're telling me this is Emma Carnot. *The* Emma Carnot.'

'Herself.'

'And you're asking me to attack the great snake.'

'What snake?'

'Up there, dammit. The great snake that slides through the back rooms. Are you calling me on an ordinary mobile?'

'No, of course not, Nolet, don't worry. My ordinary

phone's been tapped so much it looks like a woodpecker's been at it.'

'Good. Start again. You're asking me to take on someone at the very top of the system. Someone very close to the *princeps* in the state. And you know that every scale of the snake is glued to the next, so the armour is completely impenetrable. And you know the only thing I'd be able to do afterwards? Even if they let me?'

'I'll be with you.'

'Oh, thanks very much, big help,' Nolet shot back. 'And where will we both be then?'

'I don't know. In Kisilova. Or somewhere else in the mists of the beyond.'

'Christ, Adamsberg, I've always cooperated with you in the past. But this time, count me out. I can tell you don't have any kids.'

'Well, I do in fact. Two.'

'Oh, that's new,' said Nolet.

'Yes. So?'

'So nothing. I'm not St George.'

'Who?'

'Guy who killed the dragon.'

'Oh yes, I know who you mean,' Adamsberg remembered.

'Good. So you get my drift. I'm not going chasing after the damned snake that's prowling about up there.'

'OK, Nolet. Just transfer the Chevron case to me. The thing is, I don't want some guy to die because he was witness to a marriage twenty-nine years ago and one of the parties to said marriage turned out to be a piece of shit. The fact that this piece of shit has become a link in the snake's chain mail is neither here nor there.'

'A fang would be more accurate. A poisoned fang.'

'Whatever. Just drop the snake, pass me the file and forget the whole thing.'

'OK, OK,' said Nolet, breathing out heavily. 'I'm on the way to the office.'

'When will you send it me?'

'I'm not sending it, damn you. I'm taking it up again.'

'Really? Or are you just going to sit on it?'

'Adamsberg, at least do me the credit of believing me, or the whole lot goes to the bottom of the Loire. I'm that close.'

'Plog,' said Adamsberg to himself as he hung up.

Nolet was on Emma Carnot's track, and Nolet was a good cop. As long as he didn't take fright at the snake along the way. Adamsberg had no idea what '*princeps*' meant but he got the point. People used a lot of difficult words, and he wondered how they managed to command them so well. At least he could remember the *kruchema* which was something not everyone could do.

He took a shower, put his gun and two mobiles under his pillow, and lay down, still damp, under his red eiderdown, remembering the faded blue one in the *kruchema*. He heard the neighbour's door open and Lucio walking in the garden. So it must be between half past midnight and two in the morning. Unless, that is, Lucio wasn't going out to take a leak, but to find a new cache for his beer. Which his daughter Maria would pretend to discover after a month or two, marking another stage in their unending game.

Think of Lucio, Charm, the blue eiderdown. Anything, except Zerk's face, his threatening expression, his tough-guy talk, and his relentless and unthinking rage.

'A nice enough boy, with the voice of an angel,' or so Veyrenc said, but that wasn't Adamsberg's view. And yet there were some elements in the whole affair that were in Zerk's favour: the dirty tissue, the very old feet in Highgate, the convenient boots under the stairs. But the dog hairs were a formidable obstacle. And Zerk would make a perfect killer, wax in the hands of some older man, some 'Paole'. They would split the job, one going to Highgate, the other to Vaudel's place. A sick couple, combining the psychopathic and powerful Arnold Paole and a disturbed and fatherless young man. Son of nobody, son of nobody in particular, son of Adamsberg. But son or not, Adamsberg did not feel the slightest bit inclined to lift a finger for Zerk.

XLV

THE SHRILL SOUND OF A CRICKET WAS HEARD IN THE ROOM.
Adamsberg identified it as coming from his ordinary mobile
– the one tapped by woodpeckers – and picked it up,
checking his two watches. Somewhere between 2.45 and
4.15 a.m. Rubbing the sleep out his eyes, he looked at the
phone which said he had two new messages. They were
both from the same number, three minutes apart. The first
one said *por*, the second *qos*. Adamsberg immediately called
Froissy. Froissy never minded being woken at night.
Adamsberg imagined she took the chance to have a little
snack.

'I've got two messages I can't understand,' he said. 'But I
don't think they mean anything good. How long do you need
to identify a caller from a mobile?'

'For an unknown number? About a quarter of an hour.
Ten minutes with luck, but you have to add half an hour for
me to get to the office, because I don't have my equipment
at home. What's the number?'

Adamsberg read out the number, feeling on edge, sensing
there must be some urgency. Forty minutes was a long time.

'Oh, I can tell you that one right away,' said Froissy. 'Because I just identified it this afternoon. It's Armel Louvois.'

'Holy shit.'

'I was just starting to list all his calls. He doesn't make many. There had been none for the last nine days because he must have switched the phone off when he disappeared. So why has he switched it back on? Why is he coming out of hiding? He's sent you a message, you say?'

'He sent me two incomprehensible texts.'

'*Texti*,' said Froissy automatically, adopting Danglard's pedantic term for them.

'Can you pinpoint where he is for me?'

'If he hasn't switched it off again.'

'Can you do that from home?'

'I can try, but it won't be that easy.'

'Please try as fast as you can.'

She had hung up. It was pointless to tell Froissy to hurry, she always did things as fast as a fly.

He pulled on his clothes, and picked up the holster and both mobiles. He realised as he was going downstairs that his T-shirt was on back to front. The label was scratching his neck. He'd fix it later. Froissy called back as he was pulling on a jacket.

'He's at the villa in Garches,' she announced. 'Another phone is transmitting from the same address. I'm trying to identify it.'

'Keep trying.'

'I'll have to go to the office. Take me about an hour.'

Adamsberg alerted two teams and calculated the time. It would take thirty minutes at least before the first team could meet up at headquarters, then there was the distance out to

Garches. If he went at once, he could be there in about twenty minutes. He hesitated, and all his instincts told him to wait. A trap. What the fuck was Zerk doing in the old man's house? With another mobile? Or was he with Paole? And if so what was Zerk calling him for? A trap. Certain death. Adamsberg got into the car and leaned his arms on the steering wheel. They didn't get him in the vault, they were having another go here, it was pretty obvious. To stay put was by far the wisest option. He read the messages again: *por*; *qos*. He switched on the ignition, then stopped. Yes, it was clear as daylight, it was obviously and logically a trap. His fingers gripping the key, he tried to think why, nevertheless, some other instinct was telling him he should get to Garches right away, an instinct with no reason to it, which had taken over his mind. He switched on the headlights and drove off.

Halfway there, after the Saint-Cloud tunnel, he pulled over on to the hard shoulder. *Por, qos*. He had just thought – if you could call it thinking – of Froissy's ridiculous use of the term '*texti*'. That got him back to *por* again. And now he was almost sure that he had often seen *por* on his mobile. When he sent a text message and typed SMS, he often ended up with something like these words. Yes. When he tried doing SMS he ended up first with *pop* then *por pos qos sos* and finally *sms*.

SMS. SOS.

An SOS that Zerk wasn't managing to tap in properly. He'd tried again, perhaps handling a phone without being able to see it, and got it wrong again. Adamsberg put his siren and lights on the roof and set off once more. If Zerk was setting a trap, he would surely have sent a comprehensible message. If he had failed to text SOS, it meant he couldn't see the screen. Perhaps he was in the dark. Or perhaps the phone was in his pocket and he was typing while trying not to be seen. Not a trap, a call for help. Zerk was with Paole, and it was half an hour since he had sent the messages.

'Danglard?' Adamsberg said, calling while driving. 'I've got an SOS from Zerk, done blind. The murderer must have taken him back to the crime scene where he's going to suicide him. Finish things off.'

'Father Germain.'

'No, it can't be him, Danglard. How would he have known the cat was a female? But that's what he said. Don't surround the house, and don't try to get in via the door. He'll certainly shoot him at once if he sees you. Just head for Garches, and wait for me to call you again.'

Still holding the wheel with one hand, he called Professor Lavoisier.

'Lavoisier, I need a number for Émile at the hospital, it's urgent.'

'Is that Adamsberg?'

'Yes.'

'How do I know it's you?' asked Lavoisier who was entering fully into the role of conspirator.

'Good God, doctor, I haven't got time for this.'

'Nothing doing,' said Lavoisier.

Adamsberg sensed that this hold-up was serious. Lavoisier was taking his mission to heart. Adamsberg had ordered 'no contacts whatsoever', and he was being punctilious about following instructions.

'Look, shall I tell you what Retancourt said when she came out of the coma in that awful case we had? Can you still remember it?'

'Yes, of course. Go ahead.'

'To see the last Roman, as he draws his last breath,
Myself to die happy, as the cause of this death.'

'OK, *mon vieux*, I'll transfer the call for you because the hospital will refuse you access to Émile unless I put you through.'

'Yes, but hurry, doctor.'

A few crackles then Émile came on the line.

'Is it about Cupid?' he asked anxiously.

'Cupid's fine, Émile, but now tell me how to get inside Vaudel's house another way, not the front door.'

'Back door.'

'No, I mean another way, not so obvious.'

'There isn't one.'

'Yes there is, Émile. And you used it. When you came in at night to pinch a bit of cash.'

'What, me, guv?'

'Don't give me that – we had your prints on the drawer of the desk. I don't care about that now. Just listen carefully. Whoever massacred your boss is about to kill someone else tonight in that house, and I need to get in there without him seeing me.'

'Can't help you.'

The car was just getting to Garches. Adamsberg switched off the siren.

'Émile,' said Adamsberg, through his teeth, 'if you don't tell me now, Cupid gets it.'

'You wouldn't!'

'I bloody would, Émile, and stamp on him with my boot.'

'Fucking bastard cop.'

'Spot on. Now just fucking tell me, how do I get in?'

'Next door, Madame Bourlant.'

'Yes?'

'You go through the cellar. Two houses used to belong to this bloke, wife in one, fancy woman in the other. So he goes through the cellar. Door got blocked when they were sold, but the old lady opened it again. She shouldn't ought to have, but Vaudel, he didn't know, he never went down the cellar. But I promised I'd never tell on her, so she let me use it. We had this arrangement, see?'

Adamsberg parked the car fifty metres from the house and closed the door quietly.

'Why did she unblock it?'

'Scared of fires. Emergency exit. Stupid, because her life-line's perfect.'

'She live alone?'

'Yeah.'

'Thanks.'

'Don't you *dare* mess with my dog now.'

Adamsberg contacted the two teams. One was on the way, the other just setting out. No light showed in the Vaudel house, and the shutters and curtains were closed. He knocked several times next door, at Madame Bourlant's. An identical house, but in a much worse state of repair. It wasn't going to be easy to get a woman living alone to open the door just by saying 'police', which wouldn't convince anyone. Either you didn't believe it was the police, or you did, which was even worse.

'Madame Bourlant, I've got a message for you from Émile, he's in hospital.'

'So why come in the middle of the night?'

'He doesn't want anyone to see me. It's about the cellar door. He says someone has found out and you're going to get into trouble.'

The door opened a few inches on a chain. A fragile-looking

woman of about sixty was looking at him more closely as she put on her glasses.

'How do I know you're a friend of Émile's?'

'He says you have a fantastic lifeline.'

The door opened and the woman let him in, putting the chain back on.

'I *am* a friend of Émile's, but I'm also a *commissaire de police*,' said Adamsberg.

'No, you can't be.'

'Yes, I can. All I'm asking you to do is open the way through the cellar. I need to get into the Vaudel house. There are two teams of police following, and they'll need to come the same way. You will let them through.'

'There isn't a way through the cellar.'

'Look, madame, I can get it unblocked without you if I have to. Just don't cause any trouble, or everyone in the neighbourhoood will know about the door.'

'It isn't a crime, is it?'

'They'll say you were going to rob Vaudel of all his money.'

The little old woman went to get the key, muttering about the police. Adamsberg followed her into the cellar and then into the corridor which led from it.

'The police do a lot of daft things,' she said, as she unlocked the door. 'But this takes the biscuit. Accusing me of being a thief, I never heard such nonsense. And you've been bothering Émile, and that other young man.'

'The police found a handkerchief belonging to the other young man.'

'That's stupid. People don't drop their handkerchiefs in other people's houses, so why would they when they've just murdered someone?'

'Don't follow me, madame,' said Adamsberg, pushing the little old woman gently back. 'This could be dangerous.'

'A murderer?'

'Yes. Get back inside your own house and wait till the police team arrives, don't do anything else.'

She trotted off back down the corridor and Adamsberg climbed quietly up the cluttered cellar stairs into Vaudel's house, taking care not to dislodge a bottle or a box. There was just an ordinary door to the kitchen, and the lock took him only a minute to pick. He headed straight for the room with the piano. If Paole was going to engineer Zerk's suicide, that's where he would do it, at the scene of his remorse.

The door was closed and he could see nothing. The tapestries on the walls muffled voices. Adamsberg went into the bathroom next door and climbed on top of a linen chest, from where he could reach a ventilation grill.

Paole was standing with his back to him, holding a gun equipped with a silencer. Opposite him, Zerk, tears rolling down his face, was sitting on the Louis XIII armchair. All the gothic bravado had gone. Paole had literally nailed him to the spot. A knife transfixed his left hand, nailing it to the wooden armrest. A lot of blood had already been spilt: the young man must have been pinned to the chair for some time, sweating with pain.

'Who was it to?' Paole was saying, waving a mobile phone in front of Zerk's eyes.

Zerk must have tried to make his call for help again, but

this time Paole had caught him at it. The older man had opened a flick knife, taken Zerk's right hand and slashed it several times, as if he were cutting up a fish, not appearing to hear the young man's cries of pain.

'So don't think you can start that again. Who to?'

'Adamsberg,' Zerk groaned.

'Pathetic,' said Paole. 'So he doesn't demolish his father after all. First little scratch and he calls him for help: *por*, qos. What were you trying to tell him?'

'SOS. But I didn't get it right. He won't understand. Leave me alone, I won't tell, I won't say anything, I don't know anything.'

'Ha, but I need you, my boy. The police got a long way on this. So I'm going to leave you here, nailed to your chair. You decided to mutilate yourself, and you'll be found dead at the scene of your crime – a fitting end. I've got a lot of things to do, and I want a bit of peace.'

'So do I,' gasped Zerk.

'You!' said Paole, pocketing the mobile. 'What have you got left to do? Make your precious jewellery? Sing in your precious choir? Eat your supper? Who would care, you poor boy? You're no use to anyone. Your mother's left the country, your father doesn't want anything to do with you. But at least you'll accomplish something by your death. You'll be famous.'

'Please. I won't tell, I'll go far away. Adamsberg will never find out.'

Paole shrugged.

'Naturally, he won't find out. His pea brain's not much bigger than yours, he's just a windbag, like father, like son. Anyway, it's a bit late to start calling him now. I'm afraid he's no longer with us.'

'That's not true,' said Zerk, twisting in his chair.

Paole leaned on the handle of the knife stuck into his hand and made the blade move in the wound.

'Calm down. He's as dead as a doornail. He's walled up in the vault where Plogojowitz's victims are all buried, in Kiseljevo, in Serbia. So he's going to come riding to the rescue, is he?'

Paole then started to speak in a low voice, as if for himself alone, and the last hope ebbed from Zerk's young face.

'But you're forcing me to move more quickly. Sooner or later they'll trace your call, and they'll identify who you are and where you are. So they'll know where we both are. We've got a little less time than we bargained for, so prepare yourself, young man, and say your goodbyes.'

Paole had moved away from the armchair, but he was still too close to Zerk. By the time Adamsberg had opened the door and taken aim, he would have had four seconds' warning to shoot at Zerk. Four seconds to distract him. Adamsberg took out his notebook, letting fall all the bits of paper that were chaotically pushed inside. The one he wanted was recognisable, a crumpled and dirty sheet on which he had copied the text from Plogojowitz's grave. He took out his mobile and composed a text as quickly as he could: '*Dobre veče proklet*' (= Good evening Cursed one). On the next line: 'Plogojowitz'. Not very good, but the best he could manage. It would hold the man up for a minute or two, enough time to get between him and Zerk.

The phone bleeped in Paole's pocket. He looked at the screen, frowned, and the door burst open. Adamsberg faced him, having moved in front of the young man, to cover him. Paole tilted his head, as if the sudden entry of the *commissaire* was some kind of music-hall act.

'Oh, that's your idea of a joke, is it, *commissaire*?' said Paole, pointing to the phone. 'You don't say *Dobro veče* at this time of night, you say *Laku noć.*'

Paole's scornful insouciance destabilised Adamsberg. He showed no interest in him at all. As if he were no more of a problem than a tuft of grass in the road. Still covering Paole with the gun, Adamsberg reached behind him and yanked out the knife.

'Get out, Zerk! Move!'

Zerk hurtled out of the room, banging the door behind him, and they heard him run down the corridor.

'How touching,' said Paole. 'And now, Adamsberg, it's just the two of us. We're both standing here, we're both armed. You'll aim for the legs, I'll aim for the heart, and if you shoot first, I'll still shoot you, won't I? You haven't a chance. My fingers are ultra-sensitive and my sangfroid is total. In such a strictly technical situation, your door to the unconscious is no use to you at all. On the contrary, it's an obstacle. You're still making the same mistake as in Kiseljevo. Walking around on your own. Like in the old mill. Yes, I know,' he said, raising his large hand. 'Your men are on their way.'

The man consulted his watch and sat down. 'We have a few minutes, I'll easily catch up with the young man. A few minutes to find out how you traced me. I don't mean tonight and the idiot Armel's message. You do know your son's a complete imbecile, don't you? No, I mean when you came to my surgery, two days ago, for your tinnitus. You knew then, didn't you, because your head was resisting me all the time. How did you know?'

'In the vault.'

'And?'

Adamsberg was finding it hard to speak. The memory of

the vault could still immobilise him, the memory of the night with Vesna. He tried to think of the moment the door had opened and Veyrenc had come in, when he had drunk Froissy's cognac.

'The little kitten,' he said. 'The one you wanted to kick to death.'

'Yes, didn't have time for that. But it will be done, Adamsberg. I always keep my word.'

'"*I killed that kitten. Just one kick did it. Making me rescue her, that got up my nose.*" That's what you said.'

'Correct.'

'Zerk had brought the kitten out from under a woodpile. But how would he know it was a female? A week-old kitten. Impossible. Lucio knew and I knew. And you knew, doctor, because you'd treated her. Just you.'

'Ah yes,' said Paole. 'I see my mistake. But when did you realise that? At once?'

'No, when I saw the kitten again, back home.'

'Always slow on the uptake, Adamsberg.'

Paole stood up and a shot rang out. Stupefied, Adamsberg stared as the doctor fell to the floor. He was hit in the stomach on the left side.

'I was aiming for his legs,' said the anxious voice of Madame Bourlant. 'I'm not a very good shot.' The little old woman trotted over to the man gasping on the floor, while Adamsberg picked up the gun and telephoned for the emergency services.

'He's not going to die, is he?' she asked, leaning over him.

'No, I think the bullet is lodged in the gut.'

'It's only a .32,' said Madame Bourlant as if she were describing her skirt size.

Paole's eyes appealed to the *commissaire*.

'The ambulance is on its way, Paole.'

'Don't call me *Paole*,' the doctor ordered in a strangled voice. 'There are no more Paoles now that the wicked ones are all wiped out. The Paoles are saved. Understand, Adamsberg? They're free. At last.'

'Have you killed them all? The Plogojowitzes?'

'I didn't kill them. Eliminating creatures is not killing. They weren't humans. I do good in the world, *commissaire*, I'm a doctor.'

'Then you're not human either, Josselin.'

'I wasn't quite. But now I am, yes.'

'You've wiped them all out?'

'The five big ones, yes. There are two shroud-eaters still alive, women. But they can't reconstitute.'

'I only know about three: Pierre Vaudel-Plog, Conrad Plögener and Frau Abster-Plogerstein. And Plogodrescu's feet, but that's a long time ago.'

'Someone's ringing at the door,' said Madame Bourlant, timidly.

'It'll be the ambulance men – go and open it.'

'What if it isn't the ambulance?'

'It will be. Go on, for heaven's sake, woman.'

The little old woman went off, muttering again about the bad manners of the police.

'Who *is* she?' asked Josselin.

'Next-door neighbour.'

'How did she manage to shoot me?'

'No idea.'

'*Loša sreća.*'

'The other two, doctor. Who are the other two people you killed?'

'I haven't killed any *people*.'

'The two other creatures then.'

'The grand master, Plogan, and his daughter. Terrible forces of evil. I started with them.'

'Where?'

The paramedics came in and put down a stretcher, taking out their equipment. Adamsberg gestured to them to wait a few moments.

Madame Bourlant was listening hard to the conversation, shaking with fear.

'Where?'

'In Savolinna.'

'Where's that?'

'Finland.'

'When? Before Pressbaum?'

'Yes.'

'Is Plogan their real name?'

'Yes. Veiko and Leena Plogan. Dreadful creatures. He reigns no more.'

'Who?'

'I never pronounce his name.'

'Peter Plogojowitz?'

Josselin nodded.

'In Highgate. Finished. His line's died out now. Go and see for yourself – the tree will die on Highgate Hill. And the tree roots around his tomb in Kiseljevo, they'll die too.'

'What about Pierre Vaudel's son. Isn't he a Plogojowitz too? Why did you let him live?'

'He's just an ordinary man. He wasn't born with teeth. Cursed blood doesn't run in all the branches.'

Adamsberg straightened up, but the doctor caught him by the sleeve.

'Go and see, Adamsberg,' he begged. 'You know. You'll understand. I need to know.'

'See what?'

'The tree on Highgate Hill. On the south side of the chapel, a big oak tree that was planted in the year of his birth, in 1663.'

Go and see the *tree*? Obey the demented wishes of a Paole? With his idea that Plogojowitz was in the tree, like the uncle in the polar bear?

'Josselin, you've cut the feet off nine corpses, you've massacred five human beings, you locked me into that vault of hell, you've manipulated my son, and you were about to kill him.'

'Yes, yes, I know. But just go and see the tree.'

Adamsberg shook his head in disgust or lassitude, stood up and gestured to the paramedics to take him away.

'What is he talking about?' asked Madame Bourlant. 'Family problems?'

'That's exactly right. Where did you shoot from?'

'Through the hole in the wall.' Madame Bourlant took him into the corridor with her little steps. Behind an engraving, the thin partition wall had been pierced by a hole about three centimetres across, giving on to the piano room between two tapestries.

'This was Émile's lookout post. Since Monsieur Vaudel always left all the lights on, you were never sure if he'd gone to bed or not. Émile could look through the hole and see if he had left the desk. Émile, you know, used to pinch the odd banknote. Vaudel was rolling in money.'

'How did you know all that?'

'Oh, Émile and I got on all right. I was the only person round here who didn't give him the cold shoulder. We had our little secrets.'

'Like the revolver.'

'No, that was my husband's. Oh my goodness, I'm still shaking. Shooting a man, that's not something you do every day. I was aiming low, but it jumped up. I couldn't stop it. I didn't mean to shoot, I just came to see what was happening. And then, well, your police weren't arriving, so it looked to me as if you'd had it, monsieur, so I thought I should do something.'

Adamsberg agreed. Yes. He would absolutely have had it. It was only twenty minutes since he had crept into the bathroom. A ferocious hunger suddenly made his stomach rumble.

'If you're looking for the young man,' added the little old woman, trotting off to the cellar again, 'he's in my living room, trying to do something about his hands.'

XLVI

DANGLARD'S TEAM WAS FOLLOWING THE AMBULANCE, WHILE
Voisenet's was conducting the inquiry in the Vaudel house.
Adamsberg had found Zerk sitting in the next-door living
room, looking just as intimidated as he had when faced with
Paole, and surrounded by four armed police officers. His
hands were swathed in thick bandages, which Madame
Bourlant had fastened with safety pins.

'I'll look after this one myself,' said Adamsberg, hauling
Zerk to his feet by one arm. 'Madame Bourlant, have you got
any painkillers?'

He made the young man take a couple of pills, and shoved
him out towards his car.

'Put your seat belt on.'

'Can't,' said Zerk, holding up his bandaged hands.
Adamsberg nodded, pulled across the seat belt and fastened
it. Zerk sat passively wordless, shattered, as if deprived of
sense. Adamsberg drove in silence. It was about five in the
morning and almost light. He wasn't sure what to do. He
could follow the rules technically, or face what he had to
head-on. A third solution, the kind Danglard would always

whisper to him, was to steer matters to a compromise, elegantly, English fashion. But that kind of elegance wasn't in his make-up. Feeling drained and vaguely discouraged, he just drove on without thinking. What did it matter, to have it out or not? What was the point? He could just let Zerk go off and live his life, without taking any further notice of him. Or he could drive to the end of the world without saying a word. Or he could leave him there. Clumsily, with his bandaged hands, Zerk had managed to take out a cigarette. But he couldn't light it. Adamsberg sighed, pressed the cigarette lighter and handed it to him. Then he picked up the second mobile. Weill was calling.

'Did I wake you, *commissaire*?'

'I haven't been to bed.'

'Neither have I. Nolet has found the witness, a man who was in school with Françoise Chevron and Emma Carnot. He got Carnot surrounded half an hour ago. She was armed and on her way in person to her school friend's apartment.'

'There are some nights like that, Weill, when hunger stalks the world. Arnold Paole was arrested an hour ago. It was Dr Paul de Josselin. He was about to kill Zerk at the house in Garches.'

'Any damage?'

'Zerk's hands are badly cut, Josselin's in hospital in Garches with a bullet in his gut. Not life-threatening.'

'Did you shoot him?'

'No. The woman next door did. She's sixty years old, five foot nothing, weighs a handful of kilos and had a .32.'

'Where's the young man now?'

'With me.'

'Are you bringing him back?'

'Sort of. He can't use his hands yet, so he'll need some help. Tell Nolet to seal off Françoise Chevron's house, they'll try everything they can to get Emma Carnot out of the mess she's in and keep it pinned on Chevron's husband. And tell them to keep Carnot incommunicado for forty-eight hours. No statement to the press, not a word. The girl will be in court tomorrow. I don't want Mordent to have been eaten alive for nothing.'

'Naturally.'

Zerk passed him his cigarette end with a questioning look, and Adamsberg stubbed it out in the ashtray. In profile, as the light of morning came up, Zerk with his beaked nose and weak chin, apparently dreamily pursuing vague ideas, looked remarkably like Adamsberg, so much so it was a wonder that Weill had never noticed it. Josselin had stated confidently that Zerk was an imbecile.

'I smoked your cigarettes in Kiseljevo,' said Adamsberg. 'The packet you left in my house. All but one.'

'Josselin went on about some place called Kiseljevo.'

'It's where Peter Plogojowitz died in 1725. That's where they built this special vault for his nine victims, and that's where Josselin imprisoned me.' Adamsberg felt an icy shiver run down his back.

'So that bit was true,' said Zerk.

'Yes. It was freezing. And every time I think of it, I feel cold again.' Adamsberg drove for a couple of kilometres without speaking.

'He shut the door of the vault and he talked to me. He imitated your voice very well: "*Know where you are now, scumbag?*"'

'That sounded like me?'

'Very. "*Everyone will know that Adamsberg abandoned his kid, and how the kid turned out. Because of you. You.*" It sounded pretty convincing.'

'And you thought it was *me*?'

'Naturally I did. Like the little shit you were when you came to see me, "to fuck up my life". That's what you promised, wasn't it?'

'So what did you do in the vault?'

'I practically suffocated in there until the morning.'

'And who found you?'

'Veyrenc. He'd been tailing me all the time to try and stop me arresting you. Did you know that?'

Zerk looked out of the window. It was broad daylight by now.

'No,' he said. 'Where are we going now? Fucking police headquarters, I suppose.'

'Did you not notice that we're driving away from Paris?'

'So where're we going?'

'Where the road runs out. The seaside.'

'OK,' said Zerk, closing his eyes. 'And what are we supposed to do there?'

'Eat something. Warm ourselves by the sun. Look at the water.'

'I'm in *pain*. That asshole really hurt me.'

'I can't give you any more painkillers for an hour or two. Try to sleep.'

Adamsberg stopped the car facing the sea, when the road ran into the sand. His wristwatches and the height of the sun indicated that it was about half past seven. The beach was smooth and deserted, stretching out into the distance, with no sign of life except for a few groups of silent white birds. He got out of the car quietly. The calm sea and cloudless blue sky seemed very provocative, not at all suited to these last ten days of savage turmoil. They were inappropriate too for the state of things between himself and Zerk, with distress and bemusement sprouting like wild grass on a rubbish heap. A great storm over the sea would have been better, with the dawn coming up like thunder and a mist hiding the horizon. But nature had decided otherwise, and if she had chosen this still perfection, he would absorb it for an hour. Anyway, his fatigue had left him now, and he felt wide awake. He lay down on the sand which was still cool from the night, and raised himself on one elbow. At this hour, Vlad would be at the *kruchema*. Possibly as high as a kite. He punched in his number.

'*Dobro jutro*, Vlad.'

'*Dobro jutro*, Adamsberg.'

'Where's your phone? I can't hear you very well.'

'On my pillow.'

'Put it closer to your head.'

'OK.'

'*Hvala*. Please tell Arandjel that Arnold Paole's wild ride came to an end last night. But I think he's satisfied, because he has massacred five great Plogojowitzes: Plögener, Vaudel-Plog, Plogerstein and two Plogans, a father and daughter in Finland. And the feet of Plogodrescu. The curse of the Paoles is at an end, and according to him, they're all away now. Free. And on Highgate Hill, the tree is dying.'

'Plog.'

'There are two shroud-eaters left.'

'They don't trouble anyone. Arandjel says you just have to turn them face down and they'll drop like mercury to the centre of the earth.'

'I don't intend to have anything to do with them.'

'Wow,' said Vlad, apropos of nothing.

'Tell Arandjel, without fail. Are you going to stay in Kisilova for ever now?'

'No, I'm expected at a conference in Munich tomorrow. I'm getting back on the straight and narrow, which as you know does not exist and is neither straight nor narrow.'

'Plog. What does "*Loša sreća*" mean, Vlad? Paole said it when he fell to the ground.'

'It means "bad luck".'

Zerk was now sitting on the sand a few metres away, watching him patiently.

'We'll go to a medical centre to get your hands seen to,' said Adamsberg. 'Then we'll go and have some coffee.'

'What does "plog" mean?'

'It's like a drop of truth falling to earth,' said Adamsberg, miming the action by raising and dropping his hand vertically. 'And it falls in exactly the right spot,' he said, plunging his index finger into the sand.

'Oh,' said Zerk, looking at the little hole. 'And what if it falls here or here?' he asked, plunging in a finger at random. 'Not a real plog then?'

'No, I suppose not.'

XLVII

Adamsberg had stuck a straw in Zerk's bowl of coffee, and buttered his bread for him.

'Tell me about Josselin, Zerk.'

'My name's not Zerk.'

'It's the baptismal name I've given you. For me, just think about it, you're only a week old. Like a newborn baby crying in a cot. Nothing more.'

'Makes you only a week old too, so you're no better'n me.'

'So what will you call me?'

'Don't want to call you anything.'

Zerk sucked up some coffee through his straw and smiled unexpectedly, rather like Vlad's sudden way of smiling, whether at his reply or the sound of the straw. His mother had been just the same, readily distracted from the business in hand at awkward moments. Which explained why he had been able to make love to her by the bridge over the Jaussène in the rain. Zerk was the product of a moment of distraction.

'I don't want to question you back at headquarters.'

'But you're going to question me all the same?'

'Yes.'

'Well, I'm going to answer like I would to the cops because, for me, that's what you've been for twenty-nine years. A cop.'

'That's what I am, and that's what I want. I want you to answer my questions just as you would the police.'

'Well, I really liked Josselin. I met him in Paris four years ago, when he put my head right. Six months ago, things began to change.'

'In what way?'

'He started to go on at me that until I'd killed my father, I'd always amount to nothing. No, well, not literally kill, if you get my meaning.'

'All right, I understand, Zerk.'

'Before that I never bothered much about my father. I did think about it sometimes, but a cop's son? Better forget it. Now and then, there'd be something about you in the papers, and my mother would be all proud, but not me. That's it. But then Josselin started on at me. He said you were the root of all my problems and the reason I was such a failure, he could see all that in my head.'

'How a failure?'

'I dunno,' said Zerk, sucking some more on the straw. 'I don't get bothered about anything much. Maybe like you and the light bulb in your house.'

'So what did Josselin say?'

'He said I should "confront" you and do you down. "Purge the system" he called it, as if there was all this rotten stuff inside me, and the rotten stuff was you. I didn't like that idea.'

'Why not?'

'Dunno. I didn't really feel like it – all this purging stuff seemed a lot of hassle to me. And I couldn't feel any big heap of rubbish anyway, I didn't know where it was supposed to be. But Josselin said, oh yes, it was right there inside me, and if I didn't get rid of it, it would start to rot me from within. So I stopped arguing with him, because it made him cross, and he was cleverer than me. I listened. Few more sessions like that, I started to believe him. In the end, I really *did* believe him.'

'So what did you decide to do?'

'Get rid of the rubbish, but I didn't know how you did something like that. He never told me. He said he'd help me. But he said, one way or another, I'd bump into you one day. And he was right, I did.'

'Well, naturally, Zerk, because he'd planned it all out.'

'Yeah, suppose so,' said Zerk, after a moment.

Not a quick thinker, said Adamsberg to himself, feeling rather annoyed to be even a little in agreement with Josselin. Because if Zerk wasn't very bright, whose fault was that? His gestures were slow too. He had only drunk half his coffee, but then so had Adamsberg.

'When did you bump into me then?'

'The first thing was this phone call, in the night of Monday to Tuesday, after that nasty murder in Garches. This man I didn't know, he told me my photo would be in the papers next day, and I was going to be accused of the murder, and I'd better beat it and vanish from sight. And after that, things would be sorted out, and he'd get back to me.'

'That will have been Mordent. One of my officers.'

'Ah, so he wasn't lying. He was like, "I'm a friend of your father's, so for Pete's sake do what I say." Because I was thinking I should just go to the cops, and say there must have been some mistake. But Louis always told me to keep my distance from the cops as much as I could.'

'Louis?'

Zerk looked up in amazement. 'Louis. Louis Veyrenc.'

'Oh yeah,' said Adamsberg, 'Veyrenc.'

'He should know, shouldn't he? So I left home and I went to Josselin's. Where else could I go? My mother lives in Poland now, and Louis was down in Laubazac. Josselin always said his door was open to me if ever I was in trouble. And that's when he put the knife in. But I was up for it, that's for sure.'

'How did he put it?'

'He said it was now or never. He said to take advantage of this misunderstanding, it must be destiny. Destiny only stops for a minute in the station, so jump on the train. Only idiots stay on the platform. That's what he said.'

'Well put.'

'Yeah, that's what I thought.'

'But wrong. Anyway, did he rehearse you what to say?'

'No, but he told me how to act, really make you see that I existed, and you had to understand that I was stronger than you. He said what that would do would be, it'd make you feel really guilty, that was bound to happen. He was like, "This is your day, Armel. After this you'll be a new man. Go ahead, don't be afraid to come on strong." I liked that. "Go ahead, purge, exist, it's your day." I'd never heard anything like that – go ahead, purge, exist. I really liked how that sounded.'

'Where did you get the T-shirt?'

'He went out and bought it for me, he said I wouldn't be impressive enough in my scruffy old shirt. I spent the night at his place, but I was too worked up to sleep. I was going over stuff in my head. He gave me some pills.'

'Uppers?'

'Dunno, didn't ask. One pill at night, and two in the

morning before I went out. I was already feeling like a new man. And the pile of rubbish, yeah, I could see that, plain as daylight. This feeling, it kept getting stronger. I could really have murdered you. And you'd have killed me,' he added, suddenly sounding like the gothic Zerk.

The young man looked away. He took a cigarette and Adamsberg lit it for him.

'Would you really have killed me with that horrible potion?'

'What did it look like to you?'

'Some fucking poison in a bottle.'

'Nitrocitraminic acid.'

'Yeah, if you say so.'

'But what else did it look like?'

'Dunno. Free sample of aftershave or something.'

'That's exactly what it was.'

'I don't believe it,' gasped Zerk. 'You're just saying that because today, now, you're ashamed. You were locked in your study. You wouldn't keep aftershave in your study, would you?'

'You locked me up, forgetting that cops have pass keys. I went into the bathroom to get it. Nitrocitraminic acid doesn't exist. You can check.'

'Shit,' said Zerk, sucking up more coffee.

'What is perfectly true on the other hand is that you shouldn't push a gun so far down your trousers.'

'Yeah, I can see that.'

'Did you really have TB, only one kidney, all that stuff?'

'No. I did have ringworm once.'

'OK, go on.'

'Well, when I had to fish the cat out from under the boxes, that distracted me. Or maybe it was that old Spanish guy and his arm. I sort of came round as if I'd been drunk.

I was getting a bit tired of all this ranting. But I did want to go on, all the same. I wanted to carry on bullshitting until you fell on your knees and begged me to stop. Josselin told me that if I didn't keep yelling at you, I was finished. If I didn't get you down on the floor, it was all over with me. I'd have that shit inside me for ever. And it's true, I did feel better afterwards.'

'But you were still in deep trouble.'

'Bloody right I was, like the cat in the garden. I was waiting for them to find the DNA didn't match. Or for this mystery man to call me back. But nothing happened.'

'You never thought it might be a trap set by Josselin?'

'No. He was hiding me, wasn't he? I was in this box room in his apartment, strict orders not to come out because of his patients.'

'After you left me, if you'd come out of your room between nine and midday, you'd have found me with him. I came to talk to him. I imagine Josselin must have appreciated the situation. He had us both under his roof, and he was manipulating the pair of us. But he did make me feel better and he got rid of my tinnitus. We're going to miss him, Zerk, he really has got golden fingers.'

'No way will I miss him. No way.'

'So what happened next? That day?'

'He came to fetch me out at lunchtime, he made me tell him everything, he wanted all the details, what I'd said exactly, he was having a great time, he seemed happy for me. He took away the T-shirt and cooked a nice meal to celebrate. He said not to worry about the DNA, it would just be a wrong analysis and that the cops would take some time to spot it. But I was starting not to believe that. I wanted to call Louis but I couldn't switch on my mobile. Yeah, Josselin had a landline, but if the cops knew Louis was my uncle, they might have been listening in. I started to think someone was after me, trying to ruin my life. Was it him got the tissue?'

'Yes, it was easy, and the hairs from your dog, Tintin. We found them on the chair in Garches. The same chair he pinned you to yesterday. I wondered where he could have got them, though. Did he ever come to see you at home?'

'No, never.'

'When you went to see him, did he take your coat?'

'I just left my shoes in the hall, nothing else.'

'Nothing else? Think.'

'No. Yeah. A couple of times, he got me to take off my trousers to check my knees.'

'Recently?'

'No, couple of months ago.'

'That'd be when he got hold of the handkerchief and the dog hairs. You never thought anything of it?'

'No, why would I? Josselin had been helping me get my head straight for four years, why would I think he would harm me? He was on my side, with his wretched golden fingers. He got me to think he really liked me, but the truth was he thought I was a pathetic dickhead. Nobody cares if you live or die, was what he said to me last night.'

'*Loša sreća*, Zerk, he had taken on himself the destiny of Arnold Paole.'

'He wasn't making that up, it was the truth. He really was a descendant of Paole. He told me that in the car when we were driving to Garches. He wasn't kidding.'

'No, I know that. He's an authentic Paole, in the direct paternal line. What I mean is, he became as sick as the great-great-whatever-grandfather, the one who ate earth from the graveyard to protect himself against Peter Plogojowitz. What else did he tell you?'

'That I was going to die, but by dying I'd be part of his great scheme for exterminating all these people who were under a curse, and that this would be a good death for a useless person like me. What he said was, there was this horrible other family, and it had been infecting his family for three hundred years, so he was going to put a stop to it. He said he was born with two teeth, and that was proof that he had this evil in him, but it was all these other people's fault. But I couldn't understand everything he was saying. He was like, talking too quickly, and I was afraid the car was going to crash.'

Zerk paused to finish his coffee, which was now cold.

'He did speak about his mother. She abandoned him, because he was a Paole, and she knew right away, because he had these teeth when he was born. She said, "Ugh, he's got teeth!" and left him at the hospital, "as if she was getting rid of something filthy," he said. And then he started to cry, really cry. I could see him in the rear-view mirror. He didn't blame his mother. He said "What can a poor mother do, if she's given birth to a creature? A creature isn't a child." So I thought, now he's going to break down, so he might let me go, and I begged him to let me go. But he started shouting again, and the car went all over the road. Hell, I was really scared. Then he went on telling me how his childhood was ruined because he was this "creature".'

'Was he adopted by the Josselin family?'

'Yeah. And when he was nine, he opened this drawer in his father's desk. And he found a whole file on himself. He found out he was adopted, he found out his mother had given him away, and why. He was a Paole, from a whole line of damned vampires. That's what he says. A year later, the people who adopted him couldn't handle him, he was smashing things, spreading his shit on the walls. He just told me all this stuff, straight out, he wasn't embarrassed, to prove he was a damned soul. So one day in November, he said, his parents took him to this institution, and said that he was going to have his head examined. They said they'd come back, but they didn't.'

'Being abandoned a second time really fucked up his life,' said Adamsberg.

'Sort of plog, perhaps?'

'If you like.'

'Then when he was older he got married, to this woman "who was nothing much to look at, but very well set up", he said. And he started to cut the feet off of people who were a threat to him. These were other people who'd been born with teeth. He wasn't sure at first who he was looking for, he admitted that. "I was just a beginner then," he said, "I may have cut some feet off harmless people, may they forgive me. But I wasn't hurting them, they were already dead." He said his wife left him soon after the marriage. A heartless woman, he called her, "scum of the earth, as I found out".'

'He was right about that.'

'So, now, we got to the villa, and he didn't have to watch the road. He'd got into a worse state, he wasn't talking properly. He was whispering some stuff I couldn't hear, then he would like, bellow? He stuck that knife in my hand. He told me about the family tree of the Plogovitches – is that their name?'

'Plogojowitz.'

Zerk obviously had the same difficulty in remembering names. For a very brief moment, Adamsberg felt he knew him through and through.

'Yeah, right,' said Zerk, frowning with his dark joined eyebrows, just like Adamsberg's father when he was watching his soup cook. 'So he talked about "inhuman sufferings" and he said he'd never *really* killed anyone, because these were "creatures from deep in the earth", not human beings at all, and they were destroying human life. He said it was his job, cos he was this brilliant doctor, to heal wounds, and he was going to rid the world of this "filthy menace".'

Adamsberg took a cigarette from Zerk's packet.

'How did you get my mobile number?'

'I nicked it from Uncle Louis' phone, when he was working with you.'

'Did you intend to use it?'

'No, I just thought it wasn't right Louis should have it when I didn't.'

'And how did you tap in the number then? Inside your pocket.'

'I didn't need to, I'd saved it under number 9. Last of the last, see?'

'Well, I suppose it's a start,' said Adamsberg.

XLVIII

Émile came into headquarters on crutches. At reception, he had to face *Brigadier* Gardon, who didn't understand what this man was doing, asking about a dog. Danglard came up, shambling as usual, but wearing a light-coloured suit, which was unexpected enough to provoke comment, though that came a poor second to the arrest of Paul de Josselin, a descendant of Arnold Paole, the man who had had his life destroyed by the Plogojowitz vampires.

Retancourt, who was still the leader of the rational-positivist movement, had been arguing since the morning with the peacemakers and the cloud-shovellers, who accused her of having kept inquiries narrowed down since Sunday, because she couldn't accept any explanation to do with *vampiri*. Whereas there are more things in heaven and earth than are dreamt of in your philosophy, as Mercadet had pointed out. Including people who eat wardrobes, Danglard thought. Kernorkian and Froissy were on the point of giving in and believing in *vampiri*, which complicated matters. This was because they had been persuaded by the state of conservation of the bodies in the story, something which had been empirically observed, historically recorded, and how were you supposed to explain that away? On a small scale, the debate which had excited the whole of Europe in the third decade of the eighteenth century was being reopened in the offices of the Serious Crime Squad in Paris, without having made much progress in almost three hundred years.

It was indeed this detail which had unsettled some members of the squad, the horror aroused by hearing of 'pink and intact' corpses, with blood coming from their orifices, and with skin looking fresh and unlined, while their old skin and nails were under them in the grave. Here, Danglard's superior knowledge came into its own. He had the answer, he knew precisely why and how the bodies had been preserved, a fairly frequent phenomenon in fact, and he could even explain the cry of the vampire when it was pierced with a stake, or the sighs of the shroud-eaters. The others had formed a circle around him and were hanging on his words. They had just reached the moment in the debate when science was going to dispel obscurantism all over again. Danglard was just starting to tell them about the phenomenon of gases which sometimes, depending on the chemical composition of the earth, didn't come out of the bodies, but inflated them like a balloon, stretching the skin – when he was interrupted by the hullabaloo of a dish being overturned on the floor above, and then Cupid came bounding down the stairs, rushing straight through to reception. Without breaking step, the little dog gave a very particular kind of yap as it rushed past the photocopier, where Snowball was, as usual, stretched out, its paws hanging over the edge.

'In this case,' observed Danglard, as he watched the dog going frantic with joy, 'we have neither knowledge nor fantasy.

Simply pure love, unquestioning and unlimited. Very rare in humans, and very dangerous. But Cupid is a tactful dog, because he said goodbye to the cat, with a mixture of admiration and regret.'

The dog had jumped right up into Émile's arms and was clinging to his chest, panting and licking and scrabbling at his shirt. Émile had had to sit down, pressing his ugly mug against the dog's back.

'We ran the tests – the manure on his feet matched the stuff on the floor of your van,' Danglard told him.

'What about that love letter from old Vaudel? Did that help the *commissaire*?'

'Yes, plenty. It led him almost to his death in a stinking vault. Full of corpses.'

'And the secret tunnel from Madame Bourlant's house, that helped him too?'

'Yes, that got him to Dr Josselin.'

'Never liked him, poser he was. So where is he, the boss?'

'You want to see him?'

'Yeah, I don't want him to make trouble for me, we can settle it friendly like, if he wants. Help I gave him there, he owes me one.'

'Settle what?'

'For his ears only.'

Danglard called Adamsberg's mobile.

'*Commissaire*, we've got Cupid here, he's sitting on Émile's knee, and Émile wants to talk to you to settle something.'

'Settle what?'

'No idea, he says he'll only speak to you.'

'*Personally*,' insisted Émile self-importantly.

'How is he?'

'Looks fine to me – new jacket and blue badge in his lapel. When will you be back?'

'I'm on a beach in Normandy, Danglard, I'm coming back soon.'

'But what are you doing there?'

'I had to talk to my son. We're neither of us very good at this, but we've managed to communicate a bit.'

No, of course, Danglard thought, Tom isn't a year old, so he can't talk yet.

'I told you more than once. They're in Brittany, not Normandy.'

'I'm talking about my other son, Danglard.'

'What—?' said Danglard, unable to finish his sentence. 'Wha . . . *other* son?'

He was seized with instant rage against Adamsberg. How had he managed to have another child somewhere else, when little Tom was still a baby?

'How old is this other one?'

'Eight days.'

'You are such a bastard,' Danglard hissed.

'It's the way it was, *commandant*. I didn't know about him.'

'No, you never bloody know about anything, do you?'

'And you never let me finish either, Danglard. He's eight days old for me, but for other people, he's twenty-nine. He's beside me here, smoking a cigarette. His hands are covered in bandages. Paole pinned him to that Louis XIII armchair with a knife last night.'

'The *Zerquetscher*?' asked Danglard weakly.

'Correct. Or Zerk as I call him. Aka Armel Louvois.'

Danglard looked blankly across at Émile and his dog, while he tried to concentrate on the facts of the situation.

'This is a figure of speech, isn't it? You've adopted him, or some crazy stunt like that?'

'No, no, Danglard, he's my son. That's why Josselin had a lot of fun choosing him as a scapegoat.'

'I don't believe this.'

'Look, you'd believe Veyrenc, wouldn't you? Ask him. He's his *uncle* and he'll give you a glowing report on him.'

Adamsberg was half reclining on the sand, drawing on it with his finger. Zerk was lying down, his arms across his body, his hands now numbed, thanks to a local anaesthetic, and was soaking up the sun and relaxing like the cat on the photocopier. Danglard ran through his head all those photographs of the Zerk from the papers, and at once realised how familiar that face had been. Yes. It had to be the truth, but it was a shock.

'Not to worry, *commandant*. Put Émile on, will you?'

Without a word, Danglard handed the phone to Émile, who hobbled away towards the door.

'This colleague of yours is stupid,' he began. 'It's not a badge, it's my winkle pin. I went and fetched it from the house.'

'Because you're nostalgic.'

'Yeah, I suppose.'

'So what deal is this you want to settle?' said Adamsberg sitting up.

'I kept a record. Nine hundred and thirty-seven euros. Now I've got plenty of cash, I can pay it back, and then you don't know nothing about it. Because I got you that stuff about the postcard, and the door in the cellar. Savvy?'

'What don't I "know nothing about"?'

'Vaudel's money, for fuck's sake. Bit here, bit there, total nine hundred and thirty seven. I kept a record.'

'I'm with you now, Émile. Well, for a start, I've got nothing to do with that money, like I said. And in any case, it's too late. I don't think Pierre junior, since you're already getting half his inheritance, will be too happy to find out that you were pinching his old man's money and that you want to pay him nine hundred and thirty-seven euros.'

'Ha,' said Émile pensively.

'So just keep the money, and shut up about it.'

'Got you,' said Émile, and Adamsberg reflected that he must have picked up the expression at the hospital in Châteaudun from that tall paramedic, André.

'You've got another son?' asked Zerk, as they got back in the car.

'He's very, very small,' said Adamsberg, demonstrating with his hands apart, as if that made it less of a fact. 'Does it bother you?'

'Nope.'

No doubt about it, Zerk was an accommodating sort of chap.

XLIX

THE PARIS CENTRAL LAW COURTS WERE UNDER A CLOUD, WHICH was entirely appropriate to the place and the time. Adamsberg and Danglard, sitting at the terrace of the cafe opposite, were waiting for people to emerge from the trial of Mordent's daughter. It was ten to eleven by Danglard's watch. Adamsberg was looking at the gold-tipped railings which had been carefully repainted.

'When you scratch the gold, what do you find underneath, Danglard?'

'Nolet would say: the scales of the snake.'

'Coiled round the Sainte-Chapelle. Not a very suitable combination.'

'It's not such a contrast as you might think. There are two chapels there one on top of the other and quite separate. The bottom one was reserved for the common people and the top one for the king and his courtiers. Everything leads back to that in the end.'

'The great snake was already there in the fourteenth century then,' said Adamsberg, looking up at the top of the steep Gothic spire.

'Thirteenth century,' Danglard corrected him. 'Built by Pierre de Montreuil between 1242 and 1248.'

'Did you get in touch with Nolet?'

'Yes. The school friend was indeed a witness to the wedding between Emma Carnot and a young man aged twenty-four, Paul de Josselin Cressent, at the town hall in Auxerre, twenty-nine years ago. Emma had fallen for him, her mother was impressed by the name with a "de" in it, but she told us that Paul was the last of a damaged line. The marriage didn't last three years. There were no children.'

'Just as well. Josselin would hardly have been a good father.'

Danglard chose not to pursue that line of thought. He would wait and see what Zerk was like.

'There would have been another little Paole loose in the world,' Adamsberg went on, 'and God only knows what he would have got up to. But no, this is the end of the Paoles, the doctor said so.'

'I'm going to help Radstock dispose of the feet. Then I'm taking a week off.'

'Going fishing in that loch perhaps?'

'No,' said Danglard evasively, 'I think I'll probably stay on in London.'

'With a rather abstract sort of plan in mind.'

'Yes.'

'When Mordent has got his daughter back, which will be tonight, we'll unleash the torrent of mud in the Emma Carnot affair. It'll run from the Council of State to the Appeal Court, then to the public prosecutor and the Gavernan Assize Court, and it will stop there. We won't let it reach down as far as the junior judge and Mordent, since that is no consequence to anyone but us.'

'It'll cause an almighty row.'

'Of course. People will be shocked, they'll propose a far-reaching reform of the judicial system, then it will all be forgotten when they dig up some other scandal. And you know what will happen then.'

'The great snake will have lost three of its scales, after an attack, but it will have regrown them again in a couple of months.'

'Or less. We'll set in motion the counter-offensive, using the Weill technique. We won't release anything to the press about the link to the judge at Gavernan, or name him. We'll keep him in reserve for our own protection, and in order to protect Nolet and Mordent. And we'll use the Weill technique to get the pencil shavings and the cartridge from Avignon to the quai des Orfèvres. Where they can moulder away in a cupboard.'

'Why should we protect Mordent? He's acted like an arsehole.'

'Because the straight and narrow is never straight. Mordent's not part of the snake. He was swallowed whole. He's in its belly, like Jonah in the whale.'

'Or the uncle in the bear.'

'Aha,' said Adamsberg. 'I knew you'd show some interest in that story one day.'

'But what sort of idea of Mordent will be left inside the great snake?'

'A thorn in the side, and the memory of failure. That's something at least.'

'So what are we going to do about Mordent?'

'Whatever he thinks he will do himself. If he wants to, we'll take him back. A damaged man is worth ten. You and I are the only people who know about this. The others all think he's had a nervous breakdown because of his daughter, and that that explains his mistakes. They've also heard he's recovered his testicles intact, and that's as much as they know. Nobody knows that he went to Pierre Vaudel's place.'

'Why didn't Pierre Vaudel tell you about going to racecourses and the horse manure?'

'His wife was not supposed to know he was involved with the bookies.'

'And who paid the concierge, Francisco Delfino, to give Josselin a false alibi. Josselin himself or Emma Carnot?'

'Nobody. Josselin simply sent Francisco on holiday. For the first few days after the Garches murder, Josselin impersonated Francisco. He took his place, knowing there'd be a visit from the police sooner or later. When I saw him, the lodge was dark, he was wrapped up in a blanket, including his hands. All he had to do after that was nip back up to his apartment via the service stairs and get changed to welcome me in.'

'Sophisticated.'

'Yes. He'd thought of everything, except his ex-wife. As soon as Emma discovered that Josselin was Vaudel's doctor, she realised before us. Right away.'

'Here he comes,' Danglard interrupted. 'Justice has been pronounced.'

Mordent was emerging alone, under the cloudy sky. The children have eaten sour grapes and the father's teeth have been set on edge. His daughter, a free woman now, would have to go back to Fresnes for the paperwork and to pick up her things. She would eat her supper at home that night, he had already done the shopping.

Adamsberg caught Mordent under one arm, and Danglard

took the other. The *commandant* looked from side to side, like an old heron trapped by the disciplinary police. A heron having lost its prestige and its feathers, condemned to fish alone and in disgrace.

'We've come to celebrate the triumph of justice, Mordent,' said Adamsberg. 'And to celebrate the arrest of Josselin, and the liberation of the Paole clan, who will now return to their uncomplicated destiny of being ordinary human beings, and to celebrate the birth of my elder son. Plenty to celebrate. We left our beers on the table.'

Adamsberg's grip was firm, his face was tilted sideways and he was smiling. Light flickered under his skin, his expression was lit up, and Mordent well knew that when Adamsberg's cloudy eyes became gleaming orbs, he was approaching his prey or some great truth. The *commissaire* marched him over to the cafe.

'Celebrate?' said Mordent in a blank voice, unable to find anything else to say.

'Yes, celebrate. And we're also celebrating the disappearance of a certain scatter of pencil shavings and a cartridge case under a fridge. We're celebrating *my* freedom, Mordent.'

The *commandant*'s arm barely moved in Adamsberg's grip. The old heron had lost all his strength. Adamsberg sat him down between them, as if dropping a bundle. The F3 fuse has gone, he thought, a psycho-emotional shock, inhibited action. No Dr Josselin around to heal it either. With the departure of Arnold Paole's descendant, medicine was losing one of its great practitioners.

'I'm up to my neck in it, aren't I?' murmured Mordent. 'Deservedly,' he went on, ruffling his grey hair and stretching his long neck, with that movement of a wading bird that was peculiar to him.

'Yes, you are. But a cunningly constructed dam has been built, which is going to block the mud outside the doors of the Gavernan Assize Court. From there on down, there will be no visible traces of betrayal, nothing but innocent procedures. In the squad nobody else knows anything. Your job's still there. It's up to you. On the other hand, Emma Carnot is going to go up in smoke. You were taking orders directly from her?'

Mordent nodded.

'On a special mobile?'

'Yes.'

'Which is where now?'

'I destroyed it last night.'

'Good. Don't try to protect yourself by rushing to help her, Mordent. She's killed one woman, she had Émile shot at and then tried to poison him. She was on her way to bump off the other witness to her marriage.'

Ever vigilant, Danglard had ordered a third beer which he put in front of Mordent, with a gesture as authoritarian as Adamsberg's arm, meaning 'Drink up!'

'And don't think about doing away with yourself either,' Adamsberg went on. 'That would be irrelevant, as Danglard might put it, when Elaine needs you most.' Adamsberg stood up. The Seine was flowing a few metres away from them, flowing to the sea, flowing towards America, then to the Pacific, then back here again.

'*Vratiću*,' he said. 'I'm going for a walk.'

'What did he say?' asked Mordent, looking surprised, and for a moment back to normal, which seemed to Danglard to be a good sign.

'He's still got a little bit of the Kisilova *vampiri* inside him. It'll disappear in the end. Or not. You never know with him.'

Adamsberg came back towards them, looking preoccupied.

'Danglard, I know you've told me this before, but where does the Seine rise?'

'On the Langres plateau.'

'Not Mont Gerbier de Jonc?'

'No, that's the Loire.'

'*Hvala*, Danglard.'

'Don't mention it.'

'That means "thank you",' Danglard told Mordent. Adamsberg walked off again towards the river, with jaunty steps and holding his jacket over his shoulder with one finger. Mordent raised his glass clumsily, like a man who is not sure if he has the right to do so, and moved it first in the direction of Adamsberg then towards Danglard sitting beside him.

'*Hvala*,' he said.

L

ADAMSBERG WALKED FOR OVER AN HOUR ON THE BANK OF
the Seine that was in sunlight, listening to the seagulls mewing
in French, and holding his mobile in his hand, waiting for a
call from London. It came through at 2.15, as Stock had promised. It was a very short conversation, since Adamsberg had
left a single question with DCI Radstock, one to which he
had only to reply 'yes' or 'no'.

'Yes,' said Radstock, in English. Adamsberg thanked him
and snapped his phone shut. He hesitated a moment, then
chose Estalère's number. The young *brigadier* was the only
person he could think of who would offer neither comment
nor criticism.

'Estalère,' he said, 'go and see Josselin in hospital. I've got
a message for him.'

'Yes, sir, what shall I say?'

'Tell him that the tree on Highgate Hill is dead.'

'The tree in Highgate?'

'That's right.'

'That's all?'

'Yes.'

'Will do, *commissaire*.'

Adamsberg went back up the boulevard slowly, imagining the tree roots in Kiseljevo rotting away around the grave.

Where will they grow again, Peter?

www.vintage-books.co.uk